THE *Flying* GUY

John Baraniak

authorHOUSE®

AuthorHouse™
1663 Liberty Drive
Bloomington, IN 47403
www.authorhouse.com
Phone: 1 (800) 839-8640

Published by AuthorHouse 05/01/2015

ISBN: 978-1-5049-1005-7 (sc)
ISBN: 978-1-5049-1004-0 (e)

Library of Congress Control Number: 2015906762

Print information available on the last page.

Any people depicted in stock imagery provided by Thinkstock are models,
and such images are being used for illustrative purposes only.
Certain stock imagery © Thinkstock.

Th is book is printed on acid-free paper.

Because of the dynamic nature of the Internet, any web addresses or links contained in
this book may have changed since publication and may no longer be valid. The views
expressed in this work are solely those of the author and do not necessarily reflect the
views of the publisher, and the publisher hereby disclaims any responsibility for them.

Chapter 1

November 1992

Margaret Anderson stood smiling as she watched her five-month-old son crawling across the kitchen floor. She realized long ago how much fun it was to be around him. Parenting was easy when your kids made you smile and he always made her smile. His little hands plopped on the tile floor as he scooted around, his pajamas easily sliding across the smooth surface. Margaret had always been a careful person. She had a knack for knowing what obstacles stood in her way and always managed to avoid them, so having him in the kitchen with her while she worked made it more pleasant.

Somehow she knew it was going to be a memorable day. The sun had shone early and the morning had started brightly. The daily routine was smooth and on schedule. Everything pointed to a good day on the home front. Her husband, Mark, was at work, and David, the baby, was on the floor nearby. All there was to do were the usual daily chores of cooking, cleaning, and taking care of the baby.

David shuffled across the floor, stopping only to raise a small arm in the direction of the cereal box on the edge of the table. It was his favorite snack, Cheerios. O's, she called them. Margaret saw him looking to get at the box, and she knew he'd be crawling up the leg of the table to get it if she didn't get it out of sight. She poured a small handful of the cereal in one hand and managed to get the box closed with her other hand. She reached up and set it on top of the refrigerator. She settled down, sitting on the floor next to David. He saw the cereal in her hand and eagerly crawled in her lap. They sat for several minutes, as he happily gobbled the cereal she fed to him, one piece after another.

"One for my little guy," Margaret said, putting one piece on his tongue, "and one for Mommy." She took one. He smiled up at her. She continued until she finished with the small handful she had taken.

"All gone," Margaret said softly. "Maybe we'll have some later." She tweaked his nose softly.

David was still hungry, but he already knew that "all gone" meant there was no more food coming. He crawled off his mother's lap and headed for the living room, leaving in his wake a stream of drool. He grunted as he shuffled smoothly across the floor, not seeing his mother's amused smile as he headed out of the kitchen.

The living room was right off the kitchen, and the carpeted floor was covered with an array of David's toys. All of them did of course, pass Margaret's rigorous safety inspection. David loved his toys and played with every one of them. He'd move from one to the next, even at his age seeming to have picked up on what an airplane did or that he should balance blocks into a wall, clumsily stacking one on the other. He liked the brightly colored objects best.

Margaret kept an eye on him as she set about cleaning up the kitchen. She wiped all the extra food now gelling firmly to David's high-chair. He always managed to get food all over everything. Smacking his spoon on a plate and flinging food in all directions was a regular occurrence at feeding time. She scrubbed down all the way to the legs of the chair to get all the leftovers off.

David amused himself by lying on his stomach, examining a book he held in a tiny hand. He knew when Mom or Dad had it, they would talk to him. He wasn't quite sure how that all worked, but it was enjoyable enough that he liked to just hold the books.

After making sure he had thoroughly examined every inch of the brightly colored book cover, his hunger returned. He got up to his hands and knees and made his way to the kitchen. He slid across the floor noiselessly this time, coming to a stop in front of the refrigerator. His mom was now wiping down the counter and clanging dishes around. David looked up at the top of the big white refrigerator. He could see the corner of the cereal box hanging just over the edge. He looked back at his mom. She wasn't watching, so she didn't respond to his being there. He turned back and reached up toward the box and grunted to get her attention; no response.

David didn't really notice that he had lifted off the floor, even though he wouldn't have known what it meant anyway. He was intent on getting the container of his favorite food. He slowly rose from the floor, floating silently upward, his arms outstretched as he neared his box of cereal. As if he suddenly noticed he could be up that high without someone holding him, he cooed a tiny giggle.

Margaret heard him and turned to see what he was up to. Her eyes flew wide with disbelief as she saw him floating in mid-air, his little arms reaching for the box. She instinctively lunged for him, as if he were falling.

"David!" she cried out, reaching for him. He was only a few feet away, so she was able to grab him almost instantaneously. When she had yelled his name, it startled him, and he lost concentration that he wanted to go up. Gravity took over and he fell into his mother's grasping arms.

Margaret held him to her. The sight of him floating and then catching him as he fell totally shocked her. *What did I just see?* she thought to herself. She held David against her, snuggling him, patting his back as if he needed comforting. She looked at him to see if there was something – different – about him, but it was the same little smile she always got. She stepped back and turned to look at the refrigerator. She replayed the scene. *He was there,* she thought. *Right there. Floating. That can't be. That just can't be.* She looked at him again. He was the same. She had to have imagined it. *No, she didn't,* she told herself. *He was right there.*

David was still only a couple feet from what he wanted in the first place, and while his mother was trying to rationalize what had happened, he was squirming in her arms, reaching again.

"No, no, honey," she soothed him. "Not right now." She stepped back, a conscious move to get away from what was confusing her. She still faced the refrigerator, the scene being replayed in her mind. Fear mingled with the confusion.

David's squirming got at least a little freedom when she walked in and set him on the carpeted living room floor. He was within a few feet of a large, brightly colored plastic bowling pin, and he went for it, forgetting momentarily about his appetite. Margaret watched him to see if anything seemed out of place. Nothing.

Margaret glanced at the refrigerator where it happened. She looked back at him. He was okay; that's all that mattered. He was okay. Nothing seemed odd. She was still short of breath as she sat on the couch listening to the rattling of the plastic toy. She thought for a few minutes and at some point wondered not just what had happened, but what Mark would say if she told him. He'd think she was crazy. She *is* crazy! This isn't real. She thought more. He'd think she was seriously, in need of a doctor crazy. Maybe she shouldn't tell him. That's the best idea. Not tell him and keep this a secret. She did see it though, right? *Yes.* Margaret knew what she saw. She sat for many long minutes more, wondering what she should do.

Then a new thought came to her. *What if he can do that again? But it's too dangerous*, she told herself. *He's only a baby.* She'd have to be careful, but she had to see if he'd do it again. She had to.

"David, honey," she said as she rose from the couch. She headed to the fridge, taking the box from the top. "Would you like some more O's?"

He responded immediately. The word O's was always followed by eating O's. He started off in a quick crawl toward his mother, who now stood at the edge of the carpet and the kitchen floor. She had poured herself a handful of the cereal from the box. She moved into the living room to have the carpet beneath her. If she could actually get him to do that again, if he fell, she didn't want to risk him falling on the hard surface of the kitchen tile.

Margaret held out the handful of cereal for David to see. He looked up at her, one arm reaching as he gave his hungry grunts. For a moment, Margaret felt awful, almost as she were feeding or training a pet, like trying to get a dog to bark. She held out one O, but she didn't lean down to give it to him.

"Want a yummy O?" she smiled at him. He grunted again and strained a little higher. This is the point where she would have normally bent down and set one on his sloppy tongue. He let out another urgent grunt, sensing that something was different. He wasn't getting his food. He reached up and with the same unknown of what he was doing, floated up toward his mother's hand.

Margaret was speechless. David was in mid-air in front of her, taking the cereal from her hand and eating it just like he was sitting in his high-chair. He smiled and wiggled his arms, turning slightly to settle in a sitting position. Except there was no chair under him. He was simply sitting in the air.

Margaret's brain struggled to comprehend what she saw. But she didn't say anything. David looked like he always did when he wanted more food. She took another piece and gave it to him. He grabbed it like he always did and ate it. Then he reached for more. He giggled, wiggling his arms and legs. All this, while floating in the air, right in front of her. Margaret kept giving him more, slowly, one after the other. She was ready to grab him in an instant if he started to fall. A million thoughts went through her mind. She could hardly breathe.

This can't be real, she thought. *Is this really happening? What the hell was going on?*

She reached out to him then, momentarily afraid he would fall. Just as her arms went out toward him, he saw that she wanted to hold him. He floated into her arms. He settled against her chest, grasping her shirt. She held him tightly. David had a huge grin on his face. He giggled, reaching up to touch his mother's face.

Oh, my gosh, she thought. *He must enjoy that. Does he fly around all the time? Does he do this at night? No. Can't be. He's always in his crib where he was tucked in the night before.* She kept looking at him to reassure herself that he was still her little boy. Her little boy who evidently knew how to float. He had floated into her arms. She held him a bit away from her for a moment, looking at him.

"David, honey," she said. "Do you do that a lot, float around like that?" She stood looking at his little face, knowing he didn't understand the question any more than she understood why she'd ask a little baby such a question. But then why not. This isn't normal anyway.

"Please do me a favor though," she said to him, knowing he wouldn't grasp this either. "Don't do that in front of other people. Okay?" She almost chuckled to herself. *No, please don't do that in front of other people.* Except maybe Mark. If he did it for him, then she would at least not think she was as crazy as she'd be considered if she talked of this.

She gave David a big kiss and gently set him down on the living room floor. He rolled over and grabbed the same plastic toy that he had left. She stood in the doorway to the kitchen, leaning on it, watching David play.

Now what do I do, she thought to herself. *Do I leave him alone and just keep an eye on him or do I sit and constantly watch him?* After a long stretch of working out the reality of the situation, she decided that she had no choice but to do what she had been doing in the kitchen and just keep more of an extra eye on him than she normally did.

Margaret went back to the kitchen and began cleaning the final spaces that needed it. It only took about fifteen minutes and she talked to David as she scrubbed, constantly glancing in to see if he was okay. She always thought he was comforted by the sounds she and Mark made. Whether it was talking or clanging pots and pans, as she was now, he seemed to enjoy the noise. He liked to be in the middle of any commotion. Soon, he was sitting, smacking two plastic bowling pins together. Margaret smiled at him, as she always did when she saw that he was happy. *Everything will be okay*, she told herself. *Even if he can... float.*

It was getting about nap time, and when she asked David if he wanted to take a nap, he moved toward her to be picked up. As she reached down to get him, she forgot for a moment he could float and she had him in her arms before he had a chance to.

*

Margaret didn't say anything to Mark when he got home. It didn't take too long for him to sense that something was out of sorts, as she didn't do anything without keeping a close eye on David. Mark played with him, fed him, changed his diapers, and all the other normal stuff, just as he always did, but it was always with Margaret keeping an eye on them. He eventually asked her, but got the expected response. Oh, nothing, was all she said.

A few days went by since she'd seen David floating. He hadn't done it again. At least she didn't think he had. He hadn't done it when she was around anyway. Margaret didn't test him again and made doubly sure to reduce the temptations he might have to go reaching for something. She always had been doting, as Mark had pointed out, but now even she was conscious of the extra attention she gave.

One night, a few days after the incident in the kitchen, Mark got a little more pointed when asking what was going on.

"Come on, Margaret!" He always called by her full first name, as everyone else did. "You've been hovering over David lately. What's going on? Did something happen? Did he fall or something?"

Hovering, Margaret thought; *good choice for a word*. She knew she had to give him some sort of believable explanation to get him to back off.

She didn't want to lie, but didn't have much choice. She'd have to make something up. Then she'd have to back off of the hovering. Hopefully David backed off his hovering, as it seems he had, so she could get back to normal.

Unless, of course, Mark saw David float too.

She had thought of how to tell him what she saw. She thought of it a hundred times, with none of the scenarios ever ending with anything but a giant loss of trust in whether she was holding a grip on her sanity. *Flying babies!* Seeing would be the only believing. They had a close and trusting marriage and keeping a secret like this worked against her sensibilities. She needed a way to see if David would float to Mark, or to her, while he watched. A ploy came to her suddenly. She was sure it was worth a try.

She finally answered him. "David has just seemed like maybe he might have a hearing problem, and I've been wondering if he has something wrong. Then most times he seems alright. I don't know."

Mark was startled. He looked at Margaret with astonishment.

"Gees, Margaret, if you thought there was something wrong, why didn't you tell me?"

"I wasn't sure," she said. "It's just little things I notice and, I don't know. They just seemed -odd."

"Like what?" Mark asked, now concerned. "I haven't noticed anything out of the ordinary. He responds okay when you talk to him."

"Like if I say something to him, he seems to ignore me," she told him. She thought it came out okay and that he was buying it. She knew she had a chance. "Come on. We'll see what you think."

Mark followed her around the table and into the living room where David had his toys spread far and wide. He was playing, giggling and shaking the toy he held. He noticed Mom and Dad come in the room and cheerfully grunted his approval.

"How's my little guy?" Mark asked in his baby voice he used with David.

David wiggled and his smile widened. Mark and Margaret stood leaning over with their hands on their knees, as if inspecting something. They became conscious of that fact at the same time, gave each other a *don't-we-look-stupid* look, and straightened.

Margaret thought this was as good a chance as any, as David was playing and happy to see them in the room. He had flown before because he wanted something, and right now he'd probably go for some O's. He hadn't eaten for a while and it was about time for the normal feeding. She got the box and poured some cereal in her hand so David could see it as she stood next to Mark.

"Okay," Margaret told Mark. "See how he responds when you hold out your hands and ask him if he wants to come up."

Mark turned toward David and held out his hands to him as he always did. He gave two soft claps. David always went eagerly to him when he did that.

"Want to come to Dad? Want to come to your old man?" he said. He clapped again.

He started to lean down to pick him up and was shocked when David thumped into his chest. He stood holding him, just as speechless as Margaret had been.

Margaret smiled, with some relief. "That's what I meant by a little odd."

*

Mark and Margaret stood in the doorway to David's bedroom. They had just put him in his crib for the night and turned off the lights. He was awake yet, but not fussing. They thought he was probably aware that they were standing nearby. There was dim light from the plug-in night light in the socket near the doorway, and he'd occasionally glance over in their direction.

"Go to sleep, honey," Margaret said softly. She got a small grunt as he kicked his feet in response. Then there was silence. He was always quick to fall asleep.

After a few minutes Mark spoke. "So now what do we do?" he said in a whisper.

"I don't know," Margaret replied. She turned to leave, taking his arm. "Let's go in the kitchen."

They went down the hall to the kitchen and sat at the table. Neither said a word at first. Their thoughts were racing though. Mark was trying to fathom what he had just seen. Margaret had already done that days before and was now just wondering what Mark thought they should do. She was immensely relieved that David had floated for Mark. *She wasn't crazy after all.* But this whole thing was crazy to her. And now to Mark, she figured. She looked at him across the table.

"This can't be real," she finally said.

Mark nodded slowly. "Yeah," was all he could say.

"People can't fly," Margaret said. "Can they?" She asked the question as if maybe they could and she had just never been aware of it before.

"Not that I'm aware of," Mark replied. Then he added, "Does he fly or just float? Did you see him, like, flying around?"

"No. Just float."

"He levitates," Mark said, the word coming to him. "Like Superman. No gravity."

"But he doesn't always - levitate," Margaret said. "The rest of the time he's on the floor, like normal."

"Well, this sure isn't normal," Mark said. "I think we need to keep an eye on him and see if he does this again." He stared at the table. "Or how much."

"Maybe we should take him to the doctor," Margaret offered.

There was a dark silence then. *A doctor.* To see if there was something wrong with him. *God,* Mark thought, *what if there was something wrong with David. But what? People don't get sick and start to... levitate.* The thought chilled him.

"I don't think we can go to a doctor and just say '*Hey Doc. My kid has started floating around. Can you see what's causing that?*'" Mark chuckled.

"No, I suppose not," Margaret replied with a sigh. "So what options do we have?"

"Well," Mark said, after thinking a bit more. "Let's watch how things go and hope that he's at least okay, you know, health-wise, and whether he floats again or not." He looked at the window as another thought struck him. "And let's hope he doesn't float around in front of a window."

Margaret just nodded. She got up and came over to him, sitting on his lap. She put her arms around his neck and leaned into him.

"I'm scared," she said.

"Me, too."

Chapter 2

Mark Anderson was an accountant by day and now an air traffic controller by night. He had become the latter as he, and his wife, had learned that the floating "thing", as it was now called, turned out not to be a one-time thing. Together, he and Margaret, now even more happy to be a stay at home mom, had gotten marginally used to their son's aerial abilities. David floated more and more over the next few months, and since they didn't know quite how to deal with it, they just watched and worried. He was relatively good at it as far as they could tell. He didn't crash into things, and other than a couple hard thumps to the floor when he was startled, he moved around safely. Mark liked to watch him fly, but Margaret seemed on pins and needles when he went aloft. But life went on. They talked about it more as they realized this could be a permanent "thing", and they attempted to keep things as normal as they could keep them.

*

One Saturday started the way most Saturdays started for Mark. He rose early, at his usual 5:30. He made coffee, grabbed the paper from the spot on the front porch where the paperboy always landed it, and settled in his chair at the kitchen table, where the rising sun first hit. Being a Saturday only meant he'd be busier than a week day, and best of all, at home. Since he sat at a desk all day during the week, he especially enjoyed doing the little household chores on the weekends.

After the coffee and the paper, he was going to work on finishing up the window repair project he had started a few weeks earlier. Then he planned to go for a run before coming home to mow the backyard. It was going to be a perfect day, if you believed the weatherman. Margaret and David were still hours away from getting up, and the only thing they had planned together was a late afternoon meal at a Mexican spot down the street.

Mark dragged the ladder from the garage and put it up to the house. He crawled up and went to work chipping out the dirty, cracked caulk, and replacing it with a fine smooth line of replacement putty. After he finished that window and one to the left, he lowered the ladder to move it to the side of the house. Margaret appeared on the front porch with a cup of coffee in each hand.

"Brought you some coffee," she said, as she sipped from her cup. She was still wearing her pajamas. The top never matched the bottoms. She was the only person he ever thought of that could be described as cozy, just by looking at them. Mark left the ladder against the side of the house and came over to the porch.

"Thanks," he said. "I was just about to venture in to get it myself."

Without speaking they sat next to each other on the porch step, where they'd sat a hundred times before. Since David had been born it was often the three of them relaxing there, them drinking coffee and making baby talk, and David controlling the activities. The front porch was a great place to be.

"David still sleeping?" Mark asked.

"Umhm," Margaret replied, cup to her lips. "He's still out sound."

"How'd you sleep?" he asked, slipping his arm around her.

"Great. Weird dreams, but like a rock."

"What kind of weird dreams?" he inquired. He took a big gulp of coffee.

"Last night it was David flying off with a flock of birds. Don't remember what kind, but he flew away with them."

"I never really thought of that," Mark said after thinking a moment. "I never considered that we'd have to be so careful outside with a kid. And worrying about him flying off with a flock of birds."

They had spent a considerable of time discussing the ramifications of their young son's flying ability. They had learned how to deal with the occasional forays around the inside of house, but the thought of having him outside was frightening. They weren't at the point of David playing outside unattended yet, but the time would come soon enough. They knew life was about to get even more interesting for them. Above everything else they had discussed, was the overwhelming need to keep the flying a secret. They

11

thought of the media circus that would follow the discovery of a flying boy. He'd never be allowed to be a normal life, and it was obvious he was going to have a whole new definition of normal as it was.

They sat silently as they sipped their coffee. In the distance a lawnmower fired to life and Mark knew his neighbor a few doors down was beginning his usual Saturday routine also. That routine always starting with his roaring lawnmower, making sure there were no stragglers still enjoying a lazy Saturday in bed.

The sound of the machine caused some internal motivation switch to come on for Mark, and he tipped the cup up to gulp the remainder of the now cooled coffee. He set the cup on the step, eased out of the snuggle hold Margaret had on him, and kissed her cheek. She didn't resist as she stood then also, knowing it was time to get on with the rest of her morning.

"Is that all that's on your agenda today?" she asked him. "The windows?"

"Pretty much," he said. "Maybe the lawn this afternoon. I'm thinking on trying to sneak a run in between if that's okay by you." He paused for a moment. "You guys okay with me gone for a bit?"

"Of course we'll be okay. Goof," she laughed.

"Just making sure," he said with exaggerated cheerfulness in his voice. Then he headed back to his ladder. "Let me know when the big guy wakes up."

"Okay. Be careful on the ladder," she smiled at him, slipping back in the front door.

As she disappeared inside, Mark again made his way gingerly up the ladder and through the branches of the tree that seemed to have moved just to obstruct his path. He had the can in one hand and used the other to climb. He set to work at a quicker pace now. He mentally calculated the time it would take to do the side windows and he decided he'd stop after that side was done.

He lost track of the actual time, and just as he was working his way down to move it to the last bank of windows near the back of the house, Margaret appeared from the back door with David in her arms. She held him so he had a view of Mark holding the ladder and sliding it over.

"Who's that?" Margaret said to David. "Huh? Who's that guy with the ladder? Is that Daddy?"

David was squirming and reaching out toward Mark, obviously pleased to see his father. He squealed with delight when he noticed Mark smiling in his direction.

"And who's this big guy, huh?" Mark smiled broadly at David. He came toward him with arms out.

David leaned in his father's direction and was rewarded with being taken from his mother and wrapped in the strong arms of his father. He grunted happily and squealed, wiping his hands on his Dad's face. Margaret watched with a grin. She loved how the two of them reacted together. Mark smiled over at her.

"Come back to Mom now," Margaret said, taking David back. "Let your Dad finish the windows."

She took him in her arms again and stepped back as Mark went up the ladder with can in hand. She and David watched him work on the windows of the second floor bedroom.

"Dadda," David said, wriggling in Margaret's arms.

"Somebody still wants their Dadda," she said, "more than his Momma."

"He must want to help fix the windows," Mark chuckled. He didn't notice that David was squirming in his mother's grasp as he reached up for his father.

"Well, I don't think you want to be held," Margaret said.

She sat down in the soft grass, with David sitting in front of her between her legs. He leaned back in her lap, seemingly content to just sit in the cool grass with his Mom, with Dad not far away. That contentment lasted about a minute before he leaned forward and set off across the lawn on his hands and knees. Margaret let him go. She'd be more careful if he was trying to walk on the uneven ground, but he had opted to crawl. He had taken his first few steps a couple weeks back, but still preferred the four-legged method most. There wasn't anything hazardous around and she was close enough to rescue him if needed. She leaned back on her elbows and watched Mark at work above her.

"One more second floor window after this one and you're done, right?" she asked him.

"Yup. Just these two yet for today," he replied.

Margaret noticed David getting a bit too far away from her, and too close to the flower bed with her rose bushes. She didn't want him going in there.

"Davey. Sweetheart," she called to him. "Stay away from there."

"Hey, big guy," Mark called down. "Stay by your Mom."

David stopped and turned, looking up at his Dad.

"Dadda," he said extending a hand in his father's direction. Then, before Margaret could react, he rose from the ground and slowly floated up toward his father.

Margaret saw him going up and jumped up. She jumped quickly, but he was already out of reach. She stood below him, making sure not to yell.

"Mark," she said softly, not wanting to startle David, "you've got company coming."

"What?" he asked, turning to look down at her.

David was about ten feet away, squirming and wiggling and giggling, as he rose to his dad. He looked a little uncoordinated, and this terrified Margaret, but she watched as he rose up. She remained directly beneath him in case he fell.

Mark quickly and carefully set the can of caulk on the window ledge. It fell anyway, crashing down to the flower bed below. He held the ladder with his left hand and reached out with the other as David came to him. David eased into him and Mark held him close to his chest. Once he was comfortable he had him, he began easing his way one-handed down the ladder. Margaret watched from below, holding the ladder to steady it, as they came slowly toward her. She held out her arms as they neared and David went to her, flying down the last few feet from his father's grasp.

Mark looked out toward the street as he stepped to the ground. A small silver Honda had stopped in the middle of the road in front of their house. The driver, a man, was leaning forward looking at them. *Jesus*, Mark thought, *he saw that*. He stared at the man who was staring at him. The man noticed him looking back and gunned his engine, speeding down the street. Mark went to Margaret and wrapped his arms around both of them.

"Did you see that guy?" he asked her.

"Yeah," she said. She had a frightened look in her eyes. Then her eyes went wide and she said "There he is again."

The Honda came back down the road from the other direction. It slowed in front and the driver again stared directly at them. Both Mark and Margaret glared back, wishing him away. As if sensing that, the car tore down the street and was gone. Mark's eyes followed him as he disappeared.

"What the heck are we going do?" he asked Margaret softly. "Are we going have to put a leash on him?"

"That's not a bad idea," she said. "I don't think we're there yet, but we obviously need to think outside of the box."

"Yeah," Mark said, letting go. "I don't think I can find the manual for raising kids who can fly."

"We can't just fly after him if he takes off," Margaret added.

"Wouldn't that be cool," Mark mused. But he was as concerned as Margaret. They had to keep David grounded. He found himself looking around now, checking to see if maybe anyone else may have seen them. It didn't look like it, but someone could have been looking out a window at them.

"What if that guy tells somebody?" Margaret asked. "What do we do?"

"I don't know," Mark told her. "I don't know."

That night while David was asleep in his crib, both Mark and Margaret sat in his room, quietly whispering once again about how they'd have to manage their son's unusual ability.

Margaret had ideas on keeping the house safe and Mark was glad she had come up with many of those he would never have thought of. He scheduled the various construction projects he'd need to do, and then voiced a concern he had that Margaret hadn't mentioned.

"We need to make sure he doesn't fly around anyone else for sure," he said. "But gees, on the other hand - the kid can fly. That's... he should be able to, since he can, hey?"

"I know what you mean," Margaret said. Silence followed.

"I'm not aware of any flyers in my family," Mark finally said. "He must've inherited it from your side."

"Ha!" she laughed. "I have flighty relatives. And more than a few airheads. But as far as I know, no one can fly."

Chapter 3

Mark and Margaret were fairly successful in both making the house flyer-proof and at keeping their little flyer grounded. At least they did for the first few years. They used the same methods of teaching right from wrong for laying down the guidelines for David's floating abilities that they used for the rest of their parenting issues. But like any little boy, he tested his parents on the limits. Through a consistent use of the carrot and the stick, he learned those limits. Mom and Dad had the upper hand, but David still managed to float around when he could get away with it.

Mark had made a few improvements for David's safety. While he was very young, the windows on his second floor bedroom had a wood lattice-work cover put over the inside, over the glass. The only other person who was aware of the modification was Margaret's mother Delores, and she thought the decorative idea, not knowing the real reason, was just plain strange. Besides that, they never opened windows more than six inches or so, to prevent him from accidently hitting the screen and getting out. They also did the obvious things like not putting breakable things on top shelves of cabinets or ledges where David could fly into them. At least, Mark had once observed, they didn't have to worry about bird-droppings anywhere.

Despite the precautions they took, nothing still matched the effectiveness of a raised voice from Mom. David needed that on more than a few occasions. He learned as he grew, that he needed to stay away from windows, as they provided exits to the unknown world outside, but he didn't always pay attention to was the thought that someone on the outside could see him flying around inside. He knew he was safe in the house and didn't yet understand the concept, or the consequences, of being seen flying.

David was enjoying himself in the house one day, as he cruised from room to room. His mom knew he was flying, but she thought the shades were closed enough, and that the now four year old pilot was safe. He hovered around the ceiling in each room, sometimes circling the rooms, sometimes floating in the middle and doing slow, lazy somersaults in the air. He still laughed pretty regularly at his own antics and this helped him gain more freedom, as his parents wanted him to enjoy himself. He didn't yet realize that his laughing was also a signal his mother took to check on him. She always did, usually watching him with wonderment. She was still amazed at the absurdity of it all.

"David," she said, her voice more stern than she what she actually felt. "Come down from there right now. You've been up there too long."

"Aw, mom," he complained without leaving his spot above her. "I'm not hurting nothing."

"Hurting anything," she corrected him. "And I said come down here. Right now."

David still didn't budge. His back was up against the ceiling. He looked down, deciding whether to try to get away with it just to see what mom would do. She didn't look happy with him. He slowly came down.

"That's better," Margaret scolded him, "but next time I don't want to have to tell you more than once." She stood with her hands on her hips and tried to glare at him. He hung his head as he took his penance, and Margaret couldn't help letting out a little smile. *Oh, boy,* she thought, *we are just going to have a heck of a time keeping him in check.*

Being a four year old boy, he withered under the heat from a scolding mother. He didn't respond to her; his eyes were on the floor.

"Remember what we told you about flying around the windows? Someone could see you."

"No one saw me," David turned toward her and said softly.

"How do you know that?" she went on. "You have to remember to stay away from places where people might see you. You have to remember that." Her voice had softened at the end.

"I'm sorry," David moped. "Nobody saw me."

"Okay," his Mom said. "Go play, but no more flying today."

Margaret watched as he went to the living room. He was looking out the front window to see if he felt like going outside. David never cared much for watching TV, unless it was rainy and he was really bored in the house. She and Mark were glad he wasn't a stay-inside kid. He didn't seem interested in the video games that were becoming popular with kids and preferred being outside, even by himself. Their yard was enclosed and provided safety, and his parents were comfortable with him being outside as long as they could keep a careful eye on him.

They tried to keep their little flyer as normal as possible, but they were deathly afraid of the secret getting out. By the time David had turned one year old, they had realized his gift wasn't just temporary, and they started to get used to the idea. Both of them knew if found out he could become a spectacle at a minimum, but would even have to live in fear of what some kook might do. Mark voiced concern over a number of possible scenarios, from the risk of never ending publicity, to government scientists doing experiments to see what made him levitate. The fears always included having David taken away from them. As always, they decided being paranoid was a good thing, but to try to keep things as realistic as possible. They made it as clear as they could to David that flying around was only allowed with their permission, when they were around, and this especially applied to being outside. She hoped he would go outside now, though not to fly, and he decided to do just that.

David always stayed in the yard and was now learning to ride his bike. He still had training wheels, but he was working at riding without them soon. Mark and Margaret had wondered whether he even needed the training wheels, and whether his levitating abilities could make him stay up on his bike. David hadn't connected the two activities yet, and seemed like any other kid that age, wobbling from side to side on the extra wheels.

Margaret watched him now, going back and forth in their long driveway. She checked the time and saw that Mark would be home soon. She poked her head out the back door and told David to come out to the back, out of the way. She checked on him every couple of minutes as she fixed supper, and when Mark eventually pulled into the drive, David was in back, by the garage. He had his wagon attached to his bike and had somehow also attached the gardening cart to that. He started to pull his caravan out of the way when his dad drove in.

"Hey, how's my guy?" Mark yelled and waved as he eased past David.

"Hi, Dad," David said back, raising a hand in a wave. After his dad came out of the garage, he pulled his bike up next to him. "Like my new train, Dad?"

"Pretty cool," Mark told him, tousling his short brown hair.

Mark noticed Margaret in the kitchen window, watching the two of them. He waved to her and got a wave and a smile in response.

"Let's go see what's for supper, hey," Mark said waving David in.

David flew to the door.

A car went by the front of the house right at that moment and the driver had a clear view of David flying. It looked to Mark like the driver may have been able to see David. He didn't know if the person saw him or not, but his heart went into his throat. Margaret looked silently at the ceiling when he told her. Her stomach felt tight.

She looked at him. No words were spoken.

Chapter 4

The Andersons had at some point realized that if they tried to limit David to just flying indoors, there was a good chance they'd force him to sneak around outside. So, they would occasionally let him fly around the backyard, always in their presence. They made sure no one was around and kept a close eye for anyone who might come near.

They had just finished their dinner on one of those occasions, and were sitting in the lawn chairs on their back patio behind the house, enjoying the nice evening. The outdoor setting turned out to be perfect for this activity. Their yard was ringed by thick brush and trees. It was a large city lot and they had gotten it just in case they had kids to fill it with. They never realized it would be a flight practice field.

They watched him now as he flew circles around the yard. The next door neighbors, the Meyers, were out of town at a funeral. They'd asked Mark and Margaret to keep an eye on their house while they were gone. None of the other neighbors had a view into their yard. The closest house on the other side was over fifty yards away and blocked from view by a fence and tall bushes. This afforded David the opportunity to spread his wings, as Mark had put it.

"You know," Mark said, leaning back, squirming to get comfortable in the wrought iron chair, "even after all these years of watching him do this, I still have a hard time believing it."

Margaret sipped iced tea, nodding. "Yeah. It's really... I don't know the right word to use. Astonishing. Or... I don't know. Amazing seems too cliché for something like this."

Mark nodded silently. They were quiet again, watching David.

"Frightening," Margaret said suddenly. "That's what it is, frightening. The whole thing just sometimes scares the crap out of me."

Mark stayed silent. She was right, it was frightening. Terrifying actually. They'd managed just fine in the parenting department on what they both perceived as the normal things involved in raising a boy. Flying wasn't something they had knowledge of.

"Remember that first doctor's visit after we found he could levitate?" he finally spoke. He tipped his glass up for a drink. "I was pretty scared there."

"Me too," Margaret said. That memory was vivid.

"I thought the doctor was going to find some abnormality," Mark said. "Like a brain tumor or something." He was quiet again, the memory adding to the constant fear he still felt.

David had stopped circling the yard. They watched as he floated near the back by the gardening shed. They both resisted smiling when he slowly began doing somersaults in the air. He tucked his arms and legs in like he was cannonballing into water and began to spin.

"Be careful you don't hit your head," Margaret yelled out to him. "Go a little slower."

David slowed to a stop, hovering.

"I am," he said. Then he slid between the stand of lilacs separating a portion of their yard from the Meyer's yard and did a quick spin around their nearly identical space.

"Stay over here, Davey," Mark yelled to him. He stood to go after him if needed.

David came back. He drifted over near Margaret's flower garden and hung horizontally over the plants. He was interested in something down within the thick leaves. He glided slowly, as if stalking some sort of prey. Mark and Margaret studied his movements and his interest in what he was doing. They didn't think a "normal" boy wouldn't likely think of doing something like that.

"I'm not just frightened that he'd hurt himself. You know, like from crashing into something," Margaret restarted the conversation.

Mark reached over and took her hand in his. He knew what she was going to say. "I know," he said.

"I'm always so worried about if people found out?" she turned to Mark. "What would we do? He'll be going to school soon."

"I know this sounds like conspiracy theory paranoia," Mark agreed with her, "and I say this all the time, but I'm afraid of some shadowy, top-secret government agency coming and taking him away. It wouldn't just be media people interested in a boy who can fly, which would be a circus all unto itself. There'd be people who would want to know how he does it."

"Medical experiments," Margaret said. She said it ominously. The comment demanded the dark silence it got.

"It…" Marked started, but instead said, "Why us? Why our child?"

Margaret just shook her head. They'd found they couldn't have more children after David. They were saddened by that, but adjusted to the fact. They had their hands full enough with just one.

David came over to them, settling on his feet near where they sat. They looked at their little five year old marvel.

"Can I go up in the trees?" he asked. He spoke more to Mark than to his mom, knowing his chances were better that his father would approve than his mother. He'd figured that out already.

No such luck though. "No, I don't think that'd be a good idea," Mark said softly but firmly. "Someone could see you if you got up too high." He saw David's slight disappointment.

"Okay," David said, studying his feet. "I think I'm going in."

"Okay," his dad said. "We'll be in in a little bit."

They watched him walk to the back door and disappear with the usual loud slam of the door. They'd told him a million times not to slam the door, but every one of those million times was ignored. They remained silent for a few minutes, nursing their warming tea. It was a nice night and as of right now, David was safe, the secret was safe, and they could both continue to dread how this nice, neat, comfortable life could come to an end.

They held hands until they finally went in for the night.

*

A little less than nine hundred miles away, just outside of Washington D.C., in a cement office building, the kind that was the norm for government agencies like this, a new computer system was being installed. The top of the line equipment was capable of storing hundreds of times the amount of data that the previous system was capable of. The computer age was a boon to the users. Mountains of paperwork were slowly being replaced by the digital world. It was a quantum leap for their computerized record keeping.

The operators of this system were mostly long-time employees who had developed skills at putting in what seemed to be unlimited information, and then pulling out whatever was needed, quickly and efficiently. Many governmental departments and agencies within the national security apparatus relied on this information to be able to do what they do.

Some of the operators fashioned themselves to be spies, as that was in reality, one of the fundamental tasks of their employers. To them this was shadowy, top secret.

One of the most shadowy and secretive of the operators was a four year veteran of the Federal Bureau of Investigation. Even with that limited time with the Bureau, Agent C. Randall Whiting had excelled in this capacity. He had shown a propensity for the behind the scenes operations, rather than being a hands-on field agent. Unlike other FBI agents, who dreamed of glory as G-men, he liked the research and the more academic parts of this function. Also unlike many of the others in the FBI, he seemed to have an agenda. He had a purpose. He planned to use all of this compiled knowledge for that purpose. The spying was interesting, but the position was also just a rung on the ladder to him.

Chapter 5

There are a hundred ways a young boy can get in trouble in his own backyard. David had only managed to find a few and they were the basic ones. He wiped out on his bike a couple times, including into his parent's car. He was goofing around with friends and they tore enough branches off a small tree that his mom had to dig it up and throw it away. He was a pretty normal kid, with that one little exception of the gravity issue. He'd never gotten in the kind of trouble that required his parents to rescue him. But, as David had gotten used to flying around the yard under the supervision of his parents, he had also done what any kid his age would do, and tested flying on his own when they weren't looking.

David had been told enough times, as far back as he could remember, that he couldn't let anyone see him fly. While restricted to the house it was easy, since his parents covered the windows. Out in the yard, he knew they kept an eye out for him and he also knew to be watchful himself. But, he grew confident and would occasionally fly around alone.

One warm autumn Saturday, he decided to climb the tree that had always tempted him. David had stared up the tree many times before, planning how to climb the branches inside. He figured once he got up to the first lowest branches, it would be easy climbing up the other limbs extending from the solid trunk. It was just a matter of getting up the ten feet or so from the ground to the lower branches. There was nothing to stand on. He wasn't big enough to carry the ladder out of the garage, but he didn't even think of doing that.

David looked up the tree. Then he looked around the yard, listening for anyone who could be nearby and watching, and found none. He went up quickly, floating to the first couple of large branches. He settled on them and looked up again. It looked easy, so he climbed. He didn't float up.

Instead, he went from limb to limb, as far as he could go to the top of the maple where the branches got thinner. He'd never climbed a tree before. Playground equipment had been the extent of his climbing experience and that was easy when he knew he didn't have to be afraid of falling. He had never known that fear.

He sat on a branch at the top that gave him a view of part of his own backyard, part of the next door neighbor's, and of the street out front. Other than that sliver of a view, he was surrounded by branches and leaves. He felt a certain comfort being wrapped within the leaves of the tree's canopy. David had never been that high before and it excited him to be up that far. He sat on the branch, holding the trunk of the tree in the crook of one arm, idly swinging his legs back and forth. This was pretty neat for a six year old boy.

The neat experience came to an abrupt end. David spotted Mr. Meyer in the yard, looking up at him, and then walking over in his direction. This would probably mean that his mom and dad were going to find out. He knew he was in trouble when Mr. Meyer walked up to the tree.

"Davey," Mr. Meyer called up to him, "are you okay up there? And how in the devil did you get up in that tree in the first place?"

"I'm okay, Mr. Meyer," David replied. He didn't answer the second question. "I'm coming down now." He felt the need to get out of the tree.

"You be careful," he told him, shielding his eyes from the sun to watch how David came down. He had obvious concern in his voice and David had caught that.

"I will," he said as he started down. He turned his back toward Mr. Meyer and slowly stretched a leg down to the next branch. After working his way down three steps on three branches, David realized climbing trees was a lot easier going up than coming down. His original plan to float down vanished when his next door neighbor appeared, and he now realized he'd need help at the bottom. His mom and dad were going to kill him.

After a couple of minutes he found himself on the lowest branch and looking at the concerned face of Mr. Meyer.

"How the heck did you get up there anyway?" he asked again. But the question also seemed to mean how the heck are we going to get you down? The lowest branch was a little over ten feet up and that was a long way for a small boy to jump. He'd have to go get the ladder.

But David didn't seem afraid. Before Mr. Meyer could move to get the ladder, David lowered himself until he got a hold of the branch and then gently swung down until he hung by his hands. His feet were still a good six feet off the ground. Mr. Meyer reached up, his hands just barely reaching David's legs, but not too far away that he wouldn't be able to catch him as he fell.

"Okay, let go," Mr. Meyer told him.

David dropped and Mr. Meyer caught him by the waist, easing his landing.

"Thanks, Mr. Meyer," David said. He wasn't sure what else to say.

"Quite alright, Davey," he replied. "You're an awfully brave young man. I would never have climbed a tree that big at your age." He looked up the tree again and shook his head. That was a long way up. Before he could turn around a voice came from behind.

"Hi, Emery," Margaret said as she approached. "How are you?"

"Good Margaret," he replied. "And you?"

"Good also. What's my little guy up to?" she asked, sensing Emery's presence had something to do with David.

"Seems like Davey likes to climb big trees," he said, tousling David's hair so as not to make him feel like he was being tattled on. "And a darn good climber, too." He sounded like he was impressed.

He told her the story of finding him at the top of the tree. Margaret looked up the inside of the tree to where he pointed, indicating the spot near the top. He made it sound like David had a talent for climbing, as well as unusual courage. David's eyes held the ground.

"That is pretty high," she said. She looked at David. "You climbed all the way up there?" She was pretty certain she knew how he got there. She pulled him against her in a hug, knowing she couldn't voice her true concerns in front of Emery.

"I was okay, Mom," David said, certain he was in big trouble.

"Well, no more of that, okay, honey?" she told him.

Margaret thanked Emery for helping rescue David from the tree. David ran in the house while they stayed out in the yard talking. At the end of the conversation Margaret invited the Meyers over for a cookout the following weekend. Her and Mark had often talked with the Meyers about an end of summer get-together, so she suggested doing it the following Sunday.

When Mark got home that evening, Margaret told him about the tree climbing adventure. She hadn't said anything else to David yet, since she wanted to discuss it with Mark first.

They knew David was flying around on his own. He was careful when he broke the rule, but they spotted him every now and then. They could tell when he did it that he looked around first and wasn't at risk of being seen. Being caught up in the tree was probably a surprise. But the Meyers were bound to catch David sooner or later, they realized, as their backyard abutted their own and they had a view of where David played. They had to figure out what to do. They lived too close.

"Well," Mark said after they had discussed options, "I guess I sort of lean toward telling them about David. They're like grandparents to him anyway and they'd keep that secret. I think we can trust them. What do you think? Think we should we do that?"

Margaret nodded slowly. "Yeah. It's either that or completely ban all outside flying and then hope he doesn't break the rule. He's a good kid, but he's still a kid. And I'm not for moving away. We can work something out with them I think."

Mark just smiled at her remark. He was looking out the window at the big tree that his young son was found at the top of. That was gutsy for kid his age. *My son who can fly*, he chuckled.

After dinner they talked more about how to bring Emery and Phyllis Meyer in on their secret. It wasn't every day you did something like that, and Margaret and Mark shared a few unexpected laughs running through some possible explanation scenarios. In the end they decided the best way to ask for their silence and explain why, would be to have David show them right up front that he could fly.

Margaret called Phyllis to officially set the time and date of the get-together she had discussed with Emery. Before Phyllis inquired about the little tree-climber, they set up plans for the coming Sunday.

*

The Meyers brought side dishes of potato salad and homemade apple pie. Those were courtesy of Emery, the cook of their family. Each fall the scent of apple pies wafted from the Meyer's house. Margaret had prepared another side dish and Mark had the grill fired up. The cooler near the patio contained cold beer and soda, and the patio table was covered with finger-foods and snacks. Margaret had gone all out.

The adults had settled in chairs, holding cold drinks and nibbling from small plates. David stood near the table, grazing from the large snack bowls, nursing a can of Diet Coke. When he finished that, he did a pretty good job of setting up the arches from their croquet set around the backyard. He came over by the others and easily convinced Mr. Meyer to play a game while his dad did the cooking. It wasn't a competitive game, but they enjoyed themselves, smacking the colored balls through the course David had devised.

They had barely finished their game, with David winning of course, when Mark announced the food was done. Everyone took a plate, filled it from the side-dishes the ladies had just brought out, and then made their way toward the grill where Mark gave them each a perfectly charred piece of meat. Even David managed to wolf down a decent sized steak. Emery Meyer smiled at him with approval. He liked Davey.

They finished eating just as the sun was beginning to set. The warm days of autumn often turned to chilly evenings, so they all carried dishes and plates as they made their way in to the Anderson's kitchen for the apple pie desert. Phyllis had also brought ice cream and while Emery was cutting the pie and putting a huge slice on each plate, Margaret added a large scoop next to it. They moved into the living room to eat it.

"Well, it was good to get you guys over for dinner," Mark said settling on the couch. "We always talk about it, but never get around to it." He set his drink on the side table and went to work on his pie. "Yeah. There's always a million things to do when it's warm outside," Emery added, "and never enough time for the things that really matter."

"Yeah, I always get sidetracked too," Margaret said. She sat down next to Mark.

"Davey," Mr. Meyer asked, "did you have a good summer?"

"Yeah, it was great," he replied, setting his empty plate on the coffee table. He was the first one done with the desert and was nursing another can of soda. He didn't say more.

"Are you ready for school?" Phyllis joined in.

"Yeah," he replied. "It starts a week from Tuesday."

"My little guy is getting so grown up," Margaret said, patting his leg.

David blushed and didn't say anything. A short silence followed as everyone scraped their forks across their plates to get the last of the crumbs of Emery's tasty treat. Then, almost as if choreographed, they all set their empty dishes down with an identical clink of the fork.

Mark could tell that David was a little bit anxious. They had talked about what they were going to tell the Meyers and David knew he'd need to float when his dad wanted him to. Other than that, he didn't want to have to stay around for the discussion afterward. They had told him that he could go outside again since a couple of his friends from down the street might come over.

"Hey, you guys," Mark said to Emery and Phyllis. "We have a favor to ask." He leaned forward at the edge of the couch, elbows on his knees.

"Sure. What is it?" Emery replied, sensing from the way Mark had positioned himself that it was important.

"Um. Well, there's something we need to let you in on," Mark said softly.

"It's kind of a family secret," Margaret quickly added.

"And you guys are like family," Mark went on, "so you should know."

"A deep, dark secret?" Phyllis dramatically asked.

Mark and Margaret looked at each other, then at David, who was suddenly looking a little scared when they had used the phrase '*deep, dark.*'

"Well, it's not dark," Margaret said for David's benefit, noticing he looked uncomfortable, "but it's pretty deep. You'll be... surprised."

"I like secrets and surprises," Emery said. "Lay it on me."

"You have to promise us that you will absolutely not say a word to anyone," Mark said, his voice taking on a more serious tone. His face matched the tone.

Emery and Phyllis exchanged glances and then nodded in unison.

"No one will believe you anyway," Mark added, "but swear you won't say a word."

"Unless there's some serious laws being broken, I think we're good for keeping quiet," Emery said. His upturned palms indicated he was eager to hear the secret.

"Well, spill the beans," Phyllis said, even more eagerly. "You've got our attention now."

Mark looked at David to see if he was ready to go. They had discussed the cues he would get and he seemed set to go. Mark smiled at him and winked. He had warned David that the Meyers would be flabbergasted at what they saw and not to worry.

"If I told you, you'd think I was crazy, so we'll just show you. Davey?" He nodded at his son.

All eyes turned to David as he got up and stood to the side of the couch. Then he slowly rose two feet from the floor and hovered there in front of them. He looked at his mother and father to see if he was doing it as they had asked. They smiled at him and nodded, then looked at the Meyers.

It was pretty much as Mark and Margaret expected. The Meyers wore uniform looks of astonishment, their jaws dropping, and neither were able to speak. Mark filled the void of silence.

"It seems our Davey can fly."

*

David's friends showed up to rescue him while the adults stayed inside talking about the secret they now shared. Margaret took over the explaining and filled them in on the details, right back to the first time she saw him levitate. Mark joined in again when they talked of how terrified they were that word would spread of an amazing flying boy. The Meyers fully understood. They promised to keep silent.

"I guess that explains how he got to the top of that tree," Emery smiled.

Margaret nodded. "Yup. I think you're right."

Letting the Meyers in on their secret took a weight off of Mark and Margaret. They knew they would keep the secret and there was an odd sort of relief that they didn't have to shoulder the entire burden of keeping it anymore.

Both Emery and Phyllis were eager to see David fly around. Margaret invited them over a few nights later to finish the beer left from the cookout. Everyone was in the backyard watching as David coasted around in circles. He was a few feet off the ground, doing lazy arches as he maneuvered around the corners of the yard. While getting to be old hat to the Andersons, it was an exciting thing to watch for the next door neighbors.

"Boy, I wish I could do that," Emery said. He couldn't take his eyes off the phenomenon.

No one replied, but they all nodded in agreement.

Chapter 6

The following weekend Mr. Meyer asked Mark if it was okay to take Davey to the orchard to pick apples. Mark was okay with it, so he told him to go ahead and ask David. He did, and got an affirmative response. Both David and Mr. Meyer enjoyed each other's company, and with the Meyers now knowing he could fly, the comfort level increased.

It was another beautiful fall day, sunny but cool. Emery came over for David that Sunday morning at about eleven o'clock. They drove the six miles or so to the orchard, with the radio playing loud and Mr. Meyer singing along. David didn't know the words to any of the songs, but enjoyed the ride and the singing.

"Well, which way should we go?" Emery asked him when they stood looking at the long narrow rows of apple trees. The orchard was large, with row after row of trees stretched out from the parking lot.

"I dunno." David looked up at him, knowing he'd choose the way.

"Those trees look full," Mr. Meyer said, pointing off to one side. "Let's try those."

They walked over. Mr. Meyer told stories of picking apples when he was a child, getting stomach aches from eating too many, and eventually learning to make pies. He offered to show David how to bake a pie and got an excited response.

"First we gotta pick 'em," Mr. Meyer pointed at a fruit laden tree. "Let's get some from this tree here." He walked over to a tree thick with apples.

Emery took his time and enjoyed the company, having no grandchildren of his own to do this with. He found Davey to be a more than adequate substitute. He only needed a couple dozen apples and he was selective in those he picked. David, on the other hand, was adding to the bag, a lot of apples that were still mostly on the green side.

"Okay, now we need some that are really red," Mr. Meyer said to guide Davey's choice of fruit. "Looks like most of them are way up high. I think we need some poles. Why don't you go get two of the those poles in that basket over there." He pointed to where the apple-picking poles stood in a rack at the end of the row.

David looked up at the apples and then at Mr. Meyer. "Can't I just go up and get them?" he asked. "I don't need a pole."

"Hmmm. Well. I don't know if we're supposed to do that out here," Mr. Meyer said, automatically looking around. No one was nearby as far as he could tell. Still, all of a sudden the responsibility was his. He wasn't so sure about this. He glanced in all directions.

David waited for the final word on whether he could fly up to get the apples, or if he needed to get the poles.

"We don't need many," Mr. Meyer finally told him in a conspiratorial whisper, "so go ahead. But make it quick. And get only the red ones." He looked around again, seeing no one.

David went up quickly, about ten feet, to where a branch bent down, loaded with large, bright red fruit. He picked one at a time, dropping them down to Mr. Meyer, who caught each and put them in their bag. He came quickly down when he was told they had enough.

"Okay. Good job," Mr. Meyer patted his shoulder. He was confident they went unseen. He looked around again. No one saw them. "Ya'know, we probably shouldn't tell Mom and Dad that you picked them that way."

"Yeah, okay," David nodded. He was in full agreement on that.

They headed to the small store to pay for their harvest, bought caramel apples and left.

*

Emory was wrong. A very amazed man had watched them from the cover of a short, thick apple tree a few rows over.

"Hi. Can I talk to someone about something weird that I saw?" the man asked the receptionist who answered the phone at the local newspaper, the Aston Daily Sentinel.

"Can you tell me what this is regarding, so I know where to transfer your call?" the girl asked in response.

He told her briefly what he'd seen. She smirked, said okay and transferred him to Bernie Fredder, the local beat reporter. He took care of this kind of call. A fifteen year veteran on the local news beat, Bernie handled anything and everything that happened in the county. He was well known in the community and was a go-to source for information the readership wanted to know about.

"Bernie Fredder," he identified himself when he answered.

"Um, hi," the man on the other end said nervously. "I wanted to tell someone about something I saw. I don't know if I should call the cops or not."

"You can start with me," Bernie told him, cradling the phone on his shoulder while pulling out a notebook and a pen to take notes.

The man explained what he had seen. Bernie took notes, shaking his head as he did. *A flying boy. Right.* He got details anyway. How old was the boy? What did he look like and what was he wearing? Who else was around? Did anyone else see it who could corroborate the story? He finished with a few more questions, thanked the man for calling after failing to coax his name from him, and disconnected the call. Since there were no other witnesses, he was sure the man was delusional. Bernie wrote "Flying Boy" at the top of the piece of paper, the date as well, tore it from the spiral notebook and opened his desk drawer. He pulled up a file that had been in the alphabetical file N. The folder was titled "NUTCASES". He put the paper in it and shut the drawer.

Chapter 7

It was the day of Derek Dobson's birthday party. David had gotten the invitation in the mail two weeks before. His mom had checked their schedule, found nothing to conflict with him attending and called Derek's mom to let her know he'd be coming. The following weekend they'd gone shopping for a present. David carried it now as he got out of his mom's car. "Bye, Mom," David yelled as he slammed the door.

"Bye, honey," she replied. "I'll be back around four o'clock. Have Mrs. Dobson call if you need me sooner." All she saw was his back as he ran up the driveway.

"Hello, Davey," Mrs. Dobson greeted him. "How are you today?" She waved over at Margaret and got a wave in response.

"Hi, Mrs. Dobson. I'm fine. How are you?"

"Well, I'm fine thank you," she said. "I'll take the present and you go out back with the other kids." She took the package.

"Thanks. Bye," he said, running around the side of the house.

There were an even number of boys and girls at the party, but they weren't playing together. The boys were playing tag football on the large lawn, and the girls stood in small groups around the food table. The table was covered with snack trays of Doritos, potato chips, and pretzels, as well as a cooler with Coke, Pepsi and juices. David grabbed a handful of pretzels, said hi to a group of girls who first said hi to him, and went to join his friends playing football.

"Hey, Davey," his friend Perry yelled over to him as he approached, "you're on our side."

"Or maybe he wants play with his girlfriend, Amy," Calvin Burns said. "Davey and Amy up in a tree..." he sang. He'd seen them hanging out together the day before.

"Shut up, Burns," Perry defended Davey. "They're just friends."

David ran out for a pass. He and Amy Kellerman were friends. But she made him feel funny inside. Enough that he had looked for her first when he came around back. And he felt funny again when he saw her.

"Go long!" Perry urged David. "Longer."

He was reaching the point where no one could throw the ball that far. Perry lofted it to him. He had a strong arm and it carried the ball to where David ran. He had to make a diving catch, but had it in his hand when he rolled to the ground. Given his special ability, there wasn't much he couldn't catch.

"Nice grab," Perry commended him.

David was in the far corner of the Dobson's yard. The back property line ran along a deep ravine lined with trees. This was a favorite spot for Derek and his friends to hang out. They had constructed a crude tree-fort in one of the young maples that was easy to climb. They'd even tied a rope to an upper branch and built a wobbly platform on another tree, so they could swing from one to the other. The boys spent a lot of time back there.

"Hey, you guys," David yelled back at his friends. "Let's go to the fort." He pointed and tossed the ball back to Perry. His arm wasn't as strong as Perry's and the pass fell short.

"Yeah," Derek yelled, leading the other boys in a trot to the wooded ravine. In moments they disappeared in the trees. A group of girls saw them go and decided to follow. They didn't know yet that this was forbidden territory, only for boys.

David scampered up the tree to the fort. His friends were as amazed at his climbing skills as they were of his pass catching skills. He was followed by the rest of the boys and they realized too late that they had too many people in the treehouse. A couple swung over to the platform in the other tree. The boys who didn't normally hang out with Derek and hadn't been here before were enthusiastically swinging back and forth on the rope. A couple more climbed some of the other trees.

Then the girls showed up. The boys didn't like their territory being invaded and started ribbing them about not being able to climb trees anyway, and how they should go back and talk about clothes and dolls or whatever it is you girls talk about. A few of the girls decided they would show the boys that they were just as good at climbing trees as they were. In a short while, the fort and platform had girls mixed in with the boys. Suddenly, no one was ribbing anyone else about whether they could do anything and they were all having fun climbing and swinging on the rope.

David was happy to see that Amy was among them. She was pretty agile for a girl, he thought, and rather fearless. She was doing things and climbing trees some of the other boys wouldn't even dare to do. David was known to be fearless and able to outdo his friends. In fact, it was him who had crawled on the limb high above to tie the rope to, that they used to swing on. No one else even considered doing that daredevil stunt. It earned him a bit of respect from the group. No one ever questioned his courage. He now felt the same respect for Amy as he saw her navigating the branches of the trees. She didn't play it safe like the other girls did. After the ribbing he'd got from Calvin, he hesitated to join her. He stuck with the other group in the fort or hanging out at the base of the trees.

"Derek," a voice carried back to them. "Are you in your treehouse? I brought the barbeque out. Come and eat and then we'll have cake."

The kids scampered from the fort, down to join those on the ground in a run back toward the house. David was one of the last remaining in the fort. As he readied to climb down, he noticed Amy carefully working her way down from a tree only he had been able to get into. He knew more from the other boys than from experience, that it was harder coming down a tree than it was going up.

"You go ahead," he told his friend Matt, the only one left in the fort besides him. "I'll be right behind you." He kept an eye on Amy working her way down.

Matt got down and ran off to join the party. David and Amy were the last two in the woods. David climbed down and waited near the base of the tree she was in. It looked like she was having some trouble and she had a ways to get down yet. It would be a long way to fall.

Suddenly she let out a short scream. David saw her swinging by one hand, the other desperately reaching for a hold on the branch. She was seconds from falling and the certain injury that it would cause.

David didn't hesitate. He flew up to her, wrapping his arms around her waist just as she lost the final grip on the branch. He held her tightly as he slowly lowered her to the ground.

"What?" she stammered, confused. "How'd you do that?"

David didn't say anything as he stepped back. His cheeks felt hot. He looked down.

"You can fly?" she asked. "You flew up to save me?"

He still didn't know how to reply. No one was supposed to know.

"Davey," she said more than asked. "You can fly, just like Superman?"

"Uh, yeah," David said sheepishly, his eyes on the ground. "But you gotta promise not to tell anyone. My mom and dad will kill me if anyone finds out. Promise you won't tell."

"I promise," Amy said. Then after a pause she looked up at the tree. "Besides, I don't think anybody would believe me anyway."

"We should get back," David said, wanting to get away from there. He turned to go.

Amy took his hand and stopped him. Then to the complete surprise of both of them, she gave him a quick kiss on the cheek. Now they felt really hot.

"Thanks for saving me," she said softly, then headed toward the backyard. David followed.

He felt funny again. He didn't know it, but so did Amy.

They both managed to rejoin the party without being noticed together. Neither wanted the inevitable teasing that would come from any suspected activity they may have had in the trees in the ravine. Calvin Burns would never let that go.

David sat with the boys, as the group again separated into boys and girls. They ate food from paper plates. He occasionally glanced at Amy and a few times got a smile when she noticed him looking. One time, she pinched her lips together and made a zipper motion. He did the same in response.

Everyone finished the sloppy joe barbeque and the beans, and the party moved on to the cake. They sang Happy Birthday and watched as Derek opened his presents. Mrs. Dobson had arranged for some games to play afterward and all the kids were laughing and having fun. In no time it seemed, the party drew to a close and parents started arriving to pick them up.

David was walking to his mom's car and noticed Amy heading over to get in her mom's car. They each waved to the other and yelled "bye". Then Amy made the zipper motion across her lips. David did too.

"What's that all about?" his mom asked him as he got in the car.

"Just a secret we have," he replied, turning away from her inquiring gaze.

"Oh, a big dark secret?"

"Nope. Just a secret," he said. He looked out the window, hoping she would stop asking questions. No one else was supposed to know about him.

Margaret just smiled at him. "Okay," she said. "So, how was the party?"

"It was fun," David told her. "I had a good time."

And he still felt kind of funny.

Chapter 8

Each Monday at nine in the morning, Herbert Foster, the Deputy Director of the Federal Bureau of Investigation (DD), convened a meeting of the Regional Office Liaisons. The purpose of the meeting was for each liaison to update the DD, and other liaison agents, on the status of activities in their individual regions. Specifically, they gave updates on such things as crime sprees, ongoing investigations that involved the FBI, local events that could or would eventually involve the FBI, and any other topics the Regional Agents thought important to be noted at the national level. While the liaisons worked out of the national headquarters outside of Washington DC, they spent a portion of their time at their regional offices, and were in effect, second in command to the Regional Directors there.

After these meetings, the DD summarized the information he'd gathered into a report for his boss, the Director of the FBI. The Director then would share what he thought appropriate with the Director of the Central Intelligence Agency and other national security agencies.

These meetings were often boring to many of the attendees, but on occasion someone either brought up a humorous item that provided some comic relief, or filled everyone in on a high-profile case that they all followed on. Most of the agents who attended were seasoned veterans with field experience, with only one being new and recently out of training for the position.

The Deputy Director held to an agenda where each liaison, starting from the Northeast Region and moving in a clockwise rotation to the South then to the West and back, usually in the same order, would get fifteen minutes to cover news from their area. A few would run over their time limit, normally the Northeast, which covered the NY and Washington D.C. area, and the Southwest, covering a huge area that included all of California. Those whose areas were less populated and thus quieter, often

39

took much less than their fifteen minutes of allotted time, so overall, the meetings ran pretty much on time.

Not much was new in this day's meeting. After the usual reports, the Deputy Director asked if anyone had any other issues they'd like to discuss. Hearing none, the DD introduced the newest member of the Regional Liaisons.

"Gentlemen," Deputy Director Foster said, "I'd like to introduce our newest member, Arthur P. Johnston. He will be the new Liaison for the North-Central Region when Bob Bristol retires next month."

"Call me Artie," Artie quickly said, before anyone could say 'welcome Arthur'. In unison the reply came back as 'welcome Artie.'

"Artie comes to us from the Baltimore office, where last he was Special Agent in Charge of the case of the local police corruption that eventually became a federal matter. I think you all remember that one, as Bob updated us periodically on it. And a job well done there," he said, nodding in Artie's direction. Artie just nodded back. "Fourteen years with the Bureau, graduated second in his class out of Quantico, and an impressive file to back him up. Welcome to our group, Artie."

"Thanks, Herb," Artie responded. "I'm looking forward to the new post, and working with you guys." He nodded to the group in acknowledgement of their welcome to him.

"Bob will show you the ropes," the DD told Artie, nodding in Bob Bristol's direction. "That's it. Have a good day."

The room cleared out as each returned to their offices. Artie followed Bob to their for now joint office and they got to work. Bob showed him the various reports they received to review, and they spent that day and the next few days going over the various pieces of information forwarded to them. Most were from external sources, while some came from those who gathered and stored the information internally. The following week Artie was on his own.

There wasn't much going on out of the ordinary, but Artie found he especially enjoyed the oddball and unusual items that the local authorities brought to their attention. He always thought it was the little things, the minutiae, that added up to bigger things. He particularly paid attention to the police reports and local newspapers. In law enforcement, like in politics, he had learned, everything is local.

Chapter 9

As he grew, David pretty much established his own parameters on what he did for flying. His parents had explained enough about the risk of being caught, and as he matured, he understood it more and became more aware of his surroundings. He thought he was being careful.

Still there times when he was taking chances he probably shouldn't. But he enjoyed the freedom he had by virtue of his special talent so he used it as he thought he should.

One warm early summer evening just after the start of fifth grade, he had been playing football with his school friends. David had become a favorite player to have on their team. He had gained the nickname "the Vacuum Cleaner" since he was able to catch passes no one else could. His jumping abilities amazed his school-yard friends. It seemed all they had to do was loft the football in his vicinity and he would manage to get to it. He didn't actually fly, but he seemed to be able to leap unusually high and long. Fortunately, no one thought he was anything more than really good at jumping. He was considered a very good athlete, especially for his size, and like his father, he inherited a medium sized build, even as he grew. He wasn't very muscular, although he broadened at the shoulders as he got older. Adults who saw him playing football thought he was "pretty good for his size".

After they finished playing a game of four-on-four tackle, the boys all mounted their bikes and headed home. David rode a couple blocks with his friend Ethan, waved a good-bye when Ethan sped into his own driveway, then continued on by himself. The sun was setting and dusk was taking over. There were lights coming on in all the houses. People were in for the night.

David was about six blocks from home. Three blocks down and three blocks over. He knew the time and that he wasn't running late, and he was feeling good from helping win the football game. He felt the urge to fly. He looked around to see if anyone was out that might see him. He didn't see anyone anywhere. The street was deserted. He thought the coast was clear and wanted to try something. David hooked his toes under the bike pedals and gripped the handlebars tightly, lifting up about a foot off the ground. Other than being that foot off the ground, it appeared he was just riding his bike down the street. He grinned. His bike wasn't too heavy to lift using his toes and hanging on to the handlebars. He looked around again, saw no one, lifted up toward the top of a big setting of trees on his right and in seconds was over the top. He stayed about five feet above the treetops and sped toward his house. His plan was to hug the trees right up to his backyard then drop down on his driveway. The odds were that his parents were in the house. If not, David could be in big trouble. He felt the warm breeze in his hair and leaned back to enjoy it. His bike was held securely by his toes and hands. He looked up at the darkening sky, noticing the first stars to add their twinkle. In seconds he was home.

He hovered for a moment over the trees surrounding his yard, listening for activity. There was none. He stayed in the shadows as he landed on the lawn by the driveway, then waited there in silence until he was sure he was alone.

David slowly rode his bike to the garage, opened the walk in door and stored his bike inside. He felt pretty good as he walked in the back door to the house. *That was fun,* he thought to himself. *I need to do that again.*

*

Three blocks over and two blocks back an elderly couple stood on their back porch talking.

"That was just like a scene from that one movie," the woman said.

"Yeah, it was that... um... what was the name?" the husband tried to remember.

"E.T.," she said as it finally came to her. "That cute alien thing."

"That's it," he nodded. "E.T. That was a good movie." He looked up. "I didn't think it was real though."

They stood silently for a few minutes looking up, as if they expected the bike-rider to return. When he didn't, they found themselves feeling a little disappointed. The movie wasn't scary, so they weren't afraid of a boy flying his bike.

"I'm glad I'm not alone," the woman said. "You'd have thought I was going batty if I told you that I saw a boy flying a bicycle." She was still staring at the sky, her eyes scanning back and forth.

"Battier than normal," he told her as he put his arm around her. "What should we do? Maybe we should call the police."

"Let's wait until tomorrow," she said, after thinking a bit. "Think it over."

"Okay, hon," he said. "Let's go in." He motioned toward the door.

The next morning they discussed it again. The memory was still clear. They didn't know who to call, so decided on the police department. After telling the story to the officer who took the call, the elderly man hung up the phone and shook his head.

"I think he thinks we're crazy," he told his wife.

"I'm wondering the same thing," she replied.

*

The Aston police officer did think they were crazy, but as required with all incoming calls, he noted the contents of the call on the daily police blotter. The blotter was basically a diary of daily activity that law enforcement agencies used to log incoming calls, walk-ins, and whatever policing activities the officers did during their shift. Most things like this call just got noted and then forgotten. The officer noted it, and forgot about it.

Later that day the local newspaper, the Sentinel, called for the daily blotter report. They got one each day from both the police department and the sheriff's department, reviewed them, and printed in the next day's newspaper any news items they thought the public might need to know. This story didn't make the list.

Bernie Fredder, the reporter who handled the daily beat report, remembered a previous report, not a blotter report but an incoming call directly to him, of a flying boy. That was a while ago. He couldn't remember the specifics or if he had written it down, although he was sure he did. He

43

always kept written records of his incoming calls. He pulled out his file drawer for news tips, circled the story on the blotter, wrote FLYING BOY on it, and filed it under N, in the NUTCASE folder. He didn't think there was anything to this story so didn't check for the previous report. *A flying boy. Right.*

*

FBI headquarters were like almost any other office building in that Monday mornings always seemed more quiet. It was just another start to another week. Artie Johnston sipped his coffee as he went through the incoming field reports. Being the beginning of the week, the amount of incoming information was three times the normal volume, as reports from weekend days all came on the same days as the prior Friday's reports. Among the documents each liaison received were on-site field agent reports of specific active cases, crime statistics, broken out in a myriad of ways, newspaper articles, and independent agency reports, such as sheriff's department and police blotters.

He held one in his hand as he read. *A little humor to begin my day,* he thought to himself. The blotter was from a police department in Aston, Wisconsin. What was described as an elderly man had called to report that he and his wife had seen a boy flying on his bicycle, "just like in that movie". The police officer who took the report had noted the person's name and address. Artie chuckled and filed the report with the others in his blotter cabinet by date. He had bigger tasks at hand and flying bicycles wasn't among them.

Chapter 10

The next day David was reading a book in his bedroom while his father worked on fixing the screen in his window. The book was getting less attention than watching his father in the process of taking the screen off. He watched carefully as his dad carefully raised the window, then pulled the levers on both sides of the glass panel, freed it from the framework and turned it before pulling it out. He repeated the process with the screen. David only knew how to open the window by pulling the levers and sliding it up in its track, but had never seen it removed. He was watching closely now, as he learned how to take out the glass and the screen.

"Doing homework?" his Dad asked as he worked.

"No, I finished that after school," he replied. "Just reading a book."

He kept his nose in the book, but his eyes and attention stayed focused on taking out the window. As he had gotten more confident in his flying ability, he yearned to get out and do more of it. He knew the only time to be free enough to test things out was if he got out at night. Being only ten years old, he still had to report to his parents on his whereabouts, so he was confined to only certain areas and periods of time when he was alone.

David had started considering sneaking out at night, but getting out the door without being caught was virtually impossible. His bedroom was on the second floor, just down the hall from his parent's bedroom and then down some creaky steps. If he managed that without being heard, he'd then have to get out of the house without making a noise. That also seemed unlikely. They lived in an older house and the doors made noise when they closed. Going out the regular way was not an option.

He thought more and more on sneaking out and as he watched his dad working on the window and learning how to get it open, David began to devise a plan. He grinned. Sliding the window and screen up and out made considerable noise. Squeaky noise. That would surely alert his parents in the dead of the night. But the idea came to him as he thought about it. What if he took the window and screen out when they weren't around to hear it, then just lean both pieces in the frame so at a glance it would look like the window was in? He could then just lift it out at night and set it on the floor.

He smiled, staring at what was now a thirty inch by thirty inch exit from his bedroom.

"All right," his dad said as he fit the window panel back in. He slid it up and down a few times to make sure it worked in the track correctly. It did. He turned to David.

"Good book, hey?"

"Yeah, it's okay," David replied. "It's about butterflies in North America."

"Hmmm. Sounds interesting," his dad said. He walked toward the door, stopped and looked at David. "Do you like studying things that can fly?"

David thought for a moment. "Yeah, I guess I do."

"Well," his dad smiled at him, nodding, "don't get any ideas about migrating to Mexico, okay?" He turned to leave.

"I won't," came the reply. Then David's attention went back to the window. He set his book down and walked to window. He examined the track that the pane and the screen were in and the small knobs on each side that slid in the track. He had it figured out.

In the days following his getting the window figured out, David made plans for his night-time flight. He wanted to do it on a weekend night and started watching the weather reports on TV. He didn't care about the temperature, that should be fine as cold weather hadn't settled in yet, but he didn't want it to be raining. He had already learned that rain hurt. By Thursday of that first week, he was thinking the upcoming Saturday night was going to work out. According to the weatherman it was supposed to be clear and around fifty that night.

David thought about what to wear. He knew light colored clothes weren't a good idea, so he picked out a dark maroon sweatshirt and a pair of blue jeans. He set them aside in his closet so he knew right where they were when he needed them. When his parents weren't around he practiced taking out the window and screen. He had that down pat.

He lay awake the next few nights, watching the clock to see what time things got quiet. His mom and dad went to bed about ten o'clock each night and by ten thirty he was sure they were asleep. He figured eleven would be a good time. He'd get out of bed on those nights leading up to the weekend and gaze out the window, thinking of what he'd experience. At this hour, the backyard was pitch black and the adjoining neighbor's windows were dark. Beyond getting out of the house and out to the trees, he hadn't figured what he would do when he went. His main plan was to go for a short cruise over the trees and around the neighborhood. He really just wanted to have the freedom to stretch his boundaries. Until now he had been restricted to the backyard and the few times his parents had accompanied him to remote parks, where they'd keep a vigilant eye while he flew around the larger, yet still confining space.

David felt some guilt at what he was going to do, but his eagerness increased as the days slowly passed. The thought of how much trouble he'd be in if he was caught was tucked away in the back of his mind.

*

It seemed like forever to him, but finally Saturday night came. His parents didn't seem to notice he was quieter than normal, as he was lost in thought for his excursion. He couldn't wait.

He had played with friends all day, and at night the family did the usual routine of watching TV until bedtime. The weather turned out just as predicted, so everything was a go so far. He had found the opportunity to take the window out, so that part was all set. At ten o'clock on the dot his mom and dad went to bed. David would sometimes stay up a little longer to watch TV, which was acceptable only on Friday and Saturday. On this night, he didn't want to keep them awake any longer by having the TV on. He went to bed when they did.

He got the sweatshirt and jeans he'd chosen to wear from the closet and put them under his bed. When he was sure he wouldn't expect his parents to come in to his room, he quietly put them on and crawled into bed, pulling the covers over him. He waited, glancing at the clock every couple minutes, wishing it to go faster. His excitement grew as eleven o'clock came closer. He listened intently for any indication that his parents were still awake and was confidant they were asleep.

When his digital clock said eleven, he slid noiselessly from his bed. Instead of walking, he levitated to the window. He had just enough light from the clock to see what he was doing. His hands shook slightly from his nervousness, but he got the window and screen out silently, just as he had practiced. He set them on the floor near his dresser.

David floated silently for a few minutes in front of the opening to the outside. When he finally felt sure he'd get away with it, and when the courage to go had overcome his fear, he rose slightly and turned to a horizontal position. Very slowly, he left his room and went into the night.

He'd been up this high before, but he still stayed close to the roof. His window was a dormer and when he came out, he hugged the roofline near the gutter. He crept along slowly, slinking along a few scant inches above the tiled surface. He leaned over the edge to peer below. No one was there. His initial plan was to cross the side yard to the trees separating his house from the Meyer's garage. He crossed that distance quickly, then come to a stop, hovering over the trees. He waited for another moment, watching his bedroom window. No lights came on. He'd made it. He looked at Meyer's house. No lights there either.

He turned from the house and looked in the opposite direction. Having never flown this late at night before, he didn't expect what he saw. He was facing downtown and the light coming from it was much brighter in contrast to the quiet neighborhoods. The steeples of a few of the local churches were lit up, something he'd never paid any attention to from the ground before. There were only a few tall buildings in the downtown area and they stood out above the treetops. A quarter moon shone in the cloudless sky and the stars were bright.

David stayed there for minutes taking in the view in all directions. This was a whole new world to him and he marveled at the sight. Not knowing what he'd find, he hadn't planned beyond the getting out of his room. It all lay before him now. The lights of the town seemed to beckon him most, so he decided to go further than just his neighborhood and turned in that direction.

He settled into his horizontal position, put his arms out straight in front of him, and slowly cruised toward the steeple of St. Matthews Church. It was about a half mile from his house and he was familiar with the area. He knew his way around most of the town from the ground, but up here there weren't any street signs. It dawned on him that he may have trouble finding his way back without having to go down to street level to get his bearings. He figured that wouldn't be hard to get away with. The fear of that was only fleeting.

He found himself flying faster than he'd ever flown before and he enjoyed the feeling of the wind against him. It wasn't cold, so he was comfortable. His hair flitted in the wind. He came around the steeple in a smooth banking position, then back the distance of a block, to the top of a thick stand of trees. He came to a stop and hovered again, looking back at the church. *That was fun*, he thought to himself, and so decided to circle another church about a mile away. He sped toward it, going even faster this time, turning left around the tall structure in another smooth banking maneuver. When he rounded the church, he headed up even higher, coming to a stop over what he realized was the high school. He looked down at the landscape, enjoying the view from this high above. The school parking lot was illuminated by a crisscross patterns of lights and he noticed bats flitting about in and out of the light they gave off. He dropped from where he was, buzzing the empty parking lot before heading up over the trees near the neighboring houses. He headed back towards the downtown area and came to a stop over a row of taverns just off the main street. The neon lights glistened garishly compared to the soft white lights of the street lamps. Here the parking lots were full and he had to dart away toward the darkness of the nearby tree line when a pair of Saturday night revelers showed up.

They startled him into paying more attention to the fact that he was in plain view for anyone who might look up. It didn't appear to him that they did, but he needed to be more careful.

David checked his watch. It was only quarter after eleven, but he felt like he had been out for longer. The experience and the sights of this new world were almost overwhelming to him, and he knew he'd have more opportunities if he didn't get caught. He grinned at the thought of future expeditions in the safety of the night air. But now he was also thinking he should head home.

It took him a few seconds to decide on the route he'd return on. He knew the general direction, but from the air all he saw was trees, the few tall churches, and ribbons of streets. He made his way back toward his house, staying over the trees whenever possible, while following the same general path he'd take if he were on his bike. He went down Fulton Street to Bennings, then left in to his street. He was soon hovering over the dark side of Meyer's garage.

His house was dark yet. No one had noticed. The window opening to his bedroom was a dark square in the almost equally dark side of the house. David glided over to it and went silently inside. He didn't land immediately, but instead floated in the center of his bedroom, listening for telltale signs that his parents were up. Nothing. He stayed floating, putting the window and screen silently back in place. Then he removed his jeans and sweatshirt, dropping them in a pile on the floor before sliding them under his bed. He slowly settled downward.

David lay awake for a long time, replaying over and over again his adventure in the night sky. Before drifting off to sleep, he'd made plans for the next time.

Chapter 11

Two weeks later, David coasted out through the dark opening of the window. He had hovered silently before exiting to make sure the coast was clear. Once clear of the opening, he darted to the trees next door and headed in the direction of Amy's house. A veteran of more than handful of night flights, he now knew the area and had found confidence to take on these adventures.

He stayed over the trees, having figured out the layout of the canopy in the area, knowing to avoid the open spots where he could be seen. He sped along, arms outstretched, enjoying the coolness of the evening and the wind in his face. It was a clear, starry night and it felt good, especially since he was going to Amy's.

About a mile from his house he came to where he had to cross Superior Street. The road was wide and open, as it was the main thoroughfare through town. He came to a stop over a small grove of trees and bushes to check out the traffic. He had only seen a small group of cars coming north, and they were clustered together. No one was coming in the other direction, so he waited for the cars to pass and when they were a block down, he darted across to the trees on the other side. From there it was another five blocks to her house. He passed over Edison Street, navigating a few houses over to glide over his friend John's house. The house was dark. He resisted the urge to knock on his second story bedroom window and dart away. That would scare the crap out of him, David grinned. Another time.

David came to Amy's house. He stopped over a tree in the next door neighbor's yard and sat in the air for a minute. He had the funny feeling in his stomach, and he had learned a while back what it meant. He and Amy had become more than just friends, although as far back as he could remember he always thought of them as something more than friends. Friends didn't make him feel funny.

Amy had asked him to come over that night. Their friendship and mushy feeling had blossomed into a boyfriend/girlfriend relationship, and they took every opportunity to see each other. The cute little brunette girl had stayed cute, and David was, as his father once said, 'sweet' on her.

Her house was dark, with the exception of the glow of the TV in the front room. He knew which bedroom belonged to her, and it was dark. She had told him she'd go to bed before he got there, but would be in her room awake, expecting him. David was more than a little nervous as he slid over to her upstairs bedroom window. He hovered a few feet away, listening. It was quiet.

"Amy," he whispered through the screen. He waited. She didn't come. He felt scared for a second, and disappointed. "Amy," he said again, a little louder.

"Davey," a soft voice came. "Is that you?"

"Of course it is," he came back. "Are you expecting someone else at your bedroom window?"

"No, silly," she said, as she appeared in the darkness by the window. She knelt on the floor and leaned on the windowsill.

David thought she looked cute, even in the shadow. He could tell she was wearing pajamas and the thought made him feel a slight pang of guilt. The funny feeling got stronger.

They talked for about fifteen minutes. There was something secretive and forbidden about this clandestine rendezvous. Their hushed voices added to the experience. Then she fell silent.

"I think I hear my dad coming," Amy said, pulling away from the window. Footsteps neared her door.

David darted to the side and up slightly, so he was away from view and near the underside of the roof overhang. He hovered silently, listening. He heard Amy's bedroom door open.

"Amy," a man's voice said. Her dad. "Who are you talking to?"

"Um, no one," she replied, not convincingly. "I was just singing to my music." It was the best excuse she could come up with so quickly.

"Okay," her dad said. "Well, I'm going to bed. See you in the morning."

"G'night, Dad. I love you."

"Love you too." The door shut and Amy heard him walk to his bedroom. When she heard his bedroom door close, she went back to the window.

"Davey?" she whispered.

"Still here," he replied, coming down from the shadows.

"Well, I should probably go to bed," she whispered softly.

"Okay," David replied. He didn't want to go. He wanted to stay with her.

"So, I'll see you at school Monday then," David said.

"Yeah." Another moment of silence. "G'night, Flyboy."

"G'night," David chuckled, and as Amy faded into darkness, he turned and swept up over the trees. He felt happy over how the visit went, so he coasted along, arms outstretched, once again just enjoying the night air. He liked it when she had called him Flyboy. He rolled in a circle as he flew.

He checked his watch and decided he had some time outside yet. He couldn't decide where to go, but then he remembered wanting to take a cruise down Shit Creek.

Known officially as Spring Brook, the narrow creek ran through town north to south. David was near the southwest end of town, and just a few short miles from where the creek left town and entered the fields. He decided to head into the farms fields, so he turned and flew in that direction, staying over the trees the whole way. When the trees ended, he dropped to just above the fence line of whatever crop was planted in the first field he came to, and sped over. He went about a mile or so, then did a quick bank and headed back, coming to a stop in the shade near an over-lit gas station to plot his flight. He always wanted to slowly cruise down the creek, just above the water. He and his friends played down here often, catching frogs and minnows. For about a seven block stretch, the banks were a continuous old stone wall. He would stay below them. There were a few bridges he'd have to go through. They were mostly corrugated steel tubes with the road built over them. Since he'd played near the creek countless times, he knew all of the bridges.

David scooted around a bend of scrubby trees and went down to the darkness of the creek. He noticed it was cooler and the water smelled muddy, as it occasionally would. He went slowly, just as he had imagined he would, arms outstretched, pretending he was a bird scanning for prey. He dipped down to cross under Ninth Ave, feeling a little fear as he entered the cool, dark tube, but then exhilarated when he came into the open again.

The cattails were tall along the banks here, so he found himself in the center of the creek, sliding along just inches above the softly gurgling water. He went under Eighth Avenue and around the bend with the grove of trees he and his friends often climbed. David banked sideways as he made the lazy curve, then down again under Seventh Ave, before increasing speed down the next corridor. It was straight and more open. The bridge at Sixth Ave came up on him and he slowed way back to navigate through it.

The lights of downtown began to shine on him and he knew he'd have to take care up ahead. Fifth Ave was the other main street in downtown and the tunnel under it was longer and darker than the rest. Even with the streetlights, David couldn't see the other end of it. He knew from experience that he'd have to stay low and slowly went through the damp opening. The walls here were cement and smelled musty and dank. When he came out the other side, he moved over to a cluster of bushes. Here the streetlights lit the space. He waited a moment to listen, then zipped up over the embankment wall and headed out over the pond formed by the dam that blocked the creek at this point.

Being more open, David stayed low over the water of the pond. Now he sped along, worried about being seen. It was a dark night, but with the lights of downtown only a few blocks away, he knew he could be spotted. He flew over the pond quickly, through two more cement bridges, and then went up over the trees near the hospital and stopped. He checked his watch. Though only fifteen minutes had passed since he'd left Amy's, he was suddenly anxious to get home. The thought of being caught was coming back.

David worked his way over a patchwork of maples and soon silently glided back into his bedroom. He set the window back in place and hovered over his bed, taking off his clothes. Lowering himself onto his back, he listened for a moment and then smiled in satisfaction.

He thought of Amy as he fell asleep.

*

"Good Christ!" Butch Thomas exclaimed under his breathe.

He and his friend, Marc Joyce, had watched silently as the dark clad figure passed over their heads, not five feet away from where they sat on the rocks by the creek. They had been walking home from an evening spent at the bars downtown, and in their drunkenness had decided to crawl down the stone embankment to urinate by the creek.

It was dark, but some light from the corner lamps filtered down to where they sat. When the figure appeared above them, they nearly fell backward from their seats. The flying apparition was a dark silhouette against the blue black sky. They wouldn't have suspected it was a person, if the arms hadn't been outstretched like wings. As it passed over them, they also noted the white tennis shoes on the feet.

Not totally convinced it wasn't an alcohol induced mirage, they stumbled their way back up over the wall. They stood looking in the direction the figure had gone, but didn't see anything.

"Did you just see what I just saw?" Butch asked. "What I think I saw." He felt totally sober now.

"What the hell was that?" Marc asked. "That wasn't a bird."

"I don't know. Looked like a guy."

"Kinda small for a guy," Marc said. "Looked the size of a kid."

"I gotta stop drinking," Butch muttered. He turned to Marc. "What do we do? Call the cops?" He didn't really want to do that.

"They'll think we're nuts," Marc stated matter-of-factly.

"That was too freaky. We gotta tell someone. What if we're being invaded by aliens or something?" He stared at the sky for a moment, then added "I can't tell Ann though. She'll for sure make me quit drinking. Let's get out of here."

They walked mostly in silence for the remaining few blocks to Marc's house. They'd agreed they'd have a stiff cup of coffee and decide whether to call someone. Marc made a strong pot and they drank it slowly.

"I think we should call the police. That wasn't something normal," Butch finally said. The whole experience had spooked him. Marc agreed that someone should know. Butch got the phone and dialed.

"Police Department," the voice said sleepily. "Sergeant Kowalski."

"Uh, hi. I want to report something I saw," Butch tripped over his tongue.

"Okay," came the reply, "but first I need your name and address."

Butch answered some questions and at the end was a feeling like this wasn't such a good idea. He knew Kowalski personally, and that he was a no-nonsense type, and so he knew this story would be greeted with skepticism.

But, he had made the call and gave his name, and had no other alternative now except to continue.

He told the officer what they'd seen, leaving out the part about them spending the night at the bars.

"Have you been drinking?" Sergeant Kowalski asked anyway, confirming Butch's fear of being met with skepticism.

Butch lied. "No," he answered. "Neither of us were."

"Okay. Good," the policeman said. "This the second report of this we had tonight."

"Really!" Butch was surprised. "Someone else saw it?"

"Yup," Sergeant Kowalski stated. "If your stories are to be believed, there's someone flying around our city tonight." He told Butch about the other sighting, which was more than he probably should have.

"Wow," was all Butch could say.

Marc was looking at him with a puzzled expression. He mouthed "what?"

Butch covered the mouthpiece. "Other people have seen him too."

"There, we're not nuts," Marc said. "And it has nothing to do with drinking."

Sergeant Kowalski thanked him for calling and told him if they saw anything again, to be sure to report it.

"Wow," Butch said again as he hung up the phone.

*

The police report went on the nightly blotter. It directly followed the previous call Sergeant Kowalski had fielded about a flying person. One of Aston's well respected attorneys had spent the night in the hospital. The window in his room directly faced Aston Pond, and he had seen a large flying object swooping around it.

That report went to the local newspaper in the morning and also was eventually passed on to the regional FBI office centered in Milwaukee. From there it was forwarded to the liaison.

*

One of the things Bernie Fredder liked best about his job as the local reporter for the Aston Daily Sentinel, was doing the actual writing up of his stories and articles. He liked the investigating and information gathering part almost as well, but it was putting that all into words that he preferred. He felt most productive sitting in his office, at his desk, creating what would appear in the newspaper.

He had come up with a weekly news column to cover the odds and ends that he wanted to let the public know about. He aptly named it ODDS & ENDS. He didn't have any trouble selling his boss, Dan Powers, on the idea. Dan and Bernie were a lot alike in their journalistic interests. "It's what ends up on paper" is what Dan always told him. Bernie had a knack for getting out the information in a style the readership of the Sentinel liked, and Dan recognized that.

Bernie also liked to think part of his job was being a sort of a sponge. He absorbed everything happening around him, looking at it from the angle of letting others know what he hoped they wanted to know. ODDS & ENDS quickly became a favorite feature in the Tuesday edition of the paper.

Much of the column ended up being devoted to various events taking place in town. If a new store opened, there was news of it here. Noteworthy news about the business community usually dominated his column. Often, some of what ended up in the column was simply rumors that had become widespread. It was a good place for scuttlebutt and he always had the best. It was also a good place for odd little stories that Bernie hoped would add a little humor to their day.

He held one of those odd little stories in his hand, in the form of the police blotter report for the previous day. He had read the blotter through twice. Two men, both of whom Bernie knew personally, had called the police to report what they had described as a flying person. Butch Thomas was a respectable guy, and Bernie didn't think he'd be the kind of guy to make this up. As far as he knew, Butch wasn't much of a drinker, so he didn't think that was a factor to this rather absurd story. Marc Joyce was also a respectable member of the community. He knew him to be a bit of a drinker, although not to excess.

Bernie decided to call Butch and get the facts directly from the source. His ancient chair squeaked as he leaned forward reaching for the phone book. He found Butch's number and dialed it. It was a Monday morning so finding him at home during normal business hours wasn't likely. Surprisingly, Butch answered the phone.

"Thomases," he said.

"Oh, hi, Butch," Bernie said, switching the phone to his other ear so he could write. "Bernie Fredder. How you doin'?"

"Good. You?" he responded.

"Same. Hey, I just got my morning police report from yesterday, I get them every day, and you made the cut."

"I was afraid that would get out," Butch said resignedly. He knew what Bernie was referring to.

"You didn't want your name used?" Bernie asked.

"No, not really. People will think I'm crazy. You're not going to print my name in the paper are you?"

"No," Bernie told him. "I plan to put something in ODDS & ENDS about the sighting of a flying person, but I'd leave your name out."

"Okay. I just hope Kowalski doesn't say anything to anyone," Butch showed his concern. "I heard he can be kind of a blabbermouth. And this is a small town."

"True. So," Bernie got to the point of the call, "can you tell me what happened? I hate to make you go through it again, but I'd like to get the information right from the source."

Butch told Bernie the same thing he had told the police sergeant the night before. He again left out the drinking part, as he was certain it had nothing to do with what he saw. What he saw was real. Marc Joyce seeing it too proved that. So did that attorney.

Bernie jotted all the information down and after thanking Butch for his time, he laid the phone back in its cradle. He sat leaning on his desk for a minute, drumming his fingers.

Another flying person story. He vaguely remembered a report from a couple years back about the boy on his bike. The E.T. boy. And wasn't there another one? He stared blankly at his wall trying to remember. *Yes!* He thought to himself when it came to him. *A boy floating while picking apples.*

He reached for his lower desk drawer where he kept his paperwork for the miscellaneous stories. His fingers flitted the alphabetical files forward until he came to N. This is where he would have stored the paperwork. He pulled out the file titled NUTCASES. Maybe not so nutty, he thought. *No,* he reconsidered. *It's nutty. Flying people? Right.*

Bernie pulled the contents of file and set them on his desk. He stood and leaned over them, as that was easier to see the titles as he went without losing papers all over everywhere. He licked a couple fingers and began rifling through them. Since he always wrote a descriptive title of the subject matter at the top, he figured it should be easy. It was. In seconds he had pulled out the two documents he wanted.

One was his handwritten report from September of 2000. A gentleman had called in to report seeing an old man and a small boy picking apples. The boy was seen floating up to the top of the tree, picking fruit, and dropping it down to the old man.

The other document was a police blotter from June of 2002, last year. This was the elderly couple reporting that they saw a boy flying on his bicycle. Bernie laughed when he re-read that. *E.T. phone home.*

He set the two reports in front of him on the desk next to the new one he had just received. *Okay,* he thought, *this is the fun part.* He re-read them again, formulating what he'd write.

Since half of the ODDS & ENDS column for the next day's paper was already finished, he pulled it up on his computer screen. He would add this at the end. He liked to end the column with the lighter, less serious subjects.

The words came easily, as they always did. His fingers clacked away.

"This may sound like it came from a science fiction movie, but over the last couple years there have been a handful of sightings of an unidentified flying person in our fair city. Last night this mysterious being was seen flying down Spring Brook. Dressed in black, except for tennis shoes, the flying creature explored Aston Pond after the trip down the creek. This flying person, or maybe it's a thing, who knows, was seen by some prominent citizens. Does Superman live in Aston? I know they could use him on the football team!"

Bernie thought he was being funny.

*

Mark and Margaret Anderson didn't agree with him.

"David!" his father yelled up the stairs at him.

"Yeah, Dad?" he answered from his bedroom. He didn't like the stern tone of his father's voice.

"Come down here a second. We need to talk to you."

David came down the steps slowly and with apprehension. His dad hadn't asked him to come down. He'd ordered him. He went in the kitchen where his parents stood looking at the newspaper.

They laid it on the table in front of him, open to page three.

"Read this," his mother said, pointing to a paragraph at the end of a column with the heading "ODDS & ENDS".

David read it and felt the blood drain from his face. He was in trouble, big time trouble. He didn't know what to say. Denying it was him would be an obvious lie. He stayed silent, waiting for his mother or father to give him the chewing out he knew was coming.

"That's you isn't it?" his mother took the lead. "What were you doing out flying at night? When did you do this?"

David was trying to answer when his father joined in.

"Davey," he said, "you have to be careful. Other times someone saw you? It says there were other times."

"I don't know about other times," was all he could say.

"But this time," his mother's finger was on the article again, "this is you?"

He nodded.

The next ten minutes were some of the slowest in his life. He had been warned, really more like just being told to not fly in public, but this time it was after the fact, and much less pleasant. He ended up lying a little to keep from being in deeper trouble over the window, but in the end the verdict would have been the same. He was grounded for a week.

*

Artie Johnston was in the middle of his morning staff meeting that today centered around the increase in the organized crime movements in the Chicago area. These meetings used to be interesting to him, but lately they had become an unwanted burden. Just like many of the other agents seated around him, he was discreetly trying to do other things at the same time. He wasn't succeeding, so he surrendered and paid attention to the subject at hand. It went faster.

After the meeting he returned to his office to finish reading his daily police and sheriff's blotter reports from his North-Central Region. He felt half asleep from the meeting and wished he had a cup of coffee. He decided to read the inch thick stack of papers first. He didn't plan on anything more than his normal scanning through the information. When he read the report about an aerial apparition in Aston, Wisconsin, he chuckled and moved on, disregarding it. It would go with all the papers to be scanned and saved at the national headquarters building where all records were stored.

He didn't remember the boy on the flying bike.

*

Edward Gorman had recently been confirmed by Congress as the President's choice as Director of the Federal Bureau of Investigation. Known as a hardnosed field detective within the law enforcement community, he was also politically savvy enough to know the workings of the federal bureaucracy. With the recent advent of international terrorism, he was thought by many to be the ideal choice for this position. With over twenty five years of experience, he brought an in-depth knowledge of the national security apparatus within the borders of the United States. Unlike the CIA Director, who concentrated on American interests outside the borders, Director Gorman kept tabs on what happened on a more local level.

One of his main job requirements, as he saw it, was to know everything that occurred where the FBI could possibly be involved, now or in the future. He was a tenacious reader and collector of even the most trivial bits of information, always reading the fine-print. In his career, he had personally developed the internal system of Liaison reporting that brought him the information he thought crucial to doing his job.

Just as he took office, the Bureau had decided to establish a group of administrative offices separate from the national headquarters in Washington D.C. These were more secure and out of sight of the public eye. It was here, in a large underground building, that the FBI machine worked on the most important cases. The giant computer system here stored enormous amounts of information about normal, everyday citizens. If knowledge of the breadth of the information got out to the public, a loud outcry would be a certainty. Edward Gorman was aware of that and made the necessary effort to guaranty that wouldn't happen. He considered it a necessary evil.

While his official office was in the J. Edgar Hoover Building in the city, he preferred to be at the new offices in the suburbs, where he was closer to the actual internal functioning of the Bureau. He had just moved into his newly furbished office. The room was large by any standard, but was notably void of the trappings of his other office. Here there were no windows. While on the top floor, he preferred the privacy and didn't like the distraction a view of outside offered. What he did have that was not in his other office, were large banks of computer monitors. A big fan of new technologies the FBI was gaining, he made sure he had the most up-to-date equipment. While most of the other offices had the single computer monitor they were given, the Director had five. One was his personal computer and was not attached to the main computer server.

Still, he preferred reading paper reports whenever possible. The systems he had put in place in his previous role brought information from across the country to him on a constant basis. He relished the simple task of reading about what was happening in the U.S. It was said that not much got by Edward Gorman.

Chapter 12

David stopped at the top of the tree to check on activity below. Usually a bit more quiet at this time of day, the park beneath him was now buzzing with activity. Laughter and screaming came from the area of the playground, while adult voices wafted up from lawn chairs on the grassy lawn near the kids. From the parking lot came the sounds of teenagers motoring around. An occasional squeal of a car tire punctuated the noise. This rare daytime excursion was proving risky.

He carefully parted the branches at the top of the tree and peered down the trunk. It didn't look like anyone was immediately below so he slid down inside. He stayed close to the thick stem of the tree and the shadows of the leaves. He wound through the branches like a snake, carefully trying not to smack his head or hook his feet.

Suddenly, a man and a woman came into view. Holding hands and snuggling, they stopped for a moment, barely twenty feet below. David came to a quick stop, hugging tight to the tree trunk on the back side away from them. He waited, unseen, for what seemed to be eternity, although it was barely one or two minutes. Eventually the pair moved slowly off and out of view.

He resumed his descent, now more conscious of the people in the park. It was more crowded than it ever was when he returned from a flight, and he was suddenly very worried about getting down unnoticed. He checked his watch and fortunately had enough time to be cautious and wait it out if needed. He slowed even further, but continued.

David decided to move over to another tree that looked like it was easy to climb up into, coming to rest in it on a branch ten feet off the ground, out of sight of anyone below. He quickly pulled off the ski mask he'd purchased recently as a disguise, and the black shirt, and stuffed them both in a ball in his pants pocket. He had a lighter t-shirt on underneath. He climbed down the tree as if he had climbed up initially. Dropping to the ground, he looked around. No one seemed to have noticed, and if they had, he figured they'd just think he was just a kid climbing trees.

He set off across the open space of the park, checking his watch again, computing the time it would take to walk home. Having plenty of time to cover the ten blocks or so, he cut over toward the wide open soccer field at the back of the park. It looked like a number of kids were flying kites and one looked like his friend, Andrew Harkins. He walked toward him, but as he neared, he realized it wasn't him.

He stopped and peered up at the three brightly colored kites swooping back and forth against the pale blue sky. *Funny,* he thought to himself, *I didn't see those when I came in.* But coming in the from the area of the taller and thicker evergreen trees on the far side of the park, he probably wouldn't have spotted them. The kites weren't up very high.

From the edge of the field came the sound of sobbing. David watched as a small boy's mother knelt in front of him, trying to console him. A man, who was probably the boy's father, stood nearby pulling on a kite string that stretched toward a tree. David moved over to get a better view and saw what was causing the boy to cry. Stuck in the branches, string wrapped snugly around one, and fluttering back and forth in the breeze, was a bright, blue and yellow kite. Having had this problem himself, David knew how the boy felt. He also knew the more his father pulled on the string, the tighter it got stuck. But, the man kept yanking on the string anyway.

David looked up at the kite, thinking. *I could get that down. But I can't do it now, in front of everyone.* An idea came to him. He decided he'd come back that night to get it. He looked over at the little kid again. Thinking the whole thing through, he couldn't find any idea on how to get the kite back to its rightful owner though, since he didn't know where he lived. He checked his watch again. It was still early and he wouldn't need to be home for supper for a while yet. He wasn't sure what to do, so he sat on the grass nearby, waiting to see what the family would do. Eventually the boy quieted down. His mother promised him another kite. His father tired of trying to free the blue and yellow kite, and had come to the realization he probably had secured it even tighter to the branch.

The wind flipped the kite around. The boy wiped tears from his eyes as he stared up at it, struggling to keep from crying again. The other kites still flew and the other kids still laughed.

"Come on, Jacob," his mother took his hand. "Let's go home. We'll get another one."

"We'll get you a new one," his father echoed, rustling the boy's shaggy hair. He gave the kite string a hard tug, breaking it a long way up, and began to wind the loose end around the ball he held in his hands. He wound it quickly as they slowly walked off, the string trailing behind them.

David noticed they didn't go toward the parking lot, but instead walked the winding blacktopped path toward Eighth Avenue. They held hands as they moved off. The string seemed to pull at him, so David fell in behind. He figured maybe they lived nearby and he could find their house.

Five minutes later, he saw them turn off the front sidewalk to a small house just three doors down from one of his friend's houses. *Bingo.* David realized he had seen the kid before, when he had been over in this neighborhood. He looked around as he neared, checking out the tree cover on the street. Plenty of trees. Plenty of shade.

David walked past, turned left at the next corner and went home. He cut through the alley of the block by the school and was soon in his own driveway. He said hello to his mom when he came in the door, asked where his dad was, and was almost up to his room when his mom finished telling him supper would be ready when his dad got back from the store.

He went immediately to his bedroom window and took it out to be ready for the trip to the park that night. Then he sat at his desk for a few moments, thinking of what to put in a note to attach to the kite when he returned it. David pulled a piece of paper from his desk drawer and wrote. He grinned when he finished.

It was a normal night and everyone was in bed by half past ten. When he was confident his parents were asleep, David quietly dressed in dark clothes, put on his ski mask, took out the window and was on his way through the night sky to the park.

There was a small group of cars in the parking lot, with a number of teenagers having a loud party nearby, but they were well away from where the kite still flopped around from the captive branch. It was a dark night, without any moonlight, but the street lights nearby provided enough light to see what he was doing, while still not being seen.

Staying close to the dark foliage of the tree, the black clad David blended in to the shadows. He went straight to the kite. The string was too tangled to undo, so he wound it around his hand and pulled on it, breaking it about a foot from the branch. With the kite in hand, he went over the top of the trees and flew toward Jacob's house, a few blocks away.

The inside of their house was dark, but a streetlight illuminated the front porch. There was too much light for his comfort, so he landed in back near the shadow of the garage. He rolled up and attached the note he'd written to the short length of string on the kite. Sneaking alongside of the house, David edged up and set the kite on the front porch. He hooked it under the doormat so it wouldn't blow away.

Rather than risk more flying around the neighborhood, he ducked in the shadows to take off his mask, and quickly walked home. Once in his own yard, he flew up and into his bedroom window. All was quiet and he went unnoticed.

As he lay in bed, David felt a sense of satisfaction about what he had done. He liked the feeling. He knew little Jacob was going to be happy, and he was grinning to himself when he drifted off to sleep, thinking of how he'd like to help other people.

*

"Greetings from the Kite Fairy?" Jacob's father said aloud, holding the piece of paper.

"What's that, honey?" Jacob's mother said as she appeared in the doorway next to him. He handed her the note with the string attached. She repeated it. "Greetings from the Kite Fairy? What..." Her eyes followed his finger as he pointed down.

In front of them on the front porch, was the blue and yellow kite they had last seen the afternoon before, firmly stuck in the upper branches of the tree in the park, where they had left it.

They looked at each other. "The Kite Fairy?" they said in unison.

"Jacob!" his mom called over her shoulder. "Come here a sec, honey."

*

Two weeks later, Jacob's parents found themselves seated next to Bernie Fredder at a Little League baseball game. Bernie was talking to another man about a story he had covered the week before in his ODDS & ENDS column in the paper. When he finished, they told him their tale of the Kite Fairy. That would be perfect for your column, they told him.

Bernie wrote the information down. It was a great story, he thought. It appeared in the next ODDS & ENDS column.

"As usual I saved the best for last. I ran into my old friends, Terry and Sue Glass, at the Little League Park last week. They had gone kite flying with their young son Jacob, and it hadn't ended well. Their kite got stuck in a tree and they had to leave it there. The next morning, Terry stepped out to his front porch, and what does he find but the thought to be lost kite. There was a note attached from "the Kite Fairy". There was no other explanation. But, it was a happy ending for young Jacob. Where was the Kite Fairy when I needed him?"

*

"Hey, Davey. Come here a minute," his father called out to him through the window.

David had been sitting on the back patio reading a book. He was in his schools summer book reading contest, and was determined to win. His dad tore his attention away, but his bookmarker noted the spot.

"Yeah, Dad?" he said walking in the house.

The newspaper was on the table, open to page three. *This looks familiar,* David thought, *and not in a good way, if last time was any indication.*

"I'm wondering if this is you," his dad asked him. "The Kite Fairy."

He didn't even think of lying this time. "Yeah. The little kid felt really bad. I thought I was being nice." He looked at his father, who was silent. He expected another tongue lashing and was glad his mother wasn't included. Dad was always a little easier on him.

There was no tongue lashing. Instead, he got a gentle reprimand for taking the risk. Then his father said something that made him feel a lot better.

"That was a nice thing to do, David," he said, smiling at his son. "You have a good heart if you like to do things like that."

"Thanks, Dad," he responded. It was almost like his father had said it was okay to do that kind of stuff.

His mother never said anything about it, which made him wonder if maybe she didn't read the article. David was sure she would have figured it out too. When he noticed the newspaper balled up in the garbage the next day, he knew why.

*

While reading the internal Bureau reports had developed into a rather mundane duty for him, scanning the many newspapers from his region had become one of Artie Johnston's favorite parts of his job. A speed reader, he was able to flip through the papers, devoting time to studying the numerous articles that caught his interest. From this, he gleaned the information he thought necessary to pass on to his superiors and peers.

He had a few favorite newspapers that he considered far superior to the bulk of the dailies he had provided to him. Most of them were the small town papers, not part of a national media chain. The chain papers all looked alike in both appearance and content. They rarely dwelled on the minutiae of the communities. When you read one, you read them all.

Among Artie's favorites was the Aston Daily Sentinel. It spent an adequate amount of space on national issues and stories, but the best part was the way it presented the local news. There were always plenty of columns on the local page of the doings around town, with photos often being included. He particularly liked to read the Tuesday edition that had the column "ODDS & ENDS". The column had never contained anything he considered relevant to what might normally be classified as FBI business, but it gave a good feel for the social fabric of the community. This was Smalltown, USA.

He got a smile out of the paragraph about the Kite Fairy when it appeared. But, as usual, he had more important issues to watch for information on, so he added that newspaper to the growing stack of those he'd read. When he finished all the newspapers, they went with the other reports for storage

Chapter 13

The Millers lived four houses down from the Andersons. David didn't like the Millers. None of his friends did either. They were cranky, old, mean people. Even the adults in the neighborhood didn't care for them. Every now and then, David would overhear a snippet of conversation by a grown-up that he knew was referring to the Millers, and it was never anything nice. To the kids in the area, the Millers were often the fodder for their practical jokes. Their house was almost always targeted for a prank on Halloween. This year had been particularly spiteful, as on a past summer day, Old Man Miller, "the scourge of the neighborhood", as his friend George's dad once referred to him as, had taken a Frisbee that had landed on his front lawn, and burned it. The boys, including David, who had been playing catch with it, watched as Mr. Miller ran to where it landed, and right in front of them watching, picked it up, walked over to the already roaring burning barrel near his garage, and tossed it in.

"Stay offa my yard," he had growled at them. He was a little guy, but just looking at him said stay away.

"Hey, mister. That was my Frisbee," Jimmy Zimmerman had yelled back. He had guts talking to Mr. Miller that way. David always thought Jimmy would end up like this old man. He could be mean.

"Keep the next one outta my yard," Old Man Miller snarled back, "or I'll burn that one too." He turned and walked away from them. He didn't see the gestures they made.

The boys watched the black smoke curling from the barrel. Someone uttered an obscenity as they left, and during the walk back to their bikes, they talked about all the ways they could get back at the old man. David joined in, as he wanted to get even too. They all agreed something needed to be done. A couple months later, on Halloween, they finally struck.

The Millers didn't give out candy. That would be too nice of them. Instead they kept the lights down to discourage visitors. Everyone knew not to go there anyway. The boys did though. But it wasn't for treats. When it had gotten sufficiently dark, they snuck up to the house and waxed the windows. There were enough boys to do many windows at a time and they each did two or three. All the windows on the ground floor, including the basement windows, were coated by their wax bars. A few of the boys wrote obscenities on the glass. They made enough noise eventually to alert the Millers, but by the time the door flung open and Old Man Miller ran out, they had disappeared through the neighbor's yard. He saw only shadows, but he knew who it was.

The boys enjoyed watching Mr. Miller scrape the wax from the windows the next day. It was a laborious process, shaving the substance off with a razor blade. They sat on their bikes on the sidewalk across the street, laughing and yelling more obscenities in his direction.

When he finished, the old man had walked around to the houses where he knew some of boys lived. He yelled at the parents, accusing them of not teaching theirs kids to appreciate other people's property. Not a single parent yelled at any of the boys. The general consensus was that the old coot deserved to get his windows waxed. Jimmy Zimmerman's mom called him a coot.

*

One snowy, December day of that same year, David got the urge to pull his own trick on the Millers. Mrs. Miller spent a lot of time working on her gardens. In the summer they were nice looking, with bright flowerbeds and well-tended plants. The neighbors in the area were happy that at least they kept their yard up nice. That was the reason they kept people off the property, David's parents had pointed out, although his mom had also said it was just a good excuse for them to be mean.

Among the well-tended flower beds were placed a number of lawn ornaments. They had huge brightly colored reflecting balls on pedestals, Greek statues, and welded iron artwork, one a giant butterfly. In the center of their backyard, sitting on the large stump of a long gone elm tree, was the statue of a gnome. Increasingly popular as an outdoor ornament, this gnome was about three feet tall, with green clothes, white beard, pointy hat and a big cheery smile.

It was the gnome that had gotten David thinking. Snow had fallen steadily throughout the day and the forecast was for at least six inches to come down before the storm let up. Not too many people were venturing out, except to shovel. One of David's chores was the shoveling. He liked shoveling. The sidewalk in front was short and the easy part. The driveway was longer and took much more time, so he went to work when the skies lightened and flakes stopped falling.

After finishing the walk portion, David stood leaning on his shovel for moment. He looked at the driveway, deciding which end to start on. Out of the corner of his eye he saw a squirrel jumping through the snow. It was a soft, dry snow, so the squirrel would sink in when it landed, and then seem to spring out. It went from the corner of the front yard to the edge of Meyer's driveway and then it was gone. David looked at the tracks the squirrel had left. If he hadn't seen that it was a squirrel, he never would have guessed what had created the tracks. It had left just small indentations on the surface.

The idea struck him then in an instant. His best ideas always did. He grinned. "Ha!" he laughed out loud, and then again. *This would be funny.* He thought it over as he shoveled the driveway.

That night, when he was sure his parents couldn't hear, David took his bedroom windows out and prepared for a quick, short jaunt into the winter night. It was cold and still blowing some light snow around, and David had to wedge the window pane tightly against the inner frame, to keep it from rattling or blowing in. A ball of socks jammed between the frame and the pane did the trick, though some cold air still managed to seep in.

At the usual hour, they all went to bed. David lay awake, already dressed, waiting until he thought the coast was clear. Then, he floated from the bed, pulled out the ball of socks and the window, suddenly realizing he'd have to put the window back in place or cold air would stream into the room. It would likely spread under his door enough to wake his parents. With more than a little difficulty, he fit the pane back in, securing it with the socks, all while floating outside the house. It was a tentative fix on the window, so he knew he had to hurry. Besides that, it was cold. He'd only dressed to be out a short time and by the time he finished with the window, he was shivering.

71

After a quick look around, he zipped over his house and over the three houses separating it from the Millers'. David went to their backyard and hovered over the tall bushes near the back. Even though it was dark out, with the snow laying thick on everything, he knew his black attire would stand out. There were no lights on in the house, but he needed to hurry. David flew to the gnome sitting on the stump. Hovering there, he brushed the snow off and picked it up. It was made of cement and felt heavy in his hands. He got a good grip on it before he held it down to the snow. He gently brushed it through the snow, back and forth, as he lightly dragged it in the direction of the back patio doors. He watched the tracks he made as he went, seeing that he was getting the desired effect. He thought it looked like the tracks that would be left if the gnome could actually walk through the snow,

He finished right in front of the patio doors. He set the gnome down in the slightly deeper snow that the wind had drifted around the back corner of their house. He turned it to face the doors and leaned it slightly backward, so it was looking up. Then, he rose up ten feet to view the area from there. He grinned. It looked like the gnome had jumped off of the stump, and walked up to the back of the house, where it now stood looking in. There were no other tracks in the yard; just a smooth blanket of fluffy, white snow. The wind didn't seem strong enough to cause the gnome's tracks to be filled in. Satisfied, he left.

Within seconds David was back at his bedroom window, gently and quietly freeing the pane from its spot, and going in. He fit it back in place and floated in the center of the room, silently pulling off his clothes. He was still shivering, but he couldn't stop grinning as he slid under the covers.

*

He figured he'd never know the reaction the old couple would have, but the sight of a police squad car parked at the curb in front of the Miller's house the next morning gave him somewhat of an idea. His parents had joined him at the window, wondering what was going on. For a moment David thought they might ask him if he knew anything. He wished he had the courage to tell them. He didn't think the joke would end up having police over. That meant something bad had happened.

As they watched, another car pulled up behind the squad car. It was the Millers' kid, Bob, the oldest son. He got out of one side and his wife squeezed out the other. They went up the driveway to the side door of the garage and entered without knocking. They usually knocked.

"Hope they're alright," Mark said, although his voice had less concern than it would have, had that been the Meyer's house.

*

Alma Miller had walked into her kitchen at about nine o'clock that morning, intending to make a pot of coffee. He husband, Edmund, was in the bedroom getting dressed. He had his pants just about up when he heard the scream.

"Aaaahhh! Aaaahhh!" Alma shrieked. Her hands were at her face.

Edmund Miller ran to the kitchen. He found his wife standing at the patio doors, staring out.

"Edmund!" she yelled, not realizing he had come up behind her.

"What? What is it?" he asked, looking over her shoulder. He moved around her to see what the problem was. He looked out the window and saw the gnome sitting in the snow, just outside the door. Then his eyes followed the tracks back to the stump. Besides being mean, Edmund Miller was also "a little slow on the uptake" as Jimmy's mom had once pointed out, and it took him more than a few seconds to realize what he was looking at.

"Well...," was all he could get out. He stepped closer to make sure he wasn't missing any tracks in the snow. There were none. He stepped back from the window quickly. He looked down again at the gnome, which was looking up at him with the shiny, twinkling smile it had painted on its face. He stepped back again. He felt his wife's hands on his shoulders as she hid behind him, distancing herself from the statue.

"Jesus Christ," he said.

The gnome had walked to their back door.

Alma had called her son, Bob, who after having enough of her hysterical shrieking, had told her to just go ahead and call the police. He told her he'd be over when he finished shoveling his car out. He took his time. This wasn't serious enough to where a normal person might call the police, but Bob knew his mother. She'd go to the furthest extent to get to the bottom of this. She'd probably press charges against the gnome for trespassing.

73

*

Mark, Margaret, and David remained near the window looking down the street. They expected that any moment an ambulance would come flying up. None came and after a couple minutes, they drifted away, back to whatever they had been doing. They didn't notice when the police car left. An hour or so later Mark happened to see Bob and his wife walk out.

"Well, doesn't look like it was life threatening," he said to Margaret. She came over again to look out the window. They watched the couple get in the car and pull away from the curb in front of the Millers.

"Mmm," she replied. "That's good. Hope it wasn't a break-in or anything."

They both noticed David staring out the window as Bob Miller drove off. He looked scared. He looked guilty of something. They gave each other a quizzical look.

"David?" his dad asked. "What's wrong?"

There was a long pause as David considered the question. Should he lie, or let them know? He knew he'd get in trouble, but really wanted to tell someone what he had done. He didn't think he'd really hurt anyone by moving the gnome. He didn't think police would get involved. The guilt was too strong and he mustered the courage.

"I did it," he said. He stared at the street.

"You did it?" his mother asked, concern in her voice. "What did you do?" She moved toward him. She put her hands on his shoulders, looking down at him.

"David," his father said, moving closer. "Did what?"

David told them. He lied about part of it, saying he had done it just after he had finished shoveling. The window still needed to remain a secret.

Margaret was furious at first. "David Anderson," she yelled. "You are grounded for a week. You could have given them a heart attack!"

Mark remained silent for a bit, while his wife scolded David, but then he suddenly burst out laughing. He couldn't help it. He laughed loud and long.

"David," he finally said, as he then put both his hands on his young son's shoulders, "that is absolutely the funniest thing I ever heard. A gnome statue walking through the snow!" He laughed again.

David looked up at his father. He was glad they didn't think something bad had happened to one of the Millers. Things would have been a lot different if they had.

"But," his father said, feigning gravity, "you're still grounded." Then he laughed again.

From behind her hand, even Margaret found herself concealing a smile.

*

Bernie stood in the middle of his office reading, then re-reading the officer's description of the incident that had been entered in the blotter for the day before. The police officer who had visited the Millers had verified that it did indeed look like this garden statue of a gnome had walked from the tree stump in the middle of Edmund and Alma Miller's backyard to their back door, on its own, unattended, leaving tracks through the snow. There were no other tracks to be seen. This was funny, but he didn't give it a lot of thought. He remembered it later, while writing his weekly ODDS & ENDS column, so he added a one line comment about it at the end: *"AND BEWARE THE ATTACKING GNOMES!"*

It wasn't until the next day, after explaining to a friend of his what he'd meant by the remark, that he thought the whole thing through. Obviously a statue can't walk, so how would someone get it to the back door without leaving their own tracks in the snow? He grinned, as he felt puzzle pieces coming together. He liked that feeling.

*

Mark and Margaret laughed when they saw it. They knew what it referred to, and didn't think anyone would figure it out, or at least hoped no one would figure it out. They told Emery and Phyllis Meyer who had also read about it, not knowing it involved their neighbors, the Millers. They shared a good laugh. That Davey is quite a boy, Emery had said. Phyllis made a comment that it was better the Millers than them, that the prank got played on. *Imagine finding that at your back door!*

*

Amy howled with laughter when David told her what he'd done. He had been feeling somewhat bad about being grounded, although he realized if he'd kept his big mouth shut, that wouldn't have happened. Now, it was feeling like a badge of honor.

Later that evening, David's father came into his bedroom to talk to him. He needed to add some seriousness to the prank.

"Not only could someone actually have had a heart attack from something like that," he told David as he sat on the edge of his bed, "but, we also don't want the police or any reporters to come snooping around. I'm always afraid of one stopping at our front door."

"I know," David replied. His father's words at first diminished the humor of it all.

"But, that sure was funny," his dad then told him. "Only you could possibly think of that."

Chapter 14

Artie dropped his briefcase on his desk and hung his coat on the coatrack in the corner. He turned on his computer at the same time as he emptied the contents of his briefcase.

"Morning, Artie!" Bethany appeared at the door.

"Morning," Artie cheerfully responded. It was Friday. He felt good.

"The morning reports are on your desk."

"Thanks, Beth," Artie said.

"Let me know if you need anything else," she added as she turned and walked from the doorway.

"Will do." He sat down.

Artie checked to see if the computer was on. He always thought he had a lemon computer, as it took forever to fire up. He found the reports Beth had left. She had them all in order by state and the states in the order Artie liked to read them in. He read the internal FBI reports first. He was already aware of just about everything going on so scanned those quickly. Nothing new shaking there. The blotters reports took up most of the time, as they contained all of the activity noted to the police and sheriff's departments, listed by time of day reported, and were on however many sheets of paper it took. On some days Artie had a huge stack of paper, and on other days, just a small handful.

It had taken him about an hour and a full cup of coffee to get to Wisconsin. The report from the agents was limited, as there wasn't much requiring the reports in the state. The blotters were about normal. They too had been sorted into three segments, Milwaukee, Madison, and the rest of the state. He read them in that order. He swore they were the same reports recycled day after day.

Not much going on, he thought to himself as he read; nothing too noteworthy. Then something piqued his interest. It was a report from the Aston Police Department. An elderly couple reported that a garden statue, a gnome, had been found at their back door and it looked as if it had walked on its own from the normal spot on a tree stump in their backyard. A police officer viewed the scene and verified that appeared to be the case.

Artie pulled a bottle of water from his office fridge and thought about it for a while. He leaned back in his chair. How could a garden statue go from one spot to another without a person's tracks being seen in the snow? One possibility would be if they hung from a rope. But there was no report of a rope. He thought the police officer should be smart enough to notice that. *It's impossible,* he thought, *unless someone could fly.* A light bulb came on over his head and he jerked forward in his chair.

He remembered a similar previous report or two from a long while back. A report about a flying person. He chuckled. *This sure beats bank fraud and gang shootings.*

Artie thought about the previous reports he could remember. Two men had described what they thought was either a child or small adult flying past them, being approximately five feet away. "They said they knew it was human," he remembered the desk sergeant had noted, "because it wore tennis shoes." Artie again chuckled to himself as he thought of the two men being startled by something like this.

The other related report had been more credible, as the source, a noted local attorney, who had spent the night in the hospital, was lying in bed facing out toward a pond and the creek the two men had been near. Artie picked up on the proximity of the creek part of each story. Has to be the same culprit, he thought.

Then it dawned on him and he also thought that he should have thought of it before, that both the reports gave what was relatively detailed information on the exact location. These types of reports always did. The other previous reports of a flying person contained the same information.

Artie turned around and pulled out the file drawer for Wisconsin in the tall cabinet next to his desk. A conscientious filer of all his notes, the folders were neatly hanging in his preferred filing order, and the one he wanted was right where it was supposed to be. He pulled out the "Miscellaneous – Wisconsin" folder and set it on his desk. The folder was thick, as this included copies of all of what he considered the oddball reports from many years past that he had felt he needed to keep. This was the out of the ordinary file, where he would have stored the flying person reports. The dates written on the outside of the manila folder indicated the contents went back five years. He spotted the recent report of the "Kite Fairy". He pulled it out and read it. *Damn*, he thought to himself as the lightbulb over his head grew brighter. He needed to dig deeper into this. He knew there had been other archived previous reports of the flying guy or whatever it was.

"Beth!" he yelled out to his assistant.

"Be right there," she yelled back and almost immediately appeared in the doorway. "What can I get for you?"

He explained which archived files he wanted and she left to get them. Some of the files would be papers stored in cabinets in the basement storage area. Others that had been scanned would be retrieved from the Bureau's central computer in the suburbs of Washington D.C.

Artie set this report aside and finished reading the rest of the blotter and agent reports for the last few states. He grinned again at the two reports, as he stood to stretch and get another cup of coffee. *A flying person.* He couldn't remember how many reports he had, but all of them seemed consistent in that it just felt to him like it must be one person. Or one whatever it was. *What if it was an alien*, Artie pondered momentarily? He dismissed the thought. It wore tennis shoes he remembered from one old report. *The reports were descriptions of a flying person. Aliens don't wear tennis shoes.*

He had no more than set his cup down when he saw Beth standing at the entrance to his office with an armful of folders and some printed reports she'd gotten from D.C. Artie quickly took as many as he could from her and together they managed to get them on his desk without one falling and sending paperwork flying everywhere.

"Thanks," Beth said. She had been ready to drop some files.

"Nope, thank you," Artie said. "I appreciate you doing this."

"That's it for all the files," she pointed. "Let me know if you need anything else or when you want me to put them back."

"Will do. Thanks again," he said. "Oh hey, wait." He checked the dates of the reports on the kite fairy and the traveling gnome. "See if you can get me copies of the local Aston, Wisconsin newspaper for the ten days after each of these dates. It's called the Aston Daily Sentinel." He wrote the dates on a slip of paper for her.

"Okay. Gotcha," she said.

Beth left and Artie stood over the mound of folders on his desk. If he had missed anything when filing his miscellaneous stuff, it would be in this pile. Each folder was dated and since Artie was an organizational zealot, he shuffled the files in stacks by year and by month. He leaned on the desk thinking before deciding to start from when the sightings began being reported. He could eliminate some files and began the process of reading through the reports for the ones he wanted. He couldn't remember the dates, but was pretty sure it was almost as far back as the oldest file. He needed to see if he missed anything. Maybe other flying person reports had slipped through.

"Beth!" he yelled again as he sat. She came in his office. "Could you do me another favor and see if we have a large map of Wisconsin and another of Langlade County. And one for the city of Aston. Preferably on cardboard so I can set them up on an easel. I'm hoping you can procure some about three feet square, give or take. I'm going to need them with highways, and for the Aston one, I need to see the most current one with streets."

"Um. Okay," Beth said, as she tried to think of where they might be. "I think we have those. Be right back."

Artie took a drink from his coffee cup and opened the first and oldest file. The blotter reports and agent reports were in neat order, with the other items, such as newspaper articles, paper-clipped together. He skipped over reading the agent's reports. He quickly scanned each newspaper article and blotter report to see if there was anything about mysterious sightings of a flying person or object.

He had a surprisingly long two year period from the first file with a sighting, until he got the next story. After scanning to see if it was what he thought fit into his theory, he slowly read the report and looked for a description of the location. A street address was given. As he went through the files, his stack of papers pulled out grew to include other sighting besides just the ones he remembered. Artie was surprised by the number and was happy to note that each report included an address or a position near a road, highway, or other landmark. He should be able to plot them on a map.

He finished reading all the files and felt comfortable he had found all of what he had wanted, and was happy with what he had found. Beth had not returned yet and Artie thought he'd save her the work of hauling all the files back, so he took an armload and refiled them. The second load was smaller and he was soon back at his much cleaner desk, re-reading what he had pulled out.

He had newspaper articles and blotter reports of sightings over the last seven years. All had locations and if memory served him, Artie was sure they were all near or in the same city, Aston, Wisconsin.

A few things from the blotters were obvious. It was human, or looked to be human anyway, and it seemed likely to be a child, probably more likely a boy, than a girl. The description of its size was small and based on the recent report, it wore tennis shoes. The few recent stories that described the size of the flyer all indicated it was small for an adult and more like a child. The oldest story of a boy flying to get apples in an orchard, had the age then at between seven or eight, and that had definitely been a boy. He went to the last story from the day before. The description was that of a small adult or a teenage sized person.

Artie re-read them all again in chronological order and was soon certain this was a small boy who had grown into a teenager. If he were say, seven years old on the first date, and in seven more year be fourteen, he'd be about the size of a small man or teenager. He began theorizing about what or who he was dealing with here. He didn't have long to ponder as Beth walked in, this time with her hands full of maps, all wrapped in tubes with rubber bands around them.

"Sorry, all they had was rolls of maps," she told him.

"Um, good," Artie stood to take them from her. "Just in time. Thanks again for getting me all this stuff." He took the rolls from her.

"I also got an extra city street map of Aston," she said. "I thought maybe you might want two."

"Thanks," Artie said. "I might need that."

"Need any help with anything?" she asked, expecting him to say yes or at least explain what he was doing.

"No. This is fine," he said, not wanting her to know all the work she had done was because his thought was that there was a boy flying around in Wisconsin. "Just the newspapers yet."

After she left, it took Artie about ten minutes to tape the maps to his office wall. They were laminated, but weren't stiff enough out of the tubes to use an easel. He put the state map to the left, the county in the middle, and the city of Aston on the right. He fished in his desk drawer for a yellow marker and a magnifying glass. He found both, grabbed the first report and stepped to the city map. The description was at an orchard. He looked closely at the city map, didn't find it, and then looked at the county map and was thankful the orchard was clearly listed. Otherwise, he'd have to look up the address. He put a bright yellow dot there. That location was on the edge of what showed as the city limits. Then he put a small dot next to the city on the state map. He noted the spot on the state map as well. He took a pen and put the number one on each dot on each of the maps. Then he put the number one on the top of the report, circled it, and went on to the next report, report number two. He followed the same process with each report.

Artie set the marker down when he finished and stood before the maps. The hypothesis he was formulating as he marked the sighting locations, was proven by the cluster of yellow dots.

Of the eight sightings he had information on, six were within the Aston city limits, and five of those were all on one end of town. He stood closer to that map, studying the area. It was a residential area, but near an industrial park on the city limits.

Later that day Beth delivered the newspapers. Artie scanned through them, knowing where to look. He found the few of articles that he expected. The local reporter, Bernie Fredder, had commented on the Kite Fairy in his weekly ODDS & ENDS column. From the way it was worded, it didn't appear he was tying anything together. The story on the gnome, if there would be one, probably wouldn't be until the next Tuesday's column. He considered calling Bernie, but decided against it.

When he felt he had all the information straight in his head, he sat and wrote a report for the next regional office meeting. He was sure there was indeed something or someone flying around in this part of Wisconsin, but he was going to have to be careful how he'd lay all this out, so as not to seem crazy.

*

Not at all coincidentally, in the offices of the local Aston newspaper, not far from the cluster of dots Artie Johnston had been studying on his maps, Bernie Fredder was doing the exact same thing.

After thinking about the police blotter report of the gnome, and the limited possibilities for how that could have been done, he was prompted to pull his files of the previous sightings of the flyer, and he also had decided to plot them on a map. Bernie's office already had maps on the wall, although his state map was not very detailed. But he knew his area of the state and it sufficed.

He stood before them now with a hand full of colored stick pins. He pushed them in the city and county maps at the locations of the sightings. When he was done, Bernie had eleven pins in the county map, and eight more in the city map, as he also had reports that had come directly to him at the newspaper from people calling in. These had never been reported to the police or sheriff's department. Many were just the same sightings, by date, by different people, in different locations.

It had also become obvious to Bernie Fredder that this was a boy, and he was likely from the east side of Aston. He studied the area, but he wasn't sure if he could deduce from all of the pins, what might be a central location. If he put a finger in what might appear to be the center, it was pretty much right on the middle school and the high school, past the residential area. That fact cemented his opinion of what he was dealing with. *A school kid. A flying school kid.*

Bernie sat at his desk and as he stared at the map. The story he would write for the ODDS & ENDS column in the paper on the flyer began to formulate in his head. His computer was on so he began to type.

"Over the past five or so years both I and the local authorities have fielded numerous reports of a flying person in our community. I've mentioned him in this column in the past. No one has ever come up with a photo, so I tend to believe just what my common sense would tell me. On the other hand, the growing number of sightings seems to indicate there is something (or someone?) flying around us. Keep me posted on anything you might see. There must be a logical explanation somewhere. And see if you can get a picture!"

*

83

The column generated a surprising amount of chatter within the community of Aston. For those who hadn't heard of it before, the absurdity of it made it into the butt of many jokes. For those who had seen something but had never reported it, thinking they must have been just seeing things, it gave them the courage to come forward with their own stories of things they had seen. Bernie was surprised at the number of calls he now received. Many were duplicate sightings of the same ones he'd heard of already, but they added credence to what he thought was an incredulous phenomenon. The apparition became known as the Flying Guy.

*

The column also created a bit of conversation within the Anderson household. Mark had heard about the article before he had a chance to read it. He'd been standing in line at the grocery store when he overheard an older couple in front of him make mention of it. He listened intently, feeling a bit of nervousness build in the pit of his stomach. When he got home, he immediately retrieved the paper from the front porch to read the article. When Margaret got home he showed her the paragraph from the paper.

"Local authorities?" she said. "Numerous reports?" She looked pale.

"We need to put a kibosh on this," Mark said.

When David got home just before supper, he was summoned to the living room, where his parents had been waiting for him. They showed him the article, and tried to find out from him how often he goes out. David was as vague as possible, while still owning up to the obvious fact that he gets out on a regular basis.

Margaret had been furious at first, so she let Mark do the talking. They told David he had to stop going out, and if he ever did, he had to be a lot more careful. The pranks had been funny, but this was obviously more serious now. The fact that the local police and sheriff's departments were involved was cause enough to require a cutback on going out. They weren't grounding him in one sense of the word, but they were in the other.

"David," his father had solemnly intoned, "you're just a boy. I don't think you're aware of what could happen. There might be some people who would do bad things if they caught you."

The way he said it scared David. It was more than a few months before he went out flying again. He may have gone sooner, if Amy hadn't also stated her concern.

"I read about you in the paper," she had said. "My mom showed me. You aren't going to get in trouble are you?"

He assured her he wouldn't.

Chapter 15

Herb Foster, Deputy Director of the FBI walked into the meeting room. He was prompt as always and the Regional Liaison Agents in attendance made sure to be in their seats when he arrived. There were six men waiting for him and their laughter and conversation subsided when he moved to his seat at the head of the table.

"Good morning, gentlemen," he said to them cheerfully.

"Morning, Herb," came the reply, almost in unison.

"Let's get started. We need to make this quick," he told them as he set a stack of papers on the table in front of him. He reached for the decanter and poured himself a glass of water. "Bob, want to start with the Southeast?"

Bob Nicholson, Liaison Agent in Charge of information gathering for the Southeast Region of the country began his report. His reports were usually the same. He started with anything happening in Florida, then Georgia, the two largest states and then each of the others. His region experienced an increase in things like burglary strings, murderers on the loose, and crimes that crossed state lines. When he finished, the next agent started right in.

The process usually went quickly, but on occasion some crime that was getting a lot of press would generate extra discussion. Today was one of those days as they ended up going into detail on a kidnapping case in Arizona. The victim had not been found and the suspicion was that the kidnappers had long left the state, assumed to be accompanied by their captive. As that conversation wound down, they all began to look at their watches, sensing the end.

Artie Johnston, Regional Liaison Agent for the North-Central region had just finished his piece and he was the last to report today, when he decided to bring them in on the flying guy stories.

"I do have one other thing," he said. "A little lighter subject than the others. I didn't originally intend to discuss this."

Everyone waited for him to start. Artie was more skilled at this part of the job than most, and they all appreciated him for his brevity and conciseness. While he was a seasoned law enforcement agent, with years of hands on field work to his credit, he also had a real knack for sifting through stories and information to glean important details on certain events. Almost always dead serious, with a wry wit, Artie would occasionally come up with an oddball theory or news item. This was one of those occurrences.

"I've had a couple unusual local police blotters out of central Wisconsin," he started. Everyone was listening intently as they wanted to get the meeting over with. "These are weird and I hesitate as you may think I'm crazy for giving any time to it."

"Well, what is it?" one of the agents pressed him. He seemed the most anxious to get out of the room.

"I've had at least three independent reports of the sighting of a flying person in my region." He paused to gauge their reaction. As he expected, most of them smirked, others chuckled.

"I know," Artie continued. "But, I still have these reports. Most are from a police department in Aston, Wisconsin, and some are from their local sheriff's department, of people saying they saw someone flying around. There are also newspaper reports of the same."

He went through the reports for the agents. Half of the men just listened and shrugged it off as a hoax. The others listened with interest. Artie was good at laying out the story, and he matter-of-factly went through the separate sightings in detail, including one of a boy flying on his bicycle. In the end, he drew them to what might seem to be a perfectly logical conclusion, that there was indeed someone flying around Central Wisconsin.

"Sounds weird, I know," he said as he finished, putting down the last sheet of paper. "I'm just reporting what the blotters said."

After the meeting Artie went back to his office. He figured he may be needing the report again, so he pulled out the file drawer where he kept current issues. The flying person story was filed under "Miscellaneous-Wisconsin", where he kept similar information.

*

John Baraniak

The Deputy Director of the FBI was required to report to the Director of the FBI, everything that he saw fit to be relevant for the Director to be aware of. When he submitted his summarization of the Regional Liaison meeting, he attached as back-up, the individual regional reports that the agents had presented at the meeting. The flying person did not make it to the summary items, but all of Agent Johnston's back-up paperwork was attached when it went in the internal mail system envelope.

*

Edward Gorman, Director of the FBI, read about the flying guy. He always scanned the summarization, but liked to spend the time to read the individual reports that came with it. While the many reports of the flying person seemed unrealistic and funny, he made a mental note to keep tabs on any future sighting reports. Unknown people and things, especially flying things, needed monitoring. He noted that the information came from Agent Arthur Johnston. He knew of Artie. While the whole concept was absurd, he knew Artie wasn't the type to waste time on something that didn't deserve some scrutiny.

The reports were scanned and filed.

Chapter 16

"Hi Ruth. Ben," Mark said, motioning them in the door. "How are you guys doing?"

Ruth and Ben lived a few blocks away, and they had all met at one of David's school concerts. Finding a lot in common, Mark and Margaret became fast friends with them. Soon they were going to dinner and spending time together at backyard barbecues. Ruth and Ben's son Jason was a friend of David's, and they hung out with the same group of boys.

"Great. How about you?" Ben asked, offering a handshake to Mark.

"Hunky dory. Come on in. Margaret's almost ready." He closed the door when they were inside. They waited in the foyer.

"Should be a good day on the water," Ben said. "It's sunny, and not a lot of wind."

"Sounds good," Mark replied enthusiastically, then walked to the base of the stairway and yelled up. "Margaret! You coming?"

"Be right there," came her voice from above.

Margaret was in David's room. Since he was staying home alone while they went boating with friends, she needed to make sure David knew how to get hold of them. She also went through the list of rules that always needed repeating when he was going to be on his own. While he had just turned thirteen, he was still a young boy and rules needed to be repeated.

The dialogue always ended the same.

"And remember," she always repeated, "no flying. Okay?" This time she added "I don't want to read about you in the paper again."

"Yeah. Got it, Mom," he replied. He wished she hadn't said it today. Today, he fully intended to go flying. He felt guilty of the lie already, and he hadn't even done anything yet.

"Okay. We'll be home around dinner time," Margaret said. She leaned over and kissed David on the forehead. "Behave."

More guilt. David looked at the floor as she left. "Yup," was all he could say.

David stood at the window in the bathroom facing the front yard and street. His dad and Jason's dad stood by the boat, talking. It looked like they were talking about the boat. His mom and Jason's mom were chattering like they hadn't seen each other in weeks, when actually they talked all the time. Finally, they all got in the Jeep tasked with hauling the boat, and slowly made their way down the street.

David checked his watch. It was nine forty five. He'd give them about a half hour before he'd feel comfortable they weren't coming back for something they had forgotten. In the meantime, he went to double check on the clothes he planned to wear.

The guilt was still gnawing on him, and he felt like he had a stomach ache.

Since this flight was going to be during the daytime, the thought of wearing something blue came to him. He wondered if he'd blend into the sky. It was a clear day with a few puffy white clouds, and the rationalization to blend with the sky seemed logical. Then he thought of white, and figured that was an even better idea. But he didn't have any white shorts, so he joined the two ideas. He chose a pair of light blue shorts and a white tee shirt. He figured his white tennis shoes would also be fine.

David wasn't sure what to do with his mask. He always wore his black ski mask at night. Having been thoroughly drilled into him the need for secrecy about his special skill, he had been faithful to the practice of wearing the ski mask. Having no other options, he had it ready with his other clothes.

Time seemed to crawl as he waited, sitting in front of the TV with a program on that he wasn't paying any attention to. A couple minutes after ten, he changed into the shorts and shirt. He stuffed the mask in his pocket. In the other pocket was the key to the house. He was anxious to go.

The plan was to ride his bike to Edison Park. The parking lot there bordered a piece of land with thick forest on it. He hadn't flown from there before, but had gone up into a tall tree there with his bike, to scope out a place to store it. He couldn't just leave it on the ground, as someone would likely take it. He'd found a tree that was easy to get into and it had a grouping of branches, well up and out of sight, that would hold his bike while he was gone.

The agonizing wait had ended and he was soon on his way, coasting through the parking lot to the trees. The lot had a large number of cars, but they were clustered near the open park area. Families had picnic settings out and the playground equipment was overrun with kids. David gave them a passing glance, pulling up to a stop by the trees.

Then, his conscience started getting the better of him. He thought a minute, reconsidering the plan. But, as he looked around, seeing no one that would notice him, he realized it was going to be easy to get away with. He felt the guilt subside.

He rode his bicycle in a small, slow circle around one of the trees, doing a double check. Then, he hooked his toes under the pedals, held tight to the handlebars, and rose up into the tree. He slowly wound his way around some big branches, and came to the spot to leave his bike. He settled it on the two branches, rose off the bike, and made sure it was leaning securely on the tree. He hovered near it, noticing for the first time, the coolness of the shade, and the slight shifting of the leaves in the soft breeze.

David pulled the ski mask from his pocket and slid it over his head. The black mask contrasted with the rest of his clothes, but until he felt comfortable no one would see his face, he left it on.

He rose up, parting the leaves at the top, and came to a stop about ten feet above the canopy. There wasn't any way anyone could see him from where he was, so he sat in the air, again considering his plan.

David had made plenty of night flights, and knew the layout from the air of a good sized part of the county by heart. It was funny though, he thought to himself, it looks a lot different in the daylight. Resisting the urge to buzz the church steeples he'd done at night, he turned instead in a slow bank, and headed away from town, to the north. He went toward the lakes and woods. His parents had gone in the other direction, and he knew about where they were.

He flew in a prone position, as he usually did, with his arms out front. He didn't go too fast, as he would occasionally find himself approaching an open area, and he wanted to make sure he didn't accidently leave the safety of the cover from the trees. His nervousness had disappeared, and with it went more of the guilty feeling from breaking a rule his parents entrusted him with. He picked up the speed just a bit.

He flew what he was sure was northeast, and was soon near a large area of open farm field. He would be fully exposed here, so he decided to go up. In a slow arch upward, he pointed his hands at the sky and zoomed from the safety of the forest. He hoped his choice of clothing color was camouflaging him enough. The black mask might stand out, he thought, but at this height someone would have to be looking right at him, to see him.

As he rose, he noticed a very warm push from behind. He had noticed heat rising from the dark green trees as he skimmed across the tops, and the spot he was in now sent columns of hot air straight up. His tee shirt flapped around him. It felt good, and he allowed it to have some effect on his upward climb. He watched the trees grow smaller beneath him and then without having noticed, found himself at the base of a cotton ball shaped cloud. It was large and had knobs billowing out in different directions. Feeling exposed, he darted over to one side, above the area of the shifting mist. He looked down and saw white, blocking the view from below. He stopped and hovered for a minute. Other billowing clouds surrounded his hiding spot. He could still feel the updraft.

It was turning out to be very different in the daytime sky. In the evenings, the air seemed to be more still. Now, the updrafts and air currents moved him around. Most of this was all new to him, and David was enjoying the lesson. He'd never been up this far. His guilt stayed forgotten in the experience.

Deciding to visit the larger and just as puffy cloud across an open stretch, he made a slow, lazy curve around the contours of the billowing knob he'd been over. He then let the wind help him along to the next one. He flew around it, going in and out of the misty white cloud, before popping out to the clear sky. He felt a cool moisture in the cloud. Being as high as he was, he felt comfortable letting his guard down, and wasn't paying attention to trying not to be seen.

David darted from cloud to cloud. He made it like a game to stay just outside of the swirling moisture, adjusting his path as the clouds grew and swirled. He lost track of time, and when he suddenly thought of checking his watch, he was surprised to see he had been up here for almost a half hour. The longer he stayed, he knew, the greater the chance of being spotted.

Having no easy way to avoid that, he simply turned down and dove toward the ground. He again felt the heat of the day rising from below, and it washed over him on his rapid descent. In a matter of seconds, he made an arched maneuver and was again cruising above the forest. He slowed to allow warm air currents to guide part of his path. He liked that feeling.

He saw a break in the fabric of the trees ahead and figured he was coming to a lake. The glint of the sun off the water filtered through the woods below, telling him he was right. Knowing it would likely be populated by a good number of boats on a day like today, he approached slowly. He moved lower over the trees and came to the lake's edge. Without realizing it, he settled over a small cottage. It looked deserted. To his surprise, there were only two boats on this lake, and both were small and contained fisherman. The two boats were in a small weedy bay off the main body of water. David moved away from them and disappeared from view when he got to the north end of the lake. He sat in the air for a moment, studying the shoreline. Although this was a good sized lake, there were only a handful of cottages on it. He tried to think of the name of the lake, but couldn't remember it. He was sure he'd never been here on the ground.

Considering it safe, he swooped down toward the water. He came up at a level about three feet above the surface and sailed along near the shoreline, out of sight of the anglers. He felt the coolness of the lake surface beneath him, like a steely, soft blanket. At first, there was only trees and swamp coming up to the rocky shore, but ahead he saw buildings. He didn't see anyone out and weighed the risk of being seen. Feeling gutsy, he passed by, still just above the water.

Just when he was feeling safe, he encountered something he had only minor problems with before. A large swarm of small bugs was buzzing near the shore. David got some of the insects in his eyes and had to pull into the woods to wipe them out. That had hurt. When he took his mask off to wipe his eyes, he noticed it was covered with the insects.

I'm gonna need some goggles, he said thought to himself.

He slid the mask back over his head and pulled it tight. Then in a quick flip, he turned and sped out over the lake again, heading off in his original direction. He again felt the difference in temperature just above the water, as compared to the heat rising above the darker green trees. It felt comforting, so he slowed to enjoy it. He rounded the narrow end of the lake, arms out, in a slow bank. He picked up speed as he barreled down the length of the lake. The heat from the forest hit him as he approached the other end. He rose quickly to go over the trees. He hit a strong updraft and turned upward to catch the gust. David spun slowly, as he rose with the thermal.

The pleasure of the flight came to a sudden stop, as he felt the sharp impact of something on his head. He slowed and hovered. David rubbed his head. It hurt. He looked at his hand to see if there was blood. He expected there would be, but his hand was clean. He rubbed his head again, looking around to see what he might have hit. All he could think of was that it might be a bird. He didn't see any flying nearby, but when he looked down, he saw a small black shape of a bird spiraling downward. It hit the top of the trees and disappeared.

Gees, he thought to himself, *I need goggles for the bugs and a helmet for the birds.* He was going to have to figure something out. He was learning a few new things today.

Although he didn't see blood, his head still stung, and so he turned slowly toward home. He settled over the treetops and set a path for the water tower he saw in the distance.

He passed an open field with some sort of low growing crop, and dropped down to a little over ten feet above the ground. He stayed near the trees though. David was now keeping an active lookout for birds and swarms of insects. He didn't see swarms, but did notice the edges of the field, where other forms of vegetation grew, filled with butterflies. He couldn't resist going closer.

Forgetting his sore head for a moment, he cruised to a stop above a handful of large, brightly colored ones. He recognized some of them were Monarchs, but didn't know the names of the others. Most were smaller yellow and white butterflies, with no patterns. He watched the way they flitted about, quickly moving right and left. He mimicked their movements to see what it was like, but decided it was better suited for them. He sat there for a few minutes, enjoying the thought that he flew as freely as they did.

He turned and headed toward home again. At the end of the field, he rose, went over the trees, and honed in on the water tower. A long thin break in the foliage told him he was near Highway 64. He closed in on it and crossed over. There were more open fields as he neared town, so he moved south to avoid them and the increasing number of houses that appeared to be sprouting along the way. He had a couple friends who lived in this area, and he picked out the rooftop of Jerry Carlson, one of the guys he hung out with. He didn't see him or anyone else in their yard as he passed by.

David wound his way back over the patchwork of dark green to Edison Park. He knew the canopy just well enough, and settled over the tree he'd left his bike in. He stopped, hovering at the top, listening for anyone below. He heard nothing and parted the uppermost branches. It had felt cool inside the tree when he left, but now it felt warm. He moved slowly, listening, as he snaked around branches. He slid off his mask as he neared the bike. He rubbed his head again, and this time he found blood. It was drying and gooey. He turned the mask inside out and saw blood there. He tenderly fingered his scalp, this time finding the cut. Suddenly, it really hurt.

He stuffed the mask in his back pocket and that's when he noticed his white tee shirt was dotted with the black remains of countless dead bugs. He brushed off as many as he could.

David picked up his bike by the handlebars and the seat. He didn't get on it, carrying it instead, as he lowered to the ground. No one was around and he settled to the grass below.

After the long excursion, it felt funny to be walking again. Rather than getting on his bike right away, he decided to walk, so he wheeled it toward the park entrance. He saw people and cars ahead, but no one paid him any attention.

He swung his leg over his bike and rode home. It would be hours before his parents would be home from their boating excursion. He changed his clothes and washed his hair. He couldn't put a band-aide on his head, but since it scabbed over, he felt it would be okay.

He made himself a sandwich and turned on the TV. A program on Iceland was on the Smithsonian Channel, and he found himself fantasizing about cruising around the stark landscape of the faraway place. He wondered how long it would take to fly to get there.

Chapter 17

Bernie leaned on his desk studying the paperwork in front of him. He'd spread out all of the reports of the flying guy in chronological order. When he looked at all of them in total, he was surprised by the number. With the four calls he had gotten in the last two days, he now had well over a dozen different sightings on record. The dates went back a number of years. He'd previously noted tales of the flyer in his Tuesday column, but now with the number of sightings increasing, he wanted to do a full article.

He sat thinking about it. He had some doubts about wanting to do it. Sure, it was funny to throw in a little paragraph in the ODDS & ENDS column, and he did still hear people talking about it on occasion, but the whole concept of a person who could fly seemed too absurd to him. Writing a regular story for the paper would move it from the realm of fairy tale status, to reality status. It would give it a sense of legitimacy. He wanted to word it just right. First of course, he'd have to sell his boss, the Editor, Dan Powers, on it. Bernie punched a button on his phone and picked up the receiver.

"Dan," came the voice on the phone, identifying himself.

"Hey, Dan. Bernie. Got a minute to talk?" Bernie asked.

"Sure. Come on down."

Bernie went down the hall to Dan's office. It was much larger than his and befitting of a newspaper editor. It provided Dan with enough room to spread his work out around him. Slow to warm to using computers to store and view documents, he still preferred having paper copies of virtually everything. Add to that his professional need to read other newspapers, when Bernie came in, he had to clear off the chair before sitting.

"What's up?" Dan asked, sitting back.

"The Flying Guy," Bernie said.

"Ah. I heard we got quite a few calls lately on more sightings. What do you think is going on?"

"Well," Bernie started, "I have all these separate sightings from the last couple years." He set his paperwork on Dan's desk. The pile looked thick. Dan raised an eyebrow when he saw them.

"The calls I've gotten in the last couple days matches up to what the police and sheriff's departments have got," Bernie told him. "Everything seems to be consistent."

"That Superman is flying around Aston," Dan said matter-of-factly.

"Yup, that's what it looks like," Bernie said, leaning back. "Someone, or something is anyway. If these were all crackpots," he said, tapping the stack of papers, "I'd just write it off as that. But these are from people I know and they're... reliable people. Normal. Sane."

"What do the law enforcement folks say?" Dan leaned forward.

"Haven't heard them say anything yet. I get the blotters, but I haven't talked to anyone about it, other than just getting more details fleshed out. But not about any thoughts from them on whether they think there's anything to it."

"Think we should ask them?" Dan asked.

Bernie thought about it. "Yeah. I'll see what I can get. I want to do an article on the flying guy then." He looked at Dan for approval.

"Yeah, yeah, by all means," Dan nodded. "I've been hearing enough about it and I think the readership would be interested." He paused a second and then smiled at Bernie. "Hell, make them interested."

"That's the plan," Bernie said getting up to leave. "I'll keep you posted."

*

When he got back in his office, he called the Police Chief, Mike Bresky. He liked Mike and they were good friends personally, as well as professionally. He was available, so they talked about the flying guy. Chief Bresky said for now he was not doing anything except laugh about it. No crimes have been committed, so it's just a matter of people claiming to see someone flying around. No laws against that, they both agreed. The Chief said the official response would be that they've received reports from the public on something or someone flying around Aston, but have no other information on who, or what it was. And until they have the need to know, they will better use their resources and tax dollars on more important things.

Bernie thanked him, disconnected and called the Sheriff's Department. He talked to the Sheriff, who pretty much reiterated what the Police Chief had said. It's funny, but no further comments.

Bernie sat at his desk, working the various pieces of information over in his head. It was a full half hour before he broke out of his trance and began to write. He used a pen and notebook, writing long-hand, instead of using his computer. His thought process was sometimes clearer that way.

The Friday edition of the Aston Sentinel was usually in two sections. His article on the Flying Guy appeared on the back page of Section A. Official, factual local news always went on page three, along with obituaries and the local calendar. The only exception to that was the ODDS & ENDS column on Tuesdays. This article, being a bit outside of what both Dan and Bernie thought to be factual from a logical perspective, was better suited to the general interests part of the paper. The back page was still preferable to being buried in the mid-section though. More people saw the back page.

The article, titled *'Sighting of Flying Person Reported in Aston'* caught the eye of quite a number of people, if the large amount of talk on the subject was the measuring stick. Within a few days, it became the main topic of many conversations. All of a sudden, everyone seemed to know something about the flying person. Both Dan and Bernie were happy with the response to the story. They talked of future articles if sightings continued.

"I'd like to find out who this guy is," Bernie said to Dan while discussing their success. "If this is real… wow… think of the implications."

"Yeah. No kidding," Dan smiled. He saw his newspaper at the center of attention. Well, he considered, right near what was the center of attention. "Let me know what else you might need for this," he offered.

"Yup," Bernie said, and left. *Yikes*, he thought to himself as he headed back to his office, *I'm chasing flying people.*

*

David saw the article in the paper before his parents got home from work. He knew there was going to be a big discussion coming. He read the article two times, to make sure he knew what he'd have to own up to doing. Some specific instances were noted in the article. He didn't want to tell them everything. He knew the seriousness of this as it was. He knew he'd have to cut back on his flying, but he still didn't want to stop altogether. He'd considered that in the past, but it was too much fun. His parent's reaction would have to guide his approach.

His father saw the newspaper first. David heard him talking to his mom about it when she came home. They spoke in hushed voices, not wanting David to hear what they were saying. Knowing full well what it was about, he had stood around the corner in the living room, out of sight, but within earshot.

"Oh, wow! Mark!" his mom said. "This is too much. This could be trouble."

"Yeah," he agreed. "We have to figure something out. I heard people talking about this at work today, but at first I wasn't sure what it was all about."

"I don't like the law enforcement part, even if they aren't taking it seriously," his mom said, after a silence that was very uncomfortable for David.

"Yeah. Me neither," Mark said, then yelled "David!"

David came into the kitchen. He didn't ask what for when he looked at them. Double barrels of a shotgun looked back.

He thought there'd be yelling, but there wasn't. The conversation was surprisingly short. They reiterated in much stronger terms than on previous occasions, the risks involved. They said they had always feared someone would come and take him away, if they found out who it was. They'd come snooping. The way his dad always explained it scared him more than any yelling would have. He mentioned the prospect of people doing medical experiments on him, wanting to find out how he flies. His mother looked sick when he said that. David felt a little sick himself.

It ended with them telling him, in no uncertain terms, that he couldn't fly anymore without their specific permission. After what his father said, he fully intended to give that a try.

Chapter 18

The weekly meeting of the Regional FBI Liaisons was moved back an hour due to the scheduling conflicts with the Deputy Director (DD). Artie Johnson took the extra time to prepare his notes and update the official report he would file. He had a lot to cover today, which was out of the ordinary. Recent trends in drug trafficking now had Minnesota and Wisconsin showing dramatic increases in activity. The joint effort with the local law enforcement agencies was consuming more and more of his time.

Artie paged through the information he'd discuss. He was sure this would end up being a long meeting. Add to that, the likelihood that the DD will want a follow-up meeting on the drug issues, and he could see his whole day turning into an uncontrollable series of conference calls and emails.

He came to the last item he'd be bringing up for discussion. The Flying Guy. He re-read what he had prepared. It started with a summarization of what had been reported before, a couple years back. He remembered the lukewarm reception that had gotten. The other liaison agents, most of whom were still in the same positions in the Bureau and would be here today, had pretty much collectively rolled their eyes at the story of someone flying around in Wisconsin. They'd laughed it off. He would have too.

Now Artie had more sightings, as well as the full newspaper article that had been done in the local paper, the Aston Sentinel. There were no pictures of the aerial phantom, but enough people have sworn they've seen it, so there has to be something to it. Artie always hoped one of the other Liaisons would pipe up with similar information. He'd thought that over before and decided that prospect wasn't likely. It would be pretty damn weird if there were an army of flying people out there somewhere. The phenomenon was particular just to the northeastern section of Wisconsin, surrounding the small town of Aston.

Artie glanced at the clock and saw that it was time to go. He shoved all his paperwork into a folder, grabbed a pen and left. On the way to the conference room he met up with his counterpart from Houston, Jarrod McHale, who he was now working closely with on the drug issue. They both bemoaned the prospect of a long, tedious meeting.

Fortunately, Herb Foster, the DD, again ran this meeting like a well-oiled machine. He'd shown up right on time and found the room full and waiting. Extra attendees had come for the main subject, drug trafficking. They sat quietly to the side, waiting for the Liaisons to finish. While the volume of information exchanged was huge, the conversation moved briskly along. Herb Foster didn't believe in wasted time.

The DD went swiftly through the regional reports. He'd asked that the individual reports that were presented, be separate from the drug subject. That would be the final discussion. The Liaisons were to just cover the smaller issues first.

When it came Artie's turn to report, he went through what was his normal routine. There wasn't too much going on in his region. Finally, he came to the last item. He hesitated. Everyone had seemed pretty serious today. The normal banter was light, seeing as there were more senior level agents in attendance. He wasn't sure whether to bring it up today, or perhaps put it off to the next meeting. Or maybe not mention it at all. After all, he was talking about a flying person. He decided to proceed. The report was done and ready to be submitted, so all he had to do was present it.

"Well," he began, "I have one other item and this'll give you a grin. We need a little levity here today, so I think I can certainly provide that."

"Some of you may recall a little over two years ago I had reported that there were sightings of a person, or thing, seen flying around in northeastern Wisconsin."

"E.T. Phone home," Herb Foster deadpanned.

"That's it," Artie said, nodding at him. "Information I've gathered from local law enforcement authorities, and the local press, seem to indicate there remains the presence of something flying around near the city of Aston, Wisconsin. Aston is the county seat, and has a population of about eighteen thousand. It's primarily a rural community, made up of what you'd probably consider to be normal people.

"A large number of these normal people have reported what is described to be a boy, or small man, or woman I guess, dressed in black, with a black covering over his or her head, flying around."

Artie gauged the reaction in the room before continuing. The seriousness of their final subject evidently kept them from throwing out a witty comment or two, which is what would have normally happened. The senior agents in attendance didn't give any clue as to what they were thinking. They weren't smiling like a couple of the Liaisons were, and they seemed to be taking it in as if it may have been a normal topic of discussion.

"I have over a dozen recent reports, all consistent in times and details, of the flyer," Artie told them. He went into detail, moving quickly through his summarization of sightings. He did a quick synopsis of the Bernie Fredder newspaper article that had prompted this report. When he looked at the DD, he was surprised to see that he was listening intently to what he was saying.

"This is all in your printed report too?" the DD asked when Bernie wound down his presentation.

"Yes, sir," Artie told him. "I've documented everything pretty thoroughly. I realize this is a rather unusual… thing, so I covered all the bases."

"Good," the DD said. "Anything else?"

"No, sir," he replied straight-faced. "I wanted to get the serious stuff out of the way first."

There were chuckles around the room, including the DD. One of the most senior agents of the additional meeting group didn't chuckle. He stared at Artie. Behind his slitted eyes, Artie could see the gears turning. He didn't like C. Randall Whiting. Most of his fellow workers were simply dedicated lawmen, who saw their jobs as keeping the peace on a national level. C. Randall Whiting seemed to exude darker intentions. Artie averted his stare.

Two hours later, when the meeting ended, Artie squeezed quickly out the door.

One of the other Liaisons called after him. "Next time see if you can make time fly," he said.

Artie turned. "No shit."

*

Herb Foster remembered the previous time Artie Johnston had mentioned the flying person. While it was a fanciful idea, he knew that this was just the sort of thing that the FBI should be paying attention to. He was glad he had guys like Artie, who seemed to know what little things could mean to the big picture of national security. Unknown things flying around was not an insignificant occurrence. The traditional view of UFOs by the Bureau, was always to investigate if needed. Maybe this was needed.

He sat at this desk now after the meeting, looking at the report Artie had given. The last time it had come up, he included the report to the Director of the FBI, Ed Gorman. He didn't get any feedback saying not to waste his time, so he figured it either went unnoticed, or perhaps the Director also viewed things such as this as part of what he needed to know. The latter was more likely, as he knew that Gorman was known to dwell on the details of issues. He decided it would be included again. He made a copy of it for his files and put the original in with the other meeting reports, in the internal mail folder to be delivered later that morning. He wrote a comment on a post-it note that said this should followed up on.

He received no feedback this time either.

Chapter 19

David ran down the stairs from his bedroom and headed to the back door. He grabbed his dark coat as he opened it.

"I'm going to Amy's," he yelled over his shoulder. The door slammed shut behind him. His parents gave each other a puzzled look.

It was dark outside and David made a quick decision to fly to Amy's house. He could take the car as he'd gotten his license three weeks earlier, but he was in a hurry. His mask was in his coat pocket so he pulled it on, went up over the trees and on his way. He followed his normal path over the patchwork of trees to the main road.

The traffic on Superior Street was heavy, so he waited and darted across at what he thought was the least risky time. He knew any number of the cars could still have seen him. Even though he sped across, it was light in the business area and all anyone would have had to do was look up from the road. He'd been spotted here before.

David landed in the next door neighbor's yard. He'd learned from previous visits that it was the safest place to land unseen. He headed around to Amy's front door and rang the bell.

Amy's mom answered the door. "Hello, David," she greeted him. "She's up in her room. Go ahead."

"Thanks, Mrs. Kellerman," he replied and ran up the steps, two at a time. Amy's door was open and he burst inside.

"Amy," he said, holding out his arms. "I...." He didn't finish as she pressed against his chest. He put his arms around her, holding her tight.

"Davey," she sobbed, "I don't want to move. I won't ever see you again." She held him.

"Sure you will," he consoled her. "You're not moving to the moon."

Before taking off to see her, she had called to tell him that her dad had gotten a new job in Wisconsin Rapids, and they would be moving there in the next few weeks. The house was already sold and the new job started in three weeks. She had told him this through muffled sobs.

"It's far enough," she said softly. Then she leaned back and looked at him. "Hey, can you fly over to see me? Can you go that far?"

David thought a second. "Sure," he said. "I've gone up north about thirty or forty miles before. I can make Rapids."

Having just gotten his driver's license, David had become more conscious of roads and highways and where they went. He envisioned a ground route there. That would be easy enough to drive or fly. He told her that.

They sat on her bed and talked for a half hour. She told him how badly she had taken the news, when her father told the family over supper. Amy's little brother, Tony, was excited over the move. He was getting into football and Rapids high school was pretty good. Amy's mom was also excited, but Amy said she seemed more excited for her dad, than for the move. Amy had feigned happiness, but inside was torn by the news. Being in high school, she had more friends than her brother, and relationships she didn't want to end. Tops among those was David. She was afraid they'd be permanently separated.

David assured her he would not do that. The funny feeling he always had with her now hurt inside. He had never said the words before, but they came easily to him now.

"Amy, I love you," he said quietly. "I don't want to lose you."

She looked at him with tears welling in her eyes. Her arms went around his neck and she pressed into him.

"I love you, Davey," she sobbed into his coat. She trembled in his arms.

They held each other tightly, David rubbing her back to comfort her. When they finally came apart, Amy stood.

"You better come visit," she said to him. Tears still ran down her cheeks.

David rose. "I will. I promise." His eyes were wet, too.

Amy walked him to the door. Mrs. Kellerman came out of the kitchen. She gave them a wan smile as she turned into the living room. She knew what they were going through. She had been through the exact same thing once. She only saw that boyfriend one more time after moving and then it was over.

David kissed Amy, told her they'd talk more at school the next day, and went out. He ducked around the back of the house to the neighbor's yard. The coast was clear and in a matter of seconds, having not bothering to stop or even slow down over the main road, was in his own yard. He went in.

*

"David, is that you?" his mother yelled. She had stopped calling him Davey not long ago.

"Yeah," he responded. He hung up his coat and went in the kitchen where both his parents were finishing doing the dishes.

"What's up?" she asked. "You tore out of here in a hurry. And did you fly there? I didn't see you on your bike. Or did you walk?"

"Flew," he told her. "I needed to get there in a hurry."

"David!" his father joined in. "You gotta watch that. You'll be in the papers again." He didn't look happy.

"I know how to be discreet," he told his dad. He said it with a tone of authority, as if telling him he decided when to fly or not. Somewhere he hoped there would be a subtle transition on whether he needed the okay from them of not.

"What's with Amy?" his mom changed the subject back.

"She's moving," David said. He pulled a kitchen chair out and sat. "Her dad got a job in Wisconsin Rapids. They're moving in a couple weeks."

"Oh, no!" his mom said. "I'm sorry, honey." She knew how he felt about Amy. She liked Amy, too. So did Mark. The Kellermans also were good friends of theirs. Amy's mom worked near where she worked part-time at a small shop and they often passed in a parking lot. They talked a lot, mostly about David and Amy.

She pulled out a chair and sat with him. His father put the dish towel on the stove handle and joined them.

"That's too bad, David," he told him, patting his son on the back. "You guys can still stay in touch. It's not that far. You'll be seeing each other yet."

"I know," David said. He stared at the table.

"You have your license now so can drive over to see her," his dad offered. He knew what young love was and wanted to help. Although the kids were just into high school, he and Margaret had always hoped the romance would last. This could change things.

"Thanks. I'll do that," he replied. He looked pensive.

They were all silent for a bit. His parents looked at each other. They knew what the other was thinking. David probably wouldn't use the car to go see his girl.

*

Fortunately for David, the next few weeks went slowly. A bit surreal, he had thought to himself on occasion, but slowly enough for him to come to terms with the departure. It seemed to go fast for Amy, and she was "weepy," as one of his friends had pointed out.

Moving day was a Saturday and David was there to help. Mrs. Kellerman was evidently in charge, as she gave out orders on what was to be done. Being an obvious veteran of previous moves, she knew how to go about it in an orderly fashion. She had everyone carrying boxes and hefting furniture to their rental truck. David was happy that she moved everything along briskly, as it kept Amy from dwelling on the circumstances. She looked to be near tears as it was.

"Well, hey," David said to her when they had a few moments alone. "How about I come over next weekend?"

Amy's eyes brightened. "Yeah! That would be great. You can come?" she pressed against him.

"My dad said I can use the car," he told her. "If they need to use it, I'll… find another way."

She hugged him. "It'll work out," she said, finally feeling a little more comfortable with the situation. "I know it'll work out."

*

Amy had just gotten her own cellphone, and then David convinced his parents he should have one to stay in touch with her. It was an easy sell. It seemed everyone was getting one, and David's parents had planned on getting them soon anyway. They used this opportunity to get them all one.

David and Amy talked every night during that first week she was away. She had found some friends and had adjusted to the new school. Always having been considered a really nice girl by everyone in Aston, she was quickly accepted into the new crowd. Boys liked her too, and she told David how one of the school jocks had hit on her on her first day there. She had of course, turned him down. She said she let everyone know she had a boyfriend back in Aston, where she came from.

David was glad to hear that.

They made plans for David to come over that coming Saturday. The high school football team had a rare Saturday afternoon game and there was a dance to follow. Amy had to work at the game for the school's German Club, which she had just joined. David had to work at the Copps grocery store during that day anyway, so they arranged for him to come over early in the evening

Unfortunately, something came up and David's parents needed to use their car. He wasn't upset. He told them he was going to Amy's and that he intended to fly. His parents were adamant that he should not do that. It was dangerous, they said, and there was always a chance of getting caught.

David felt it was time to come clean on some of his flying experiences. He left out a lot of details he wanted kept secret, but he let them know he had flown enough times to be confident in what he was capable of. He explained his methods for determining where to fly from, wearing a mask, avoiding sight by staying over trees or going up so high that no one would see.

They already knew he snuck in some flying, but were surprised by the amount of times he had done it. They were amazed at what he said he could do. And, they weren't even getting the whole story.

"You be damn careful, David," his dad told him, punctuating the air with a pointed finger. And with that, David felt he had gotten official approval for any flying he wanted to do, now and in the future.

His mother remained silent. She wasn't so convinced. "Tell us when you go though, and what time you'll get back, so we know when you're gone," she said finally. She didn't look too enthused.

When David was gone, his parents looked at each other with a resigned expression.

"We knew the day would come," Margaret said. "It still scares me though." She hoped her fear would sway Mark more in that direction. It didn't seem to work this time.

"On the bright side," Mark said instead, "it seems like he's done it enough to figure out how to get away with it – other than the few things in the paper. And that was awhile back."

"Yeah, he got away with it" Margaret interrupted him, "other than the few times he *didn't* get away with it."

"He's pretty level-headed though," Mark said. "Hopefully we've imparted some common sense into him." He was envisioning his son flying over the countryside. Since coming to grips with the phenomenon, he had often wondered what it was like to have that exceptional freedom to just go anywhere. But he knew it wasn't that simple. He couldn't be found out. The thought of being subjected to medial experiences had subsided, since he wasn't a little boy anymore and it didn't seem so sinister, but what could happen if he was found out, was still a great fear. He tried to balance Margaret's concern with his own wonderment at what David could do.

They stood and held each other for a long time.

*

David bought himself a road map of Wisconsin and pinned it up on his bedroom wall. Having got what he considered carte blanche approval for flying, he figured he'd need one.

He scanned the map. He knew where Rapids was and studied the route there. He saw which highways he'd take if he drove, but was looking for the easiest way to fly there. To do that, all he had to do was get some major landmarks to follow. He wasn't familiar with that area, or what trees and forested land might be on the way. If memory served him right, it was a lot of wide open corn fields. He traced his fingers over a couple different potential routes he could take.

In the end he settled on flying directly to Wausau, which was easy. All he had to do was go up high enough to see the glow of their city lights, and head southwest. He couldn't miss it. He had seen that glow before. Then, from there he'd watch for Highway Fifty One running south. It was a major highway so would be easy to follow. He'd follow that south to Stevens Point, and then turn west from there. It looked to David like there were some pretty big electrical power lines that ran directly to Rapids from Stevens Point. He'd pick them up and follow them in. He figured he could make it in around fifteen to twenty minutes, unless he wanted to get there sooner.

A lot depended on how cold it was. He flew faster when it was really cold, just to get out of it sooner. Temperatures were forecast to be in the forties. Not bad, he thought.

Amy had given him directions to a park where she would meet him. If anything got messed up, they now had cellphones to stay in touch.

Whenever David came into his bedroom, he re-traced the path he'd take. *Piece of cake*, he thought to himself. The week whizzed past and he was thankful for that.

David had to work on Saturday morning, so he gave all the arrangements about his trip to his parents before he left. They would be going out of town around noon and he'd miss them when he got off work. He showed them his map and traced the route he'd take. He explained how he'd avoid being seen. His parents listened intently, seeming to grow more comfortable with the plan.

"I'd like you to call us when you get there, to let us know you made it okay," his mother told him. Even though she had said she was okay with him flying there, her voice said otherwise.

"Okay," he agreed.

"And then call us when you get home," she added. "We'll be home later than you. We want you home by midnight."

"Sure. Okay," he told her. That timing was what he had thought of anyway.

"David," his dad said, putting a hand on his shoulder, "we're counting on you to be smart, be safe." He made it sound like his son was going off to war.

Before David could respond, he found himself in a slightly awkward embrace with his father. Then his mom joined in, wrapping her arms around them both. The awkwardness went up a notch.

"Thanks. For trusting me," David said, as they broke apart. "I'll be okay."

David was dressed and ready for work, and it was time to go. A friend and fellow grocery stocker he usually rode with, was already at the curb to give him a ride. He left after promising again to be safe. His parents stood at the window watching him go.

The day went slowly for David. He was anxious to make his trip and that seemed to be what caused the day to drag. At five o'clock, he and Greg, his ride, left work. David hadn't planned to make any food at home, so they stopped at the local Pizza Hut for an Italian sub. He told Greg he was going to see Amy. He was bumming a ride with someone, he told him. Greg said that was cool. Amy was a nice chick. David smiled.

*

The plan was to meet at a park, not far from the high school. The school was on the edge of town, a couple blocks off the main highway on the south end of town. David was sure he'd be able to find it. Schools were easy to spot from the air.

His heart was beating pretty fast when he locked the back door to go. He slid his black ski mask over his head. His backyard was all shadows and the coast was clear. He went quickly over the trees. He kept envisioning the map route in his mind, as he wound along his usual path from home. In a couple short minutes, he was out of town and into the flats to the west. It had been dark for over an hour, so his chances of being seen out here where there were no streetlights, was pretty slim. He cruised along at a steady speed. He flew horizontally and had his gloved hands out front. It was cold enough to where he needed to hold his hands where they'd break the wind flowing against his head and face. It had felt comfortable on the ground, but it was definitely cooler higher up.

About ten miles out of town, he went up about two hundred yards higher. When he looked to the southwest, he could see the glow of nighttime lights in Wausau. He went straight for them. In no time he reached the eastern edge of the city. He knew where Highway Twenty-Nine met Highway Fifty-One and that was his next point of reference. He saw the headlights of the cars on Twenty-Nine and kept them on his left. He saw the intersection, so he turned left, going south. Stevens Point wasn't far from there and from that altitude he saw the glow of that city right away. A few more minutes and he located the power lines that led to Wisconsin Rapids. To Amy.

The swath the power lines cut through the wooded areas was easy to follow even in the dark and he found himself coming up to the city limits of Wisconsin Rapids. David slowed and then stopped, sitting in the air. At the height he was at, no one could possibly see him. The sky was clear and black. And cold.

David could see the whole town from his vantage point. It looked smaller than Aston. The downtown area was brightly lit. The main roads that went through the town, were easy to follow. There was plenty of traffic. His eyes followed the road he thought was the highway, and he located what he thought must be the school. He banked and flew slowly in that direction.

It was the school. David came to a stop directly over the building. It was lit up from all the lights in the parking lot and there were a number of cars in the spots up against the back of the building. Must be people back from the football game, he thought.

He scanned the area around the school and found the gas station Amy had said to look for. The park was a few blocks over from that and just down from the school. He checked his watch. He had ten minutes before the pre-set time to meet Amy. He couldn't wait.

David went to the park. He dropped down from the altitude he had been at, until he was just above the trees. No one could see him there. He listened and didn't hear any noise from below. He decided to skip going into a tree and winding down through the branches and instead went toward a gap between the trees. It was all shadows, so he slowly descended and came to the ground. He looked around. There was no one. He slid off the ski mask and stuffed it in his coat pocket, then dragged a comb through his hair.

He walked over to the picnic table Amy had described. It was the only one between the kiddie playground and the bathrooms. David sat on the table and waited. He suddenly remembered he needed to call his parents. They were relieved to hear he had made it, and were eager to get more details about the trip when he returned. He ended the call quickly in case Amy would be calling.

Two minutes later a car pulled in and took the parking spot closest to him. A honk on the horn confirmed it was Amy, so he started walking over. She got out and ran to him. She wrapped her arms around his neck and gave him a very long and very wet kiss.

"Boy," David told her, "I don't think I'll be able to wait a week at a time to get that!" He grinned.

"Well, maybe you can visit more often" she said, taking his arm and walking to the car. She held tightly.

"Ooh," David said as they approached the vehicle. "Parents gave you the Buick, hey?"

Amy had her parent's new car. She had gotten her driver's license a couple weeks before David. Now she drove that car more than her parents did. She was starting to pester them for a car of her own. She told them then she could go see David and her old friends once in a while. Her parents weren't sold on that yet.

"You get limo service tonight," she said, as she opened his door with a flourish.

They drove to the local Elks Club, where the dance was being held. Amy introduced him to all her new friends. A couple of the guys gave him what he called 'the hairy eyeball', as if sizing up the competition. One in particular kept staring at him. David mentioned that to Amy and she laughed. That was the jock who hit on her.

"Don't worry," she told him. "My flyboy is the only one for me."

David felt as funny inside now as he had the first time she had called him that.

They liked the band and danced almost every dance during the night. When it broke up, they joined a number of Amy's friends in going out for pizza. Everyone seemed to like David and he liked them in return. He was comfortable with this new crowd. He promised he'd see them again and even invited them to come to Aston for a visit. They all said good-bye when David and Amy headed out. The guys now knew she was unavailable.

Amy drove back to the park. She found a dark spot near the back of the parking lot and turned the car off. No words were spoken before their lips met. They enjoyed the ending to what they both thought was a very nice night, as they made out in the Buick. They shared one last kiss outside, then Amy watched as David rose into the night sky and disappeared.

David went straight up, until he was probably five hundred yards over the school area. From there, he could see past the harsh glow of the downtown and all the way to the glow of Stevens Point. He turned into his cruising position and sped toward there. It was now even colder than before, but he wasn't noticing. He still felt the warm, fuzzy feeling he'd gotten from having been with Amy.

From this altitude, he could see Wausau illuminated in the distant sky. He increased speed. Once he got just to the east of there, he spotted the faint glow of Aston, a much smaller city than Wausau. He went in that direction. Before he knew it, he was slowing to a stop over the fields on the south end of town. He crossed over the last farm field and passed over Shit Creek, where he recalled the previous flight through, resisting the urge to do it again. Too cold.

David followed his normal path through town and soon swooped down over the maples in back of his house. He landed near the back door. He'd purposely left the backlight off when he left, so he'd have the cover of darkness.

He went in, checking his watch as he pulled off his coat and mask. He was surprised to see that he had made it back in less than ten minutes. *Man, he thought to himself, that was fast.* That was good. Knowing the route now and knowing it was only a ten minute flight, he could see Amy more often. He felt good thinking about that.

David called his mom and dad to let them know he was home safe. They breathed a sigh of relief and asked briefly how it all went. He told them great and would fill them in on the details tomorrow. Then, he called Amy to let her know he was back. She told him she loved him and was happy he had come over. He said the same. They set a time to talk again the next day.

He went to bed thinking of the trip, that it was a lot of fun. He realized his ability made it possible to go virtually anywhere very easily. He planned to go again the next weekend.

*

Mark and Margaret felt relieved he'd made the journey safely. When no police or news media showed up after a couple days, even though they didn't expect any, they gave David their okay to go again the following weekend. He just smiled. He would have gone anyway.

Chapter 20

David had told Amy he could come over Friday night for the high school football game in Stevens Point. She didn't have to work an away game. She had use of her parents Buick again and they'd agreed to meet at the same park. They'd ride together with one of Amy's new friends and her boyfriend.

This flight was just as successful as the first had been, and when he got to the park, Amy was already there, sitting at the park table. She greeted him as warmly as she had the week before. A few minutes later, they picked up her friends and were on their way to the game. David was in command of the Buick this time.

The Wisconsin Rapids team creamed the Stevens Point team and now only Merrill High School stood in the way of a conference championship. All the kids were pumped over their school's success and couldn't wait for the game the following week. David joined in the revelry and was rooting for Amy's new home team.

They ended the evening the same way they had ended the last one together. He had the warm, fuzzy feeling. After promising Amy he'd call her when he got home, he was up and gone.

David felt pretty happy as he sat momentarily high above Wisconsin Rapids. The two visits he'd made here had worked out pretty well. He made new friends and had a good time with them. He chuckled over how excited they were over the football team. His own high school was having a so-so season and were out of contention for the championship. David looked down at the high school below him. A light still shone on the school flag. The banner, a dark flag of black and red flapped in the breeze from the pole at the end of the football field. One game and you're the champions, he thought. Merrill, he knew was straight north of Wausau. He looked in the direction it would be, but couldn't see any glow from here. That had to be eighty or ninety miles from here, he estimated. Only the glow of Stevens Point stood out in the dark.

Suddenly, an idea came to him, as he sat staring at the rippling flag below. He thought it over and as preposterous as it seemed, he couldn't find a reason why it couldn't work. The fans in Rapids were pretty enthusiastic and would really get a kick out of it. Actually, he smiled, they were rabid football fans and they would love it.

David circled around the school beneath, going lower with each lap. No one was around. There were no cars in the parking lot. He came to a stop directly above the building, then decided to land on it. He stood on the edge of the flat roof of what he didn't know was the chemistry lab. He peered out at the flag.

Looks just like a regular flag, he thought. He looked all around. There was no one on the school grounds. David dove into the air and went directly to the top of the flag pole. *No sense taking it down to remove it,* he thought, *when I can just take it from where it is.* He freed it from the two clips that secured it to the rope. He almost lost it in the wind, but managed to get it off, wrap it under his arm in a ball, and then zipped back to the darkness high above the school. His heart was beating like crazy. *This should be cool,* he thought.

David didn't know how long it would take, so found himself going as fast as he'd ever flown. He went faster even than his return flight the week before, except this time he wasn't speeding home. He was going to Merrill.

By the time he had passed over Rib Mountain on the west side of Wausau, he had picked up the glow of Merrill. The flag was balled up in his arms, but the edges flapped in the breeze trying to free itself. David struggled to hold on to it. His face felt cold from not having outstretched arms to divert the airflow that now hit him straight on. He went faster to get out of the cold.

He didn't know the layout of Merrill at all. He came to a stop and hovered over the south side of the city. He looked right and to the east, and saw the glimmer of Aston twenty-five miles away. That's the direction he'd be going when finished. He looked back at Merrill. He didn't know where the school was, but figured it would be on the periphery of town somewhere. He began to go around the outskirts of town watching for the campus.

David spotted it and dove down to the treetops of a residential area right next to it. He flew slowly to the edge of those near the school parking lot. The lot was brightly lit and to David's dismay, there were a number of cars in it. Lights shone from several windows of the school. He found that odd at this hour, but they were lit up.

"Shit," David mumbled. He sat in the air watching. After a couple minutes, he came to the conclusion it wasn't safe to do. The flagpole was right out in the open. Any one of those lit up windows had a view of the pole. *Great*, he thought, *now what do I do?*

Slowly, without changing from his sitting position, he floated higher. He couldn't think of anything to do. He'd have to return the flag to the Rapids high school flagpole. He spun slowly around and looked out at the top of the city, thinking.

And there, right in front of him, was the dome of the county courthouse. And right at the top of the dome was a flagpole, currently flying the American flag. He looked around. This was the highest flying flag in the city.

David thought about it for a minute. *Yes*, he thought, *this is going be great!*

He leaned toward the courthouse and started in that direction. The courthouse dome and flag were well illuminated. Made out of copper, the roof of the Lincoln County Courthouse glinted in some spots, while reflecting green in others. The light from below made it look a little spooky.

It was likely he'd be seen putting the new flag in place of the other one, if he flew up and did it from the top. He surveyed the big building. The base of the mast was set on a small crow's nest at the top of the dome. The lights at the edge of the building shot their light upward at the flag, creating shadows above. It looked safe.

David skirted along the edge of the trees on the courthouse lawn, then darted over to the crow's nest. There was a door leading down into the dome and he checked and found it was locked. Good, David thought. Now they'll really wonder how the flag got there.

He watched traffic on the side streets surrounding the building. Traffic was light. It was too cold and too late for people to be out walking. He looked up at the American flag above and then at the rope that it was secured to. He figured he'd have to be fast and hoped it would be as simple as quickly lowering the one and attaching the other, hoisting it up and securing the rope. It occurred to him then that this was the American flag he was taking down, so he'd have to give it the respect others would expect of it.

David checked that the coast was clear and went to work. He quickly untied the rope and pulled the length that brought the flag down. He removed the American flag, relieved to see that it was virtually the same size as the replacement banner that he had brought. He carefully set the American flag on a small ledge attached to the railing, perhaps intended and used for just that purpose. He secured the Wisconsin Rapids school banner, a black and red flag depicting their mascot, a Red Raider. He pumped his arms, pulling the rope that took it to the top. He secured the rope and looked up to see it flapping in the breeze. He grinned.

This is too cool, he thought. Then he realized he needed to get out of there fast. He didn't want to stay up at the top to fold the flag he'd removed, so he took it down by the back area of the courthouse. There was an outdoor seating area that was dark compared to most of the courthouse grounds. He landed there, spread the flag over a table and swiftly, but carefully folded the flag in the triangular shape he'd learned how to do as a boy.

David left it on the table where it should be easily noticed the next morning. He dove into the sky and flew about a half mile to one of the darkest spots he could find. He looked back at the courthouse dome and the flag flying above. He grinned even wider. He'd have to tell Amy.

He got his bearings, went straight up to avoid detection, and peeled off in the direction of Aston's distant glow. In scant minutes, he landed in his yard. His parents were up yet, waiting for his safe return. He gave them the abbreviated version of his trip. He specifically abbreviated out the flag part. They'd probably guess it was him if they heard about it. Or, as he was sure, when they heard about it.

Before going to bed, he called Amy to tell her he'd made it home safely. In the end, he decided not to tell her and have it be a big surprise to her, as well as all the rest of the Wisconsin Rapids fans. He went to bed with the secret.

*

By noon of the next day, pretty much anyone in the entire country who watched any of the national news networks knew about the school banner that had been moved from its home at the school in Wisconsin Rapids, Wisconsin, to the courthouse dome of the city that was home of their big opponent for the high school conference football championship game the coming weekend.

The local TV stations from Wausau had taken footage of the flag flying brazenly over the courthouse, and the story and that footage was picked up by the major networks: ABC, NBC, and CBS, as well as CNN. Most of the coverage was on the upcoming football game, and how this was a stunt of tremendous originality, forethought and courage. Everyone wondered who had done this, and initial thought was that it had to have been some high school boys.

But what no one could figure out, and this eventually became a bigger part of the story as more details came out, was how it could have been done. The door to the crow's nest at the top of the dome was locked from the inside. They shot footage of the locked door. Only two people had keys. They interviewed them and both denied doing it. They both said they had the keys in their possession, and no one could have taken them. There was no evidence that the lock had been picked. Besides, as it was pointed out, whoever did this would have had to also break into the courthouse, just to be able to get up to the crow's nest. There was no evidence of that having happened either. Scaling the outside of the building would have been virtually impossible due to the shape of the dome, and that would have left some telltale signs. There were none. So everyone was wondering, how was this done?

But, as most news commentators had opined at the end of their reports, at least whoever did it had folded the American flag appropriately and left it behind.

*

The citizens of Wisconsin Rapids were abuzz with joy over this national headline story of their town and school spirit. Whoever had done this would be infamous in local lore. But no one stepped up to lay claim to the heroic deed. No one could even venture a guess as to who was responsible.

Except for one person. Amy figured out who it was. But she wasn't talking.

*

Bernie Fredder had hardly been in his office for one minute when Marsha was at his door.

"Morning," Bernie said cheerfully. He had slept a little later than usual, since it was a Saturday, and had breezed in at nine o'clock.

"Morning," Marsha responded. "Did you hear about the flag thing in Merrill last night?" she asked him. She seemed eager to talk about whatever that was.

"No. What was that about?" he asked, hanging his coat over the back of a corner chair. He sat with creak in his wooden desk chair and waited for Marsha's response. She told him.

"You're kidding!" Bernie exclaimed. He sat wide-eyed at his desk, while she recounted the story of the flag.

When she left, Bernie called Ann Granger at the Merrill Herald. She was his counterpart at their local newspaper. Ann gave him pretty much the same list of facts as Marsha had. Bernie asked if she had any photos that she could share and she said she'd get some to him right away, via email. He thanked her and told her if anything breaks, to be sure to give him a heads up.

Bernie wrote the story for the Saturday paper. It was on the front page with the headline "FLAG STUNT HAS AUTHORITIES BAFFLED". The picture of the flag flying over the courthouse accompanied the article. The article raised the same questions that the TV networks had: Who did this and how did they do it?

Bernie had his own ideas. It appeared that after a lull, his Flying Guy was back. He laughed to himself, as he sat back in his creaky chair. He put his hands behind his head and smiled at the ceiling. My flying guy also has a great sense of humor. But, what was he doing in Rapids and Merrill? All previous leads had pointed to Aston as this person's home base. What's the connection?

He pulled out the maps he had used. They had been had stuffed behind a file cabinet. He went to the state map he used for tracking the flying guy and marked the locations of Wisconsin Rapids and Merrill. The playing field had just widened. Bernie was sure that also must be able to provide some sort of clue. He was sure he was dealing with a teenaged boy, and now he was connected somehow to these other cities.

*

Mark and Margaret Anderson were watching the evening news together. They'd seen the newspaper article and heard that it earned national attention. They wanted to see the coverage on CNN.

They hadn't had an opportunity to talk to David about it yet, but they knew he was behind it. There was no other explanation. Amy lived in Rapids. He flew there last night. They watched now to see the level of interest the story got. While it had been a while since the chatter of a flying person had settled down, this could re-ignite the curiosity.

The television version of the story touched first on the originality of the feat and the football rivalry of the two town's schools. The flag flapped in the breeze in the background of the commentator. Then they asked the expected question of how it was done. Mark and Margaret were at least a little relieved that no one seemed to have come to the conclusion that it was someone who flew to the top of the courthouse. And, they knew that on a national level, this was just a cute, one day human interest story. Locally, it could be different.

When David got home a half hour after the newscast, he knew he'd need to discuss this, so he joined his parents in the living room. They were expecting him and turned the TV off when he entered.

"I assume you heard about the flag," he asked, dropping into his usual spot on the couch.

His mom gave him a slight scowl. His dad was fighting a grin.

"You know David," his dad spoke first, "if you could get paid for this stuff, you'd be rich."

His mom gave his dad an incredulous look. "Mark," she said. "This is serious. This made national headlines!"

David held back. It was looking like maybe his father would be coming to his defense, so he wanted to let that card play out first.

"Yeah, I know," his dad said, "but no one said anything about the flying person. They think it's someone from Rapids who did this. Kids. A prank."

"Well, they could eventually connect the dots," she countered.

"We'll see," he said. "I'd be surprised."

121

His mom turned to David. "Why didn't you tell us about this last night when we asked how the trip went?"

"Well, gees, Mom," he replied. "Then you would have chewed me out last night. I was kinda enjoying having done it. I knew they'd never figure it out."

"You knew we'd figure it out though, didn't you?" his dad chimed in.

"Yeah, I guess. I didn't think it would make national news though."

The conversation that followed was similar to previous ones. David's mother expressed concern. His father did too, but still with a touch of understanding that while he may sixteen years old, he was also the practical joker he'd always been. They didn't seem to use the scare tactics as much as they used to. He hadn't been caught yet, and there didn't seem to be any indications he would be.

Chapter 21

Artie Johnston grouped the papers on his desk together in order of what he'd cover at the meeting today. As with recent meetings the bulk of the conversation was on national security issues. He missed the good old days when all they had to worry about was drugs, gangs and organized crime, an occasional kidnapping. Everything seemed less ominous before.

He stopped at putting the reports on the potential return of the flying guy in with the other reports he'd cover today. He reconsidered. He'd never gotten any response on the previous reports he'd given, but the Deputy Director hadn't told him to ignore the weird stuff. Artie considered the subject to be serious enough. Someone, or something, had been flying around central Wisconsin. Now, after a lull in police reports and newspaper articles, it appeared it was back. Artie had thought that through. The almost two year stretch without further sightings had started just after the newspaper article was printed. That probably spooked the flyer into laying low. The fear must have worn off now.

The latest report reawakened his interest. Based on his previous assessment, he thought the flyer had to have been a boy or a small man. It could have been a woman, he had to remind himself. Now he was sure it was a boy, a teenager. Someone had taken a high school flag from one city and got it up on the courthouse in another city. Artie had checked, then re-checked all of the available sources of information, and had come to the conclusion that others had apparently not yet come to. The only way this stunt could have been pulled off is if someone had flown to the top of the courthouse. The most likely culprit for a prank involving a high school football rivalry, would be a teenaged kid. A boy, most likely. It fit his theory.

Artie had summarized his information to be presented. He added the report to the stack.

Five minutes before the meeting was to start, he got himself a bottle of water from the small refrigerator outside his office and headed off. In the hallway, he met up with Herb Foster, the Deputy Director.

"Morning, Herb," Artie greeted him as he fell in step. Herb was short and stocky so Artie had to slow to keep pace.

"Artie. How goes the battle today?" Herb smiled up at him.

"Same stuff, different day," he replied. "But, I do have a question for you before we go in the meeting. Remember the flying guy from a while back?"

"Yeah. In Wisconsin."

"Yeah. He's back," Artie told him. "I never heard back before on that, so I was wondering if I shouldn't keep bringing it up."

"He's back?" Herb slowed, raising an eyebrow.

"You must've seen over the last week or so, the stuff on TV about the flag that got moved from the high school to the top of a courthouse."

"Yeah," Herb said. He stopped walking and faced Artie. There was a pause as he put the pieces in place in his mind. "That was your flying guy?"

"I think so. I don't know how that could have been done any other way. I checked everything out on this."

Herb was silent again, thinking. Artie waited for guidance.

"You have a good summarization of everything, I presume?" he asked Artie.

"Right here," he tapped the file.

"Give the report," Herb told him as they resumed walking. "You always have a way of making that stuff seem logical."

Artie gave the report at the end of his normal allotted time for his North Central Region report. As usual he got a couple chuckles and a few eye rolls. He gave the DD a hard copy of the report, and after the meeting had put the issue in the back of his mind. He left for another series of more pressing meetings.

*

The DD did a summarization of the meeting and attached the individual liaison reports as back-up. He forwarded that on as he always did, to Edward Gorman, Director of the FBI.

Ed Gorman read through the summarization and picked which subjects he wanted more detail on. He looked for the information on the flag stunt.

He remembered the Flying Guy. He remembered it well. He didn't like the idea of unidentified flying people or things. While a flying person was outside of what he considered reality, the reports had been convincingly conclusive that there was something strange going on. He needed to know more.

"Carol," he said, pushing an intercom button on his phone.

"Yes, Mr. Gorman?" a voice came back.

"Get me Randy Whiting. Tell him I'd like to see him in my office at…" he looked up at the clock, "one o'clock."

"Yes, sir. I'll get him," she said.

He pushed the button to end the call. C. Randall Whiting, Randy to only the director, as C. Randall expected everyone else to call him Agent Whiting or Sir, was Special Agent in Charge of National Security Programs. This internal department within the Federal Bureau of Investigation was charged with keeping tabs on all national security issues. While the bulk of the Bureau's workforce worked on the normal, unglamorous everyday crime, this department was more secretive due to the sensitive nature of their function. C. Randall Whiting had experience in many different internal departments and was perfect for his role as being Agent in Charge.

He arrived precisely at one o'clock and was shown into the Director's office. Ed Gorman liked Randy Whiting well enough, but he had realized long ago that it was primarily because he was his boss. If he had to work with, or for Randy, he knew it would be different. He was well aware of what others thought of C. Randall Whiting.

Director Gorman slid Artie Johnston's report over to Randy as they sat around his desk. Without a word, he took it and read through it. His face didn't offer any clue to what he thought of the subject matter. Two minutes later he looked up. He had read it twice.

"I saw this on CNN," Randy said, "and there was even something on it in Time magazine this week."

"What do you think?" the Director asked him.

"I remember being at one of the Liaison Regional meetings a couple years back. What was his name? Artie Johnston. He gave a report on a flying guy. Same guy, right?" he checked the paperwork. "Yeah. Arthur Johnston." He squinted his steely eyes at the Director.

"I'm thinking we need to look into this more," the Director said.

"I agree, sir," Randy replied quickly. "This could, theoretically, be considered a threat. Something, or someone flying around unidentified is not an issue to be overlooked. Pranks are pranks, but what's next?"

"If there actually were such a thing as a flying person…" the Director started.

"We could certainly use them for more than childish pranks," C. Randall Whiting finished the sentence.

Edward Gorman swore he felt a chill when Randy said that. But, he had thought the same thing, and if Randy picked up on that, then he didn't feel as apprehensive about pursuing it.

"I know Artie Johnston," the Director said. "He's a good agent. Others wouldn't have dreamed of bringing this… subject up to the Bureau."

"That was my impression of him also," Randy agreed. "He was a no-nonsense guy." He waited for specific instructions from his boss.

Ed Gorman pursed his lips, looking at the report. Finally he leaned forward and stabbed a button on his phone.

"Carol. Come in for a second."

"Yes, sir," she said and came to the door to his office.

"See if Agent Artie Johnston is in the building. He's the North-Central Regional Liaison. If he's not in, get me Herb Foster. I want one of them in my office now. Not on the phone. If you get Artie, I don't need Herb."

"Yes, sir, Mr. Gorman." Carol turned and left.

A minute later, Carol called in to say Artie Johnston was on his way up. When he showed, she led him into the Director's office.

"Come in Agent Johnston. Have a seat." The Director motioned him to a chair next to C. Randall Whiting. "I assume you know Agent Whiting."

"Yes, sir," Artie said. He resisted the urge to offer his hand. No hand came at him, so he sat.

"Agent Johnston," the Director started, "we've been reviewing your reports on your flying person."

There was a pause and Artie immediately thought he was going to get reprimanded for wasting the Bureau's time on something so frivolous. But then, he thought, why would C. Randall Whiting be there? In the hierarchy of the Bureau, Agent Whiting was only two levels down from the Director. There was more to this.

"Yes, sir," was all he said, waiting.

"Interesting theory," Agent Whiting took over unexpectedly. He fixed his emotionless gaze on Artie. "A flying person."

There was a silence then, a cold one, brought on by Agent Whiting's tone. Artie wasn't sure if he should say something or if Whiting was going to continue. He returned the gaze and then looked over to the Director.

"Yes, sir," Artie said. "I'm not sure what to make of it. It certainly seems out of the realm of logic, but, as I've documented in the files, there is something there."

"Yes, your reports," C. Randall Whiting said. "For future purposes, please submit them directly to the Director and myself. No more reporting this through your regular Liaison meetings. Do not pass them through Herb Foster. Directly to us. Understood?"

"Yes, sir," Artie nodded. "I'll do that." He didn't like the sound of it though. This was a departure from normal procedure.

"Good. No one else is to know of this. Don't talk about it with anyone, including Herb, or any of the other agents, even the ones senior to you. If anyone asks why, tell them you were ordered not to waste your time on this... silly, flying guy stuff." Agent Whiting had the ominous tone again.

"Good," the Director said. He punched the phone again as he stood. "Carol. Please come in."

The door opened and Carol entered. "Yes, sir?"

"Agent Johnston will be reporting directly to me on a matter that also involves Agent Whiting. He is to have immediate access if needed."

"Yes, sir," Carol said. That meant that if Agent Johnston requested time with the Director, he was to be put through or shown in immediately. Other calls got screened, and very few ended up getting through on the first try.

"Thanks, Carol." The Director turned to Artie, holding out a hand. "Keep your ears to the ground. We want notification of any future activities."

Artie shook his hand. "Yes, sir," he replied. Then, without even wanting to, he shook the hand C. Randall Whiting offered. It was cold and clammy. Carol escorted him out.

"A flying guy! Jesus!" Ed Gorman said, dropping in his chair. "We're playing hush hush over people seeing flying people. What's the world coming to?"

Agent Whiting leaned forward toward him. "We'll get to the bottom of this, sir. I've always held to the adage that where there's smoke, there's fire."

The Director of the FBI stood, signaling the end of the meeting. He shook Randy's hand and walked him to the door. He wiped his hand on his pants before sitting again.

*

Artie Johnson sat in his office, pondering the directive he had just been given. He'd only been in the Director's office once before, in a group of agents being commended for a job well done for a long ago solved case. This meeting today was slightly bizarre. C. Randall Whiting being involved made it doubly so. The absurdity of a flying person was now replaced by a feeling of apprehension. He began pulling all of his flying guy information to put in one central file. He almost felt like he needed a secret hiding place.

Chapter 22

David was just coming into Wausau on his way to Amy's house when it occurred to him. A part of him was going to miss the flying to visit her there. Since it rarely took him more than ten or fifteen minutes, it had never turned into a really big hassle. It actually took him just a little more time to fly from Aston to Wisconsin Rapids, than it did to drive from his house to where Amy used to live. Numerous stoplights and stop signs slowed him down. No stoplights up here, he thought. No traffic.

As he passed by, he looked to the west at the hulking shadow of Rib Mountain against the sky. He'd made a couple laps around there a few times, on some of his return trips. One winter night, he had hovered over a dark section of leafless trees there, watching night-time skiers maneuvering the slopes. Many of his friends skied, but he'd never tried it. Watching the graceful descent of the figures below had him reconsidering. Now he again made a mental note to maybe give it a try. He'd have someone to do it with.

Amy was moving back to Aston.

She had called him about a half hour prior to his departure to visit. He had noticed that her reaction to this news now, was a complete one eighty from her reaction when she learned she was moving to Wisconsin Rapids. This time, she'd been bubbly and buoyant.

"Davey," she had gushed when he answered, "you'll never guess. You'll never guess in a million years."

"Guess what?" he had responded. He didn't have a clue what she was going to tell him.

"I'm moving back," she told him. "I'm moving back to Aston!"

"What!?" David exclaimed. "How? When?" He was flabbergasted. Pleasantly flabbergasted.

John Baraniak

"This summer," she told him. "My mom and dad said I could live with my grandma during my senior year if I want. She sort of needs someone around and can't afford other people to check in on her. Mom and Dad knew I wanted to get back to Aston. My dad has to travel a lot and now my mom works a rotating shift, and is either at work or asleep whenever I'm home, so they don't see me much."

David listened to her go on about the move. He wore a big smile the whole while she talked. Amy was coming back. Now he'd be able to see her every day at school. He wanted to see her now.

"I'll be over around seven," he had told her, when she finally stopped talking.

He hovered over Amy's next door neighbor's yard waiting for the car below to pull out. If he'd arrived about ten seconds earlier, he may have landed in their yard just as the car pulled out and bathed him in the headlights. When the headlights disappeared down the street, he landed. He went into Amy's yard and then around front.

"Hi, David," Mrs. Kellerman greeted him at the door. "I sort of figured you'd show up tonight." She was smiling.

"Hi, Mrs. Kellerman. Yeah," he replied, "I can't believe it. This is great." He paused a second before heading up to Amy's room upstairs, suddenly thinking of how she must be feeling. Her smile did have a touch of sadness to it. "How are you taking it?" he decided to ask.

"Well…" she considered. "It'll work out, since we rarely see her with our work schedules, and I get over to Aston more now since my mother isn't doing so well. Amy will be a big help with her. It was her idea."

Amy came bounding down the steps from her room. She threw her arms around David's neck and gave him a big kiss on the lips. Her mother raised one eyebrow and her smile turned happy.

"Hey, David," Amy's mom asked as she shut the front door, "how did you get here? I don't see your car."

"I bummed a ride with my cousin," he fibbed. His usual story.

Mrs. Kellerman left them in the front foyer. She had found his frequent rides with his cousin to be a bit unusual. She never saw car lights when he was dropped off, or picked up. She didn't say anything and it never crossed her mind to consider any alternatives.

130

"C'mon," Amy said, taking his hand and leading him upstairs to her room.

When they got there, she threw her arms around his neck again and hugged him tight.

"I'm so excited," she gushed again. "I get to come back."

"Mm," David said, holding her around her waist, lifting her up. "So am I." They kissed again.

They sat on her bed, talking for over an hour. It seemed she wouldn't stop, but he didn't mind. He was here with her and she was happy. And best of all, she was coming back. Like most times when alone and near each other, they found ways for their bodies to touch. She was practically on top of him tonight. Being teenagers, their closeness usually led to other thoughts, and feeling as celebratory as they did now made them wish her mom and dad weren't home.

Normally when he left Amy, they both felt the slight pain of separation. Even though he came almost every weekend and an occasional weekday, it still hurt to be apart for those days. Not tonight. David kissed her at the door and felt like flying directly off her front porch. Not a good idea, David considered, since Mrs. Kellerman was a little suspicious of his comings and goings with no car. She had, on a few occasions, watched through the window as he walked off, before he ducked around back. He told her he meets his cousin at the gas station a couple blocks over.

This trip home took a little longer. When he took off from the normal departure point, instead of staying over the cover of the trees until out of town, he had gone straight up. He rose quickly into the blue black sky, and when he was high enough where he knew no one could hear him, he threw his head back and let out a yell.

"Yeah!" he yelled as loud as he could. He held his arms out to the side and gently rotated as he rose. He felt good. It grew colder the further up he went. But, he didn't notice it.

After a couple laps around Rib Mountain, he flew home. He told his parents the good news.

"Oh, David. That's wonderful!" his mom hugged him. She was really happy for him.

"Yeah," his dad added. "That'll make things easier now." He wasn't just thinking of it being easier on David. It would be easier on him and Margaret also. They worried every time he left, that something would happen to him or that he'd get caught. They'll definitely breathe a sigh of relief.

"Yeah, thanks," David said to both of them. "She'll be moving back at the end of May when school gets out. Well, I think I'm going to bed. 'Night." He was all talked out and went to bed.

*

The day after the Wisconsin Rapids schools let out for summer vacation, the Kellermans loaded all of Amy's worldly possessions in their car, and brought her to Aston. David met them at her grandmother's house and helped carry things in. He had met her grandmother before and liked her. She was a nice, little old lady. She seemed to like him too.

He found himself checking out the landscape around her house. It was an older home, in an older neighborhood, and there were a lot of wooded lots, with big mature trees in the yards. He was happy about that. He found a handful of spots he thought would work for coming and going.

He had driven his parent's car to the house and was now wishing he had flown. He felt so happy to have her close again that he wanted to take off into the sky, even if it was broad daylight.

*

David had visited Amy in Rapids twice in her last week there. He hadn't deviated from his routine flight path on all his previous visits, but on the these last two he had. Instead of coming in to town over the zig-zagging maze of trees lining the streets, he'd gone directly over the downtown business district. It was at night on both occasions and he had been up over five hundred yards. He was sure he went undetected.

He was wrong. On the second trip, Larry Ogden, owner of Ogden's Barber Shop, the only barber shop still in the downtown area, had seen the dark shape of a person cross overhead as he was getting into his car. He thought he was either seeing things or maybe it was a bird, so he didn't think much of it. He mentioned it the next evening while cutting the hair of Earl Gummer, Editor of the Wisconsin Rapids Register, the local paper.

"Well, I'll be," Earl Gummer, Editor of the Wisconsin Rapids Register, had said after Larry recounted the sighting during his haircut. "I thought

132

that was mainly an Aston thing. Maybe whoever it is comes over our way once in a while."

When Earl got in to work at his office the next day, he made a point to call Bernie Fredder up at the Sentinel in Aston. It had been awhile since they'd last spoken, and this was a good reason to reconnect.

"Hey, Bernie," he greeted his long-time friend and colleague. "How they hangin'?"

"High and tight," Bernie responded, recognizing Earl's voice right off the bat. "What can I do for ya, Earl?"

"Remember your flying guy?" Earl asked.

"Hard not to," Bernie said. "Why do you ask?"

"I think he's been to Rapids. My barber saw something the other day." Earl passed on the information from Larry Ogden, and then ended with his theory that maybe it was the Aston flyer who'd pulled the flag stunt. How else could someone get to the top of the courthouse without going through the inside, except to fly?

"That had me wondering too," Bernie told him. He was already pretty sure those dots connected.

Bernie did a short paragraph for the next weeks ODDS & ENDS column:

"Earl Gummer, my compatriot at the Wisconsin Rapids Register reported the possible sighting of a flying person over their fair city a few days back. His barber had spotted the aerial apparition when leaving his shop one evening. It was flying right over their downtown district and had gone right over his shop. Has our flyer been visiting them or is there another one like him...? That certainly could explain how their school flag would show up over the courthouse in Merrill. Who knows?"

Chapter 23

Nearly a year passed by before more reports of the flying person began coming in to Agent Artie Johnston. When they did, they came in somewhat of a deluge. These differed from previous reports though. Previous reports were from the Aston, Wisconsin area, with the glaring exception of the flag incident. That had involved Wisconsin Rapids and Merrill, Wisconsin. The new batch of sightings were from the police and sheriff's departments in the Wausau, Stevens Point, and Wisconsin Rapids areas.

Artie stood before his map. While never having been any further north into Wisconsin than Milwaukee and Madison, he was growing familiar with the area on the map. If he drew a line between Aston and Wisconsin Rapids, it would pass near both the other cities. He didn't have to think too hard to figure out what was going on.

The flying guy was travelling back and forth between Aston and Wisconsin Rapids. The sightings indicated different movements in both directions. The previous day's blotter from Wausau said someone driving on Highway Fifty Two had seen something moving toward the southwest, toward Stevens Point or Wisconsin Rapids, at around seven PM. A later, and separate report, said there was a sighting of something flying in the exact opposite direction at approximately eleven thirty the same night. So, Artie surmised, Aston was still the home base. Whoever this is, has been visiting Wisconsin Rapids for some reason.

He took the better part of the morning preparing a report for the FBI Director Ed Gorman. He made sure he was doubly careful in what he included, considering that this correspondence would also go to C. Randall Whiting. He felt that uneasy feeling when he thought of him.

At four o'clock that afternoon he was shown into the Director's office. Thankfully, Agent Whiting was not in attendance.

"Have a seat," the Director motioned to a chair. "I thought maybe this issue went away since we haven't heard from you in… what? Almost a year?"

"Yes, sir," Artie replied. "Our sighting reports seem to come in streaks. It's back."

Artie handed the report to the Director. He took it and sat back, reading it slowly. Minutes passed before he spoke.

"This is just too weird to believe," he finally said. "Let me ask you this, Agent Johnston: Do you think this is in any way, a threat to our national security?"

"No, sir," Artie shook his head. "I'm glad it's just us here today, so no one else could hear me say it, but I think there is indeed someone flying around in Wisconsin. As whacky as that sounds. But all information points to it being a kid, a teenager. There's nothing even in northern Wisconsin that could possibly be threatened by this person or thing. There are no military bases. It's just general population. That's it. It's… Wisconsin."

"I'm pretty much in agreement with you there," the Director said. "We need to continue to keep this quiet for now. Keep me posted on anything else that comes up."

"Yes, sir. Agent Whiting also?" Artie asked.

"Yes. I'll pass this on to him." He held up the report.

"Thank you, sir," Artie said standing to leave. The Director opened the door for him.

Chapter 24

David looked out the front window at the leaves accumulating in the yard. They had just started falling and his dad had suggested he get a jump start on raking. They had a heavily wooded lot and there were plenty more to follow. Autumn tended to come quick and leave early, he had learned, and the cold and snow weren't far behind.

Today was a glorious day though, as his mother had said when she had earlier stood in this exact same spot, enjoying the bright sunshine and the red and gold leaves it illuminated. David remembered his mom liked fall the best out of all the four seasons. She said that every year. This year she had again taken the wheel of the car, with David and his father along, and gone for the annual drive through the northwoods to view the changing of the leaves. David liked that, and he'd acquired her appreciation for this slice of nature. During that drive, he had decided he wanted to see what the leaves looked like from above. There had been the usual TV reports of the percentage of peak color change in the state, and they almost always included an aerial or panoramic view of the vibrant orange forests. Since he had the ability to fly, he wanted to see it up close.

"C'mon. I'll help you rake the back," his father said, coming up behind him.

"Yeah. Okay," he replied. He liked doing this with his dad and any help he could get with the backyard was welcome. He knew this was only the first of many times he'd be raking that stretch of lawn. There were a lot of leaves on the ground now, but there were even more still on the trees.

They had a system for raking that had been developed years back, when David was officially assigned this task as one of his chores. Back then, both his parents shared in the work, and the three of them always enjoyed it. The work went quickly and at some point always included flinging the crisp, dry leaves at each other. Today, it was just him and his father.

David was thinking of the trip he had worked out for his autumn ride. As he was going in broad daylight, he'd need to start from somewhere other than his own backyard. They weren't the only ones out raking today and he'd surely be seen. He figured he'd see if he could borrow the car and head out to a spot east of town, where he figured it would be safe to leave from. It was a spot a lot of his high school friends frequented for night-time parties, and was well off the beaten path. It was getting increasingly easier to get his parent's permission to go, even though he'd learned already that he could pretty much go as he wanted. They trusted him enough now.

"Dad," David asked, "is it okay if a use the car this afternoon?"

"Uh. Yeah. I guess so," his dad replied. "What's your plans?"

"Well," David said, leaning his chin on his rake, "I think I'm going to fly up north. Over the Nicolet National Forest. Look at the leaves."

"Where we went the other day?" his dad asked. He leaned on his rake, resting for a moment.

"Yeah, around there," he replied. "I was going to drive out to Woods Flowage and park, and leave from there. Should be safe."

His father considered that. As far as he knew, David had been seen only a handful of times, at least according to the papers, and so far no one came knocking on their door. There was always a part of him that he knew should say no, but it was usually overridden by his feelings that David should be able to enjoy his skill. He knew that if he had the ability to fly, he'd be gone all the time.

"Okay," he nodded. "Just be careful. I imagine there'll be a lot of people enjoying the scenery on a day like today."

"I will. Thanks, Dad."

They finished raking and went in the house. David went to change clothes for the flight, while his dad made them each something to eat. When they sat at the table, his father smiled over at him.

"You're a lucky guy, Davey." His dad still sometimes called him that. "Being able to do that. I'd love to be able to. But every time I jump in the air to take off, I land on my feet."

David looked at him, then grinned. "Somehow I can picture you doing that."

"I have. Honest," his dad smiled. "Every time, I still hope." He looked out the window at the bright orange and red colors that bathed the backyard. "Should be even prettier from the air, than from the ground.

"Yeah," David said, stuffing the last bit of a sandwich in his mouth and getting up. "I'm looking forward to it."

They each helped to clean the table and put the dishes in the dishwasher. Margaret was gone for the day and they always made sure to keep things clean for her. David grabbed the car keys, said good-bye and left. He saw his dad standing at the front window when pulled out onto the street. He looked envious. David wished his parents could fly like he did. For whatever reason, he was the only one with that talent. He often saw that look on his father's face. Not so much his mom, but his dad for sure.

*

David drove out to his planned departure point. There was another car there, but a short walk down the trail leading into the woods revealed a couple kids goofing around. He thought he recognized one, so got out of sight to avoid conversation.

When he was comfortable that he wouldn't be seen, David rose through a small gap in the trees. It was a warm day that could be called Indian Summer, if there had been a cool spell recently, but it had stayed consistently warm for the last couple weeks. The air was dry and the crisp smell of autumn stayed with him as he started on his way.

He came out of the forest and settled over a large sugar maple. The foliage of the tree was like a bright red flower. He turned and looked to the north, toward the direction he planned to go. The TV stations had said this area was at the peak for leaf color, and what he saw in front of him proved that out. The woods he was over were in full bloom. Here and there, an almost equally bright green spire of a pine tree jutted above the canopy. He saw distant breaks in the color, and knew these were farm fields that rolled gently toward the thicker forest further on.

David turned horizontal and headed off. He coasted slowly along, trying to keep the comforting scent of the fall leaves in his nostrils. He came to a stop near the edge of the woods. Below him lay a long expanse of honey colored field corn. It was getting to be harvesting time, he knew, but for now, the dried tassels leaned gently in the breeze. To the side, David saw the brilliant magenta of the sumac bushes that lined the sides of the road. Most of the roads that they had driven a week ago had also been bordered in red. Everything was coming to their seasonal conclusion at the same time.

He didn't see anyone, so he went down low over the corn. He flew fast, crossing the field to another copse of woods. Not knowing the landscape, he proceeded cautiously. He thought of going up a couple hundred yards or so, but was content in simply going slowly and enjoying the ride. There was only a slight breeze that he detected, and it was warm.

After crossing two more fields, one a since harvested potato field that was now just flat and dusty, he came to the beginning edge of the thick forest that hugged the hills going north. David stopped. It was a brilliant orange vista. He rose to get a better view, and subconsciously moved in further over the deep forest to avoid being seen.

He was amazed at what he saw. The scenery from the ground was awe inspiring enough, but up here it was much better. He slowly set out on a path to the national forest. It looked like one long orange shag carpet, David thought to himself. Occasionally he'd spot what appeared to be a slit in the fabric, and he knew they were the country roads winding throughout. It was much hillier here, and there were no farm fields.

After crossing a long stretch, he started noticing holes in the color. He came to one and slowed to the edge, overlooking a small lake. It's more like a pond, he thought. There were no buildings around it and no boats. As far as he could tell, there were no roads leading into it. He went down. There was no wind here and the surface of the water was smooth as glass. The brilliant colors of the surrounding trees glinted off. David slowly circled the lake near the shoreline. When he looked across the water, he could barely tell where the real woods ended and the reflection began.

Sure wish Amy could see this, he thought, or *Mom and Dad. Or anyone for that matter. This is incredible.* Thoughts of floating over this hand-in-hand with Amy, arms outstretched, filled his mind. If only she could fly. *I want her to see this.*

David spent well over an hour swooping around above the national forest. Occasionally he would stop, point his arms skyward and roar into the light of the blue sky. He'd look down at the glory beneath him, knowing why people like his mom loved this season. He was glad he'd decided to do this.

When he turned to head back, he realized he'd lost his bearings. He knew it was pretty much straight south, so he kept the now setting sun on his right, and flew off. He zoned in on a distant water tower and got his location from the name spelled on it. He took his time, and twenty minutes later descended through the gap in the trees to his parked car. The other car was gone now. He drove reluctantly home.

"How was it?" his dad asked when he dropped the car keys in the bowl by the back door.

"It was awesome," he said, thinking that sounded too cliché for what he'd just experienced. "I wish you could have seen that." He saw the faint look of envy return to his dad's eyes.

All his dad could do was nod.

Chapter 25

Bernie went to work early on this Monday morning. He'd been at the city council meeting held on Saturday, and now needed to prepare an article for the afternoon paper. It had to be done by ten o'clock to make the print, and he'd be pressed to get it done by then. In addition to that, he had to finalize two other stories that he'd thought were done, but now needed revision. Some facts had changed. Bernie never liked facts that changed.

When he set his briefcase bag on his desk, he noticed the stack of pink phone messages sitting under a paperweight. Marsha, his assistant, had to have put them there. He picked them up and flipped through. They were all people who had called, most prior to eight o'clock, about seeing the flying guy. The last message slip was from Mike Bresky, the Chief of Police. Bernie looked at it. The Chief wanted to meet with Bernie about the recent sightings. Evidently, some of the people who had seen what all the messages referred to, had also contacted the law enforcement community.

Bernie sat at his chair re-reading the messages. He wished he could call now. He set them aside and pulled out the other writing he needed to do. Even though it seemed to go quickly, it took him right up to the ten o'clock deadline to finish. His mind had been creeping back to the request from Chief Bresky to meet on the flying guy. He wondered what had changed to get the Chief's interest. After filing his articles for the day's paper, he called the police department.

"Chief Bresky, please," he inquired of the receptionist. "Tell him it's Bernie Fredder." There was a long wait.

"Hi, Bernie. How are you?" the Chief, Mike Bresky greeted him.

"Good. You?" he responded.

"Great. Hey, have you heard anything about your flying guy from yesterday?"

"Well, as a matter of fact, I have," Bernie told him. "I had a stack of messages from people saying they saw him out yesterday. I haven't had a chance to get back to anyone yet. That was my next step after my call to you."

"Ah. Good," Mike Bresky said. "Can you bring those and meet me in a half hour? Here at my office? Let's talk before you call to verify your sources. Can we do that?"

"Uh. Sure. I guess," Bernie said checking his watch. A half hour would work. He wondered what the Chief wanted.

"Good enough. See you then," the Chief signed off.

Bernie sat back for a moment, wondering what this could be about. The Police Chief had only shown an amused interest in the past, but was now summoning him to discuss it. And Mike wanted to talk before Bernie did any calling to verify the people's stories. He found that somewhat odd. A slight sense of foreboding came and went. He'd find out.

Five minutes before he was to meet the Police Chief, Bernie instructed Marsha to keep any new incoming calls of the sightings in one folder for him. She gave him with a quizzical look when he headed for the door.

"Does this have to do with your meeting with Mike?" she asked.

Bernie looked at her and nodded. "Yeah. Wonder what he wants."

The Aston Police Department was only one block away from the Sentinel office, so Bernie walked in right on time. The front desk sergeant buzzed him in. He knew his way around the building so headed for the Chief's office.

"Bernie!" a voice came from an open office door he passed by.

He stopped and swung back, poking his head around the corner of the doorway.

"Hey, beautiful," he said when he saw who called to him. "How are you?"

"Peachy," Cindy Hill, the Department's Lead Investigator smiled. "What brings you in?"

"Meeting with Mike."

"Mm. I think it has to do with your flying guy," she said.

"I believe so," he said, noting the time showing on the wall clock behind her. "Need to go. I'll stop back when I'm done." He smiled at her. He liked Cindy Hill.

"Don't be a stranger," she called after him.

The door to Mike's office was open and he saw Bernie as soon as he appeared there.

"Hey, Bernie. Thanks for coming. C'mon in," he motioned him in. "Shut the door please."

Bernie closed the door, noticing the County Sheriff was already sitting in front of Mike Bresky's desk. A big man, the Sheriff always dominated a room.

"Hey, Bill. How are you?" Bernie asked, extending a hand to Sheriff Bill Lippmore.

"Good. You?" the Sheriff stood to shake hands. He towered over Bernie.

Bernie liked Bill Lippmore. He was a good cop, and well liked within the community. He and Bernie got along personally, as well as professionally. Like his counterpart Mike Bresky, he had been a friend of Bernie's before taking the position in law enforcement.

"So," Bernie said, settling in a chair. "What's the scoop? Has our flyer gotten in some more mischief?"

"Not so much mischief," the Sheriff said. "There was a complaint that he vandalized some property."

"Really?" Bernie said. He was surprised and the expression on his face showed it. He was also disappointed. So far he thought the flyer was simply a prankster, someone who provided an unusual sort of entertainment for the community. Turning into a vandal would change everything. Bernie felt almost heartbroken with the news.

"Well, that's what we're checking out, and why I asked you to come in before calling your sources," Chief Bresky said.

Bernie sat quietly while the Chief and the Sheriff filled in the blanks. Hank Holshuh, a local farmer, reported that vandals had spray-painted graffiti on the side of his barn. The barn, a huge and ancient structure, was just off County Highway A, on the southwest side of town. The Sheriff's deputy who investigated, had noted the graffiti was pretty close to twenty feet off the ground. There was no obvious means to get up that high, that could be found in the area of the barn. The graffiti was amateurish and consisted of the just the words 'Aston sucks'. They were big letters, easily seen from the road.

Bernie thought about it. That changed his whole opinion of the guy. Having gained the collective attention, and even goodwill of the town as their anonymous claim to fame, he might now become a black mark on the community. A vandal. *No. It can't be.*

"I'm a little disheartened," he finally said. "So far I thought all we had was a mischievous kid on our hands."

"Me, too," Sheriff Lippmore said, nodding.

"Actually, that's why we wanted to talk to you," Chief Bresky added. "We're not really sure this was done by him. It's out of character for one thing, and the other is that Hank Holshuh has a troublemaker for a son. I'd guess it was him, before the Flying Guy."

"I know him," Bernie said. "Dennis, right? Little guy. Likes to fight. I've seen his name in the blotter now and then."

"That's him," Chief Bresky said. "The old man, Hank, called it in. Claims he confronted his son first, but the boy denied it. Swore he didn't do it. Hank said he wasn't totally convinced."

"So, we have to go on what we know for sure," the Sheriff went on, "and the fact that its twenty feet off the ground can only make you wonder."

Bernie felt a little better. Maybe it was the kid and not the flyer. He hoped that were the case and said so. Twenty feet off the ground or not, this didn't seem like something a Kite Fairy would do. He told them that.

"Yeah," the other two said, nodding in unison.

A thought occurred to Bernie. "Have we ever had any other reports of wrongdoings that involved… height? You know, things that were high up, that could only be done by a… flyer?"

"Way ahead of you on that," Sheriff Lippmore said. "I have a couple guys doing a quick review of vandalism cases, window peeping, or any breaking and entering that might fit the bill. I hope not."

"So, what do you want me to do when I call on the reports I got in?" Bernie asked. He held up the stack of pink message slips.

"Can I see those?" the Sheriff asked. Bernie didn't see a problem with that, so he let Bill scan through them.

"First, check on where the sightings were at," Bill said. "All of the reports we got here came from the northeast side of town, not the southwest, where Hank lives. Then check for the time of day. Our reports were all from the daytime. The barn was painted at night. Hank was around during the day."

"Okay," Bernie sat looking through his stack of message slips. He looked at the names. A couple were familiar, but he only knew where one of those lived. The northeast side. He felt a little better.

"Let us know what you find," the Sheriff said.

"Okay," Bernie said again, standing to leave. A thought occurred to him. "Is it okay if I call Hank Holshuh? Any issue there?"

"Sure. Go ahead," the Sheriff said. "Maybe the story will change."

Bernie said goodbye, forgot to go back to say hi to Cindy Hill on the way out, and walked back to his office. His head was down, as he considered the circumstances. Vandalism. *No. Please don't be true.* Bernie hated vandalism.

*

When he was back at his desk, he started calling the people back. Marsha had added three more while he was gone, so he now had nine calls to make. Evidently the flyer had opted not to be as discreet this time. Normally, the sightings indicated at least some mention of the Flying Guy hiding or trying not being noticed. Nine calls was a lot.

After reaching and talking to the first five messages he needed to return, Bernie had a better picture of what probably occurred. The prior day had been an extraordinarily beautiful fall day, and it could have been that the flyer simply went out for a flight over the autumn scenery. All five of those people lived on the north side or east side of Aston. All described the same thing. Same color clothing. Black mask. The usual. He was flying over and around the wooded areas. One person said he wasn't moving real fast. Bernie noted the times of the sightings, and they were all within an hour of each other. Nothing at night. Nothing on the southwest side of town. He was feeling better.

When he finished calling, having reached eight of the nine tipsters, he was growing confident the daytime excursion was probably unrelated to anything done at night. There were no calls about anything at all at night, nor on the southwest side. Bill and Mike had said they too only had messages from the other side of town, with the exception of Hank.

Bernie called Hank Holshuh. Hank's wife answered, saying Hank would have to call back when he came in from the barn. He was too busy now. Bernie left his direct dial number. Time dragged while he waited.

145

Half an hour later Bernie's phone rang. "Bernie Fredder," he said when answering it.

"Hello, Mr. Fredder. This is Hank Holshuh."

"Hi, Mr. Holshuh," Bernie greeted him. "Thanks for calling back so quickly."

"Sure. Call me Hank," he said. His voice was gruff.

"Thanks, and call me Bernie." He decided to be direct. "Hank," he said, "the Sheriff's Department reported the act of vandalism on your barn last night. I see that report from them every day. I was wondering if I can get some information from you."

"This ain't gonna go in the paper, is it?" Hank asked.

"Well, yes, normally it does. Do you not want it in the paper for some reason?"

"Well, I'm kinda thinkin' it was that dipshit kid of mine," Hank explained. "Denny was out last night with the usual group of kids he hangs with, and I never put anything past them. Or him. They've done this before, spray-painting and stuff. That, and my big ladder looked like it had been moved. You know. It was still in the corner I store it in, but just didn't feel like it was in the same spot as always."

"Hmm. I see," Bernie said. He was taking notes.

"That's why I don't want it brought out. I'll take care of this myself."

"Okay. Fair enough," Bernie told him "I'll keep it out of the paper."

"Thanks…uh, Bernie," Hank said.

"No problem. Good luck with your son," Bernie said.

"Thanks," he snorted. "I need it."

Bernie hung up the phone feeling better than he had when he had placed the call. He was sure the Flying Guy hadn't spray-painted the barn. He called Police Chief Mike Bresky and filled him in. The Chief agreed that it wasn't likely the flyer. They exchanged some of the information Bernie had gained in his calls and agreed to stay in touch on the subject. Both Chief Bresky and Sheriff Lippmore were now paying more than just bemused attention. Bernie hoped he wouldn't have too many conversations like the one today.

Chapter 26

Artie Johnston sat at a table in the sun in the lunchroom, one level below his office. He'd come in early and already had three hours of laborious meetings out of the way. He decided to take a bit of a break, so moved to a location that afforded him a little of the sunshine he'd missed in the morning. It was still only nine thirty, so the bright light streaming in the window cast long shadows across the room.

He set the stack of newspapers he'd brought to read on one of the other chairs. He put the prior day's police and sheriff's department reports in front of him. He took a sip of the scalding coffee in the cardboard cup and set it aside to cool. It was too hot for his taste. He started paging through the law enforcement reports. He had over seventy different blotters in his stack. Today, it seemed there was nothing but the routine events that had come to the attention of the local cops.

That was until Artie hit the reports from Aston. As soon as he turned over the preceding page, and saw the name Aston at the top, for some reason he knew something was going to be there. When he saw the name, he'd immediately pictured C. Randall Whiting. It had to be karma, he thought. *Bad karma.*

The Aston reports, from both the law agencies, consisted of one suspected break-in, two auto accidents and the Flying Guy. Most of the individual notations in the reports centered on the Flying Guy. *Dang*, Artie thought to himself. *Now I have to do a report for the Director.* He read the information through once more, then set that paperwork aside. He finished reading the rest of the blotters for Wisconsin, paying extra attention to whether there were other sightings in other towns. There weren't. He clicked his pen and wrote a note on the Aston Police blotter that there were no other reports elsewhere.

Artie put those aside and set the newspapers on the table. He ignored his now cold coffee as he paged through one after the other. He knew where to look in most of the papers, so the process went swiftly. Not much jumped out at him as relevant to anything he was currently involved in, so he breezed through them. He noted on the Aston blotter, that there was no mention in the Aston Sentinel of the Flying Guy. He made a mental note to be doubly sure to check that newspaper over the next few days, to make sure he'd catch if anything was written on it. This would probably make the ODDS & ENDS column the following Tuesday at the very least.

The sun streaming in the window was now hot, and it was the catalyst to get him up and on his way back to his office. He made note of the time and decided he'd have enough to get his report done right away and sent off to the Director, with a copy to C. Randall Whiting. When he finished, he called the Director's office to set up a time to meet. Carol, the Director's secretary, penciled him in for one o'clock that afternoon. The Director was out right now, but was expected to be back in his office by one.

*

At ten to one, Artie made his way up two floors to see the Director, Ed Gorman. He was already in and the door was shut, so Carol had him wait in the small seating area of the outer office. Carol didn't talk much, but she had a friendly smile that she offered whenever she glanced at Artie. At one on the head, the intercom phone rang. All Artie heard was Carol saying "Yes, sir. I'll send him in."

Artie rose and was shown in. To his dismay, C. Randall Whiting was in the room . Surprisingly, he rose from his chair to meet him. He held out a hand. Artie took it and said hello. It wasn't as clammy this time. The Director offered a hand then.

"Agent Johnston," the Director said. "Have a seat."

"Thank you, sir," Artie said and settled in a chair.

"So. I assume our guy is back at it?" the Director began.

"Yes, sir," Artie said then handed each of them a copy of his report. "Would you like to read it first, or should I go on?"

"Give me a sec," Agent Whiting said as he began to read.

They both finished at the same time and Artie noticed the glance they exchanged with the other. He hesitated for a moment before starting. He didn't like the look they'd shared.

Artie reviewed the sightings listed by the Aston law enforcement agencies. He noted there was no newspaper mention of it, but would be watching and fully expecting it to be noted in the next few days. He told them about weekly column. The sightings were all consistent, he pointed out. Same dress. Same size. Same side of town. Everything meshed. They listened in silence as he laid it all out for them.

"The newspaper guy in that town," the Director finally cut in. "What's his name?"

"Bernard Fredder, sir," Artie told him. "He's the guy who handles their local beat. He's the only one who writes about it there. He seems to take great interest in the flyer." He saw them exchange another glance.

"I wonder if he has more information than just what ends up in the newspaper," the Director said.

"That's very possible, sir," Artie said. "I'd imagine in a small town like theirs, a lot goes unreported to the police."

"What do you think, Randy?" the director asked Agent Whiting.

"Well, sir," Agent Whiting began, "as odd as this all seems, these sightings are all consistent in their description of the flyer and that there is likely only one of them. Unfortunately. There have been so many sightings, what'd we have here – nine sightings in one day, yeah. There has to be something to this."

There was a pause, that at the end seemed sinister to Artie.

"And I want this guy," Whiting said, confirming Artie's feeling.

The Director nodded in agreement. "Yeah. We have to check this out a lot closer."

"Sir," Agent Whiting leaned forward to ask. "Perhaps it wouldn't be a bad idea to send Agent Johnston to Aston to meet with this Bernard Fredder. And to get a feel for what we've potentially got."

"What are your thoughts on that?" the Director asked Artie.

"Yes, sir. That's a good idea," he said. "I've been wanting to talk to him and it would be better to go there than to talk over the phone."

The Director told him to clear his calendar and go immediately. He said he'd have Carol notify the Deputy Director that he was going to be gone for business, on the instructions of the Director. Agent Whiting added that Artie should try to make it look like he was perhaps in the area on other business and just wanted to drop in and see what the deal was with a flying person. Downplay it, he said. Artie felt like he was being sent on a secret mission.

*

He went back to his office to make travel arrangements. He'd fly into Mosinee, Wisconsin, their central airport up there, then rent a car to go the fifty or so miles to Aston. He cleared out his appointment calendar, notifying whoever needed to know that he'd be missing meetings for a few days. He didn't expect this to require him to stay more than two days at the most.

Then it occurred to him that he should have checked to see the availability of Bernie Fredder for a meeting. He rifled quickly through the daily newspapers from his morning review, and pulled out the Aston Sentinel. He went to the editorial page where they printed contact information. There was a list of the main executives at the paper, the Editor, News Editor, Sports Editor, and others. Under that was the street address, mail address, email address and phone numbers.

Artie dialed the number shown. He sat thinking while it rang, wondering if he should go if Bernie Fredder was not around. He'd have to double check with the Director.

"Aston Sentinel. How can I help you?" a pleasant voice asked.

"Bernard Fredder, please," Artie told her. He always figured he went by Bernie, but wasn't sure.

"I'll check if he's in. Can I ask who is calling?"

Artie almost gave his usual official sounding name of Agent Arthur Johnston of the FBI, but opted to stay anonymous to the receptionist. She didn't need to know he was from the FBI.

"Artie Johnston," was all he said.

"Thank you," she said. "Please hold."

A couple seconds later Bernie Fredder answered the phone. "Bernie Fredder," he said.

"Hello, Mr. Fredder. My name is Arthur Johnston. I'm a Liaison Agent with the Federal Bureau of Investigation."

"Yes, sir," Bernie said cordially. "What can I do for the FBI?"

Bernie had on previous occasions spoken to FBI agents over matters that required their involvement in Aston. Most of the occasions were for getting information on activities in the area that were somehow tied to outside events. Otherwise, Aston didn't require outside assistance. It had been many years since he'd had contact with anyone from the FBI.

"First, perhaps I should explain my function with the Bureau," Artie said. "I am a Liaison Agent for the FBI's Northcentral Region, which includes Wisconsin. I basically keep tabs on what's going on in that region, that might be of interest to us."

Bernie listened to the explanation and sensed where this may be going. Knowing there wasn't much else happening in this neck of the woods, the only possible thing could be the Flying Guy. Since the local authorities were paying more attention, perhaps the big guys were too. He didn't like the thought of that.

"I'm going to be in northern Wisconsin tomorrow on other business, and was hoping to meet you and talk about…uh… your Flying Guy."

"Ah. Our Flying Guy," Bernie said, his suspicions confirmed. "The FBI is interested in the Flying Guy." It was a statement, not a question.

"Well, yes, I guess so," Agent Johnston tried to think of a way to downplay it. "I've read about the sightings and am naturally curious of what it could be. I'm sure you'd agree that if this is real, then there are people who'd be interested in getting to the bottom of the matter. UFOs are taken seriously until proven otherwise."

Artie didn't realize it that the way he had said that, automatically sent up warning signals to Bernie.

Bernie was silent for a moment, so Artie continued. "I'm wondering if we could meet some time tomorrow, in your office perhaps?"

"Yeah. Uh. Yes, sir," Bernie said. "What time works for you?"

Artie almost said any time, but he thought that might undo the story he'd given of being in the area for other business and just wanting to chat. He'd wanted some time in town to look around anyway.

"I'll have time in the morning. Later morning. Say eleven o'clock?"

"Eleven sounds good," Bernie said. "I'll see you then, Agent Johnston."

"Thank you, Mr. Fredder," Artie responded.

"Bernie. Call me Bernie."

"Thank you. And please call me Artie." He hung up.

*

Bernie hung up the phone and leaned back in his chair. He fixed a blank stare at the wall in front of him. *The FBI is interested in the Flying Guy. Wonder why.* He thought it over. Actually, he considered, the reason should be obvious. Unidentified flying objects would be of interest to them. They wanted to know what or who was at the heart of the matter. The more he thought of it, he wondered why they hadn't come knocking before.

But our flyer isn't a threat to anyone, Bernie reasoned. A few childish pranks may have been attributed to him, but nothing else. The spray-painted barn had now been attributed to the no-good son. *Well, we'll see,* he thought.

"Marsha," he yelled out the door.

"Yeah. What do you need?" she said, walking in.

"I have an eleven o'clock appointment tomorrow with an FBI guy. Make sure I don't end up with anything to conflict with it."

"Sure," she said. "What do the Feds want?"

"Not sure," he lied. He didn't want word to get out that the FBI was interested in the Flying Guy. Word of that would get around fast. People might start thinking if the FBI was looking for him, then there must be some threat. It would be best to keep this under wraps. He pushed a button on his phone. He still needed to let Dan Powers, his boss, know what was going on.

*

Artie Johnston entered the office of the Aston Sentinel at a minute before eleven. He'd been in Aston since eight o'clock that morning, having spent some time driving around reconnoitering the area. Before he'd left Washington, he'd reviewed on his maps the various locations of the sightings, and wanted to visit some of those spots. He'd started at Spring Brook, getting out of his car to peer down in the stone-walled banks where two men had noticed tennis shoes on the flyer. He pictured it. He visited a couple other sights, including driving to the northeast side of town where the most recent incident occurred. He felt he had a good sense of the landscape. He jotted down some notes he thought important for his report back to his superiors.

"Can I help you?" the receptionist greeted him when he came into the lobby.

"Artie Johnston to see Bernard Fredder," he told her. "I have an eleven o'clock appointment."

"Hold on. I'll see if he's available." The receptionist didn't call Bernie, but instead walked down a short hallway to the side past a number of offices.

"Hey, Marsha," she said stopping by a desk. "Is Bernie in?"

"Yes!" a voice came from one of the offices. "I'm in."

"Hey, Bernie," the receptionist swung around the doorway, "I have an Artie Johnston here to see you."

"The FBI guy," Marsha whispered.

"Ooh. FBI," the receptionist said. "What'd you do now?"

Bernie rolled his eyes. "What haven't I done? Show him in. Thanks."

She saw that Artie had been watching them converse and motioned for him to come back. He nodded and walked back to where she showed him in to Bernie's office.

"Bernie," he said holding out a hand. "Artie Johnston."

"Agent Johnston. Come in," Bernie said, shaking his hand. He noticed the FBI man didn't carry a briefcase, or anything else for that matter. He wondered if he had a gun concealed under his coat.

"Please. Call me Artie. This isn't official business."

"Artie, have a chair." Bernie motioned him in and closed his office door. He noticed Marsha looking at Agent Johnston suspiciously. "You're not officially looking for the Flying Guy?" he asked, sitting.

"No, but I thought I'd check it out," Artie started. "Things like this can often seem trivial and harmless, I mean we're talking about a flying person here, but you never know. We're wondering whether this is legitimate or not. Pretty farfetched, isn't it?"

"That would be my take on it also," Bernie told him. He studied Artie as they talked. He seemed like a nice enough guy, but somehow he didn't believe this subject wasn't the main reason Agent Johnston was in town. The 'being in the area' story was feeling sort of hollow, as the conversation went on. The FBI was asking more pointed questions than would normally be asked if this were just done in passing.

They discussed many of the sightings over the years. Bernie was surprised at the amount of information Agent Johnston had. But then Artie explained that he gets the identical local law enforcement blotter reports as he did. Bernie determined there were many sightings Artie wasn't aware of and kept them to himself. Although they shared a few laughs over the Kite Fairy and the gnome incident, Bernie was getting the sense that the interest level ran much deeper.

"Do you think you'll ever find out who it is?" Artie asked.

Bernie wanted to know who the flyer was, but immediately felt the need not to tell Artie that. When he looked into Artie's eyes, he tried to read his true intentions. While they were friendly eyes, there was definitely something there he wasn't saying. Bernie wanted the meeting to get over soon. All of a sudden, he felt the immediate need to find the Flying Guy. To find him first. He was sure this casual meeting with the FBI Liaison, as he said he was, wasn't going to be the end.

The conversation drew to a close. Agent Johnston gave Bernie his card and asked that he call if there were more sighting, or if there was any other information on the flyer. Any information at all, he said.

"Will do," Bernie told him. He wanted to throw the card away.

"Thanks, Bernie," Artie said as they walked to the front door. "And you have a beautiful little town here. I came from a town like this."

After Artie left, Bernie mulled over the conversation. This is more than a casual interest. Artie had shown a surprising grasp on the flying guy saga. And how did he know this was a beautiful town, unless he had already checked it out? *Just in the area, my ass*, Bernie thought. When both Marsha and the front end girl had asked what the Federal Bureau of Investigation wanted, Bernie told them he couldn't say.

"It's double top secret," he winked. "If I told you, I'd have to kill you." He hoped they wouldn't connect Agent Johnston to their hometown celebrity.

*

Artie Johnston stayed in town for the rest of the day. He drove around the high school area, even stopping for a while to watch students leaving at the end of the school day. No one took off flying though, and he realized after a moment that unless the Flying Guy was spotted in a location or situation that could definitely tie him to something that would lead to a positive identification, the odds of finding out who he was, were relatively slim. He thought of C. Randall Whiting, and found he considered that a good thing, at least from that angle. This is indeed a nice little town and if this is home to the Kite Fairy, then maybe it should stay that way.

He completed a report to the Director when he returned to his office late the next day. He gave a detailed account of the trip to Aston, his findings while driving around, conversations he had with a couple of the locals, and finally the chat with Bernie Fredder. He ended with his assessment that the Flying Guy was indeed real, but as of now, did not appear to be a threat to the United States government or anything else.

Artie received a call from the Director just before leaving for the day. He thanked him for his concise report and told him to continue to keep tabs on it, and still report anything new. He, or Agent Whiting, would be in touch if they needed him.

Chapter 27

"So, are you a good witch, or a bad witch?" David mimicked the Witch of the North from the Wizard of Oz.

"Well, if you play your cards right," Amy purred in response, "I can be a bad witch. A very bad witch."

"Ooh," David said. "A naughty, bad witch?"

"A naughty, naughty, bad witch" she said.

"Okay, count me in! What time will you be here?"

"In about ten minutes," Amy told him. "I just have to say bye to Mom and Dad, and I'll be over."

"See you in a bit," David said. "Love you."

"Love you. Bye."

David set his phone on his dresser. He had his Spiderman costume laid out on his bed, as well as two pair of long underwear. This year Halloween was colder than normal, and he'd need the extra insulation under the thin fabric of the costume. He took off his pants and began putting them on.

David and Amy were going to the school costume party dance, and then to Julie Petrone's bonfire afterward. They were looking forward to the dance. There were prizes for best costume, which they didn't expect to win, but some of the other kids had plans for elaborate costumes, so they should enjoy it. As he slipped on the second pair of long underwear, his mother came to his bedroom door.

"Good idea, the long underwear" she told him. She leaned on the doorway, crossing her arms.

"Yeah, I think it'd be too cold with just the costume."

"When's Amy coming?" his mom asked.

"Couple minutes," he told her as he slid the costume pants over the underwear. They fit snug over the layers. "She's gonna get ready over here."

"Let me know if she needs any help," she said as she turned to leave. "I can't wait to see her costume."

"Me, too," David replied.

As his mom's footsteps faded down the stairs, the doorbell rang. *Wow, that was fast,* David thought, slipping the Spiderman top over the two long underwear t-shirts he wore. But then he heard the loud chorus of "trick or treat" a second later, as the continuing flow of kids came for their annual dose of candy. Two doorbells later, he heard his dad welcome Amy in and direct her upstairs.

"Well, hi there, Spidey," she said, carrying an armload of the witch costume into his bedroom. She set it on the bed and appraised his costume. "Don't you look all Halloweeny." She kissed him on the cheek.

"You're friendly neighborhood Spiderman," he grinned.

David helped Amy put on the witches robe over her jeans and sweatshirt, noticing that like him, she had dressed appropriately. The dance in the gym would be warm, probably too warm for what they wore, but the bonfire after would be chilly. With the robe in place, she put the long cape over it and planted the pointy hat on her head. She stood in front of his dresser mirror, shifting the hat to get the best angle. Satisfied, she turned to show David.

"Wow," David smiled at her. "You make an awfully good looking witch." He eyed her up and down. The long robe fit her slender body, flaring out at the bottom.

"Well, thank you" Amy said. "I've already got a spell on you, don't I?"

"Yes, indeed," he kept grinning.

"Hey," she asked him, "do you think I should put on this makeup or not?" She picked up the container with the pointy prosthetic nose, wart and all, and the small tube of the garish green face paint. The costume was disguised to resemble the bad witch from The Wizard of Oz.

"I think I like you the way you are" David told her.

"Well, let me touch up my non-witch make-up real quick." Amy primped in front of the mirror just as David's mom appeared in the doorway again.

"All set?" she asked the kids. "Need any help?"

Amy turned from the mirror, spinning around to display the costume.

"Well," Margaret said, her eyebrows arching. "Don't you look nice." She had always thought Amy was a beautiful girl, and all dolled up in the Halloween costume made her, oddly enough, even more beautiful. She thought David was a lucky guy to have her for a girlfriend. And such a nice girl too.

"Thanks!" Amy smiled. "I'm just about ready."

"We have to get some pictures before you go, so no sneaking off," Margaret told them as she headed back downstairs.

"Okay," David yelled back. "We'll be down in a couple minutes."

Margaret and Mark stood smiling, as they snapped pictures of the pair in their Halloween attire. David's face was covered by the mask, but they could still tell that he was grinning beneath it, hugging Amy to his side. She looked great in her witches outfit.

"Okay, so what's the agenda for the evening?" Mark asked, as they headed to the front door. He held it open for them.

"The dance until eleven o'clock, and then the bonfire after at Julie's," David told him. "We'll probably be home about one o'clock."

He opened the outside door for Amy.

"Have fun!" Margaret and Mark said in unison as they watched them leave.

"Don't you wish you were a kid again?" Mark asked her, as he put his arm around her and closed the door.

"Yeah. Sometimes I do."

They watched out the front window as David helped Amy into the car's passenger seat. He stowed her broomstick in the back seat of her Escort and in seconds they were gone.

*

Mark was dosing in his usual spot on the couch when the front door opened. Half asleep, he leaned his head up to check the time on the stereo clock. It said ten thirty.

"Margaret?" he called. "Is that you?"

"No," came her distant reply. "I'm up here in the office."

David and Amy came in, shutting the door behind them. They were wrapped up in a conversation that Mark could only get snippets of real information out of. Someone at the dance evidently said something to someone that they shouldn't have.

"You guys are home a little early," Mark said, slowly getting up to his feet. "Everything all right?"

"What's up?" Margaret said at almost the same time, as she came down to greet them.

"You want the long version or the short version?" David asked.

"Whatever," Margaret said, with some concern in her voice. She thought it a little unusual that they came home so soon.

"You want to explain it?" David looked at Amy.

Amy took off her witch's hat and set her broomstick up against the wall near the door. Mark and Margaret listened to the story of the two girls, one a friend of Amy's, the other obviously not, who nearly came to blows at the dance. David had broken up the fight, but the argument they were having, over another boy, had continued. A teacher had to step in to settle the pair down, but not until enough damage had been done so that half of the kids who had been invited to the bonfire, had been pretty much uninvited. The girl, who was obviously not Amy's friend, was Julie Petrone. Amy stood behind her friend, who now found herself without a boyfriend, as he had decided Julie Petrone was a better deal.

"Well, that's not good," Mark frowned. "What are you going to do now?" He motioned them Into the living room.

"Not sure," David said, as they all moved into the living room. Each found a spot to sit. "We might go down to Pauline's for pizza with Jimmy and Derek and some other guys." He checked the time.

"I'd like to go to Julie's and give her a piece of my mind," Amy stated. "I can't believe she'd do that. I knew she was a witch with a capital B, but this is pretty low even by her standards."

"Too bad you couldn't jump on your broomstick and go put a curse on her," David kidded her, lightening the mood a bit. He knew Amy was loyal to her friends. He gave her a one armed hug.

"Well," Mark said, "people like that usually get what they have coming."

Amy didn't seem to hear him, as her face brightened and she sat forward. In a second, she was grinning. She looked at Mark and Margaret, then turned to David.

"I couldn't jump on my broomstick and fly over there," she said and then paused, "but you could."

There was a moment of silence before Amy continued. "You could put on my costume and go buzz the bonfire." She was pointing and smiling at him. "They'd never know it was a guy in the costume."

Another moment of silence ensued.

"Oh, Amy," Margaret started. "He will absolutely not do that. We've worked so hard at keeping his secret a secret."

"Yeah, you're right Mrs. Anderson," Amy said apologetically. "I just would like Julie Petrone to get a little comeuppance."

David sat silently imagining the scenario. He could easily don her witches costume and fly to the bonfire. He grinned. It would be funny to see. To his surprise, his dad spoke those exact words.

"That would be funny to see," Mark said, leaning forward, looking at Margaret. "In that costume, in the dark, they'd never recognize him."

More silence, but they all looked at each other, the wheels in their minds churning their imaginations.

"We still have the rubber nose and the makeup upstairs," Amy added. More silence.

"No," Margaret said, but not as emphatic as before.

"That would be hilarious to see," Mark urged. "Even better if Mike Petrone was there to see it. He was always a bit on the uppity side anyway."

David was still silent, but the smile on his face showed that he was all in for this little charade.

"Let's do it," he said, standing abruptly. "Aha ha ha ha..." he cackled in his witch imitation. "I'll get you and your mangy dog too. Aha ha ha ha."

"That's good," Mark egged him on. He looked at Margaret. This would require her approval to go forward. He was all for it, but he wouldn't try to over-rule her if she was adamant. She had always been more unwavering over the subject of keeping David's flying a secret. But, he thought, she seems to have been softening lately.

"Oh, okay," she said, relenting. "I never cared much for Mike Petrone either. But you be careful."

"Yeah!" David exclaimed. He stepped over to where Amy's broomstick leaned in the corner. He tucked it between his legs and rose slightly from the floor, coasting around the edge of the room.

"If only I had some flying monkeys too" he said.

"Come on," Amy stood and moved toward the stairway. "Let's get you made up." She looked at Mrs. Anderson. "Want to help?"

"I guess," Margaret rose from the couch. "In for a penny, in for a pound."

"Hey, Dad," David said, landing back on the floor and setting the broom against the wall. "Do we still have those sparklers leftover from the Fourth of July?"

"Yeah, I think so. Why?" His dad looked at him quizzically.

David explained why, and as he went upstairs with Amy and his mom, his dad went out to the garage to get the package of sparkler boxes. He found them just where he thought they were and brought them inside the house. He spread a newspaper on the kitchen table, opened the boxes and began scraping the silver sparkler material off the wire posts with a paring knife. Soon, he had a small mound of it.

Upstairs, David sat on the edge of his bed as Amy dabbed the bright green costume makeup on his face. In minutes, he was the dark green color of the witch on the costume box. His mom looked at him from different angles, making sure his whole face was covered. Amy had done a good job.

"Try the nose," Amy said, pulling it from the package. It had self-adhesive glue on the edges and when she pressed it on, it stayed in place. The green rubber nose was long and hooked down.

"Oh, my gosh" Margaret said chuckling. "I wouldn't recognize you!" She pressed the nose attachment tighter to his face. "This won't come off when you fly will it?" She was still concerned.

"I'll test it in the backyard" David replied, standing. He took the robe Amy had removed and shrugged it carefully over his head. His mom put the cape over his back and tied it loosely around his neck. Amy handed him the wig and the hat.

They watched, silently smiling, as he fit the pointy hat over the wig on his head and faced the mirror. With the makeup, wig, and the nose, you couldn't tell if it was a guy or a girl. David turned and pointed a crooked finger at Amy.

"Who killed the Witch of the East? Was it you?"

"This is going to be so cool" Amy said excitedly. "I wish I could be there to see it."

"Why don't you go over there?" David said, as he thought for a second. "Petrone's backyard has a lot of trees around it. In fact, I think the next door neighbor has a bunch of bushes you could hide behind."

"Okay," Amy eagerly agreed. "I just gotta see this! They're going to shit their pants!" Her hand flew over her mouth and she turned to Margaret. "Oh, I'm sorry Mrs. Anderson. That just slipped out."

"That's okay," Margaret laughed. "I think you're right. I can't believe I'm saying this, but I want to go too."

"Make that three of us," David's dad said, appearing in the doorway to David's room. "I'm not missing this."

"Well, then," David said, checking his watch and seeing it was after eleven. The bonfire was probably underway already, as everyone had left the fracas at the gym at the same time as David and Amy.

They all filed down the stairs, David having to lift the robe so as not to trip on it. At the bottom, he collected the broomstick and again put it between his legs, cruising around the living room. They were thinking the same thing: David definitely was passable as a stereotypical witch and he was going to put a fright in those kids. He settled down in front of them.

"I got the sparker stuff ready," his dad told him. "What do we do with it?"

David thought for a moment and then they all followed him to the kitchen. He pulled two pieces of paper towel from a roll and laid them flat, one on the other. He scooped up the pile of silver sparkler dust and put it in the center of the paper towels, folding up the edges. He dug in the junk drawer and found a long twist tie, and wound it around the paper towel so it formed a ball.

"What's that for?" his mom asked.

"You'll see," David said. "If it works, they'll really freak."

They carefully laid out the plan and the timing. David could fly there in a minute or so, but for the others, it was a twenty to thirty minute walk. It was suggested that they drive and park near the library, then walk the three or four blocks to the Petrones. Amy was evidently more schooled in this sort of mischief as she suggested they bring along a dog leash, in case someone asked them what they were doing lurking in someone's yard. Searching for a lost dog was a logical explanation. They synchronized their timing and set off, stopping only to watch David do a test flight around the backyard.

David took his time flying to Petrone's, since he had more time than the others. He took the usual route from his backyard. Since it was late autumn and the trees had lost their leaves, he had to pay closer attention in some spots that used to afford him more cover. It was cool in the air and he felt the long robes flapping in the light wind. He was glad he still wore the two pair of long undies under the jeans he had thrown on.

In minutes, he was hovering above the grove of trees that he expected Amy and his parents to arrive in shortly. From his aerial vantage point, he could see the glow coming from what had to be a sizable fire in the Petrone's fire pit. He heard voices and laughter, although he couldn't make out any conversations. It didn't matter. That would come to a halt shortly. He took the time to make sure the witches hat was secure, and then pulled the paper-towel pouch from his shirt pocket. Seconds later he saw the shadows of what had to be his partners in crime, sneaking into the bushes. David flew around the back of them to make sure it was indeed them, then whispered from above that he was here and ready.

Amy signaled back and they watched David bank back away, before he slipped up and over the trees, into the darkness.

David had devised a plan as he had waited in the chilly air. The Petrone's backyard was long and deep, bordered by a fence lined with shrubs and trees. The fire pit was near the far end away from the huge brick home. There was a back light on near the patio, but it offered little illumination anywhere but near the back door. He decided he'd come from the house side, and fly back toward the party in the rear. He stopped for a couple seconds to make sure the cape and robe would flow behind him. The front of the hat tipped down. There wasn't that much of a breeze, but he didn't want it flipping off the back of his head as he flew.

In the bushes, Mark, Margaret, and Amy crouched down, silently waiting. They weren't sure where David would come in from, but they also thought he would come from the area close to the back of the house. They were eager with anticipation. They listened and watched closely for a sign of anyone seeing them, but were confident that they were safely hidden.

The kids at the bonfire were rowdy and boisterous. Most still wore the costumes from the dance. It was fairly obvious there was alcohol present. While it was a cold night, the fire and the active conversation kept the temperature at bay, and some weren't wearing coats. Most stood around the crackling fire for the heat.

Amy saw him first. "There," she whispered, pointing at a moving shadow.

Mark and Margaret saw him then, too. David came down from the dark sky near the trees on one side of the house. He flew about five feet off the ground, down the center of the yard, straight at the bonfire. He was going slow, wanting them to see him.

"What's that?!?" someone said, but no one else was paying attention to the approaching vision. Most were lost in their unsupervised alcohol consumption.

"Hey," someone else yelled seconds later. "What is that?" This voice was louder than the first. A few conversations stopped. Heads turned to see what they were talking about. From the air came what would later be described as a hideous cackle.

"Ahahahaha..." came the voice.

Everyone else fell silent, looking around. Fingers pointed to the air. All heads turned toward the sound and all eyes went wide in disbelief. Coming straight at them, flying on a broomstick, was what looked obviously like a witch. They stood stunned, not moving, as they watched it pass, dipping down over the fire. The figure dropped something into the flames and suddenly the bonfire flared even brighter, a white hot flame, and sparks began to shoot off in all directions. The shape of the witch slid over their heads, like an oily serpent against the black sky. The shocked teens didn't need any more prompting and every one of them took off running toward the house. They screamed as they ran.

In the shadows behind the edge of the yard, Amy clamped a hand to her mouth to stifle a laugh. Mark and Margaret also struggled to hold off from laughing. They watched the screaming teenagers head for the safety of the back door.

Near the back of the yard, David banked and then zoomed down at the rear of the scattering group. He spotted Julie Petrone, and in front of her, the new boyfriend leading the way.

"Cody," she called after him, wanting him to protect her. But bravery was obviously not one of his strong suits, and he put his star athlete speed to good use as he approached the back door. He wasn't thinking of Julie at all. In seconds, he was the first in the house.

David decided to give the party host a little extra attention. He sped up to her and kept pace just above her. He pointed a finger at her terrified eyes.

"I'll get you," the witch warned, "and your pussy boyfriend too."

Then David flew up and back over the trees to the spot from where he started. He hovered there watching the frightened throng frantically pushing each other out of the way in their efforts to get out of the open yard. He fought hard to keep from laughing.

The trio in the bushes saw the last of the kids claw their way in the door. They could barely make out David in the dark, but then saw him slowing as he slid up to a spot over the trees. Now he was just a shadow against the inky sky.

Short minutes later the back door opened, and slowly and tentatively, Julie's father, Mike Petrone emerged. He eased his way out, staying close to the house. His head swung back and forth, his eyes scanning the sky over his backyard. He didn't see anything and even from the distance of the length of the lot, the trio in the bushes could see the relief on his face. Surely the kids must have seen a bird. And who knew what drugs some of them may be on. He knew they were drinking.

David wasn't done having fun yet. The bonfire raid went so well he was feeling confident in what he was doing. He dove down and came to a quick stop barely ten feet away and a few feet above the now petrified father of Julie Petrone. He hovered in front of him.

"Well, well," came the witches voice. "What have we here? A hero to save the children?"

"Who...who...who are you" the wavering voice asked David. The fear was back.

"Well, I know who you are," the witch responded. "Baloney Petrone. You're a hotshot, aren't you?"

No response. He was backing up to his house. Mike Petrone was a big man and known to be a bit of a bully even as an adult, but he didn't look to David to be too tough right at the moment.

"Cat got your tongue, hotshot?"

David slowly came closer. The expression of fear grew and the blood drained from Mike Petrone's face. He stumbled backward.

"Want to go for a little ride?" David asked, inching closer.

Mike Petrone was in the door in a second, letting it slam behind him as he ran up the steps inside. The cackle of the witch faded in the air behind him.

David zipped around to the rear of the yard again and settled down to the ground near Amy and his parents. He stepped back into the shadows. They pulled back from their vantage point to join him.

"That was great," they almost said in unison. They could hardly contain their laughter.

"We should get out of here," Margaret urged. "David, we'll meet you at home." She turned to leave. Amy and Mark started to follow.

"Okay," David replied, kissing Amy on the cheek. He put the broomstick back between his legs and disappeared into the night sky.

Twenty minutes later they were sitting in the Anderson's kitchen sharing a laugh, as they regaled each other with the highlights of their evil charade. As David stood over the kitchen sink washing off the green face paint, he described how it looked like Mike Petrone was about to pee his pants.

*

Bernie hung up the phone and sat back. The giant springs of the ancient wooden editor's chair squeaked as it reclined. He always liked the sound. It gave him self-inflating gravitas.

"Baloney Petrone," Bernie said softly.

He put his hands behind his head, as he replayed the story he had just heard. The call came from his nephew, Justin Cavers. As Justin had explained, he had been to a bonfire the night before, Halloween night, at the Petrone's. There were a number of kids there, mostly high school classmates of Julie Petrone, Mike "Baloney" Petrone's daughter. While they partied around the fire, what Justin described as a witch, flew right through their gathering. The witch was on a broomstick, pointy hat and all. It flew over the bonfire with an explosion of sparks, and then chased the kids indoors. Old Baloney himself went out to check and he was also confronted by the Halloween spook, and then chased back indoors. Justin had finished the call by trying to make sure his name was kept out of it. A story like that, he said, was too weird to be believed. But, he swore he saw the witch.

Bernie thought it through. *A witch appearing on Halloween night, terrorizing a group of high school kids.* He laughed to himself. Then he thought maybe it was hoax. But, Justin wasn't that kind of kid, and he was obviously serious about what he said. *I suppose*, Bernie pondered, *a witch on*

Halloween was logical from a certain point of view, but why go after kids? As he tried to picture the scene in his own mind, the intuition settled over him. He saw someone flying around on a broomstick. *Flying.* We seem to have our own flying person in town, based on all the sightings over the years. Maybe they did have a witch amongst them. Bernie had always thought it was a man. The descriptions he always got, although he now realized he never asked pointedly for enough detail to determine the gender of the person, were always assumed to be male.

He contemplated that. *So, we either have a witch living in the area, the old fashioned, stereotypical witch on a broomstick, or maybe some drunken, drugged up story of one, or maybe someone who can fly and decided to pull a Halloween trick. It was a bunch of kids,* he thought. *The witch visited them for a reason.*

Since it occurred to him that the town flyer was always just assumed to be male, he figured maybe he should back-check with a few of the previous witnesses. His journalistic senses were stirred.

Bernie opened the lower right file drawer of his equally ancient oak desk, and found the folder he wanted. He pulled the file out and plopped it in front of him. It overflowed with paper, but Bernie knew exactly what was in it. He flipped through groups of paper held together with paperclips, until he came to the one he wanted. This inch thick sheaf was held together with large clasp. It contained all of the notes, blotters, and copies of the articles he had written over the years about the flying man. Or woman. *Or witch,* he thought now, as he pulled the clasp off.

He flipped through the papers. They were in chronological order and he was looking for something from five or six years ago, the sighting by the two guys down by Shit Creek. They had seen it as up close as anyone had. He scanned the papers quickly, looking for the notes he had taken from the two witnesses. He found it, and the name he was looking for: Butch Thomas. Bernie remembered the story and he knew Butch well enough to know he was still around town. Maybe he'd remember.

Bernie pulled out his phonebook and got Butch's number. He dialed and sat waiting while it rang. A female voice told him Butch was at work, but he could be called there and she offered up the number. Bernie thanked her and dialed the new number.

"Butch!" Bernie greeted the answer enthusiastically. "Bernie Fredder from the Sentinel. How are you?"

"I'm good," Butch responded. "What can I do for you?"

"Remember the flying guy down Shit Creek?"

"Yeah. Actually I was thinking of that this morning," Butch replied. "I heard a story about a witch flying around. Is that why you're calling?"

"Yeah," Bernie said, feeling better about Justin's story. "Where'd you hear about it?"

"My sister's kid was there," Butch told Bernie. Then he re-told the story as his sister had told it to him. It matched the one Bernie had gotten from his own nephew. There wasn't any new information. It saved Bernie from having to verify Justin's story, as he normally did. He never liked to take just one person's word for something. Especially something as bizarre this.

"Well," Bernie said after listening, "that brings me to why I called."

"Did I see a witch?" Butch asked the question for him.

"That is indeed the question," Bernie said. "Was your flyer on a broomstick?" He flipped a paperclip around as he waited for the answer.

There was a moment of silence as Butch thought about it again. He had dredged up the old memory earlier in the day, when his sister had called to tell him what her son claimed to have seen. In his still clear memory of that night, the apparition had not been on a broomstick, and against the night sky did not at all resemble what he thought as the stereotypical witch profile. The person he saw flew flat, horizontal, the way Superman was portrayed as flying. He told this to Bernie.

"Well, let me ask you this," Bernie inquired. "Could you tell if it was a male or a female? I mean, I always assumed it was male, and didn't see where I noted you saying either way."

Butch pictured the scene in his mind again. It had been pretty dark. All he really saw was the silhouette against the dark sky above.

"I couldn't really tell," he said finally. "It didn't have any obvious boobs. I suppose it could have been a female, but I always thought it was a guy too."

Bernie had gotten the answer he had been looking for, although it didn't offer any new clues on the new chapter in the flyer saga. He asked Butch to call him if anything else came to him, and he hung up.

He reclined with another squeak of the springs. Bernie stared at the stack of papers with all of the sightings. He remembered most of them without having to read through anything. None of the other witnesses would likely be able to venture an accurate opinion of the gender of the flyer.

Bernie leaned forward. He moved the paper work idly around, thinking. *How could this be related? A witch buzzing a bunch of kids. This sounded more like a teenage prank.* The thought struck him in an instant.

He dropped the paperclip he had now been biting on and he again dialed Butch's number.

"Butch," he said. "Sorry to bother you again. One question I forgot to ask."

"Shoot."

"How old do you think your flyer was?" Bernie asked him, then after a short pause, "I mean you probably can't tell that, but was the flyer adult sized, teenager sized, or could it have been a little kid?" He hoped this information would be remembered.

"Well, as I think of it," Butch said slowly, "It wasn't real big. I guess small, by adult sizes. Yeah. Small. Coulda been a kid."

Bernie thanked him again and ended the call. He sat again, flipping the paperclip in his fingers.

"Marsha," he called at the door.

Seconds later Marsha swung her head around the doorframe. "What's up?" She was cheerful.

"Can you rustle me up a copy of last year's high school yearbook?"

"Sure," she replied. "We have those around. What do you need that for?"

He told her what had happened the night before. He left out his own feelings on the tie to the prior sightings of the flying person. She laughed at the thought of a Halloween witch.

"Do you think you'll find a picture of the witch in the yearbook?" she asked, and then felt sort of stupid for asking what she thought was a stupid question.

"If only it would be that easy," Bernie replied.

Bernie stacked the papers together again, as Marsha disappeared to look for the yearbook. Satisfied the file was back in the chronological order it had been in, he set it at the side of his desk. Then he rose from the desk to get his local city map he had long ago plotted the sightings on. It was now on the floor, half shoved behind one of his file cabinets. He had to move other cardboard placards out of the way, but finally pulled out the map and brought it to his desk. He stood over it, noting the spots indicating where there had been sightings. As he reviewed them he recalled as best he could the story that went with each. Finally he reached for a felt-tip marker from the coffee cup he used as a penholder, and he located Petrone's neighborhood. He knew where they lived and he put a small dot on the spot on the map.

He studied the markings on the map. The new one was not in the same area as the largest grouping of the others were. It was on the opposite side of town, although near other sightings. Bernie smiled. "Well, well, well," he said to himself.

Marsha walked in then, holding out the yearbook. "Here you go," she said cheerfully and handed it to him. "Good luck finding your witch."

"Thanks, Marsha," he said to her, as he continued to study the map.

"Hey," he kidded her, putting his finger to the map. "Where do you live?"

"Oh, thanks," Marsha feigned indignation, but returned Bernie's smile before she turned and left.

Bernie noticed his finger was on the park where there was a pin marking the location. He thought of it momentarily. *The Kite Fairy*. He smiled broader. *Or a witch. Maybe it wasn't human.* Nah. He shook his head.

He sat again with the yearbook open on his lap, thumbing through until he got to the photos of the juniors. The seniors from last year are obviously gone, and most of the kids at the Petrone's party were from the next graduating class.

Not sure what exactly what he'd expect to gain from looking at the class photos, he began slowly going through the rows of pictures and the names for each. He paused at the few names he recognized as having been at the party, and he made note to get a full and accurate list of the attendee's names. He studied Julie Petrone's picture, noting the resemblance to her father. They had the same smug look.

Nothing jumped out at him when he finished the first run through, and he didn't expect anything from the second scanning either.

Bernie closed the yearbook and again called to Marsha.

"Did you find the witch?" she grinned at him, as she again leaned around the doorway.

"Yeah," he said. "Do you have a twin sister in high school?"

"Ha, ha," she shot back.

"Hey," Bernie said holding up the yearbook, "can you either get me a list of the juniors, well now seniors, from the school, or take the book and type all the names into one list for me?"

"The school will need a reason," she told him. "They don't like giving that out."

"You're right. Can you type the list?"

"Sure." She took the book and left.

Bernie sat at the desk studying the map some more, the paperclip flipping in his fingers again. He studied the dots.

"Hmmph," he muttered. "I need to connect those dots."

He put the map up against the wall, sat again and took a long swallow of his now cold coffee. He went to the file on his computer where he stored the ODD & ENDS articles, pulled up a blank page and wrote a few paragraphs about the witch sighting. It would at least be a nice Halloween story for the folks in town. He gave Baloney Petrone a break and kept his name out of it.

"Halloween has always been one of my favorite holidays. Just like Christmas and Easter, but unlike the other mundane Mondays off, it has a slight sense of the supernatural to it. You get to dress up in a costume and pretend to be someone you're not. As a little kid, I liked getting treats and playing a few tricks. I waxed many a window as a lad. Other tricks, I can't tell you about.

A party of teenagers had a pretty nifty trick pulled on them on All Hallows Eve this year. While warming themselves around a bonfire, they were visited by a Halloween witch. Pointy hat, pointy nose, green skin, and flying on a broomstick. That's right. This witch flew on a broomstick. It buzzed their little gathering and sent sparks flying from the fire. Of course they were terrified, but thankfully, no one was hurt. An adult in the home came out to check on the witch, and sure enough, he was confronted also. We've had many reports of a flying person in Aston, but no one had ever described it as a witch on a broomstick before. Is our flying guy maybe a witch? This adds a new twist to our continuing saga. And sort of a spooky one at that!"

*

Mark was in the living room watching the evening news on TV. He'd made a small pot of chili for supper and it was warming on the stove. He was waiting for Margaret to get home before eating. David was already home from school, and was upstairs in his bedroom doing his homework.

He heard the back door open and glanced at the time. Margaret came and went like clockwork, and was right on time for supper. He clicked the remote to turn off the TV and joined her in the kitchen.

"Hi, Hon," Mark said, kissing her cheek. "How was your day?"

"Good," she replied. "But boy, was there a lot of talk about the witch. It was in the paper this afternoon."

"I know. I saw it," Mark said. "That was funny. We'll have to cut that out and save it."

"Yeah, but people are talking like they want someone to figure it out. Find out what it is." She stood looking at Mark. "A flying person seemed funny, but evidently some people are actually afraid of witches."

Mark didn't say anything. He hadn't heard anyone talking about it where he worked. As in the past, the chatter he heard was more along the lines of amused interest in their own local hero. The Flying Guy, as the public referred to David, hadn't done anything bad, so no one really wanted to get rid of it. Stunts like the kite and the flag had made people seem to want more. People actually believed in witches? *But why not,* he thought. *There is such a thing as a flying person.*

"We really need to be more careful now, I guess," Margaret said.

"Yeah. We should let David know," Mark said.

"Let me know what?" David asked, as he joined them for supper in the kitchen. The smell of chili had brought him down. He pulled a bowl from the cupboard for each of them.

"Your mom said she heard people talking that they want someone to find out what the Flying Guy is all about. If it's real. After the witch appearance, people have evidently gotten scared of the unknown."

"They want someone to catch the flyer," his mom said.

"Oh," was all David could say.

They sat at the table and ate supper. The conversation continued on what they, David in particular, should do. As with the numerous past discussions, it was agreed that David would lay low on the flying for a while, until this stopped being a topic of discussion around town. As in the past, the depth of his parent's concern seemed to wane a bit more as time passed without being discovered. The older David had gotten, the lesser the prospect of horrible medical experiments on a little boy had become. Years of worry now turned old hat. Before they finished eating, they had moved on to other subjects, and the witch-hunt was soon forgotten.

Chapter 28

Bernie sat flipping the small card around in his fingers. It was the business card that Agent Arthur Johnston of the FBI had given him. The card was very official looking. It had the FBI emblem under the words 'Federal Bureau of Investigation', with the agent's contact information just below that.

He had just met Agent Johnston, Artie he'd said to call him, a couple weeks back. The FBI was interested in the Flying Guy, and while Artie had been a nice enough guy, there was something unnerving about his intentions. He hadn't said what the FBI wanted with the flying guy, beyond normal national security concerns of monitoring UFOs or anything that could be a threat to the country, but Bernie had an active imagination and it was working now.

He stared at the card. He wasn't sure if he wanted to call. He pictured a swarm of G-men coming to Aston to try to catch the Flying Guy. Or witch, or whatever it turned out to be. They'd take him or her away in a cage. Well, no cage, he thought. Handcuffs and chains would likely do the trick. Unless it was a witch, he smiled. Then maybe they'd have a fight on their hands. But no matter what, Bernie considered, *I'd like to find the Flying Guy first. Maybe just to warn him.* Agent Artie had asked that Bernie not mention the FBI's interest to anyone, so he couldn't just put something in the paper about the flyer needing to be careful because the Feds were looking for him.

Bernie felt the urge to throw the card in the trash can. That wouldn't be wise though, he thought. Agent Artie said he gets the police and sheriff's blotters, as well as newspapers, and so is privy to pretty much the same information as he is. The only exception is the calls directly to him, at the Sentinel. Bernie had already decided those would remain known to him only. No need to feed more information to the FBI.

He stared at the card, flicking it with a finger. Then his finger punched the phone number of Agent Arthur Johnston into his phone. He waited as it rang.

"Good morning," a curt female voice said. "How may I direct your call?"

"Uh, yes, is this the FBI?" Bernie asked. She hadn't identified herself or the business she was in when she answered.

"Yes, it is," she said. "How can I help you?" Her voice was all business.

"Agent Arthur Johnston, please," Bernie said, reading the name on the card as he told her.

"Who's calling, please?" the cold voice asked.

"Bernie Fredder with the Aston Sentinel in Aston, Wisconsin."

"Hold please." Only a short pause followed the click of the transfer before it was picked up.

"Agent Johnston," a male voice announced. "Is this Bernie Fredder?"

"Yes, it is," Bernie answered him. "Is this Agent Johnston?" It didn't sound like him.

"Yes, it is. Call me Artie though," he said.

"Well, Artie," Bernie began, "we've had another sighting. I figure you'd hear about it through the police reports, but you'd wanted me to call if I heard anything."

"Yes. Thank you for calling, Bernie. I didn't think it would be so soon," Artie said. "What have you got?"

Bernie went through everything he'd heard and seen on the Halloween witch. He opted to include calls directly to him, as they didn't give away any other clues to what may really be going on. He decided to keep Mike Petrone's name confidential though. Baloney Petrone was the kind of guy who would try to convince the FBI to come to investigate. He'd pester them until they found the flyer. No, he didn't want one of Agent Artie's business cards in the hands of old Baloney.

"That's interesting," Artie said after Bernie told him the story. "A witch. Ha! That's funny."

"It is," Bernie agreed, and he almost felt his guard going down when Agent Johnston saw the humor it in it too. But, he was still wary and wanted to get the phone call over with. Artie didn't need to know about his own investigation. He didn't want to risk saying something he'd rather keep to himself. He'd done his civic duty by calling as he'd promised to do.

"Thanks, Bernie," Artie said as the call ended. "I appreciate your calling. Let me know if anything else comes up."

"Will do," he responded. "Thanks."

Bernie threw the card in his top desk drawer and hoped he wouldn't use it again.

*

Artie watched for the police and sheriff's department blotter reports to come in from Aston for the previous night of October Thirty First. There were several calls on it to the police department, but none to the sheriff's. The witch sighting had been within the city limits of Aston, so the calls would have been put through to them, not the county law enforcement folks. Some of the calls were from kids who'd been at the bonfire party that the witch had appeared at, but some came from parents who had called on their child's behalf. That, Artie considered, was probably because the kids didn't want police involvement in their lives, especially being at a high school party.

He thought it all through. *A witch.* The Director was going to wonder if Artie was playing games with him now. And C. Randall Whiting. What will he think? He'll probably salivate at the prospect of getting his hands on a witch. He'd want the recipes to the magic potions. Artie had no alternative but to write up a report for the two of them, so he set other things aside to get it out of the way.

When he finished summarizing his written report, he called for an appointment with the Director. The Director wasn't in and would be unavailable for a few days. His assistant, Carol, asked how important the matter was, and if she should set up a meeting with Agent Whiting in the meantime. Artie told her he'd send up copies of his report for the Director and Agent Whiting, and if Whiting wanted to meet on it before getting the Director in on it, he should just let Artie know.

Later in the day, Artie walked back to his office after a short meeting a couple floors down. He almost jumped out of his skin when he found C. Randall Whiting sitting in his office waiting for him.

"Jesus, you scared me," Artie said, after his obvious reaction. He offered a handshake. "I hope you haven't been waiting long." He didn't really care.

"I'm sorry I startled you," Agent Whiting said, standing to greet him. "I just preferred not to be seen waiting out in the hallway."

That was logical, Artie thought.

"So, you read my report about the witch?" Artie asked.

"Yes. I spoke with Director Gorman also," Agent Whiting told him. "He asked that I talk to you, in case there was anything little that may have been overlooked. And I had a few questions."

Artie and Agent Whiting spent over a half hour re-hashing some of the previous sightings, with emphasis on whether the flying person had exhibited any other strange powers. Witch-like powers, Agent Whiting had said. Artie chuckled and asked what witch-like actually meant. To his surprise Agent Whiting laughed also, something Artie thought him incapable of doing. Like in the movies, he said.

The general consensus, after they discussed it, was that this was one of three possible scenarios. First, it was the Flying Guy, dressed as a witch. Second, maybe previous sightings were of a witch, dressed without the stereotypical trappings of a witch. And third, maybe they had two different flying people, or things.

"A son of a witch," Whiting said. A grin then followed.

Artie chuckled again. *He has a sense of humor*, he thought. *I still wouldn't want to be strapped to a chair, with him in charge of the interrogation.* He thought their parting handshake was clammy again, but then he thought he was probably just imagining it.

*

A day later, C. Randall Whiting was at the official FBI building in downtown Washington D.C. He found his way to the office of Ed Gorman. He was expecting him.

"So, what have we got, Randy?" the Director asked when they were seated.

Agent Whiting filled him in on what Agent Johnston had given him. Anticipating the Director may think his time was being wasted, he'd brought copies of the blotter reports, as well as the newspaper from Aston where the witch sighting was noted. The Director read them all as they talked it over. He didn't think his time was being wasted. He didn't even chuckle over the absurdity of it.

"We need to figure out to a way to catch him. It. Whatever," the Director said.

"Or her," Agent Whiting added. His eyes seemed to glisten.

"Come up with something," the Director told him. "Make sure we have only Agent Johnston involved for now. I'd also recommend you get one internal information analyst assigned to this. There's a guy down in Records who I've used before, and he keeps internal requests confidential. He already thinks he's a spy when he reports only to me on something."

"Yes, sir," Agent Whiting said.

Ed Gorman gave him the analyst's name, and they set a goal of having a more solid idea of what they could do by early the coming spring. C. Randall Whiting already thought of what he could use a flying person for, and wanted this to come to some sort of fruition sooner than that. But, this would take time. They weren't dealing with normal things here.

Chapter 29

Later that same year, David again got the urge to head out to enjoy the wonders of nature. The fall ride had opened his eyes to the beauty that he was virtually the only person to be able to see from that aerial vantage point. That heightened the appreciation. His routine forays now always included occasional breaks just to enjoy the scenery. He found himself stopping often, just to sit and look around. He began to notice things he'd never noticed before, like colors, the symmetry of the parcels of land, and railroad tracks and power-lines that now served as directional routes to faraway places, replacing the roads others had to use.

When the first snow came in early December, he stood by the front window looking out at the sparkling landscape. David had immediately wanted to go flying. It didn't help that his mom, the great appreciator of all things nature related, had commented on how beautiful it was outside. The first blanket of snow had gleamed in the front window on the two of them that early morning.

"Sure looks pretty when it's fresh snow and there aren't a lot of tracks in it yet," she said, standing next to David looking out.

"Yeah," was all he could say. His mind was elsewhere. He was working on a flight plan for the afternoon.

"So smooth, so fresh," his mom said. She almost seemed to be urging him on.

David dressed and went out to shovel. It was cold, probably only about twenty degrees, he estimated, when he started on the front sidewalk. But, within about ten minutes, he had started to work up a sweat. He formed neat snowbanks along the walk, just like his mother liked. She had often commented on how nice it looked when there was a long, straight, even snowbank holding back the rest of the new fallen snow. David had learned to make the job look aesthetically pleasing for her.

He finished that and went to work on the driveway. He had a method for that too. He shoveled a path down the middle, parting the driveway. He'd done this many times before, and although the simple beauty of it usually kept his mind occupied, today he was thinking of the flight he planned to take.

It was cold enough to where that was the first consideration he took into account. He'd flown in the cold before, and knew that whatever the temperature was on the ground, it felt a lot colder in the air. Add to that the wind chill from whatever speed he went, and it could get downright frigid. Today would be one of those days. He went through a mental checklist of the clothing he would need. Being bright white everywhere and with an almost equally bright baby-blue sky, the usual black attire was going to be easily visible. He thought it through as he worked and found he had no other choice but to wear black. His snow-pants, which would be a necessity, were black. A couple pair of long underwear and jeans under that would be enough, he thought. But, they were black snow-pants, and he had no other options. He figured a couple sweatshirts under his regular winter parka coat would do on top. His black ski mask wouldn't be sufficient for his head, so he'd need a stocking cap to go over that. All the clothing was black or dark colored. He'd have to be careful.

David finished the driveway and took a few moments to cool down before going in. He was moist under all his clothes, and would break out in a full sweat if he went in right away. He leaned on his shovel with his coat unzipped, proudly surveying the job he had done. The sidewalk and driveway were now neat corridors through the snow. Mom will be happy. Down the street he could see snowblowers roaring, as they shot long sprays of white. He thought of doing the Meyer's drive for them, but knew Emery enjoyed shoveling and would be out soon enough. He had always said snowblowers were for women and old people. He didn't consider himself old yet.

After staring at the sky with a grin for a couple minutes, he figured he had cooled down enough. A slight chill had come over him, as the cold air worked its way into his sweaty shirt. He went inside.

"What's your plans for the day?" his father asked him when he shucked off his coat and scarf.

"I'm going flying," David told him. He kicked his boots from his feet, setting them on the rug near the back door to dry.

"Ooohh. That's going to be cold," his dad said.

David smiled at him. He could see that little look of envy in his eyes. He knew the cold wouldn't get a second thought if it was him being able to fly.

"Yeah," David replied, "but I can dress warm enough. Only problem is that all my winter stuff is dark colored." He looked out the kitchen window. "I'm gonna have to be careful."

"You better," his mom said, joining the two of them in the kitchen. "Do you have to go?"

David was silent, as they all stood staring out the window, squinting their eyes from the glistening backyard.

He nodded slowly. "I want to see what it looks like." He looked at his parents, as if it should be obvious to them. He saw the look in his dad's eyes, that it seemed like the logical thing to do. Even his mom now looked envious.

"Where are you going go?" his dad asked.

"I was thinking of going to Woods Flowage, but I don't think the roads will be plowed out to there," David answered. "I think I might try Edison Park. I don't think there'll be anyone there on a day like today."

"But, you can't just leave the car," his mom said. "There won't be any footprints in the snow. It'll look suspicious with car tracks, an empty car, and no tracks coming from the car."

"I thought of that. I was thinking of walking over," David told her. "That'll warm me up before I go. Then there's tracks in, and then out when I get back. As long as in between no one checks where the tracks went when I go. Or, I can just mess with people's minds." He smiled.

His dad smiled too.

His parents told him to be careful, and he went up to his room to get ready. He pulled on the many layers of clothes and went back down to put on the rest of his gear. When he walked out the back door, he was already wearing his ski mask and had to catch himself about to dive skyward, since that was the usual thing to do just after donning the mask. Instead, he walked to the front and headed in the direction of the park.

Not all the sidewalks had been cleared of snow yet, and he found himself trudging through the eight inch blanket of white. The air was dry and the snow swirled up from his footsteps. The initial twinge of cold he'd felt when he returned to the outdoors subsided and was replaced with the heat from the exertion required to walk. It took him over fifteen minutes to reach the park, and he was breathing heavily when he got there.

The park was quiet. The snowstorm had cloaked the park in white and since it was early yet, it had not been plowed. There were no tire tracks. David kept glancing around as he headed for the trees in the area he usually used for his comings and goings. No one else had walked in either, so the path he made through the snow was the only evidence of activity. He hoped no one else would come the way he did until after he returned, as they would see tracks leading up to the trees that then came to an abrupt and mysterious end. He grinned when he remembered the prank on the Millers.

The trees were now bare of their leaves, so he was missing the comfort of the cover they normally would provide. He felt little concern though, as the park was large and there were no houses around. He'd still be able to ascend unseen. He looked around one last time and then quickly shot up to a height of about five feet over the tree branches. Through the branches, he was a dark shape against in the sky to someone below.

He had to squint his eyes. The goggles he'd worn were clear. The sun shone glaringly on the white surface below and David wished he'd brought some sunglasses. He checked his pockets, hoping maybe to find a pair. His pockets were empty.

He took off to the east. He followed the straight line of the snow covered trees along Artic Street toward, the edge of town. He'd only taken this route a small handful of times before. There always a little risk of being seen up until he reached the beginning of the flat potato fields there. Then, he was right out in the open. On a normal summer day, this would be far riskier.

He stopped at that point. He stayed back, just inside the trees. He knew it didn't add much cover. He hoped he was just a large black spot in the spindly gray branches of the trees. There were no cars on any of the roads that he could see, and the few farm houses and other homes, all were silent. Smoke curled from their chimneys. A pair of horses stood in a small fenced enclosure near a large red barn. They wore blankets. Even from his distance, David could see their breath in the still air.

He set his sights on the hills to the northeast and sped off. There wasn't much of a wind, but his barreling across the field at this speed was cold. Even with all his layers of clothing, he felt it seeping into his bones. *I'm going to have to keep this short,* he thought.

He dropped down to a level five feet over the crystalline surface. Even with his goggles, the cold air stung his eyes and they started to water. He nearly clipped a fencepost because of the blurred vision, and he decided he'd need to go higher to avoid hitting something else. He was familiar with barbed-wire fences bordering fields.

He came to the woods and the end of the field. He was right out in the open, but decided to stop anyway. There was very little movement anywhere. He could see cars in the distance, but all of the homes visible here were quiet also. No one was out.

David rose slowly to a point over two hundred yards above the ground. He looked toward town, to the west. It was a stunningly beautiful scene. The long expanse of smooth snow revealed only the occasional colored side of a house. Smoke rose from most chimneys. The water tower stood out only slightly in the distance, as its white blended in to the surroundings.

He felt the chill settle in further. It went far enough in to spur him on. He decided again, he'd be making a quick trip out of this. He turned and sped off to the north. The gray leafless treetops whizzed by beneath him. He saw a long break in the trees and went down. It wasn't wide enough to be a road and when he dipped below the tree line, he saw signs indicating it was a snowmobile trail. No tracks could be seen, so he dropped even lower and slowed, as he wound down the path through the woods. He held his arms out to his side, as he coasted through the snow covered branches and bushes. The beauty amazed him.

As he'd grown and matured, David noticed his increased appreciation for the ability to see things in a way that was different from what others saw. Everyone else could only view things from the ground level. Not him. The beauty of his special vantage point always gave him a slight sense of awe. Other teen-aged boys may not be as in to nature as he was, and this was why.

He wished he could share this with his parents. And with Amy. He knew they'd love it.

After cruising around the forest and zipping over a number of large open fields, the cold began to dominate his consciousness. He checked his watch and discovered he'd been out for over an hour. It didn't feel like he'd been out that long. He turned and headed back to Aston. This time, he went up well over a thousand feet. He knew he'd be just a dark speck against the sky to someone on the ground. He sped along, his eyes stinging more as he went.

No one had ventured out to the park yet, and he landed in the exact same footprints in the snow from which he had departed. He walked home, welcoming the movement in his stiff and numb limbs. He walked briskly to warm up. It wasn't working, and he was still feeling it when he was indoors, sitting to take off his boots.

"How was it?" his father asked, coming to the back hall where he sat. He watched David shed his coat.

"It was great," David told him. "Colder than a witch's…" he stopped, almost saying the word he didn't think his father would find appropriate. "Petuna," he replaced it with.

"I imagine," his father smirked. He knew the right word. "Pretty though, I'd imagine, hey?"

David joined his father as they sat at the kitchen table. He described what he'd seen flying, as he sat rubbing life back into his stiff legs. His dad listened and tried to picture what David was describing. His mom overheard and she joined them. Now, even she had a look of envy in her eyes. She was gazing out the window as she listened.

*

When he finished regaling them with the details, they filled each other in on what their plans were for the rest of the day. His parents were going grocery shopping, since they figured few people would be out, and David decided to call Amy to see if she wanted to go to the library. He had homework that required a visit there and hoped she'd come along. She agreed, and they met an hour later.

Amy finished the little bit of homework she had to do, then found some magazines to read. David finished the term-paper for his history class and stuffed it back into his backpack. He'd type it on the computer at home.

They sat whispering, trying to figure out what they were going to do later on, before deciding they'd go to the school basketball game that night.

Since they had both walked to the library from different directions, they left together to go to Amy's grandmother's house, where she'd borrow the car to give him a ride home. Amy had shoveled the front sidewalk, but not the driveway, so they decided to finish that together. When they were done, they took a rest near the back of the garage. They were out of sight of the house and soon found themselves in each other's arms, kissing.

David wrapped his arms tightly around her, and with their lips still joined, picked her up off the ground. He rose a foot from where they stood. When she noticed he wasn't standing on the ground, she wrapped her legs around his waist and held tightly around his neck. David reached down below her and held her by her legs. They floated in that position, looking into each other's eyes.

"Is this hard to do?" she asked. "Carry me like this?"

"No, actually," David replied. "It's not hard at all."

He held her up, and it didn't feel any more difficult than if he were standing and holding her. He looked around to make sure no one was watching, then turned horizontal on his back. She was now lying across the top of his levitating body.

"Um. Well…" she purred. "This could get interesting." Amy put her lips to his again, and they kissed long and slow.

David enjoyed the kiss, but his mind was now imagining other things. When he brought himself back to reality, he started wondering if he could take her out for a flight. But, how could he hold on to her? They were clinging to each other now, and if he had a loose grip, she would probably otherwise fall.

"Mmm. That was fun." Amy snuggled into him when they were back on their feet. "We'll have to do more of that."

"Yeah. Yeah!" David repeated. He was thinking this could lead to a number of different things. "Hey, try this," he told her, turning his back to her. "Put your arms around my neck, like piggyback."

Amy reached her arms out and circled them around his neck from the back. She leaned against him and then jumped, wrapping her legs around his waist. Slowly his feet left the ground, and she felt him turning forward onto his stomach, horizontally. She lay across his back on her stomach.

"Hold on," David told her. He did another quick look around, not seeing anyone.

Amy's grandmother's yard was small. There were trees, bushes, and other garages that gave some privacy even, now with the leaves gone. But, it was big enough for a little jaunt around the outer edges.

David slowly glided around the perimeter of the yard. He stayed low, only a foot above the snow. Amy didn't feel heavy at all. He figured she felt about the same as if he were lying down while she lay on top of him. Her added weight didn't have a great effect on his anti-gravitational ability. He grinned widely, holding his arms out like a bird. His mind was racing.

"Oh! Oh, my gosh, Davey," she gushed. "This is so cool. Oh, my gosh!"

"Thank you for flying Davey Airlines," he intoned.

Slowly, he cruised to a stop back by the garage. He turned and they settled back on their feet."Oh, wow!" Amy said excitedly. "Can we do that again? Can you take me up in the sky?" Her arms went around his neck.

"I don't know," he replied. His mind was searching for a way to do it. "We'd have to maybe strap you on somehow. That's a long way to fall."

"Oh," she sounded disappointed and her smile faded.

"We'll figure something out," David told her. He saw her eyes brighten again.

Chapter 30

David and Amy took only a few short and very low flights together over the next couple months. They never came up with a way to safely and securely have her be attached to him. More than a couple times she almost fell off him. She was small compared to him, and otherwise able to stay on him when flying straight, but when they turned, she sometimes tipped sideways. Still, they both loved it that he could now share his ability to fly, even if only briefly.

It was a cold, early spring evening when a solution presented itself. David had just finished his homework and had joined his parents in the living room to watch TV. Both of them were reading, not paying attention to what was on, and surrendered the remote control to him. He surfed through the stations. He didn't see any movies he cared to watch and no regular network program held his interest. He kept clicking.

He eventually came to a program showing how elderly people were finding ways to stay active in their retirement. He was about to flip past it, when his face lit up and he was grinning as big as he figured he ever had in his whole life. An elderly man had taken up skydiving while being in his eighties. The program showed him leaping from an airplane, attached to his diving instructor by use of a harness. The program narrator went on to explain the use of the tandem parachute. David stared at the screen. There it was. There it was! *A tandem parachute harness!* It securely held one person hanging in front of the other, as they parachuted down to the ground. *No need for a parachute though,* David thought.

"I'm going up on the computer," David told his mom and dad abruptly, and ran upstairs.

"Okay," they said in unison, looking up from their books for a glance at each other.

David turned on his computer and signed onto the Internet. He searched on the words 'Tandem Parachute'. A number of sites came up. He went through most of them. He was looking particularly for pictures that were close up enough to where he could get an idea on how the straps worked, and to see if the parachute could be detached. It could. They could be interchanged, and thus removable. He went through dozens of photos. His excitement grew the more he read.

He started looking at websites that sold the tandem parachutes. There were also a number of those, and he quickly learned that to get one of them was going to be expensive. The prices ranged from a couple hundred dollars for a used one, on up to thousands of dollars for brand new ones. A used one was the only option. He went through his options then for those. All of the websites would require a credit card for use as payment. He didn't have his own. He'd need to use his parent's card and then pay them back. That would involve letting them know. He wasn't sure they'd be okay with him spending three hundred dollars for this. He had way more than that in savings, but they had instilled in him a sense of frugality when spending money. David thought it was worth it, but it would be a hard sell for his parents. Especially his mom.

He remembered that there was a skydiving club in Wausau. He passed it a couple times, when he used to drive to see Amy when she lived in Wisconsin Rapids. He didn't remember ever seeing anyone actually skydiving there, so didn't know if anyone used tandem chutes. He considered stopping there to see if anyone had one for sale.

David went on Craig's List and did a search. He thought the god of flying must be looking out for him today, when he found exactly what he was looking for. Someone in Wausau had a used tandem set-up for sale for only two hundred dollars. There was a phone number to call. David reached for his cell.

It turned out the guy selling the parachute was an instructor at the Wausau flight school at the airport right next to the skydiving club. He was a member of the club and David could meet him there most weekdays after five o'clock, or Saturday mornings until noon. They made arrangements for the next day.

*

After school that day, David went to his bank and withdrew three hundred dollars. The cost of the equipment was advertised at two hundred, but he didn't know if that covered all the incidentals, whatever they may be. He was a little nervous about this as it was, and he didn't want to have to make a return trip. He stuffed the wad of twenty dollar bills in his pocket.

He'd already arranged to use the car that day and was on his way to Wausau by four thirty. It was about a forty five minute drive and he found himself speeding to shorten that up. When he pulled into the parking lot, there were three men standing near an airplane, talking. They gave him the once over as he walked to the small office. It was just a small shack next to the runway on the far edge of the airport. The planes must taxi over here to load, he figured. The door slammed behind him when he went inside.

"Hello!?" David yelled when he didn't see anyone. No reply came. It didn't appear that there was anyone inside. He felt nervous again. He looked around and saw a rack up on a side wall from which hung various types of skydiving equipment. He didn't see anything that resembled what he had seen on the Internet or on TV. He didn't really have much knowledge of this sport or its equipment, other than what he had gained from his search, and he was sure he was going to sound stupid in their conversation. The guy is going to be suspicious.

The door slammed from behind him, startling him. He turned to see one of the guys from the conversation outside stepping inside.

"Howdy," the man said. "What can I do for you?"

"Howdy," David replied. "I'm looking for Pat Blaser."

"That'd be me," the man said offering a hand. "Are you Dave?"

"Yes," David shook his hand. "Came to look at the tandem parachute."

"Yup. Right over here," he said, signaling for David to follow him. He bent down and picked up a large black nylon tote bag. He unzipped it and pulled out the harness and parachute, setting them on a long, broad table.

David walked over and looked at it. He didn't know what questions to ask and was relieved when Pat went into a bit of a sales routine.

Pat explained what kind of chute it was, how old the equipment was, and did some snapping of the clasps attached to the belts and straps. David closely watched what he was doing. It looked pretty simple to him, so he only asked a few basic questions that came to him. He hoped he sounded like he knew something about this. How many jumps had been made with it? Were there ever any problems?

"None," Pat told him. "Works great. I just had the opportunity to get a new one pretty cheap and don't need this one anymore. Didn't have any takers here at the club."

David nodded.

"Where do you skydive?" Pat asked. "I've never seen you around here before."

It was one of the questions David had anticipated getting and he had a lie prepared just in case.

"It's not for me," he told Pat. "My brother skydives over by Green Bay, and he's always trying to get his wife to go. He had talked about maybe getting himself one of these."

"Ah, well, this is a good starter chute," Pat said. "Cheap. Works just fine."

"Great," David said. "I'll take it. If he has questions, he can call, right?" David thought that question added weight to his lie.

Pat packed the chute and harness back in the tote bag and zipped it up. He held it out to David. "He can call any time," he said.

"Two hundred, right?" David asked, fishing the wad of bills from his pocket.

"Yup, that'll do," Pat said taking the ten twenty dollar bills he offered. "Tell your brother to let me know if he ever needs anything else. I can fix him up with just about any equipment he might need."

"Will do," David smiled and offered his hand.

Pat took it and they said good-bye.

The whole way home David kept glancing over at the bag with the tandem parachute in the seat next to him. He was anxious to give it a try. The first thing he was going to do was to call Amy. He hadn't told her about his idea yet and he was going to surprise her. He wanted to set up a ride for the coming weekend.

David called her on his cell as soon as he pulled in the driveway. They made plans to meet on Saturday morning. He told her it would just be a short ride out in the woods they liked to go through, leaving her with the impression it would be like before, where she would more or less just lay across his back.

After he stuffed his phone back in his pocket, he did a quick double check of the kitchen window to make sure neither of his parents was watching. The coast was clear, so he took the parachute into the garage. He pulled it from the bag and held it up. It was much heavier than he thought it would be. Most of the weight was in the parachute. He studied the straps that attached the bag containing the parachute to the belts of the harness. He had it figured out. Pat had been thorough in his demonstration. He laid it on the garage floor and disassembled it. When the chute was off, he picked up the harness. It was much lighter.

David held it in front of him examining it more closely than he had the opportunity to at the skydiving shack. He saw just how he'd get in and then how to attach Amy. He was ready. He felt both anxious and excited. She was going to be thrilled!

He stashed the parachute bag behind some boxes standing in the back corner of the single stall garage. He'd find a permanent home for that later. Or maybe he could sell it, he considered. The harness went back in the nylon bag, and he stashed that in a cabinet his parents had little reason to go into in the next few days. He figured he was safe.

Each night of the three days leading up to Saturday, David found time to take the harness out to get more comfortable with it. It wasn't lost on him that Amy's life would be dependent on the reliability of this gear. He'd snap it on and set the length of the straps to fit himself. He'd have to adjust the straps for Amy when she was in it. He was sure she'd be as excited as he was.

Chapter 31

At nine o'clock on Saturday morning, Amy picked up David in her grandmother's car.

"What's in the bag?" she asked when he stored the harness in the back seat, closing the door with a bit of a flourish.

"Just a little surprise," he grinned at her. He buckled his seat belt and at the same time leaned over and gave her a kiss on the cheek.

"Ooh, I like surprises," she said. She backed out of the driveway.

David just grinned. *This is going to be so great!* he thought.

Fifteen minutes later, Amy pulled the car into a grassy spot just off the road, near one of the many entrances to their favorite trail. They had found from experience that few people ever parked here. She could tell David was excited about the surprise and that got her more excited too. She figured it had something to do with flying, but she wasn't sure what. Maybe he got them costumes to wear, capes and things, like the super heroes wore. Davey was like that.

David made sure they were alone. He pulled the bag from the car and set it on the ground. He thought his nervous excitement must be visible to Amy. He couldn't wait.

"Okay. Turn around," he told her. She complied.

Amy didn't say anything. She heard the zipper of the bag open and the rustling of the belts and clasps as he pulled out the contents, but had no idea what was making that sound. It didn't sound like capes though.

"Okay," David said, holding the harness up for her to see. "Turn around."

She turned around, and as David expected, there was no recognition in her eyes of what she was looking at.

"Do you know what tandem parachuting is?" he smiled at her.

"Yeah. I think so," she replied slowly. Still no spark of recognition.

"This is the harness that connects the two people together."

Her eyebrows went up. Her eyes lit up and she smiled. Now she got it.

"Connects *us* together," David said. He would cherish the look on her face forever.

Amy was speechless. She looked at the harness. They could be attached to each other with this. No more falling off. He could take her up in the sky!

"C'mon. Let's give it a try," David said anxiously. "Here, hold it out like this." He gave it to her and she held it so that he could strap into his section of the straps and belts. When he had it fastened, the collection of belts and nylon straps that would hold Amy hung down in front.

"Turn around," he instructed her.

"Oh, my gosh," she said. "This is going work, isn't it." It wasn't a question. She was confident that David knew what he was doing.

David stood against her back and wrapped the harness around her. He told her where to attach the clasps and how to tighten the straps. They fumbled a bit at first, but five minutes later they were tightly secured in the harness and against each other, both facing in the same direction.

"Are you ready?" David asked. He put his arms around her and nestled his head on her shoulder.

"Yes," she said softly. She turned her head to the side and kissed him on his cheek.

David rose slowly from the ground. An instant later, the harness pulled the weight of Amy up with him. As he had expected, parts of the harness chafed his skin in a few spots. He figured the same thing was happening to Amy.

"Let's turn this way and adjust the straps," he said. He turned horizontally, with her hanging a scant foot above the trail. They each tugged and jiggled a couple belts until they felt comfortable in the harness.

"How's that?" David asked, feeling more than ready to go.

"Good. I'm good," she replied. "This is so cool, Davey."

"And we're off."

David took them up so that Amy was five feet off the ground. They were securely in the harness, with four inches of slack between them. She hung down, not even in contact with his body. He leisurely took them down the trail.

"Oh, my god," she said. "Davey. This is so great!" She held her arms out like wings.

They flew silently down the trail through the thick woods. The beginning of the trail where they were, was long and straight. David cruised along at a gentle pace. Amy was obviously as excited as he'd expected and he wanted to savor the moment. He held out his arms like she was doing as they sailed smoothly along. There was no problem with his ability to levitate with the added weight in the harness. After a couple minutes, he felt like she was a part of him. He wished he'd thought of this before.

They wound through the curving trails. Amy would lower one arm and raise the other in a banking maneuver that told David which way to turn. He went up and down a couple times, just a few feet each time as they went, getting a feel for how flexible it felt with her below. No problems. The harness worked exactly as he'd hoped it would.

"Can we go up?" she asked after a while. "I want to go higher. Way up in the air."

"Okay. Let's give it a try," he said. "Are you comfortable about being safe?" He slowed to a stop, hovering in a small clearing.

"Yes. Yeah," she eagerly responded. "I want to go way up."

They checked all the equipment again. Everything was tight and secure. Still, David didn't want to take any chances. He put his arms around Amy, holding her close as they turned to a vertical position. She hung down only slightly in his embrace.

They rose through the break in the branches above.

"Oh, wow!" was all Amy could say as they broke through the treetops. "Oh, wow."

For her first time she saw woods and fields and houses and everything from a bird's eye view.

This was all new to her. She soaked it all in.

David knew what it was like to see this for the first time and he felt pretty happy to be able to give this opportunity to Amy. He hugged her a little tighter. She wrapped her arms around his and leaned back, kissing his cheek again. It was a great day.

Amy loved it so much that, in the days following, she felt like she was starting to pester David too much to take her out. His happy agreement each time told her he didn't mind though. They went as often as they could.

One night, David decided to surprise her again. He took her out for a night flight to Wisconsin Rapids to visit her parents. There were a number of fibs required to get away with that. She showed him her appreciation later that night.

*

As the comfort level rose for him, David started to think of telling his parents about the harness. He was sure he could take his mother up, as she was a petite woman and didn't weigh much more than Amy did. He had some concern with his dad, who had a few pounds on David. Not many though, David computed, and he didn't think too many that it would be a problem. More than anything, he wanted to take his dad. He wanted to wash away the years of him getting that look in his eyes. His dad had always made sure he appreciated his special gift. He deserved this.

*

David was now in the habit of following the weather reports on TV. He didn't like flying in the rain and only went when it was clear. His normal bedtime, by his own choosing, had always been ten o'clock. Now, he waited until the local news stations gave the weather report at ten after ten. On virtually every weekend where it wasn't raining, he and Amy were able to get out.

The harness had been a godsend to him. It had allowed them to spend special time together. David often thought about how lucky he was to be able to take his girlfriend out flying. Who else could do that? He had known for a long time now that he wanted to spend forever with her. The secret of his aerial ability helped keep them close. When they flew, he felt like they were one single person. One unit. She had said the same thing.

A couple months later, when spring started to bloom into summer, he began thinking more and more about taking his mother and father. On an early June night, he decided the time was right. The weather forecast for the coming weekend was for sunny, seasonal temperatures. It would get up to about sixty five by Saturday. Amy had to go to Wisconsin Rapids to see her parents that day, so it presented the opportunity he was looking for.

When David turned off the TV to go to bed, he started considering how to broach the subject with his parents. He wanted to ask them the next day.

David came in to the kitchen the next morning to fix a bowl of cereal before school. His mom and dad were already dressed for work and sitting at the table with their breakfast.

"Morning," his dad offered.

"Morning," David replied.

"Morning, honey," his mom added.

"Morning," he said again. He took a bowl from the cupboard, filled it with cereal and milk, pulled out a chair and sat. His parents were talking about something he wasn't paying attention to. He was thinking about how he'd get them to come with him on Saturday. He wanted it to be a surprise like it had been with Amy. He waited for their conversation to dwindle to an end.

"What are you guys up to this weekend? Saturday?" he asked when he had the opportunity.

"Not sure," his father said. "Too far ahead to make definite plans. Probably yard work. I don't have anything else going."

"Why?" his mother asked. "Do you need the car?"

"No. Well, yes and no," he responded. "I was going to go flying on Saturday and wondered if you wanted to come along." He didn't give any specifics. There was a moment of silence.

Mark and Margaret looked at each other. It was sort of an odd request. They had stopped taking him out to fly years ago, when he had become responsible enough to go alone. He'd never asked them to accompany him before.

"Well, yeah. I guess," his father said. "Why do you want us to come along?"

"Yeah. That's kind of a funny thing to ask us," his mother added. "Something you want us to see?"

David smiled. "Yeah," he said. "I was thinking you guys would get a kick out of it. Amy can't go, since she's going to Rapids, and I thought maybe you'd be interested. You'll like it. It's a surprise."

"Okay," his father said, giving his wife a puzzled look.

"Great!" David said. "Be ready to go by eight Saturday. We need to get out early."

His parents agreed. They didn't ask any more about what he might possible surprise them with. They finished breakfast and went their separate ways. David was feeling as anxious and excited as he had when he first took Amy out. He couldn't wait to get their reactions. His mom would probably be a little scared, but he knew his dad wouldn't hesitate. This was more for him.

When they all piled in the car that Saturday morning, precisely at eight o'clock, David got the identical question that Amy had asked. What's in the bag? He told them it was the surprise and said nothing more. They left with David at the wheel and his dad next to him. On the drive to the trail, he noticed his father glancing at the bag in the back seat next to his mom. He could tell he was trying to figure it out.

Being early for a Saturday, there weren't any other visitors to the trail. Usually, once the weather warmed up, this became a popular spot for hikers and bikers. David figured pretty soon he'd have to start looking for a more private place for future landing spots.

"Okay. So you've got me wondering," his dad said as they got out of the car. He pointed at the bag David had pulled from the backseat.

"You'll see," David replied. "C'mon. Let's go down the trail a little."

They walked about fifty yards into the woods to get out of view of the road. Not all the leaves had popped out on the bushes yet, and the three of them were too visible by the car.

David dropped the bag on the ground. His parents stood looking at him, waiting for him to explain. They had no idea what he was doing. He bent down and unzipped the bag, feeling a sense of déjà vu as he pulled out the harness and held it up for them to see.

"Do you know what a tandem parachute is?" he asked. It was exactly the same way he had presented it to Amy.

"Yeah," his father said. There was no puzzled look on his face though, like there had been when Amy saw it. He looked at the harness and knew exactly what David came here for. He started grinning immediately.

"No, not really," his mother replied. "What's a tandem parachute?"

"Two people skydive together," his father eagerly took over. He reached for the harness, eyes wide with excitement. He took it and held it like it were a prize. "They both put this on and only need one parachute when they jump, because they're held together by this."

197

"Oh," was all she could say. It took her a second longer before she understood. "Oh," she said again.

David looked at his father. He got the same rush he had felt when the lightbulb had gone on over Amy's head. His dad was reacting just as he'd hoped and expected. He felt the need to explain the harness, more for his mother's sake.

"This is the harness from a tandem parachute," he told them. "I took the parachute off obviously. I got it a couple months ago. I use it to go flying with Amy. I take her up."

"Is it strong enough?" his father said, a momentary look of worry clouding his face.

David knew he was wondering whether he could be carried. Amy was much smaller than he was, and he was thinking he may get his hopes up only to be unable to be carried.

"I'm pretty sure I can do it," David told him, hoping to assuage his concern. "I don't have any problems at all with Amy." He saw the hope in his father's eyes.

"I… Are you sure?" his mother asked. She stared at the contraption. She didn't appear to be sold on the idea.

"Yup," David said taking the harness from his father. "And we're going to find out right now."

He showed his father how to hold it so he could strap in. When all the belts and straps were fastened, he had his dad turn around. No words were spoken as they secured themselves in the harness. David tugged on all the straps and was satisfied. His mom stood watching, her face showing concern.

"Okay," he told his dad. "Let's see what happens."

David rose slowly off the ground. The belts pulled tight, tighter than they ever did with Amy. But, up his father came. He was heavy, but not that bad. David knew then that he could do this. He saw his mother put a hand over her mouth. Her eyes were wide. His father didn't say anything right away.

"No problem," David said. "Let's turn this way to adjust the straps. It pinches when you first go up." He used his hand to indicate a horizontal position.

David turned so they were parallel to the ground, his dad hanging below him. He was feeling extremely happy that this was working out. All the years, all the times he had seen the look of envy on his father's face when he left to fly, could now be swept away.

"Okay," his father finally spoke after fidgeting in the harness. "I think I'm good."

"You're not going to fall out of there are you?" Margaret asked him.

"I sure as hell hope not," Mark answered her. "God, I hope not."

"I don't think so. This feels comfortable," David added. He could tell his father's concern wasn't so much for his own safety. It was for being able to go up or not.

David didn't waste any time thinking about it. He slowly turned to the right and headed down the trail, leaving his mother standing there in amazement.

"We'll be right back," he yelled back over his shoulder.

They coasted down the path in silence, gliding a couple feet about the forest floor. David knew his father was in seventh heaven over this and he left him to his thoughts. After about a minute, he noticed his father had mimicked what Amy had done on her maiden voyage. His arms were out like wings. David couldn't see his face, but he was pretty sure it held a grin.

David rose and fell a couple times and then turned his body slightly in each direction. His father swung in the harness beneath him.

"Oh, man," his dad said, sounding emotional. "This is just how I imagined it would be. And I imagined it a lot. I never thought I'd be able to do this. I mean, you'd be able to do this. Take me along."

"I always wished you could fly, Dad," David told him. "I knew you'd like it." He resisted the urge to hug him. Maybe later. For sure later.

They flew down the trail to the clearing where he and Amy would ascend, to get over the trees. The forest was bright green with fresh new growth, and they brushed against branches as they rose. The sun shone brightly in the cloudless sky when they finally popped out into the open. They hovered there for a few seconds. David's father looked all around. He looked at the tops of the trees, realizing he'd never seen this perspective before.

"Boy, I wish I could do this all the time," he said. "You are so lucky, Davey."

"I know," he replied. "I know."

David took him for a ride over the woods. As they flew, he explained how he stayed low over the trees to keep from being spotted. They hovered at the edge of an open field, as he told him how he always checked for activity and when he thought it was safe. He had told him this before when he had to make him comfortable to let him go flying, but seeing it was a better way to understand.

"Want to go up?" David asked him. "Way up?"

"Uh, yeah, absolutely," his dad said. He showed no reservations. He was willing to try anything.

"See anyone around?" David asked, looking around himself.

"Not that I can see," his dad replied after a quick scan of the ground below.

David moved back toward the middle of the tree's canopy. He turned vertical and felt the harness straps pinch his thighs again as his father's weight pulled down on him. They hovered there a moment to readjust. Once the squirming stopped, they slowly rose. They picked up speed as they went.

"Hold your arms up like Superman," David told him.

David put his arms up also and then shot them skyward. He didn't know how fast he was going, but things on the ground grew smaller and smaller very quickly. He estimated they were up a couple thousand feet, so he slowed to a stop. They floated silently. David spun them in a slow circle, letting his father soak in the view.

"Wow. This is really something," his father said, his voice full of awe. "Thank you for taking me along."

David knew there would be a sincere hug later on.

"We'll do it again," he told him.

They went a little higher and flew faster, in a wide circle. Then David dove back toward the surface of the forest cover. He turned up and sailed over the woods, back to where the clearing was.

"We better get back, so Mom's not worried," he said. "We've been gone a while."

"Yeah. She's probably thinking something happened to us by now," his dad replied.

They descended through the trees and back to the trail. David slowed before making the final bend in the path. He always stopped there and peeked around the corner to make sure no one was on the trail. All he saw was the distant figure of his mother. He told his dad to hold onto his hat and roared down to where she stood. They landed in front of her.

"Are you guys okay?" she asked Mark, concern in her voice. "You were gone a long time. I thought something might have happened."

"I'm fine. No, I'm great," he told her. "Margaret, you're going to love it."

"Your turn," David told her, waiting as his dad disengaged himself from the harness.

"Okay," she said. "My turn it is."

Both Mark and David were surprised by how eager she now was to go. She stepped into the harness and let Mark snap her in. Neither David, nor his father, sensed any apprehension in her at all. They all worked to fix her securely in place, and in minutes were ready to go. There was a long moment of silence when they were done.

"I remember the first time I saw you floating," she said softly.

David wrapped his arms around her in a warm embrace. Then he rose and took her to where he had just taken his father. He soon realized it must be a normal human reaction to hold your arms out like wings when moving through the air.

Fifteen minutes later, after they had both removed themselves from the confines of the harness, David got the hug from his father. He was happy to return it. His mother joined in and everyone was misty eyed.

They drove home in silence. When they got out of the car, his father was the first to speak.

"We should find a way for you to use your power, you know," he said. "Without being found out of course…"

David smiled at him. He'd begun thinking the same thing.

Chapter 32

Gerald Wainwright was being dragged through the park by his one hundred twenty pound chocolate Labrador. It was all he could do to keep his arm from being pulled from its socket. He liked taking the dog out, but often found it to be strenuous of work. The dog found a tree to urinate on and they finally came to a stop for a couple minutes. Gerald stood holding the leash, watching his dog take the first of what will probably be a half dozen potty breaks in the park. He liked to mark his territory.

Movement in a tree off in the distance caught Gerald's eye. The tree the dog was using partially blocked his view, but in the distance, he still was able to see what looked like a man climbing out of a tree. He thought that was odd. Kids climbed trees, but not grown men. At least he didn't know of any who did. And it was getting dark. He wasn't sure what to make of this.

He watched as the man swung down from a branch that was well over fifteen feet off the ground. At least it looked that high up from his vantage point, fifty yards away. The man leaned down, got his hands in a good grip, and then slowly dropped until he hung from the branch.

Gerald thought that was still pretty high off the ground to be preparing to jump. His feet were a good eight or nine feet up yet. The ground was soft, but that would be a risky thing to do anyway. That was a good way to break an ankle. He figured the guy would have to hit the ground and roll to break the fall.

The man let go, but didn't crash to the grass below like he should have. Gerald watched as he came down quickly, but when his feet hit the surface, there was only a slight bending of his knees. It looked more like he floated down the last few feet, rather than dropping with the full force of gravity pulling on him.

The dog started off after finishing his duty, and Gerald strained to hold him back. He saw the man better now. It wasn't so much an adult, he thought, as it looked more like a big kid, a teenager. He had curly brown hair, and was medium height and thin. He couldn't see his face well in the early dusk, but the kid wore the type of clothing that indicated his likely age. He saw him look around before he started walking toward the Eighth Avenue exit out of the park.

Gerald needed two hands to hold his dog from pulling him out in the open. He didn't want the tree climber to see him, so he held tight. Only after the guy had rounded a corner of a stand of bushes did Gerald relent and let the dog pull him forward. He steered the dog as best he could in the direction the guy had gone. He wanted to see who he was and where he was going. There was something definitely unusual about the way he had descended from that tree. He had heard of a flying person, but that didn't immediately register as being related to this. There was just something discomforting about the way he landed. That wasn't normal.

Unfortunately, his one hundred twenty pound dog had other ideas and by the time Gerald was able to tug him in the direction of the street, the brown haired teenager was out of sight. Gerald pictured the way he'd landed in the grass again as he walked home. It dawned on him that this could amount to something. Aston had reports of a flying person, and a claim of a witch, he now recalled, so seeing unusual things was not out of the ordinary nowadays.

It was after seven o'clock when Gerald got home. He unleashed the dog, which went promptly to the large water bowl and began loudly slurping enough water to quench the thirst it had just worked up. Gerald was going out of town the next day on business, so decided to call Bernie Fredder at home tonight. He knew Bernie personally and didn't see an issue with calling now. He pulled the phonebook from the drawer of the coffee table and sat paging through it. He found Bernie's number and dialed.

"Hello," came the answer.

"Hey, Bernie. Jerry Wainwright. How are you?"

"Good. You?" Bernie asked.

"Great. Hey, I just saw something weird and thought you may be interested. I hate to call at home," Jerry told him, "but I have to go to Madison tomorrow and wouldn't have time to call at all during the day."

"That's okay," Bernie said. "What's up?"

Gerald recounted what he'd seen at the park.

Bernie had just poured himself a glass of wine and had settled on the couch for a little nighttime reading. His book was on his lap, a slip of paper marking the spot he'd just been pulled away from. He often got work related calls at home and rarely minded. There weren't that many to where it was a nuisance. He'd realized long ago that being the local reporter at the paper was a twenty four hour job.

"Interesting," Bernie said after Jerry finished his story. "He floated down."

"Yeah," Jerry told him. "I think normally a person would have landed hard and rolled. That was a ways down."

Bernie asked a few questions, then thanked him for calling and slowly hung up the phone. He sat for a while thinking it over. The book slid off his lap untouched. He sipped his wine as he considered the scene that Jerry had described. The guy had come out of a tree. The tree was in Edison Park. Edison Park was where the kite had been freed from years back. There had been sightings of the Flying Guy in that general vicinity before. This was his guy. He knew it.

Why would he climb trees, he wondered? He could just fly over them or around them. Unless he didn't want to be seen taking off and landing right from the ground. *That's it!* Bernie grinned. That's what the flying guy was doing. He'd go up through the trees and then come down the same way. Then people wouldn't see him fly in to land. He could just fly into the trees and make it look like he was climbing up or down. Jerry had said the guy had looked around when he landed, as if to see if anyone was watching. He didn't want to be seen, so he'd have to do this only when the park was deserted. He didn't see Jerry there when he climbed down, because he was blocked from view.

Bernie poured another glass of wine and drank slowly. A plan formulated as he rolled it over in his mind.

*

The next night at six o'clock, Bernie steered his car toward Edison Park. He planned to watch for the flying guy, to see if he could spot him coming down from a flight through the trees. He parked on the street near some houses, rather than in the parking lot located in the park. There were no other cars there that he could see, so he set off through a long expanse of lawn toward the area Jerry had indicated the tree climber was seen. Bernie stayed near the edge of the open grassy field in as much shade as he could. The sun was already setting, so long shadows darkened the edge of the trees. He came to where he thought was the spot Jerry had been and stood looking around. There was no activity anywhere, so he sat beneath the tree. Only then did it dawn on him that he could spend quite a bit of time just sitting in expectation. His original thought had been to do this each night until he saw something. After sitting for over a half hour in the moist grass behind the tree that afforded him both cover and a view, he realized his odds of catching the flyer coming or going were pretty slim.

Two long hours later, Bernie was walking back to his car. He had not seen anything tonight. He decided he'd determine whether he'd continue coming here, on a day to day basis. He didn't want to waste a lot of time for what was not likely to happen when he was here. Jerry seeing him was just luck.

Bernie visited the park nine times over the next month. Sometimes he'd sit for an hour, sometimes for over two hours, but rarely more. He never saw anything. A couple times he saw rustling in the leaves and branches. Nothing came out though. Probably just squirrels jumping through the trees. He was disappointed, but the more he'd thought about it, the more he was sure his theory was correct. He'd reviewed his information on all the sightings, and there was almost always mention of being seen over some trees or near them. He tried to put himself in the Flying Guy's place. How would I go about it? *I'd use trees for cover*, Bernie thought. *That's what I'd do.* Thick trees, like in a park. Reduce your chances of being seen taking off into the sky by climbing into a tree, then exit at the top. He was sure he was on to something.

It occurred to him that he could let Agent Johnston of the FBI in on his idea. It was something he'd be interested in knowing. Bernie decided against that. There would be secret agents lurking in the park.

When Agent Johnston called Bernie about three months later, just to see if he'd seen or heard anything new, Bernie told him there was nothing happening. He kept his theory to himself. Agent Johnston thanked him for his time and asked to be notified when there was.

Bernie had hoped the FBI would lose interest. There hadn't been any recent sightings, but he expected them to continue again at some point. He hoped the calls would come directly to him if they did start again, rather than to the law enforcement folks. Artie had said he had access to those. That way, he could keep the FBI out of the loop.

Chapter 33

Both David and Amy had somewhat of an idea of what careers they wanted to go into when they got out of high school, and since their romance was still as strong as ever, they wanted to be able to go to the same college. His flying to Wisconsin Rapids from Aston for that one year they had been separated had been fun for him, but the risk had proven costly. The newspapers were on to him. Neither he nor Amy were going to have access to a car while being freshmen in college, so David flying to visit her at a different school would be their only way of seeing each other. It may have worked okay logistically in the past, but it had too many drawbacks. They hoped to avoid that by finding a college that worked for both.

The decision to attend the University of Wisconsin in Eau Claire was made after their families had met to discuss the subject over a dinner at the Andersons. Margaret had maintained her friendship with Amy's mom, and since the kids had made it clear they wanted to go to the same school, they all decided to meet and discuss options. The dinner was a great opportunity.

Amy was interested in nursing and had a list of schools that were known for offering excellent programs in that field. David had expressed interest in accounting or business. Most of the schools in the Wisconsin university system covered both, but there were a only few that concentrated on both of those two fields. Amy's parents had attended the university in Eau Claire, so they lobbied for their alma mater. It matched the criteria they needed. David's parents were familiar with the school and the city itself, and liked that idea. They discussed other schools, but kept coming back to this one. By the end of the evening, it was pretty much set that this was the direction they would go in. The kids were in agreement.

After David and Amy had gone out to a movie for the evening, the parents remained to talk. Both sets of parents figured at some point there would be a wedding and felt that by both attending the same school, it would reduce the chances of them going their separate ways. They could see that David and Amy were happy that they had all been in agreement. Everyone was all smiles when the night ended.

Over the next few weeks all the arrangements were made to attend UW-Eau Claire. They submitted the necessary paperwork, and as it turned out, both David and Amy got their acceptance letters on the same day.

*

The time to head off to college snuck up on them. They'd graduated from high school, worked through the summer and before they knew it, it was time to pack up and leave the home nest. Since their parents continued to maintain their close relationship as well, they planned a joint effort to move Amy and David the one hundred plus miles to Eau Claire.

David's parents had an older van that Mark used mostly for recreational and utility purposes, and together, everyone packed it full of the personal belongings they felt college freshmen would need. When they finally had it ready to go, Mark and Amy's father, Adam Kellerman, decided to drive together in the van. There wasn't any room for anyone else in the crammed vehicle, as the back seats had been removed to accommodate everything.

Margaret and Amy's mother, Sandy, together with the two kids, piloted the Kellerman's Jeep Cherokee behind them. After a three hour drive and two hours of lifting and carrying all of the boxes containing their clothes and other necessities to their respective dorm rooms, the six of them took a break, sharing a meal at the university student union. Tearful goodbyes followed, and finally David and Amy were left behind to begin the first stage of their adult life.

"So, Flyboy," Amy said to David as they walked hand in hand from the Student Center back toward the Towers, David's dormitory, "maybe we could take a flight some night and check out the area."

"Definitely," David said. He was happy that she liked to fly with him. "It's really pretty here. I only wish we could go during the day. It would be fun to buzz the dorms."

"Yeah," Amy grinned. "They'd freak." They both laughed at the thought.

The two of them sat together on the small rectangular patch of grass just outside the entrance to David's dormitory. They watched as the steady stream of new students and parents hauled cart after cart of belongings into the building. Across the parking lot, they watched the same parade going on at Amy's dorm, Sutherland. They had hoped to get into the same co-ed dorm, but it didn't work out. It didn't matter though, as it turned out the windows of their respective rooms faced each other across a small parking area. They could wave to each other when they were talking on the phone.

Classes started on the Tuesday after Labor Day, and they soon were buried in their school work and other activities. Everything worked out as planned and they were able to see each other every day. Being in different degree programs meant they didn't share any classes together. They hoped maybe at some point to be in a common class each needed to take, but for now their days were separated by their class schedule. Fortunately, they had meal plans at the same food center and were able to meet that way to share most evening meals.

Chapter 34

Near the end of an unusually warm October of that first year, the city and university had turned to a vibrant shade of autumn orange. David still had a clear memory of his past adventure to see the fall colors north of Aston, and wanted to get out again. This time it would be in his new town. He wanted to take Amy with him, but decided he'd check it out alone first. He wanted to get the lay of the land and figured he'd go out for a solo flight, to get a feel for where it would be safe to go.

There was a park about three miles away that he'd liked from the first time he'd seen it. The layout and heavily wooded landscape of Carson Park had immediately struck him as a good spot to use for coming and going. There were number of parking spots along the sides of the road that wound through the park, where it wasn't uncommon to leave a vehicle while walking through the trails. He decided this would easily give him adequate cover. David and Amy had spent an earlier warm autumn day strolling around the area. While there was a lot of car traffic going through the main road, the trails in some spots were much less crowded.

David got out of his last class at noon on Fridays. The day had turned out perfect for him to go for a flight. The sky had been clear and sunny as soon as the sun rose in the morning. The temperatures were slightly above normal and comfortable at sixty five degrees. The conditions were perfect.

Amy had class until three thirty that day, and then was going to dinner with some new friends at a small sandwich shop in the area of town that catered to the college crowd. David had the time to go flying. He planned to meet Amy later in the evening, so that afforded him the opportunity to go now.

By one o'clock David was steering his bicycle over the bridge from one side of campus to the other. From there it was about three or four miles to

Carson Park. He'd thought about it and didn't plan on taking his bike up into a tree. That would take too much time scoping out the area for both a good spot to go up and one that had a good layout of branches where he could hang the bicycle unseen. He decided instead to chain his bike in a rack near the football field, in the center of the park. His college team played here. In fact, he recalled there was a home game the next day that he planned to go to. From the football field, he decided to take a trail that didn't go very far, dead-ending against the rear parking lot of a local business. This trail was only a couple blocks long. The area around it was heavily wooded. Just to the east of that area was a lengthy stretch of trees heading toward the downtown district. From there the tree cover ended, so he would need to go north from there, over the residential area.

David had gotten up unseen and was easing his way over the city of Eau Claire. He stayed as low to the tree canopy as possible and went very slowly. He could tell where the breaks in the trees were before going over them, but still being new to the city, he had to creep up to the opening to see what was below. After a little over a mile, he realized it would take a considerable amount of time to weave through the city, and it also dawned on him that he didn't know the area well enough to know if he wouldn't have to go over a crowded area at some point. Being broad daylight didn't give him the cover he needed.

He stopped over what he thought must have been a city park. The square city block was a solid mass of trees, with no rooftops peeking out. If he went up a little higher to get a view, he'd be in airspace visible from a couple different angles. He wished he'd been able to start from an area perhaps on the edge of town or in a rural area. Not having a car left him at a disadvantage though, on transportation needs.

He hovered there, looking around in all directions. He checked his watch. It had taken almost a half hour to get to where he was and as far as he could tell, he had about double that time, at the rate he was going, to even get to what looked like the edge of town. He only had one alternative.

David pointed his hands to the sky and soared straight up. He went as fast as he could ever remember going. His goggles felt like they may get ripped off his face. After what was just a scant five seconds, he slowed to a stop and sat in the air. He estimated that he was over three thousand feet up. No one could see him from here.

Below him stretched the city of Eau Claire. He saw first how the Chippewa River snaked its way through town. He knew from the part of it that flowed through a beautiful area of the campus, that this was a wide, but very shallow river. It looked even wider from the air. This river was bigger than any he'd been over in the Aston area, with the possible exception of the Wolf. But, this was more of an urban waterway. He wanted to dive down and wind his way over the water where it slid through the downtown. Unfortunately, that wasn't an option in the broad light of day. He'd do that some night, he decided.

He sat in the same spot for almost fifteen minutes, slowly turning, as he memorized the layout of the city from the air. His eyes followed the highways into the distance and he made a mental note of which ones he didn't know the names of. He'd get that information later from a road map, so he'd know where they lead to. He noticed the landscape was much hillier here than near his hometown. Aston was flat. Here, there were gently rolling hills going off to the north, south, and west.

David paid particular attention to the tree cover. Eau Claire was a very pretty city and had a lot of trees. The density of the canopy, even in the residential areas, was greater than that of Aston or any of the other cities and towns he'd flown over. He easily spotted the university and looked for a tree-lined route from that area, so he wouldn't have to travel too far to just find a safe place to use as a base. He found a couple of spots that from the air looked like good candidates. The foliage was thick, and the wider more open streets were at a minimum near most of them. He'd check these out from the ground when he had the chance.

He decided he'd gotten a pretty good lay of the land and banked to the northeast. He knew from the highway beneath him where he was going. There was a large lake in that direction. He figured he'd check out that area to see what was there. He stayed at the same altitude and headed off. The air was unusually still and the sun peaked from behind low clouds. He took his time, hoping no one would look up as high as he was. Dressed in his usual dark attire, with the black ski mask, he'd be a small dot in the sky. He'd be visible, but probably not distinguishable as a person flying. He curved around the lake, decided he'd like to come back again when he had more time, and then worked his way back to Eau Claire.

Fifteen minutes later, he was again sitting high above the city. He found the spot he had risen from, but upon further examination, discovered he could probably do a rapid descent straight down to a part of Carson Park not far from his initial departure point. He zoomed down to just over the trees. For a moment he was disoriented on the direction he'd need to go to get back to that exact same spot. He had to go down into a tree, to look around to get his bearings. Moments later, he settled to the ground unseen, on a trail near the one he'd left from. He stuffed his mask in his pocket as he walked back to the football field. He was confident he hadn't been spotted anywhere.

*

Two weeks later he wasn't so lucky. He'd gone out alone for a night flight. He'd scoped out a couple of the potential base spots he'd seen on his maiden voyage, and found one that he thought would work well. When he left, he didn't see anyone around. He was comfortable he had gotten off unnoticed. It was his first night flight over Eau Claire, so he paid special attention to the open spots and roads. But, being a city of many trees, he found an easy path to get to his destination. This time though, he was able to go faster and dart across the roads that now had considerably less traffic than they had when he went during the day. He got through town unseen and was soon at the farthest point that he intended to go. He could see his ultimate destination below him, just to the east. The Chippewa River entered Eau Claire from the north here, after exiting the smaller city of Chippewa Falls. This is where he was going. David saw headlights on the Highway Twenty Nine and Highway Fifty Three interchange. He didn't sit in the air for long, though. He wanted to cruise down the river. His hope was that he may be able to get all the way to the campus unseen. He was already familiar with the route it took through the downtown area, having studied that on walking visits during the evening. It was a pretty long haul from the dorms, but he and Amy had found they liked to explore their new home on foot. On their way, he'd figured out which side of the river to stay near and where he needed to stop and watch for either car or foot traffic to clear. He was sure he could do it.

After a short moment enjoying the vista, David dove down to a dark stretch of the river. He slowed, then arched up to a cruising position about five feet above the water. The edges of the river were heavily forested in this part, with an occasional break for a backyard of a huge house. All of the houses in this stretch of the river were huge. Most were brick mansions. There was nothing like this in Aston.

The river curved where it came to the downtown district. In some spots, the banks of the river were steep and dark. He stayed in those shadows. He could smell the water. It smelled like the wet leaves that floated along the edges where they had fallen. Since this was his first time here, David was extra cautious. He stopped under every bridge, hovering just beneath. He peered out from his viewpoint, hugging the cement pillars. When he thought it was clear, he'd zip over to the next area he thought was safe. Slowly but surely, he worked his way through the town toward the campus.

David figured there would only be one spot where he'd have real trouble. That would be the campus area itself. It was coming up now. The Chippewa River was very wide at this point. It came out of the urban downtown area, through some humongous and expensive houses, mostly professors he'd learned, and then curved right to go through the lower level of the campus. There were a number of university buildings on the right, just at the curve, and in the middle of those was a walk bridge. During the day, the walk bridge was always crowded with steady flow of students moving between classes in those buildings and the other classrooms on the other side. It was a weekday night, so David hoped the traffic on the bridge would be light. If it were a weekend night, that wouldn't be the case. Since the dorms were all on campus on the far side of the river, students flowed over to the nightlife on the small stretch of Water Street a couple blocks down. This is where the bars and restaurants were.

David hovered under the road bridge that went to Water Street. Up ahead and to the right, he could see the lights over the foot bridge. He floated slowly through the trees that covered the yards of the big houses closest to campus. He cruised between the blind spots he'd studies days before. When he was sure he'd be okay, he shot out from where he was and roared around the bend. As he went along, he scanned the walk bridge he was approaching, and figured he was good to go. There was no one on it. Staying in the shadows as well as he could, he rounded the bend and zoomed over to a dark spot on the south side nearest the dormitories. The lights of Water Street were on the other side.

He sat in the shadows for a few minutes, reconnoitering the area. He listened for people and heard none. He always listened for someone saying "what's that?" All he had was silence above the gentle gurgling of the water below. The walking trails here were deserted at this hour.

From where he was, he could go up over the trees that lined the edge of the river and he would be on the upper part of campus near the majority of the dormitories. Amy's dorm would be right there. He didn't even consider the idea of flying around there though. Too many windows. Too many students. Too few trees and hiding spots.

David knew the river went straight for a stretch that paralleled Water Street. He shot down that stretch, going from dense shade to the ribbons of light given off from the streetlights and businesses along the way. He hoped he was going too fast to be seen. As far as he could tell, no one was around that would be looking in his direction.

When he finally slowed down, he moved over to a clump of bushes he'd earlier identified as a potential ending spot for his excursion. David had decided to end at a different place than where he had taken off from. He wasn't far from the main entrance off Menomonee Street that went in to Carson Park. He could land on the river bank here and still be in the shadows as he climbed to the sidewalk. He peered over the top of the bank, saw no one and crawled up. He walked the roughly two miles distance back to campus. He crossed the walk bridge he'd just buzzed by, and after climbing the hill to the upper campus, he went to Amy's dorm to visit. He still had enough time to tell her about his trip before he had to get to bed.

*

Rose Ward lived in one of the brick mansions on the Chippewa River. Hers was close to town and within walking distance to the northernmost business district. The lawn behind the huge house stretched out to the manicured flowerbeds near a patio by the river. There was a seating area set up here, and on most sunny, warm days and evenings, she and her husband Timothy, a local doctor, would enjoy a cocktail and their view of the Chippewa.

On this night she sat alone, enjoying the cool but comfortable night sky. Her dog, a playful white poodle, scampered around beside her. The yard was large by any standards, and she didn't need to keep the dog on a leash. It had learned the boundaries and stayed within them.

She heard the dog growl. It had stopped running around and now stood still, staring out at the river. Normally, the dog had a shrill bark that annoyed Timothy to no end, but now was uncharacteristically silent.

"What's the matter with you?" Rose said to the dog. She peered out to where the dog was watching.

The river was dark here, with little light filtering down to it from her house. The sky held only a quarter moon and was little help. Rose still had enough light to see the black shape glide by. It wasn't more than thirty yards away from where she sat. It looked to her like it was cigar shaped, or maybe like a bullet, she thought. It flew by, barely five feet above the water. As it passed, she could just barely make out what looked like feet at the tail-end of it. Shoes. The dog continued its low growl. She was sure it was about to bark. She shushed it as quietly as she could and was successful in keeping it from yipping. She and the dog sat still in the darkness of her yard.

When the shape had moved on down the river she got out of her wrought iron chair and almost ran to the house. The poodle followed, now yipping unbridled. She opened the back door and held it for the dog to come in.

"Tim!" she yelled when the door shut.

"What?" came an exasperated reply. She must be interrupting something important. Timothy didn't like to be bothered most times.

"I saw something flying down by the river," she still yelled. "Something flying. Something big."

"Well, so what?" Timothy said as he came out of his office. The glasses he wore were pushed up on top of his head and indicated he had indeed been pulled away from something. His tone was slightly angry. "There're all kinds of things that fly around the river here. What's the big deal?"

"This wasn't a bird," Rose said. She didn't care if he was perturbed by the interruption. "It was bigger. It looked like a person."

"A person?" Timothy almost snickered. "What are you talking about?"

"I saw someone… or something that looked like a person flying down the river," she told him. "It wasn't a bird. I know what birds look like. I'm not stupid. This didn't have wings. And it had feet. Human feet. Even the dog saw it."

Timothy looked at the dog, who was standing behind his wife. He almost spoke to the animal, asking it what he saw, just to end the conversation with Rose. But, then the dog would probably come over to him and want some attention. And Rose would be pissed that he spoke to the dog like a person, while obviously trying to end her conversation. He opted for a quick out.

"Maybe you should call the police," he told her. He stared at her, wanting to get back to work.

"Well. Maybe I will," she said harshly, and turned back toward the kitchen, stomping away.

Timothy returned to his office and the work he'd been so rudely torn away from. Rose went to the kitchen to get her purse and the cellphone inside. Since she was a little mad over her husband's lack of concern, she didn't think of just calling the police department. She dialed 911 instead.

She explained to the officer what she had seen. The police officer, a woman at the emergency call center who answered, was at first upset that someone was wasting their valuable time that was supposed to be used only for emergencies. But, she forgot about that as she noted the details of a sighting of a flying person. I suppose, she considered, something like this could be considered an emergency. Who knew what it could have been? Since this wasn't going to require an ambulance or police cruiser to go out, there was no expense to the call. She bit her tongue over what she wanted to say and told Rose to contact the local police department directly if she ever saw it again.

The police officer at the call center logged the call on her shift report. This went out in the daily blotter to the Eau Claire Herald, the local newspaper, and to the state and federal law enforcement services, including the FBI. The next day, the blotter report was included in the stack of paperwork that sat on the desk of the FBI's Northcentral Liaison.

*

Agent Arthur Johnston strode into his office after returning from the now daily anti-terrorism meeting. It felt like a long meeting, but when he looked at the clock he saw it was exactly ten o'clock on the head. Perfect, he thought. That will give enough time to review the material for his region that needed to be done before the afternoon meeting. In addition to that, he had meetings at two o'clock and three o'clock. He was prepared for those.

He decided to read the newspapers first today, so he took the top one off the stack. It was the Chicago Sun Times, the biggest paper. He flipped it open and scanned the local news articles. Nothing much going there he determined, so he went on to the Minneapolis paper, the Milwaukee and Madison, Wisconsin papers, and then the smaller ones. Fifteen minutes later, he closed the last one and set them aside. He'd only found one article of note and had added the information from it to the report he'd present at the Liaison meeting.

Next, he moved on to the regional FBI office reports. Everything contained in them was already common knowledge to the Bureau and he didn't add anything to the list of what he'd need to disseminate. He set these aside, putting a post-it note on the stack saying to send down to be scanned.

Artie moved on to the blotter reports. He glanced at the clock and saw that he was moving along faster than he'd anticipated. That was a good thing, since the stack of blotters was over two inches thick today, well above the normal amount. He'd need the extra time for these. He went through those for Illinois first. As usual, the Chicago area had the most to report on. He found a couple items of interest that might concern the other liaison agents, adding those to his report.

When he came to Wisconsin, he did Milwaukee first and then would go through Madison, Green Bay, La Crosse, Eau Claire and Wausau in that order. They were the biggest cities when it came to police activity. His otherwise routine review of his region came to an unexpected halt when he read the Eau Claire Police Department daily report.

A woman had called 911 to report seeing something, or someone, as she was sure it was a person, flying along the Chippewa River behind her house. She had described it as being all black, shaped sort of like a missile or bullet, except she'd seen feet at the back end.

Artie thought about that, picturing what she may have seen. It could appear missile shaped, if it was as person flying along with arms out in front, like Superman. The lady had said it was about thirty yards away and in the dark, so she couldn't positively identify it as a person.

He sat back with the paper in hand. He considered the possible scenarios. It could just be that she was under the influence of something and was seeing things, or he supposed, it could have been a large bird. But, that wouldn't explain the feet. He sat staring at the paper. The other possibility is that it was the Flying Guy. Or, he thought, another flying guy. Wisconsin seemed to be turning into the Twilight Zone, he mused. He chuckled.

Digging in the small closet off the side of his office, he found the maps he had been using to plot reports of sightings of the flying person. He pulled out the roll containing the state map. He spread it out on his desk, using a stapler and his coffee mug as paperweights to keep it laid out flat. He sat down and reviewed the map.

Aston was in northcentral Wisconsin and that part of the map had yellow dots all around that city. He traced his finger straight west, to the western portion of the state and found Eau Claire. That was quite a distance away. There were no other yellow dots other than around Aston, with the exception of a handful near Wisconsin Rapids and Wausau. That was as far away as the sightings went. Eau Claire was, as he eyeballed it, about one hundred fifty miles from Aston.

Artie pondered the thought. The new report indicated that this time, the flyer hadn't been seen out in the open flying, as it had been in most of the previous reports when outside of Aston. It was seen down by the river. What the open air flying meant to him was that the flyer was traveling when he was spotted. The sightings around Aston were almost always of him being in specific situations or locations. Those, and the flag incident. This new report from Eau Claire said he was gliding down the river. He recalled the sighting on the river in Aston. Shit Creek it was called. Bernie Fredder had called it that.

It occurred to Artie that he hadn't seen any newspaper or law enforcement reports from Aston in months. He wondered if Bernie Fredder had anything new. He hadn't had a call from him lately. He pictured Bernie, remembering him as a nice guy, easy to talk to and very helpful. He had called once with news of a sighting. Artie decided to call him just to check in. Maybe he'd heard something about the Flying Guy that might connect him to Eau Claire somehow.

Artie pulled up his contact list on his computer email system, found the number and called. Two rings later he had him on the phone.

"Bernie," he greeted him. "Agent Johnston with the FBI. How are you?"

"I'm good. How are you, Artie?" Bernie remembered he preferred to be called Artie.

"The same. Say, I was just checking in to see if you had any recent sightings of our flying guy."

"Nope. Nothing recent." Bernie didn't like the sound of *'our'* Flying Guy. It was his Flying Guy. "The last time was that last time I called you." He remembered he was omitting the sighting of the guy climbing out of the trees from reports to the FBI.

"Mmm," Artie said. "I thought there might be a recent sighting. Or I was hoping there may have been."

"Really?" Bernie said. "Why is that?" It seemed odd that out of the blue Agent Artie thought there would be something. This didn't sound good.

"Last night there was a report of a flying person in Eau Claire," Artie told him. "It was similar to Aston sightings in that he was seen flying down a river, the Chippewa in this case."

"Really," Bernie said again, slouching down in his chair. *Eau Claire?* he thought. *Why Eau Claire?* He had long ago discounted the notion that there may be more than one flyer. Every sighting could logically be determined to be just the one, sometimes flying in different places.

"What do you make of that?" Artie asked, hoping maybe Bernie might have some unthought-of insight on it.

"Eau Claire you say." Bernie was silent then, thinking. He didn't have to think too hard before coming to at least one conclusion. Eau Claire was a college town. The general age of the flyer, from what he had computed based on the pranks and the various sightings over the years, would make it very possible that the flyer was now college age. It struck him that he didn't want to tell Artie this.

"Yeah. I'm wondering if there may be two of them," Artie said. "But, if he was seen recently, I was thinking he may be on the move. Just the one I mean."

"Yeah. I see what you're thinking," Bernie replied. His mind was going off in a different direction that he didn't want to share with the FBI.

"I found it interesting," Artie continued, "to note that he was seen flying down a river. He wasn't out in the open like he was heading somewhere. He was reported as slowly floating down the river."

Bernie listened, wondering if the FBI agent would mention Eau Claire was a college town and connect those dots. So far no indication of that. He pulled a piece of paper over and wrote himself a note: *check to see who from*

Aston now attends UW-Eau Claire. He added several large exclamation points after the words.

"I'm not sure what to make of that," Bernie told him. "I never thought there was more than one, but... who knows?" He hoped Artie would go in that direction.

"The FBI would certainly be quite a bit more interested if there were more than one," Artie responded.

"I imagine they would," Bernie chuckled. He was getting the same unsettling feeling he had experienced the first time he'd met Agent Johnston, and now wanted to end the call. "Tell you what, I'll keep my ear to the ground and let you know if something comes through."

"Okay. Thanks. Much appreciated," Artie said.

"Oh, can you send me a copy of that blotter from Eau Claire?" Bernie asked. "I can get one from the Eau Claire PD myself, but if you have it handy, can you scan it and email it to me? That would be quicker."

"Sure," Artie agreed. "What's your email address?"

Bernie gave it to him and thanked him for that.

"No problem," Artie said." Let me know ASAP if you hear anything."

"Will do. Have a good day." Bernie hung up. He sat back again, drumming his fingers on his desk.

He stared at the note he had written for himself. He smiled. He finally felt the net closing in on the Flying Guy. He hadn't felt that before. If his thought was correct, the Flying Guy graduated from Aston and was now attending the University of Wisconsin in Eau Claire. *That sounds logical. Very logical.* He chuckled to himself. He was applying logic to a situation where a human being could fly. How logical is that?

He sat forward and yelled. "Marsha! Can you come here a sec?"

His assistant appeared at the door. "What's up?"

"Can you get me a list of all Aston graduates from the last school year who are now attending UW – Eau Claire? The school should be able to get that information."

"Sure. I think they can give that out."

"Oh, and also ask for a list of students attending La Crosse, Point, and Madison. I only need Eau Claire, but I don't want anyone connecting any dots to Eau Claire." Bernie expected her to ask what this was about after he said that, but she didn't and left to get the information.

221

Bernie could only dedicate a portion of his attention to the article he was working on for the next day's paper. He waited anxiously for Marsha to get the list. He figured the list would be short and it would contain the name of the Flying Guy. Then all he had to do, he now pondered, was figure out which one.

It took almost an hour for Marsha to get the lists for him. He set aside all but the Eau Claire list. He set that in front of him. He leaned his elbows on his knees, his face just above the list. There were eight boys and eleven girls. He was sure the flyer was a male. He slowly went through their names. Nothing jumped out at him. He knew three of the boys, as he knew their parents. One had been a paper carrier for the Sentinel. He didn't think it was any of them, but, he thought, he couldn't rule anything out.

"Now, what can we do here?" he said aloud to himself.

*

After Artie Johnston had ended the call with the Aston newspaper reporter, he summarized all of his information for the FBI Director and Agent Whiting. He called the Director's direct line and was told by his assistant that the Director was out of town for at least a week. Artie asked if she knew if Agent Whiting was available. She wasn't sure, but thought he was also out of town. He told her he would send two copies of his report to her for them and if either wanted to meet, he was as always at their service.

Artie put the two copies of the report in the envelope to send up to Carol, the Director's assistant. He put them in an inter-departmental envelope that indicated it was for the Director's eyes only.

After a week, Artie had almost forgotten he'd sent the report up. He knew the Director was back in this office and hadn't heard from him. He wondered if the infrequent sightings was causing him to lose interest. Then he thought of C. Randall Whiting. Not much chance of him losing interest.

Chapter 35

David swung his backpack over his shoulder and headed out the front door of his dormitory. It was cold with the threat of snow, but he only needed to cross the parking lot to get to Amy's dorm. They had planned to spend the night inside, watching a movie. Amy's roommate, a girl from Minnesota, spent most of her evenings at her new boyfriend's dorm. She rarely returned before eleven, so they had the room to themselves.

He had an older friend get them a bottle of wine to share while they watched a DVD of a recently released movie. It was a love story, something David never minded watching with Amy. He was only marginally interested in seeing this particular one, but didn't tell her that. He thought it was too much of a "chick-flick". Still, love story movies and Amy had always combined well in the past. Add to that a bottle of wine and a private dorm room, and he was looking forward to an enjoyable night.

David signed in at the front desk of Sutherland Hall and was allowed to go directly to her room. Recent changes on visitation were overlooked. The girl at the front desk was a new friend who lived on Amy's floor, and she didn't have him wait for Amy to come get him as she was supposed to. He bounded up the steps to her floor and knocked on her door.

"It's open," David heard her say from inside. He opened the door just as she was reaching for the handle.

"Hi," she greeted him and leaned in for a kiss.

"Hi," he smiled back, obliging her. He came in and set the backpack on her desk table. The wine bottle inside thunked on the surface.

"What have you got there?" Amy asked when she heard it. "A present? For me?" She knew what it was.

"Yup. Vino for the lady," David said, unzipping the backpack and pulling out the bottle.

"Mmm. I'll get glasses."

Amy opened a cabinet and pulled out two plastic cups. David pulled off his coat, stuffed his gloves in the pockets and hung it over the back of her desk chair. He came over to Amy and put his arms around her from behind.

"Got a wine bottle opener?" he asked.

"Right here," she held it up. "Want to do the honors?"

"Allow me," he said. He took the corkscrew opener and began working on the bottle.

Amy got the movie and put it in the DVD player. She sat on the edge of the futon across from the TV, working the remote control to get the movie set to play. David came over with two glasses of wine and sat next to her. She took the cup he offered and sipped a bit of the sweet wine.

"Mmm. This good," she said.

"Hey! What's that? Go back," David said, pointing at the screen. While she was changing to the channel that her DVD player required for watching movies, she had passed one that showed the 'BREAKING NEWS' alert indicating something major had happened. She flipped back to it.

"Well, Bob," the on the scene reporter was saying, "right now the police and emergency units are attempting to bring up bodies and, they hope, some survivors from this horrific crash."

In the background, David and Amy could see the flashing lights of numerous police and emergency vehicles. It was dark in the rural Virginia community where this accident had taken place. They could make out the silhouette of a large vehicle behind the reporter. Looks like a bus, they both thought. It was lying on its side, well down a steeply sloping embankment that seemed to end in darkness.

"What we do know," the reporter continued, "is that this bus, filled with students returning home from a high school basketball game, had slid on this treacherous, ice covered stretch of highway, hit the guardrail, and then plunged down the embankment behind me." The reporter pointed behind him without turning his face from the camera. "We're told there are some fatalities, but that there are survivors they are working to bring up. What their conditions are is not known. Authorities think some are likely to be critically injured."

"Wow. Hate to hear that," David said solemnly.

Amy turned to him. "If you were there you could help." Her eyes were boring into him.

David looked at her. He didn't know what he should say. He was sure she was saying that he could fly down and rescue the injured survivors. Her eyes held his for a long moment. He tried to read them.

"Have you ever thought of what you can do with your power to fly?"

Power to fly. He rolled the words over in his head. *I've always thought of it as the ability to fly. Not power to fly. Although I do consider it a power,* he thought. Combine them, and it takes on a different context, like it came with responsibility. He'd thought of this numerous times before, but still being so concerned over being caught had kept him back.

"Yeah," he said. "Sometimes I think I should try to do things. I've always been scared of getting caught. My parents have always drilled the need for secrecy into me." He wanted Amy to continue.

"But that's when you were a kid," she said. "They were afraid someone would come and take you away. You're an adult now. You'd know how to get away". She paused. "You could be Superman, you know." Her eyes bored into him.

David didn't say anything at first, his eyes mesmerized by the flickering red and blue lights on the TV screen. He considered what she'd just said. She was right. It was different now. He looked at her.

"What do you think I should do?" he asked.

"I don't know," she replied. Then she was silent, watching the lights on the TV. "But if something like that happened nearby, I'd want you to go help," she finally said.

"Yeah," David said. "I could. I mean, I should." He sat thinking of the concept. Using his ability, no, *power to fly*, to help other people. He never had envisioned himself to be a superhero. Sure, there were times he'd seen things like this and pictured himself swooping in to save the day, but that well pounded in concern over being caught always drove the thoughts away. Maybe it is time. He looked at Amy.

"I'll need a cape," he deadpanned.

Amy rolled her eyes at him. "Think about it," she said, flipping a button on the remote. "Let's watch the movie."

During the movie David daydreamed about pulling the people up from the crashed bus, rescuing kittens from trees, or children from burning buildings. He held Amy tight against him. Amy, he thought. *My Amy, who wants me to save people.* He kissed the top of her head.

"What's that for?" she asked, looking up at him.

"I was just using one of my super-powers."

"One of your super-powers?" she asked, eyes twinkling. "You have more?"

"Yes," he gave her an exaggeratedly lewd grin. "My x-ray vision." He eyed her up and down.

Amy put her arms around his neck and pushed him down on the futon. It was a good movie.

*

Three weeks later, David and Amy were back home in Aston for the semester break from college. Amy had asked David to ask his parents to have her over for dinner. They were delighted to do that. They were certain it was going to be to announce their plans to get married. Why else would Amy ask to be invited over? But, after they thought about how Amy had seemed so satisfied in school, and her eagerness to be a nurse had increased, they didn't think marriage was appropriate for this period in their lives. They were only college freshmen, so it couldn't be that. Maybe she's pregnant, Mark had said. Margaret looked at him. Let's hope not, she told him. Secretly, she smiled at the idea.

Amy had brought up the subject of David using his "power" a couple times since that first mention. David had continued to be in agreement, but wanted to talk to his parents about it first. While he was now an adult, this decision affected everyone. Amy wanted to be in on the discussion with them and had him make the dinner arrangements.

The dinner was a very pleasant affair. Everyone was dressed in holiday attire and the mood was light. Mark and Margaret were expecting some announcement, or at the very least, some explanation. The way David had suggested the dinner implied something like that would take place.

After dinner, they remained at the table talking. Mark poured himself and Margaret a glass of wine, while David and Amy watched in envy. They wanted a glass too, but being underage, they knew they wouldn't get one. The Andersons were sticklers over things like that. They nursed their water.

"So," Mark said, sipping from his long-stemmed glass. "It seemed like there was a purpose for this dinner. Is there something we should know?"

After he said it, Mark got a glance from his wife. He knew what it meant. She thought what he said came out too much like "so, are you pregnant?"

"Yes, sort of," Amy started.

She didn't look at David as she may have, if looking for support to say something like "I'm pregnant". For that, Mark and Margaret felt a pang of relief. It must be something else.

"David and I have been talking about his ability to fly," she continued.

"Power," David interjected. *"Power to fly."*

"Power," Amy said, sticking her tongue out at David. "Anyway, we're thinking he should use his... power, to do things. You know, help other people." She left the thought hanging in the air, waiting for them to respond.

Mark and Margaret were quiet. They looked at each other. Thoughts of babies were gone. This was kind of a surprise. The years of concern over David's flying were now evaporating and any previous thoughts on how he'd handle his flying could be considered.

"Well. Wow. Didn't see that coming," Mark said.

"Mr. and Mrs. Anderson, I know you've always been concerned over David being caught. Taken away. I was always scared of that, too. Things are different now. You know... different."

Mark and Margaret looked at David, as if signaling him to speak.

"Yeah. I think I should use my flying to help out other people where I can," he said. "I still want to stay anonymous, of course, but I think we can figure a way to do that."

There was silence again. Margaret took a long pull on her glass of wine. Mark instinctively refilled her glass. David and Amy were even more envious now.

"So, what are you thinking?" Margaret piped up.

They told his parents of the night they saw the bus crash. It was that sort of thing, they said, doing the kinds of things David could do easily, where normal human efforts that were required would be too huge and too time-consuming to where lives were at risk. Being able to go where other people couldn't easily get to.

John Baraniak

David could tell he was winning them over on the idea. Amy would add comments and they liked the way she wanted to help other people. In the end, Mark and Margaret agreed it was a good idea. David noticing his father smiling throughout the discussion and knew he had thought of this many times before. That's probably why he had always been supportive of his flying.

Mark nodded slowly. "You're right," he said. "It is a power. It's a gift. You should use it."

Amy stuck her tongue out at David again. "See!" she said.

"But, you still have to be careful not to get... found out," Margaret said. *'Found out'* was a much better way of thinking of it than being *'caught'*.

"We'll figure something out," David said. He picked up his water glass in a toast. "To saving the world," he said.

"Oh, lord, we've created a monster," Amy laughed as she clinked glasses.

"I'll need a cape, you know," David smirked.

"And a cool name," his father added. "The Kite Fairy won't do." They all laughed.

"Oh, come on," Margaret said, remaining more serious than the others. "I'm just wondering how you'll be able to be an accountant, or have any regular job, and still be a superhero. Couldn't this take you away from work sometimes? People will wonder. And, how will they, the authorities, get a hold of you when they want you, if you still want to be anonymous?"

"I guess we still have wrinkles to work out," David said.

"To saving the world," Mark said, raising his glass. He noticed Margaret was actually smiling. It was a slight smile, but a smile none-the-less.

Chapter 36

C. Randall Whiting read the report a second time. He was familiar with most of Wisconsin, especially the northeast corner, but not so much the western side. In his many different duties with the Federal Bureau of Investigation, he'd had opportunities to visit Milwaukee, Madison, and Green Bay. That was years ago. He wasn't familiar with Eau Claire. In fact, he realized he was so unfamiliar with the state, that he'd never heard of virtually any of the towns in that state until the flying guy issue came up.

His initial anger over getting the information so far after the fact was subsiding, as he looked at the blotter from two months ago that was attached to the report that had been sent to the Director. It had originally gone to Ed Gorman from the Liaison Agent Arthur Johnston. Gorman, for reasons unknown to Agent Whiting, had sat on the document. It wasn't until another meeting on a totally different subject that he gave it to him. He was then asked what the status of the Flying Guy search was. All Agent Whiting could tell him was that Agent Johnston was continuing to monitor the situation and anything that came up, came to them in these types of reports. There were no other reports covering this and he took the opportunity to slide in a sideways scolding of the Director for not forwarding this one to him quicker. He was one of very few people who could get away with that. Ed Gorman claimed to have been extremely busy on other things and ended up apologizing to Whiting.

Whiting thought about the information from the Eau Claire Police Department. A woman had called 911 and reported seeing the same type of flying apparition as was common in Aston, the home base of the other sightings. The flying person she saw was coasting down a river behind her home. He wondered what the connection to water was. He pictured the scene going down a river. He'd been on a few canoe trips over the years and he had a clear picture of what the scenery would be. It's probably aesthetically pretty, he determined, so maybe it was just a matter of the flyer liking nature. He had his notebook open to where he jotted down his private thoughts and he wrote on a page: NATURE LOVER? SEEMS TO LIKE RIVERS. He thought about it more. Many of the previous reports indicated the flyer was seen over wooded areas, often just seeming to be goofing around. Gorman and Agent Johnston were in agreement on the general age of their quarry, figuring it was a teenager. Agent Whiting was thinking about seventeen, maybe eighteen years old. Usually kids that age aren't into things like tree-hugging, he almost snickered, they're stuck to their electronic devices. When he thought electronic devices, it reminded him that perhaps he should do some electronic surveillance. If there were two flyers, which seemed to be a definite possibility now, there was added incentive to get his hands on them. Or, at least one of them.

Agent Whiting sat quietly in his huge, sterile office. No sound filtered in, so he was alone with his thoughts. He liked to sit alone, preferably in the dark, when he formulated his plans. He was thinking of what he would do if, no, *when*, the flyer or flyers were caught. Tops on the list was to figure out how they fly. No one had ever described the flyer as having wings, or even of flapping his arms. Why doesn't gravity affect them? But, he considered, they have to walk around sometime. They must be on the ground like anyone else when they're not up in the air. It's not like they'd have a nest. He shook his head momentarily to clear out that thought. No. We've determined whoever this is, is most likely an otherwise normal human, who just for some undetermined reason can become airborne.

He'd want to do some sort of testing. Medical tests. Perhaps there was a medical reason for this strange power. He wondered if the flyer could be cloned. Or bred. He felt almost lightheaded considering the ideas. Above all that, at the immediate time, though, he wanted this kept secret. He realized now, since this has been happening for years, that perhaps he could have enlisted other help. He could have used more of the Bureau's assets to find the flyer. Maybe he'd already have him. Either way, it was becoming evident other people would need to be involved. It would have to be done discreetly. He certainly didn't want others to think that C. Randall Whiting believed in witches and people who can fly.

For electronic surveillance, he'd have to get help from the National Security Agency, the NSA. They were the proprietors of the equipment used to do phone taps, computer hacking and monitoring, satellite imagery, and virtually every other form of spying on someone's life. If the flyer was talking with someone about flying while on an electronic device, they could hone in on them. Even C. Randall Whiting was afraid of the NSA. On the other hand, he considered, they were now going to be my new best friends. *I'll find out what they're capable of.*

Agent Whiting picked up his phone and punched one button. That was all he needed to do to get through to the Director. His assistant, Carol came on the line almost immediately.

"Good morning, Agent Whiting," she said when she answered.

"Hello, Carol. How are you?"

"I'm fine," she said. "Are you looking for the Director?"

"Yes. Can you see if he has a moment?"

"On the phone or are you coming up?" she asked.

"Phone. Thanks." Agent Whiting didn't like small-talk.

Carol put his call through and after almost a minute of waiting, Ed Gorman picked up.

"Randy," he greeted him. "What can I do for you?" He seemed distracted. The tone was too curt, like he was being interrupted.

"Sir, I'd like to do a low level electronic watch on the Flying Guy."

"You found him?" The Director perked up.

"No, sir. I want to do a blanket on the city of Aston to see what we might get." A *blanket* was the commonly used term for a mass surveillance effort. It basically entailed tapping all the phones in an area and monitoring all computers, with the emphasis on email messages and social website contact. The NSA supercomputers made this look like child's play. They could select just the calls that contained certain words, out of the millions of calls made. They would simply tap every phone, all at the same time, and let the computer do the work to filter to what was needed.

"How do you think that will somehow net the Flying Guy?" the Director asked him. He knew how the system worked and couldn't think of anything off the top of his head that could somehow track a flying person. This was electronic spying. A thought occurred to him and he asked Randy another question before he had time to answer. "Can this guy be picked up on radar?"

"No. He's too small. Radar picks up objects about the size of small aircraft, hang gliders, that sized things. If we caught him in the air, carrying a cellphone, we could track him with cellphone towers. But, that's a shot in the dark."

"Yeah. I suppose. So what type of surveillance are you thinking and what do you need?"

"Well, sir," Randy started, "I want to get a NSA analyst assigned to me. We'll need one that has top security clearance, so that the subject matter remains confidential."

"Ask the Deputy Director (DD) of the NSA for that," Ed told him. "He doesn't pass things on to his director. I don't want him to know about our guy. It'll stay quiet then."

"Thank you, sir. I fully agree with that. I'll then have a blanket done. I'm thinking we'd have such search parameters as the words flying, sky, airflow, weather, and other similar terms that someone flying might use in conversation. I'll review all of the reports to get other ideas and work on that more. Then maybe a parameter also by age. I'll narrow the initial phone tap field to teenagers, if that's possible. Maybe just at first, to see what we get and then widen that if nothing pops. We're still thinking this is a younger kid."

"Okay. Sounds logical," the Director said. "Similar parameters I assume on the computer system searches?"

"Yes, sir. I'm holding off on satellite usage. They can do the infra-red scans, but we can't do that unless we can catch him flying in real time and also be lucky enough to have a satellite overhead at the exact same time. That would require other people knowing to watch for a flying person. We don't need them knowing that. Perhaps at some point down the line that could be useful, but not now. So, that'll be it."

"You got it. Let the NSA DD know that this has my approval and is hush-hush. He's a good guy. He'll help you out."

"Thank you, sir," Agent Whiting said.

"Keep me posted," the Director told him and disconnected.

*

Agent Whiting visited the Deputy Director of the NSA personally to make his requests. They both had secondary offices located in the same huge intelligence agency building where the analysts did their work. This would work out well he thought, as he would also be able to meet the designated analyst and lay out everything he was looking for. He could get a feel for the analyst's reliability at the same time.

When he got on the elevator to go back to his office more than three hours later, he was feeling confident, almost cocky, that the plan he had just put into place would net something.

"Yes, indeed," he said to himself aloud, alone in the elevator. He had visions of cloning the flying guy and having a network of flying FBI agents. Things would definitely be interesting then, he was sure. He thought for a moment of the current move toward using drones for covert spying. It would be even better with a live FBI agent to hover where the drones might otherwise go. Hell, the entire United States military could become airborne.

"Yes, indeed," he said again when the door clanged open.

Chapter 37

All agents with the Federal Bureau of Investigation, from the new recruits right up to the Director, were required to take an annual physical fitness test. The lower echelons, who were mainly in the field, needed to pass the rigorous tests with at least a minimum score that had been set based on what an agent was expected to be able to do as part of their individual jobs in the Bureau. The higher level agents, who were in reality nothing more than the equivalent of business managers in the real world and who sat at a desk most of the time, had somewhat more lenient guidelines. No one was going to tell the Director he was out of shape and had failed a test. The higher the rank, the lower the required score.

At the same time as the physical tests were done, agents were also required to do weapons training and qualifications. The Bureau issued a standard firearm, a .45 caliber pistol, and it was a requirement that they pass the test on target shooting. This was the part most agents liked.

Agent Arthur Johnston had just finished his weapons test. While he had never had the opportunity, thankfully he had always thought, to use his weapon in the line of duty, he was diligent in staying proficient as a marksman. His score on the firearms test was not too far off the record score for all agents. Artie was pretty pleased over that fact. He figured someday that may come in handy.

Now, he set his sights on also getting a respectable score on his physical fitness test. There were a number of different individual components to this test. There was an obstacle course where the agents were timed for completion. They had a strength test where they had to carry the equivalent of the weight of an average person, for a certain distance, in a prescribed period of time. The test that everyone trained most for, the one that was also the easiest to train for, was the twenty five mile run. Many of the agents,

234

certainly a higher percentage than in the general population, were avid runners. They knew by running regularly that they stayed in good enough physical shape to pass the other tests. They also knew they'd be in shape as needed for their jobs. Sure, there were slackers just like anywhere else, but by and large, the vast majority of the FBI force took physical fitness seriously.

Artie was in the category of those who took it seriously. He liked to work out and stay fit for the job. Based on his position within the Bureau, he could have fallen in with those who were able to get by with lower scores. But, he wasn't going to let his desk job turn him into a fat-body. That was the name the physically fit agents gave to the ones who weren't fit. Fat-bodies gave the Bureau a bad image.

The weather was exceptionally mild for an early spring in the Washington D.C. area, and after his weapons test Artie took the opportunity to go out for a run. He wanted to stretch out a bit before doing the official run the next day. He wasn't alone. The huge FBI training ground included miles of running trails and on most days it was crowded with runners. Today was one of those days. Many of the agents that were out were in the same position as Artie in the testing schedule.

Artie fell in with a group of regulars. He knew two of the four agents and was introduced to the others. FBI agents were a tight knit group and while they may have just met, they had heard of each other. They bantered back and forth as they ran the paved trail. Like any group of hardened law enforcement professionals, tales of their own exploits were the main subject and those tales became exaggerated. They had a good laugh, exchanging wild stories. They all knew the others were embellishing their stories and tried to outdo them.

As they rounded a curve in the trail, they came upon the remains of a snowbank that had melted onto the pavement. The snowbank was small and one of the few still left standing. It created a huge puddle on the trail that required running through soggy wet grass to avoid. The leading agent on the run saw the puddle at the last minute and took a giant leap left to avoid it. The grass was slippery and when he came down, his foot went sideways, his momentum sending him sprawling to the ground. He threw a spray of water up when he hit.

Artie was right behind him and hadn't seen the puddle coming either. When the man in front went down and he saw the water, he instinctively tried to jump it also. He hooked his foot on the already soaked agent on the ground and fell over him. He got his hands out in front of himself, but they connected with the slippery grass and slid sideways. The pain in his left wrist was immediate and excruciating. He only had a split second to experience the pain, as his head slammed against the corner of the paved path. He saw a blinding white light and then nothing. His last thought as he faded to darkness was that the sound he heard, a dull "thuck" from his head hitting, was not good.

*

When he woke up two days later in the Walter Reed Hospital, he had a blinding headache. He had to keep his eyes closed to keep the sharp stabs of light from making his head feel like it would pop. He drifted between consciousness and semi-consciousness for hours, and it took him awhile to realize other parts of him besides his head had sustained some damage in the fall. He squinted to see the large cast on his left arm. He remembered that part. His body was sore all over, but when he squirmed to assess other possible wounds, he was at least happy to have feeling in all of his extremities. That was a relief.

The doctor making the rounds that evening saw that he had regained consciousness, and filled him in on his medical status. He had a several abrasions and contusions, a severely broken wrist, and a concussion. They had done MRIs and CAT-scans, and had found no internal bleeding around his brain. However, the fact that he was in a coma for two days was a cause for concern. He'd remain in the hospital until they were comfortable he was capable of leaving.

Artie found out later when a Bureau approved doctor examined him, that he would be laid up and off work for a minimum of thirty days, longer if needed. He was demoralized. If he had been hurt in the line of duty, it wouldn't be so bad. But he had simply fallen while running on the Bureau's exercise ground. He felt embarrassed. What would the other agents think? He thought about that often in the first few days of what he considered his incarceration in the hospital.

Days later, when he was comfortably at home, he called his immediate supervisor at the Bureau, Sandra Fowling. Agent Fowling had temporarily replaced Herb Foster as Deputy Director. Herb had his own health concerns and was thought to be ready to retire. His replacement was a no-nonsense taskmaster, who most thought was simply overcompensating for her gender. Artie liked Agent Fowling though, and they got along well. He had discovered early on that she was not interested in the politics or side talk that went on, and simply did the job that needed to be done. She had Artie prepare a list of what he'd need to have covered in his absence and sent the replacement agent to Artie's house to have them go over the information.

Despite the medication for his headaches, Artie felt twinges of pain from the light outside when he showed his replacement into his living room. He was learning his recuperation just might take the thirty days and then some.

"Agent Jance, I presume?" he said offering a hand to the big man standing in the doorway.

"Yes, sir. Thanks for seeing me so soon," the man said.

He didn't sound happy and Artie wondered if he was perturbed that he had to come all the way out to his apartment building on the outskirts of Arlington to get up to date on what his new functions would be. It didn't matter. Either way, Artie wished he could have gone into the office to do this, regardless of the doctor's orders and his condition. He directed Agent Jance into his dining room, and to a seat next to where he'd been sitting while reviewing what he was to cover with him.

The table had a row of neatly stacked papers spread across it. Each stack was for one of the many individual issues Artie had been working on. There was more paperwork to back up each of these summarizations, but he figured this would suffice.

The two men exchanged small-talk that centered on their respective backgrounds and careers. Agent Jance was a ten-year veteran of the Bureau, with almost all of that time spent in the field as a Special Agent in the Major Crime Division, primarily working on cases involving organized crime murders. He liked that work, he said, and had hoped to stay in that arena. Being pulled away to be a temporary Regional Liaison had been presented to him as a reward for excelling in what he was doing, but was to him instead, a blow to his career ambitions. He was hoping this assignment would be short and uneventful.

Artie found himself liking Agent Jance. He was a hands-on crime investigator. While Artie liked what he himself did, he had a great respect and admiration for these guys. His own work in the field had been a very rewarding experience. While Jance was a bit sour-grapes over the move, he figured he'd be more than capable of filling in for him for a while. After a good fifteen minutes of feeling each other out, they got to work going through the paperwork and issues.

Agent Jance listened closely and appeared genuinely interested in the subject matter they covered. He asked good questions and Artie was impressed with his insight on many of the cases he'd now be working on. This wasn't the detective work he was used to, but he gave the impression he'd do his best to make the effort to cover all the bases.

Artie held off on covering the Flying Guy with Agent Jance. He was sure Agent C. Randall Whiting wouldn't want him to be discussing that with a temporary replacement. Since he anticipated being back to work in a month's time, he figured the subject wouldn't come up anyway. What he did do along the lines of wanting to keep track of this unusual issue, was to ask Agent Jance to just pay particular attention to anything happening in the Aston, Wisconsin area. He didn't tell him anything about the flyer and tried to leave the impression that what he was watching for was outside of Jance's need-to-know. He was to just advise Artie of anything happening there, anything at all – no matter how unusual.

Agent Jance nodded, as if strange events and secrecy were all in a day's work. Artie figured it probably was for him and was glad he didn't question anything further.

After Jance left, Artie called into the Bureau and asked for C. Randall Whiting. When he had him on the phone, he explained what had happened to him and that he was off for medical reasons for at least thirty days. He advised Agent Whiting of how he'd left the subject of watching for the Flying Guy with Agent Jance. Agent Whiting was appreciative of Artie having simply told his replacement of the need to watch for unusual events, while not telling him specifically what to watch for. He asked Artie to continue to advise him if and when the flyer was seen. When Artie hung up, he realized he had become comfortable dealing with Agent Whiting. *Still,* he thought, *I get a weird feeling around him.*

*

Agent Jance did an excellent job of filling Artie's shoes while he was gone. Even though he was used to more action and less desk-work, he managed to stay interested and focused. He handled everything as Artie had wished, with a minimum of calls to him for help.

Artie asked on a few occasions if there was anything from Aston, Wisconsin. Agent Jance told him he had been paying extra attention to Aston, being sure to read the newspaper and blotters closer than he otherwise did for the other municipalities. He mentioned the ongoing problem the area had with drug busts, but his assessment was that the drugs were just normal activity by small town users. Nothing else jumped out at him. He didn't think police reports of people saying they saw unidentified flying things was what Artie was looking for, so never mentioned those. The newspaper even played it up as something humorous and non-threatening.

Artie thanked Agent Jance each time and reminded him to be sure to file all of the data he had been receiving. He hoped he'd be able to go back and review the information at some point after his return.

Chapter 38

Bernie Fredder found a message on his desk the same day Artie had first met with Agent Jance. It said to please call FBI Agent Arthur Johnston at his earliest possible convenience. Agent Artie must have used that phrase, he thought, as his assistant Marsha didn't talk like that.

He called the number given, which was different than the number on Artie's business card. When Artie answered, he told him it was his cellphone and to use that for the immediate future if he needed to reach him. He explained why. Bernie offered his sympathies over Artie's physical condition and assured him he'd call him on his cell if needed. After thinking on why Artie would want that, he came to the conclusion he probably wouldn't be calling at all if something came up on the Flying Guy. Maybe Artie's replacement would miss the information if there was any that went through the normal channels. Or at the very least, Bernie could say he lost the phone number. The "only call me on my cell" request gave him that bad feeling again about what the FBI wanted.

Chapter 39

Besides tracking the Flying Guy, C. Randall Whiting had numerous other higher profile issues he was involved in. Most of those other issues were more immediate and time consuming. With no new reports coming from Agent Johnston or his replacement, Agent Jance, Whiting had to put the flying guy on the back burner. He didn't completely forget about it, though. Once each week, he contacted his assigned NSA analyst for an update on how the blanket search was progressing in Aston.

The analyst indicated the system was working as required, but that at some point in the near future they should meet to discuss how they would be able to review the data the surveillance had pulled up. The analyst indicated there was a huge amount of communication data being netted by the programs, even with the parameters used to narrow the search. Nothing exactly matched those parameters, so he suggested adjusting what they were looking for. Agent Whiting agreed, making slight adjustments. All of this information would continue to be stored in the computer system, in a secured area that only the analyst could get to. Agent Whiting told him to continue to work the blanket program as redefined and that he'd be in touch soon.

He hoped to get to it sooner, but it was months later before he had the opportunity.

Chapter 40

Even at this time of day, the sidewalk felt like it was putting out over a hundred degrees, and the downtown crowd trudging into work that morning seemed to be slowed by the heat. They dragged themselves from comfortable cars into office buildings to start their work days.

Bernie had to push his way through the shuffling foot traffic of the back parking lot to get into the Daily Sentinel building. Once inside the door, he was welcomed by the coolness the air-conditioning provided in contrast to outside. He took a moment to stand under the vent to feel the relief. He pushed the door open leading to the reporters den and was met by the din of loud voices on telephones and in over the cube wall conversations.

"Hi, Billie," Bernie said as he passed one of the sports writers. "Who's on first?"

"What's for lunch?" came the grouchy reply. Their normal greeting.

After the usual early morning hellos, Bernie was at his desk turning on his computer and making notes on what his schedule would be for the day. Every day was different, although there were always certain things that needed to be done. He had one story nearly finished and it had to be in by the next day to make the Sunday edition. He pulled the story up on his screen and at the same time hit the play button on his phone voicemail. He had eight messages.

The first three were internal, reminding him of a meeting, even though he had also been emailed on it, an after work party, that he'd also been emailed on, and the usual reminder about the upcoming department meeting, which should have been emailed. Bernie deleted all of them.

Message four was from what sounded like a drunken man claiming to have seen the flying man following him around. The man didn't leave a number, which was probably just as well. Delete.

Bernie sat up straighter, more alert, when he retrieved the next message. It sounded like it could be a worthwhile call right from the start. He didn't feel the urgency to delete it right away.

"Yes, hi," the message began. "My name is Andrew Cook. I read in the paper some of your articles on the flying man." There was a bit of a pause, and Bernie made sure he had a pen ready to write, anticipating what may be coming.

"I saw the guy flying around this morning," the voice continued. "It was the darndest thing I ever saw. And I thought maybe you'd like to know about it."

I would, Bernie thought. *Give me a phone number.* This guy sounded sane. And then the guy left his phone number.

"Anyway, my name is Andrew Cook," he said again before disconnecting.

Bernie wrote it down with the usual anticipation over another flying man lead. Something about this one, though, felt more legitimate than the previous call and many others that never panned out. He collected the rest of his messages, then went back to this one. He forgot for a moment about his Sunday story sitting on his computer screen. That could wait.

He punched the number in his cellphone, bypassing the newspaper phone system. He got better reception this way.

"Hello?" a cheerful voice answered.

"Hello," Bernie said. "Is this Andrew Cook?"

"Yes, it is," was the reply. "Who's this?"

"Hi, Mr. Cook. This is Bernie Fredder, from the Sentinel. You left me a message." He didn't want to do the talking. He was brief in his introduction to let Mr. Cook establish his legitimacy.

"Please, call me Andy," the man said, both friendly and professional in his manner. There was a moment of silence in which he realized he was to continue. "I've read your articles and when I saw the guy, I thought I'd let you know."

"What did you see, Mr. Cook? I'm sorry. Andy," Bernie said. He started making some notes, and as Andy Cook explained what he saw, Bernie found himself sitting up even straighter, eagerly jotting down what he told him.

"Mr. Cook, umm Andy," Bernie almost tripped over his tongue, "can we meet? Today?"

Andy Cook agreed and gave him directions in elaborate detail. His place where they'd meet was about seventy miles north, and it sounded like it was in a remote forested area. Bernie considered the remoteness as he closed out the computer with the article he was supposed to finish, and instead pulled up his favorite map-finder website. He plugged in the address and got pretty much the exact same driving instructions that Andy gave him. He printed a map, double checked the route, highlighted it in yellow, and checked his watch. He had enough time without having to rush. He headed out.

"Hey, Dan," Bernie said, leaning into the editor's office as he passed by. "I have to go see a guy out past Laona about the Flying Guy story. He said he saw him and this story sounds better than the other ones."

"How long you be gone?" Dan asked.

"Most of the day," Bernie replied. "I'm not sure when I'll be back. It's a ways away."

"Will your article for Sunday be done?" Dan had to make sure. "And are you still doing the story on the west-side housing thing?"

"Yes and yes. I'll fill in everything when I get back."

"Okay. Have at it," Dan dismissed him with a wave. Dan was good that way. He trusted his reporter's instincts, and even better, he had good enough instincts of his own to sense there was something behind the flying man mystery.

*

Bernie stopped at a Marathon station, filled his tank with gas, grabbed a bag of sunflower seeds to snack on and a quart of cold orange juice, and was soon on his way heading north. He wouldn't need the directions for a while yet, so he rolled down the window for some air flow, turned up the radio, and thought about what Andy had told him. He tossed seed shells out as he drove.

The directions he was given, and map he'd printed, both proved accurate, and after only one small wrong turn, Bernie found himself turning into the narrow gravel road leading to Andy Cook's cabin. It was definitely a secluded backwoods retreat. Bernie had driven the last three miles or so without seeing a single house. If the map and handwritten directions hadn't specifically indicated he was supposed to be in the middle of nowhere, he would have turned back after bouncing down the rutted road just off County TT.

The cabin was rustic, yet well cared for. The clearing it sat on wasn't a well mowed lawn, but still it showed some effort was put into keeping it aesthetically pleasing. Bernie's first impression, as he saw it from a distance, was that he'd probably be met by a field of broken down appliances and lawn mowers. Seeing wash machines would have burst his bubble of hope that this was a good lead. He was relieved that there was no junk to greet him, as it had been a long drive to get here.

Instead, the door of the cabin opened and a man who had to be Andy Cook came towards Bernie's car. Bernie pulled his car in next to a little Subaru. Also a relief, Bernie thought, that it wasn't a rusty old pickup. He stepped out of his car.

"Bernie Fredder, I presume?" was the greeting, along with an offered handshake.

"Yup. And you'd be Andy Cook?" They shook hands.

Bernie sized him up, as he did with every lead he had for a story. What you saw is usually what you got. Hopefully, Andy wouldn't disappoint. He was about fifty-five or so and in good shape. He was short, maybe five eight, and wiry. He looked like he stayed physically active. He had a pair of high-top hiking boots, with dark socks peeking out the top. He wore a pair of green cargo shorts with numerous pockets and a light yellow tee shirt. The clothes were clean. That's a good sign. He had short salt and pepper hair and was clean shaven. Bernie was happy that he didn't look like some hermit backwoodsman.

"Boy," Bernie chuckled, "you weren't kidding about being well off the beaten path!"

"Yeah," Andy smiled, as he led Bernie in the direction of the cabin. "It's pretty secluded up here. I like it. Wouldn't have it any other way."

"Nice cabin," Bernie noticed.

"It is. I don't get a lot of company, as you may have guessed, so pardon any mess you see."

Andy led him into the cabin. Contrary to what that comment may have led him to expect, the interior of the cabin was anything but messy. It was larger than what the exterior appeared and very clean. The walls were wood logs, the opposite side of the outside logs. There was a good sized stone fireplace and a neat stack of logs nearby. The furniture was sparse, but in good condition, if not expensive looking. It wasn't at all run down. Bernie was feeling good about that.

"Get you something to drink?" Andy asked as he went to the kitchen area. "I have juice, soda, water, beer? It's all cold."

He opened the fridge and Bernie noticed it was well stocked with food. It looked like mostly fruits and vegetables and juices. There were a few two-liter bottles of what looked like ginger ale and a jug of milk, and a couple bottles of beer. He always checked out other people's dietary habits.

"A cold beer would be great," Bernie replied as he checked his watch. It was just before noon, but he was hot and the orange juice he had on the way up had been warm by the time he got here. A cold beer would be good right now.

Andy pulled two beers out, opened a drawer to get a bottle opener, cracked them open and handed one to Bernie.

"Here's to the guy who can fly," Andy said, holding up his bottle in a toast. He had an easy smile."The guy who can fly," Bernie echoed as he toasted in reply. *Nice guy*, he thought to himself. *So far, so good.*

They both took a long, slow pull on their bottles, savoring the icy beer in a moment of silence. Bernie was feeling good about being here and hearing more of Andy's story. What he'd told him on the phone was just the very short abbreviated version, and he was eager for details. Andy must have been reading his mind.

"Come on outside and I'll tell you what I saw," he said, gesturing for the door. He held it open and they stepped back outside. They started walking toward the water.

"Sure is beautiful here," Bernie said, taking in the surrounding. The woods were thick, with a mix of towering evergreens and mature maple trees. Everything was lush and green. The grassy area wasn't mowed, but was the only thing growing in the area up to the edge of what looked to be a small lake. They followed a worn path and stopped near the bank. There was a lone wooden Adirondack chair set next to a small fire pit, where a tumbled stack of wood lay off to one side. A shed nearby revealed a newer model All-Terrain Vehicle.

"I own from that big tree right there," Andy said, pointing, "right out to the lake over there." His arm swung in the other direction. "And then from there, back to that old barn foundation you passed on the way in."

"Wow," Bernie replied. "That's a chunk of land." Andy obviously had some money. The barn foundation was an easy two miles back. This was some serious acreage.

As if sensing he should explain, Andy went on. He told how he had inherited the land from his parents. He retired two years ago just after his wife had died. There was still a house in Milwaukee that was his office and official residence, but this is where he spent most of his time now. He'd been a dentist in his working years and was now just taking it easy. He liked being outdoors, and even though it had taken some getting used to, being alone in the wilderness suited him just fine. He didn't have any children, so he had no real reasons for being back in civilization.

"I hope someday to find my own piece of happiness," Bernie said, more to himself than to Andy, he realized.

They both took another long drink on their beers while they soaked in the serenity of the setting. The bay was long and narrow, although it widened where they stood at the furthest point inland. The forest surrounded the inlet all the way around. As far as Bernie could tell, there were no other clearings on this water than this one.

"Well," Andy began, "I'll tell you right from the beginning."

Bernie nursed the remainder of his beer and listened intently as Andy told of the events of that morning. He was soon smiling, nodding his head as he wrote some notes, and quite certain it wasn't the beer making him feel so warm and fuzzy. He jotted down as much as he could as the story unfolded.

"I'm an early riser," Andy began. "I'm usually up with the sun, about five thirty or so. I go to bed when it sets, so it's easy to get up. I brewed a pot of coffee and had a mug while I walked out to about right where we are. It's really beautiful in the morning. There's mist and fog in thick patches here and up further by the bay. The water is still and smooth as glass. There's a couple pairs of loons that live here and I like to watch them in the morning. Other than that, there wasn't anything else moving."

"I was looking down to the opening to the lake, when I noticed something flying along the trees. Right over there." He pointed. "It was big, and my first thought it was maybe an eagle or heron. They're pretty big up here. I've seen eagles I swear could pick me up. But, this thing didn't have wings. As it came in this direction, still along the tree line, it looked more like a missile. I didn't know what to make of it. When it got to about right there," he said, his hands continuing to mark the flight path, "I realized it was actually a man. Or woman, I suppose. But it looked human. Arms, legs, all black. It was wearing all black. Even on the head."

"I ducked back a bit, slowly, so as not to be noticed, and crouched behind these weeds." Andy motioned toward the brushy area just to the right of where they stood.

"How high up was he?" Bernie asked.

"About thirty feet," Andy said. "He came around the end of the bay here at about the same height on the first pass."

"He came by more than once?" Bernie asked.

"Oh, yeah," Andy smiled. "He cruised around a couple times. The first time, he was just slowly gliding by. Couldn't have been doing maybe fifteen to twenty miles an hour. Just… coasting. Sort of banked around the turns." He used his hand to describe the position. "He was prone, like this. Just like Superman flies. Arms out front."

"He didn't have a cape, did he?" Bernie had to ask.

"Nope," Andy chuckled. "No cape. No S on his chest."

Bernie wrote as much of the story as he could. Andy continued.

"When he came by, I thought he'd see me. Fortunately, I wasn't wearing this yellow shirt. I had an old gray sweatshirt, since I was going to do some yardwork later on. He came by about twenty yards from shore and so I got a pretty good look at him. He was all in black, and had what looked like a ski mask and either sunglasses or goggles. At first I thought, well maybe he's some sort of alien and those were his eyes, or maybe it was a spacesuit or something. I'm not used to seeing flying people so, you know…" He paused and took a sip of his beer and set the bottle on the arm of the chair.

"Anyway," he continued, "he went by and kept going down to the end. I thought he'd head out from there, but he banked again and came back. This time though, he came down lower. He couldn't have been more than two feet above the water. And here's a funny part. He seemed to be aiming for the patches of fog. He shot right through them. Weaving from one to another, working his way around again."

Bernie looked at him, quizzically. Andy provided more detail.

"At this time of morning, and when it's real still, like it was, there's lots of fog shrouding the bay. He weaved around a little to go through the thickest patches. He came by me again, and it seemed like he wasn't paying attention for anyone else, and I dunno, I suppose... what are the odds of being seen around here?"

"He didn't notice your cabin and this clearing?" Bernie inquired. He turned to look back, trying to see what the Flying Guy would have seen. From this position, the cabin was set back, but still potentially visible.

"I'm thinking maybe in the morning, since the sun comes up over there," Andy pointed east, on the other side of the trees behind the cabin, "and with the mist, maybe he missed it. Or maybe he expected smoke from the chimney and since there wasn't any, he felt safe. Anyway, it didn't phase him."

Bernie nodded his head, picturing a man in black soaring around the bay.

"One time," Andy went on, "he came to stop right in front of a larger, thick patch of mist. Just floated there, right in front of it."

"He stopped flying and just floated?" Bernie asked. "You mean levitated like there was no gravity?"

"Yup," Andy said, pointing. "Right about there. He stopped, and he turned from flying in a flat, prone position so it was almost like he was sitting in the air. Sort of eyeing up the patch of fog."

"Wow. And then what'd he do?" Bernie was picturing it. It was almost as he could see it happening himself.

"This is another funny part," Andy explained, "and this is when I stopped feeling scared. At first I was a little scared, but after a while I was just... kind of numb with amazement."

"He straightened up vertical, like he was standing, spread his arms and legs out, like this," he struck that pose, "then just zipped into the cloud of fog real quick. He came out the other side, stopped and turned around to see, at least I think it was to see the hole he poked through the fog. Like, if it had the shape of him or something. It sort of did, but the fog swirled all together."

"He was just playing around," Bernie said, more of a statement than a question.

"Yeah," Andy nodded. "And you know, I think that's all he was doing out here. Just goofing around. He looked like he was having fun."

Bernie looked out over the water, nodding. "Yeah, that would probably be fun."

"That's what I started thinking," Andy agreed. "How cool is it to be able to fly around like that?"

They stood silently for a short moment, both lost in their own imagination.

"Then what?" Bernie broke the silence, eager to hear more. He had his pen and pad at the ready. Andy Cook was telling a good tale. This was way more interesting than any other accounts he'd gotten.

"After he went through the fog, he slowly turned and headed back out the mouth of the bay. I thought he'd leave again, but no. He turned again. But that time, he went up about fifty yards, and here it looked like he stopped, then banked back on the other side and back down to just above the water."

Bernie's eyes followed the path.

"This time he was going faster though," Andy said. "A lot faster. He was screaming along the water. If I had to guess, I'd say he was doing fifty to sixty miles an hour. He whipped around here and when he headed out over the bay again, he disappeared into just a small dot on the horizon. Then he was gone."

"That was it?" Bernie asked, not wanting the story to end.

"I thought so," Andy replied, "but no. He came back. I saw the black dot appear again and get bigger as it came. He was about ten feet above the water and really moving. I thought for a minutes he'd smack right into that tree. That one there." He pointed.

"What'd he do?" Bernie asked.

"This is where I knew for sure he was goofing around," Andy continued. "He came by here, sort of arched his back and went up. Not straight up, but in a, what do call it, loopty-loop?" His finger spun in a circle a couple times.

"Yeah, I think so," Bernie nodded.

"He just looped around in a big circle on his back, arms out to his side. He was about a hundred yards up, and came back around. Came down along the trees over there and did another fast circle around the bay."

"You're making this sound so real, I can picture it," Bernie told him.

"It was as real as you and me standing here now," Andy said. "If I hadn't come out of those bushes with all these scratches on my legs, I would think maybe I dreamt it." He showed Bernie the red scratches up the side of his left leg.

"Those look real to me," Bernie chuckled, nodding.

Another moment of silence ensued. Bernie stared at his notebook. He hadn't realized he'd filled so many pages with notes already.

Andy went on.

"He made another couple laps around the bay, all at good speed, then on the last one he just headed over those trees over there and was gone. I stayed here about ten more minutes, but he never returned. I was kind of hoping he'd come back."

They both stood looking out over the bay for a couple minutes. Then a question occurred to Bernie that he thought he should have asked sooner.

"You said you owned the land up to that tree over there," he pointed. "Who owns the land on the far side?"

"The county," Andy told him. "That whole side is part of the county forest. A part of it is for recreational use. There's a couple campsites out on the tip by the water. Really remote sites. You'd have hike a ways to get to them."

"Campsites?" Bernie's eyebrows went up, as if a lightbulb came on over his head. "That you have to hike to get to." It wasn't a question.

Silence again, but when Andy's eyes met his, they knew they were thinking the same thing.

"Or fly," they both said in unison.

Bernie checked his watch. So did Andy. It was almost two o'clock.

Bernie was thinking there was no way he was going to check out the campsites and then get to his office again today, and he considered the things he was supposed to get done. He'd have to call Dan to let him know and then Marsha, his co-worker, to cover for him.

Andy was thinking about whether they'd be able to hike to the campgrounds today, and then back out again. It was a long drive to the parking lot, and then a long walk from there.

They discussed their options and it was decided that Bernie would spend the night and they'd go in the morning. Bernie was willing to go now, but Andy knew they couldn't do it and convinced him otherwise.

There wasn't enough time to go and come back before it got really late and really dark. The odds were that if the guy they were looking for was indeed camping, he'd be there in the morning too. Bernie wasn't fully prepared for the trek and they needed some time to do some preparations. He reluctantly agreed to wait.

Bernie called Dan and explained. Dan put him through to Marsha who agreed, as she usually did, to finish the article for the Sunday paper, although there wasn't much to do to finish it, and to write up a summary of his notes on the concerns of west-side residents over a rise in home break-ins. He was so excited about what he was doing here, he didn't feel the usual pangs of guilt that he often felt when he dropped things on Marsha.

Andy was anxious for the adventure also. Since seeing the unbelievable spectacle that morning, he was eager to tell someone, and Bernie Fredder turned out to be a pretty decent guy, although he was definitely going to need some guidance through the woods. The hike wouldn't be easy.

Over the remaining beer and a couple large fish Andy had caught the day before, they laid out their plans for the next morning. They had found another chair and sat by the bay enjoying each other's company. The conversation continued on flying and they each fantasized about what they would do if they could fly. The tales got crazier by the minute.

Then Andy asked Bernie a question he hadn't thought of before.

"What are you going to do with him when you catch him? I mean, he doesn't seem to want to be caught."

"Hmmm," Bernie mused. It hadn't occurred to him what would happen if he found him. He never thought he would. "That's a good question. I guess I was always thinking on bringing everything out in the open. Now I'm not so sure."

"Like catching the big fish," Andy smiled. "Once you have it, you think of mounting it for a trophy. Or you can let it go. Either way, you caught it."

*

David had hugged the top of the trees when he returned from his morning cruise around the bay. Since he'd been there before a couple times, camping and hiking, he knew the terrain of forest canopy and where the campsites were hidden below. There weren't many breaks in this forest at all and there were none in the area of the campground. The road was a long way back and the trail didn't widen to form a gap. He had gotten to know the trees.

He slowed and hovered over the area he was going to descend through. The forest made many sounds, but he was listening for the human kind. Satisfied that no one was on the ground beneath him, he parted the leafy branches and slowly crept inside. It was early morning and the sun was up, but not too much light filtered into the thick woods. His eyes grew accustomed to the level of light and he wove through the branches, easing to the ground. He settled near the base of a big tree. He checked again to see if anyone was around, finding no one. He took off his mask and goggles.

This spot was forty yards from his and Amy's campsite. The other campsites were on the other side from here, and the trail was even further away in that direction.

David always made sure he got the most secluded of the sites, so that his coming and going would go unnoticed. They had company this time, with two other campsites being occupied. He thought they were far enough away not to be a concern.

He'd occasionally sneak up on Amy when he arrived by air. There were some great tricks he'd played on her over the years, but today he landed, and since she had been left alone at the site, he signaled his arrival by calling to her in advance of arriving.

"Hi. You're just in time," Amy greeted him.

"What's up?" he kissed her as he took her in his arms.

"You can start the fire. You're better at it than me."

David laid his mask and goggles on the chair nearby and set to work on getting a fire started. There were logs and newspapers nearby, and in minutes had a flame crackling in their fire-pit.

Amy busied herself fixing a pot of coffee to brew. They both loved sitting around a morning fire with a cup of freshly brewed camp coffee from their beat-up, old camping pot. It was rustic cookware, and they agreed that the inevitable abundance of coffee grounds that ended up in their cups just added to the camping experience. The words gritty and shitty had become synonymous when discussing this coffee.

"How was your excursion this morning?" she asked, sliding her chair closer to where he was sitting. They both faced the fire.

"Great. It was really pretty," he replied. "Lots of fog. But a lot of bugs, too." David had his head mask and goggles in hand. He leaned over to the table to pull off a paper towel, and began to clean the goggles.

"Are we going tomorrow morning?" Amy asked. She was okay with letting David have their first morning here to himself for going for a ride. He loved flying around mist shrouded lakes in the morning and looked forward to this part of camping more than the camping itself.

"Yup," he said. "Make sure you bring yours." He held up the goggles, then went back to picking bugs off. He finished and set them aside.

"You have some on your shirt too," Amy told him, pointing to his shoulders.

David looked at both shoulders and then stood to pull the shirt off. The bug spray he'd put on his arms before leaving the tent that morning wasn't keeping the mosquitos from zeroing in on his bare skin now. They swarmed near him. He hastily found a sweatshirt to pull on and settled back in his chair. He took Amy's hand, and they sat, quietly watching the coffee pot over the fire to see when it started to perk.

David was thinking of the fun he had coming around the bay. And the nagging feeling that he had been watched. He hadn't seen anyone, but his instinct about being seen had grown keen over the years. He'd have to be careful the next time.

The coffee finished brewing and he poured them both a steaming cup. They sat back, savoring the smell and the taste. After long minutes of silence, conversation started over the plans for the day. It was decided they'd hike the trail along the shore that circled around the western most side of the camping area. It would be an all day trek and they looked forward to it. If they had enough light left in the day when they returned, and if the other campers didn't get in the way, they planned a joint flight over the forest and maybe over the bay out to the lake when the sun was setting.

Chapter 41

Bernie and Andy developed a solid friendship in the afternoon they spent together. They didn't have a real lot in common, with the exception of being great conversationalists. They took great interest in each other's stories of their lives and past times. They shared more than a few laughs as they sat by the bay, and time flew by. The sun had set behind the trees, although it would be another hour or so before it dropped below the horizon. The trees cast long shadows over the water. The wind, which had been light all day, was non-existent now. The surface of the bay looked like a mirror, reflecting clear images of the lush, green trees.

"This has to be one of the most beautiful places I've ever been to," Bernie said, nodding his head slowly as he enjoyed the change in light.

"Yeah," Andy said. "I can see how my grandfather fell in love with it. Although he must have liked mosquitos." He swatted away one that had been buzzing by his ear. The lack of wind brought them out in droves to the two sitting in the open.

"They don't seem to like me," Bernie said. "Haven't got a bite yet."

"Maybe that gigantic bug will have a taste of you."

"What bug?" Bernie asked, looking around him, checking the space around his chair.

"That one," Andy pointed out.

Bernie saw what he was pointing at and his excitement came back. *There it is*, he thought. *There it is! The Flying Guy. I'm going to see it with my own eyes!*

"Come on. Let's get out of sight," Andy said, sliding off his chair to the weeds nearby.

Bernie was quick to follow him. Neither said a word, as they crouched in the tall reeds where Andy had been earlier in the day. Their attention was on the dark shape flying at the edge of the treetops. It didn't look like the flying man, they both thought. What it looked like was two flying men, one on top of the other. They watched the form cruise around the curve of the innermost edge of the bay, and go right by them about thirty yards overhead. They ducked down further, hoping not to be seen. The form moved slowly toward the mouth of the bay and the open lake.

"That was it? That was what you saw this morning?" Bernie asked in an excited whisper.

"Not exactly," Andy replied. "There was only one of them this morning." He paused. "There were two people there."

They watched in silence as the form disappeared into the diminishing light of dusk over the lake. They pictured the form they had seen pass over them.

Bernie spoke first. "That looked like some sort of harness contraption they were wearing."

"Yeah," Andy replied. "I think the guy on top was doing the flying and the one on the bottom was just along for the ride. The bottom one looked like they were suspended, you know, hanging from the other one."

"That's what I thought," Bernie agreed. "And the one on the bottom looked like a female, even with the mask on."

Andy just nodded in agreement. Their eyes were still gazing east to the lake, hoping the flying pair would come back. They sat for another fifteen minutes before assuming they weren't going to return, and then they worked their way out of the brushy reeds.

"I think our theory of the camping might be a good one," Andy stated. He checked his watch and waved for Bernie to follow him back to the cabin. "Let's crash now so we can get up early."

Bernie didn't fall asleep right away. The guest bed was pleasingly comfortable, but his mind wasn't relaxing. He was excited for not only seeing the flying man himself for the first time, but even more thrilled to see that he had taken someone else up with him. Since the sightings came to his attention years ago, he had on more than a few occasions gazed at the sky and wondered what it was like to fly around freely, like a bird. He had grown to envy this man.

Seeing that the Flying Guy could take someone else along made Bernie want to find him even more. Forget the story, he thought. *I want a ride!*

Bernie was still asleep when Andy came in to shake him awake. He momentarily forgot where he was, and gave Andy a puzzled look as he sat up.

"Morning!" Andy cheerfully greeted him. "Want to go see if they show up again this morning?"

The cobwebs disappeared and Bernie remembered why he was here. He swung his legs off the bed.

"Yeah. Yeah!" he said, standing. "Let's give it a shot."

"Coffee's on. Come on in when you're ready," Andy told him. "There's a clean toothbrush and all the sundries you'll need in the bathroom. Make yourself decent."

Bernie thanked him and went to the bathroom to clean up. The previous day came back in a flood and he found himself rushing along. He finished and came out to the kitchen, and a hot cup of coffee. It smelled great and tasted even better. He was just about to slide onto a stool, but didn't have time to get settled.

"Let's go outside," Andy said, checking his watch. "It's about the same time as yesterday."

*

David and Amy snapped themselves into their harness. They went through the checklist to make sure all of the belts were attached and tight. They rose off the ground a couple feet and turned horizontal to their test position. They re-checked everything and then settled back to their feet. Amy handed David his mask and goggles, then slid hers on. Easing back into the horizontal, they did the final adjustments so that they were both comfortable and not being pinched. Satisfied that they were ready, they both instinctively looked around to be sure no one was watching and then they were off.

"Take me away, Davey," Amy said. She always loved the initial takeoff.

"Shall we sing?" David kidded her, knowing she'd say no.

"Only if you must."

Thankfully he didn't, and they were soon cruising about fifteen yards above the treetops in the general direction of the lake. The sun had just burst above the horizon of the big lake and was now a huge ball of glowing orange. They sped into it. When they reached the shore, David took them down toward the water. They settled at an altitude ten feet above the surface, going at about fifty miles an hour.

"We're not crossing, are we?" Amy asked him.

"Nope. Just about to turn around," he replied.

They eased into a long, wide turn, and were soon doing the same speed back toward shore. David aimed for the bay, slowing as he entered. It was pretty much the same as he had found it the previous morning. Fog shrouded the long cove and trees closed in around them. The air was still and cool.

He kept them to the right side at about fifteen feet up. Occasionally he'd swoop down to glide through a cloud of mist. He knew Amy enjoyed this as much as he did. Her arms were out to the side as if they were wings, steering David around the bay. They flew as a team. When she lowered an arm, he knew to turn in that direction.

This morning was a peaceful one. They coasted in slow, lazy circles around the water. Dipping into the mist, then up then back down again. The air was cool just above the water and they breathed it in deep, savoring it.

They didn't notice the two men in the tall reeds.

*

The flying duo was gone. Bernie and Andy came out of their hiding spot in the brush.

"That is just so cool!" Bernie said excitedly. Seeing the flying man taking someone else up again had him wanting even more to find the flying guy so he could maybe get a ride.

"We're going to have to move sort of quickly, I think," Andy said. "It's going to take us an hour or so to get to the campsites from here. I don't think they can pack up and leave in that time, but they might head out hiking or something.

Bernie checked his watch. It was barely after six o'clock. He wasn't used to being up this early and already on the job. But what had started as the usual routine search for more of the story, had now become a personal quest to just meet the flyer. *And maybe get a ride.*

"So," he asked Andy, as they walked back to the cabin, "what all do we need to do?"

"Well," Andy replied, looking at Bernie's feet. "We'll need to find you some better shoes to hike in. And I think I have some clothes that may fit you. You'll be uncomfortable hiking around in what you got on now, and we'll be doing a fair amount of walking through the woods."

They went back in the cabin and Andy outfitted Bernie with the appropriate attire for their journey. Bernie was a bit taller than Andy and had bigger feet, but Andy found a pair of old, sturdy sandal shoes that fit him okay and would be comfortable to walk in. While being taller, Bernie wasn't much larger around the waist, so he was able to find a pair of shorts that did the trick. Andy grabbed a backpack and added two bottles of water and a couple apples. Soon they were heading to their cars.

"I need to get back to town right away then," Bernie said. "Do we need to go in the same car, or can I take mine and follow you?"

"That'll work," Andy told him. "There's a small parking lot at the trailhead, and you'll be three miles closer to the main road."

"Lead the way," Bernie said cheerfully.

Almost an hour later, Andy eased his little Subaru into a spot just off the road by the trailhead, in the tall grass. There wasn't a lot of space there for parking, and this area was used when the space a short way down the trail was full. The trail was wide enough at the beginning for a vehicle to get down, but then it narrowed to where it would be tough to get through. Andy opted for this area, as cars could get scratched further down, and you could only get out by backing out. Bernie found a spot nearby.

They didn't waste any time and were on their way toward the campsites in a matter of minutes.

"There's a parking area just down here," Andy pointed as he walked. "Maybe we'll be lucky and they left a car."

"Like those." Bernie also pointed.

Nestled in tall grasses of the main lot were three vehicles. The two men stopped, looking from one vehicle to another. They were surprised there that many cars. There was a rusty Plymouth Grand Voyager, a newer Jeep Cherokee, and an older model Ford pickup with a cap. Old, but in good shape.

"I wasn't expecting a crowd," Bernie said.

Andy nodded silently. He was looking in the window of the van. Then it occurred to him that they could look like thieves if seen, so he leaned back toward the trail, looking quickly down in the direction they'd be heading.

"Anyone coming?" he asked Bernie in an unexpected hushed tone.

"Nope. All clear as far as I can tell."

They both walked around the vehicles, checking them over. They weren't really sure what they were looking for. Maybe just something different. Nothing seemed out of the ordinary. In fact, all the vehicles could have been driven by the same people. They were all relatively clean inside, although they all bore evidence of having been packed with some type of gear. When they finished snooping, they stood back, looking at them again. Nothing jumped out at them.

Then a thought occurred to Bernie, and he was annoyed he might have forgotten in the excitement. He pulled out the small notebook he never went anywhere without, and wrote a description of each vehicle and the license plate number.

"Aha," Andy observed. "Doing the obvious, hey?"

"Hey, I didn't get to be a crack reporter by guessing on everything," Bernie smiled back. He finished his notes, stuffing them back in his pocket. "Let's head out."

They set off down the trail again. It narrowed to a well-worn dirt path. It wasn't wide enough for a car, but an ATV could easily navigate it. There were no tracks from a motorized vehicle though, so the owners of the vehicles they'd seen were carrying their own hiking gear and their camping equipment, in by hand.

"How far do we have to go?" Bernie asked.

"If I remember right, "Andy replied, "about a mile and a half. It's been a couple years since I've been here, but I remember this as being a bit of a hike. If anyone is camping, they have to really be into it to haul stuff all this way."

"I've never been that adventurous," Bernie stated, then added, "but our guy evidently is."

They walked in silence for a while. They weren't racing, but kept a good pace. Bernie was thankful Andy had provided different clothes and shoes. His normal clothes that he'd worn when he came to the wilderness were not suited for a journey through the woods.

"It's just ahead I think," Andy eventually said, slowing and then stopping. "What's our plan of attack?"

"Not sure," Bernie said. "Should we just walk around, posing as hikers?"

"We don't really look the part of hardcore hikers," Andy replied. "Why don't we just see if we can find a path we can spy on them from?"

"You lead and I'll follow," Bernie told him. "You've been here before." He was enjoying the hunt.

Andy found a path that led off the main trail and thought it may circle around the campsites. His memory was that there were about a half dozen campsites that were really nothing more than small clearings with a fire pit. They were situated in a row, not far from the shore of the lake. The sites were about forty yards apart from each other, separated by thick woods. Unless someone was making a real ruckus, you'd never know if you had neighbors. If the path they were on was the one he remembered, they'd pass by the string of campsites from a safe enough distance not to be seen if they didn't want to be. They walked in silence, and without consciously noting it, they stepped lighter, so as not to snap twigs or rustle leaves.

They passed the first site and found it unoccupied. The next one had a small dome tent and from what they could see, there was obvious activity. They crept closer to get a better view. They saw cooking equipment set up on a small folding table, with two collapsible chairs nearby. Smoke rose from the fire pit, but there was no obvious flame. Andy checked his watch. It was eight thirty. Bernie noticed him checking and raised his eyebrows in a silent question.

"Must've finished breakfast and went out for a walk or something," Andy whispered.

Bernie just nodded, but as they turned to leave, movement caught their eye. They both ducked down behind a large bush.

The tent flap opened with an audible zipping sound. Through the branches of the bush they saw a young man of about thirty step from the tent. He looked the part of the hardcore camper, wearing cargo pants, hiking boots, and a loose fitting long sleeved tee shirt. A light green cap completed the picture. He was tall and lean. Bernie thought he looked like he came out of a catalog.

"Should I put everything in the tent?" the man said, evidently to someone else in the tent. "I think we can leave some of this out."

"I think we can leave it out," came a female's voice, and that was followed by her stepping out into the campsite. She also was appropriately dressed in similar attire, except she had a brimmed straw hat. She was much shorter, but still lean and muscular.

From their vantage point in the bush, Andy and Bernie sized up the pair.

"Think that's them?" Andy whispered to Bernie.

"I don't know," Bernie replied. "I didn't see such a big difference in height between the two when they were flying. Did you?"

"I see what you mean," Andy said. "But the dark clothing could have made them seem closer in height. And we didn't see them actually standing up."

They watched silently as the pair readied themselves for a hike. Andy and Bernie both realized they had gotten themselves stuck here, unable to leave without not only being noticed, but found out to be spying. How else would they explain it? They hoped the pair left quickly. It looked for a second like they were, as they pulled on their backpacks and headed off. But from another trail that fed into the one through the campsites, came another pair of campers. The two men hiding in the bush were within seconds of being discovered, when the departing campers noticed the approaching pair and waved a hello. They all stopped to talk.

"Come on," Andy whispered, as he started to crawl out of the bush toward a tree with a wide trunk. Bernie followed as silently as he could. They glanced back and were relieved to see that the others were looking in the opposite direction as they chatted. They got to their feet without being noticed.

"You know, Andy," Bernie said good naturedly, "I've had enough bushes for a while." He brushed himself off.

They waited a bit to see if the new pair of hikers came their way, and in a few minutes they did. It was another young couple. Other than being younger, closer in height and having different colored clothing, they could have been clones of the two who had just left their campsite. They approached Bernie and Andy, who were suddenly looking and feeling conspicuous as they stood in the trail talking. Bernie had been in this type of awkward position before, and as the couple approached he became more animated talking with Andy, as well as when offering a greeting to the approaching couple.

"Good morning!" Bernie said, almost too enthusiastically.

"Hi," Andy chimed in, adding a head nod.

"Howdy," the man replied. "Setting up camp?"

"No. We're just checking it out for now," Bernie said. "I heard it was a great place, so we decided to check on it. Plenty secluded."

"That it is," the man replied. "If you like getting away, this is the place."

"Yeah," the girl added. "This is the most crowded I've ever seen it."

"Lots of hikers, not many campers," the man said. "Too far to haul all the gear."

"That's the first thing I noticed," Bernie told him.

"I suppose the trick is not to take anything you don't really need," Andy said.

The man laughed. "That's about it, yeah." He paused and then said, "Well, we need to get going. Nice to meet you. Enjoy your day. It's a beauty."

The girl smiled and waved goodbye, and they set off in the direction of the next campsite up the trail.

"You too," Andy and Bernie said in unison as they passed.

"That could have been them," Bernie said when they were out of earshot.

"Yeah," Andy agreed, and they watched the couple go to their campsite, take off their packs, and each fixed themselves something to drink. "I'd bet it was them more than that first couple we saw," he added.

"Yeah," Bernie said, "I think the flyer is younger than the first guy. More like the second guy. But we don't know for sure if it's any of these guys. It's not like we can walk up and ask them."

"True."

They set off to the far end of the campgrounds, and as they neared where the trail veered right and then swung back toward the main trail heading out, they came upon another tent. It was the last campsite. Two men sat in chairs around a crackling fire. They turned to look in their direction.

"Morning!" Bernie called over as they passed by. The two men just waved. Both held up beer cans like a salute.

"Okay," Andy said, turning in the direction to head back to their cars, "it could be them too. We thought the pair included a girl, but it could have been two guys."

When they were out of sight of all the campsites, they came to a stop.

"I guess we don't know any more than when we started," Andy said. "Just some campers we saw that could be them."

"Except," Bernie smiled, "I have license numbers, and license numbers have names. And addresses."

They set off back down the main trail in the direction of the parking lot. They walked in silence for a long while, both lost in thought over whether any of the campers they saw could have been the flying man and his passenger. They both figured it could very well have been any of the three couples.

*

"Shit," David said as they entered their campsite.

"What?" Amy asked, pulling her pack off.

"Those guys," he responded. "The one with the black socks."

"The one who didn't look like a hiker?" she asked.

"Yeah."

"What about him?"

David turned to her. His face was almost sad. "Bernie Fredder."

Amy didn't say anything, but her eyebrows arched and she mouthed a silent "oh".

"Yeah," David said resignedly, dropping into one of the chairs near the fire pit. "Shit." Then, he was lost in thought.

*

Bernie and Andy said their goodbyes at the parking lot. They exchanged phone numbers and email addresses, and promised to stay in touch. Both fully intended to do that, having enjoyed each other's company in the day they'd spent together. And Andy wanted to know how everything panned out in the end.

After a bumpy thirty minute drive out of the forest, Bernie had his car back on pavement and was soon on the highway headed back to town. He pulled out his cellphone and dialed the number of the downtown police headquarters.

"Hi," he said when the desk cop answered. "Can I talk to Cindy Hill?"

Cindy Hill was an old friend and sometimes girlfriend, and one of the lead investigators for the department. They had a long history, which included helping each other out when needed. Cindy's boss, his friend Police

Chief Mike Bresky, was okay with her trading information, as Bernie had proven to be a useful asset for the police, and had provided help solving a number of cases over the years. She came to the phone.

"Detective Hill," she said.

"Hey, beautiful. How's my favorite policewoman?"

"Hi, Bernie," she recognized his greeting. "How's my favorite reporter?" Their conversations usually started this way.

Bernie gave her the three license numbers and vehicle descriptions, and she said she'd email him back in a couple minutes. They ended the call with the usual promise of getting together soon. If everything worked out with the information he got, Bernie intended to keep the promise.

He got back to his office an hour later. He checked in with Dan and heaped thanks on Marsha for helping him out with the work he'd left her to do. She said she was okay with doing it, and he made a mental note to get her some flowers or dinner or something to show his gratitude.

He fired up his computer and checked his email. He'd gotten ninety seven in the day he'd been gone and the third to last one was from Cindy. He opened it and stared at the names and addresses she had provided. The addresses were all local. He printed the email.

Okay, he wondered. *Are any of you my guy?*

He checked for the list of students who had been seniors at Aston High School, then also pulled the list of UW – Eau Claire attendees. He resisted the urge to cross-check the names now, but decided instead to put the paperwork in his briefcase for later, and went to work clearing out the other emails and catching up with the work he'd left behind. It took him the balance of the afternoon. Adding to his workload was a new assignment from the editor, and an early evening school board meeting. He did his duty by attending and writing a quick, yet detailed article for the morning paper.

Chapter 42

At seven thirty that night, Bernie walked in his back door. He had brought his Aston map and all of the paperwork on the Flying Guy with him from work. Now he had the time and could work uninterrupted. He carried his work briefcase bag and map to his bedroom office. He set them on a chair while he cleared off the surface of his desk. He needed room. He pulled out the manila folders holding all of his information on the flying guy and sat heavily in the chair. He propped the map up in front of him, leaning against the wall.

"Okay," he said to himself. "Let's see what we got here."

He laid the paperwork across the top of the desk in chronological order, with the oldest on the left. He ended up with two rows of papers, and most of the piles had numerous documents with different, yet close calendar dates. He was amazed at the volume of evidence he had on the Flying Guy.

Bernie opened his notebook to where he had jotted down general notes on his feelings and gut intuitions on what was going on. He paged through those notes first. He read slowly, deliberately taking his time, so that if he had had any thoughts not already on paper, maybe they would come back to him now. He began writing on a fresh page.

He jotted down the things he thought were obvious. The flyer was human, or at least looked human. He thought a second on what that meant. He never had figured that out. Human was good enough he decided. It's a male. He's around nineteen or twenty years old now. When he wrote that, he did a quick shuffling through his paperwork, looking for notations of the age of the flyer at different times over the years. He thought that was about as accurate as it could be. The flyer had grown from a boy at the time of the apple orchard incident, right up to the sighting in Eau Claire, and then just recently at the lake and campgrounds. Over the years, the description of the size was consistent with a child growing up. The times he'd played the pranks as the Kite Fairy and the walking gnome, would have put him at the age that someone would so those sorts of things. Bernie laughed, as he thought again of the sense of humor this guys has. There was the flag thing too. That was great. That was genius. And the witch. He grinned.

His excitement grew as he made his notes. He pictured the guy from an old TV show who always said: *I love it when a plan comes together.*

He sat back for a moment, thinking. He heard a noise outside on the street, but the sound didn't fully register, as his thoughts began to gel. It faded and left him in silence.

He took the list of students in the Aston High School class he had determined to be the one the flyer was in. He stared at the long list. Step one, he thought.

Okay, now to narrow that down. He set the list of students at the University of Wisconsin in Eau Claire next to the other. It was much shorter. He slowly read the names. What I need to do here, Bernie determined, was to get the addresses here in Aston for each of those. This, he figured, was the list that contained the name.

Bernie held the list of names and addresses of the campers he had just got from Cindy Hill. He stared at it. There had been three vehicles in the remote parking lot. Three sets of campers. He had three names and three addresses next to the descriptions of the vehicles. The list had the names of two males and one female.

He picked up the list of the UW – Eau Claire students and read through the names. His breathing stopped. He felt slightly dizzy and his eyes blurred momentarily. He had a match. It was only the last name that matched, but it had to be a connection. This had to be it. But he didn't get that satisfied feeling of making the ultimate discovery. The match was one of the girl's names. *The flyer was a guy, not a girl.* Sure, today it had looked like a girl was attached to the guy flying, but it was still the guy doing the flying.

The light bulb came on over his head immediately. It isn't the girl. It's the guy with her. He stared at her name on the UW list. Amy Kellerman. Amy Kellerman attended UW – Eau Claire. He checked the list of Aston graduates. She was there. The Jeep Cherokee was registered to an Adam Kellerman. Bernie checked the phonebook and found two Kellermans listed. One he knew personally and he was very old. The other one listed was Adam. Adam lived at an address on the west side. He knew the area. *That could explain some of the sightings flying over Superior Street.*

It's his girlfriend, he figured. He thought more. *I'm close.* Getting close. He looked at the list of the other college students from Aston. The list of boys was short. There were only eight names. Could it be one of them? Did the boyfriend go to college at the same place? Maybe he just came to visit, he pondered that. No, he decided. The flyer was seen going down the river in Eau Claire, over water, just like today. Goofing off. The Flying Guy had been seen, or not seen for that matter, while pulling pranks, flying around in one area, mostly Aston, or he was traveling. Bernie had always thought the sightings in Wisconsin Rapids and Wausau were when he was going to or from somewhere. *But, why Rapids?* he again thought. That piece of the puzzle was eluding him. He hoped it wasn't needed.

Bernie slowly and carefully re-read the numerous police reports to verify his thinking. When he finished, he leaned back again, staring at the wall.

Okay, he figured, *I think I've got it. The guy is one of the boys on the college list, and he's the boyfriend of Amy Kellerman. So, how do I get that information, Amy's boyfriend's name?* That would take some real investigation he considered, trying to find out who a college girl's boyfriend is without drawing any suspicion.

He sat up suddenly in his desk, as a thought came to him. He can maybe narrow that down more, and if he were really lucky, he could hit just the one name. What was needed were the addresses for each of the eight boys attending UW – Eau Claire. If he could pinpoint where they live, he may have just one on the east side of town, where the largest portion of the sightings occurred. A phonebook search might reveal that, but if not, he'd need to enlist outside help to put those pieces together.

Bernie leaned up and studied the city map of Aston at the head of his desk. All of the marks he had made were clear and indicated the vast majority were in the one area of town. He looked at the street names of that area and then back at the list of names. He might need Cindy Hill's help again. He figured she'd be able to put addresses with those student's names. He didn't want to involve her more though, since she was a smart girl and could put two and two together on what he was doing. He'd managed to get the three camping vehicle owners from her without explanation, but he was sure she'd spot the Kellerman name and ask what this was about. He pulled the phonebook over and flopped it open.

He looked at the first name on the college list of boys, David Anderson. He flipped pages in the phonebook until he got to the Andersons. There were thirty two of them listed. So, it wasn't going to be that easy. He looked at the other names. At least they weren't as common as Anderson.

He slowly scanned through the names and addresses for Anderson. He knew most of the streets in town, as he had most likely driven every one of them at some point in his life. As he went through, he was able to disregard many he knew to not be on the east side. He took a pen and put a checkmark next to those he knew could be eliminated. When he finished that process, he reviewed the addresses of those remaining that he either knew were on the east side, or was unsure of exactly where the street was. Some streets in Aston ran all the way across town, so he needed to also check house numbers.

His eyes stopped on one street. He stared at it. *That sure looks familiar,* he thought. He'd seen that street name on one of the sighting reports, one of the funny ones, he remembered. It came to him. *The gnome. That's it.* Bernie went through the papers in front of him until he found the police blotter from nine years prior. He saw the address. He double checked the phonebook. *Yes, this could be it.* He felt almost breathless again. There was a Mark Anderson that lived at 934 Ninth Avenue. Edmund and Alma Miller, whose gnome walked, lived what must be just three or four houses down, at 907 Ninth Avenue. Neighbors. It didn't seem like a coincidence.

Bernie looked at the map in front of him and found the street. He traced his finger down the length of Ninth Avenue, as he estimated which would be the nine hundred block. His finger came to a stop. This spot was centrally located to the sightings. Shit Creek was about five blocks away. Edison Park was also about five blocks away, but in the opposite direction. He took his pen and drew a circle over where he figured that address to be.

He stared at the other piles of paperwork and tried to remember if there were any other sightings that referenced Ninth Ave. Nothing came to mind, and he was sure he'd plotted on the map everything he'd heard or received. He had just that one tie. He double checked and found that the Kite Fairy thing happened on Eighth Avenue, just a block over, but about seven blocks down. *So,* he thought, *is David the son of Mark Anderson?*

He looked again at the names on the college list. While he was feeling confident David Anderson could be the guy, he would still need to check out the other seven names. It was possible that one of them could also be from ground zero on that side of Aston. Slowly, he followed the same process. The phonebook lists of names of the others were shorter than for the more common name of Anderson. Three of the boys had names where there were only a few entries in the book. Two of those had all the names showing what were obviously rural addresses, and the other listed names all had street addresses on the north side of town.

The other four names had longer lists, so he took his time checking each and every address in the phonebook to see where it was.

"Shit," Bernie said aloud. "Shit." He slouched back.

He had found one of the boy's last names that had an address of 806 Eighth Avenue, one block over and one block down from the Millers. *Damn,* he thought. It's possible this kid lived there and so now there were two names. He squinted at the name. Jeremy Liggit. There were Liggits at 806 Eighth Avenue. He put a mark next to that name on his list, and then a mark next to David Anderson's name. He didn't want any more marks by names.

Bernie finished the process with all the names, with no more connections. He had, in his mind anyway, narrowed it down to the two people. What he needed now, were the exact addresses of them, and he thought, he might as well get them for all of the boys, just to make sure he hadn't missed anything. It's possible his logic was off.

Or, he just needed to know who Amy Kellerman's boyfriend is. He felt he was closer than ever and was feeling excited. He was going to catch the Flying Guy! At last it was all coming together. Suddenly a slight feeling of apprehension came over him. What if Agent Artie and the FBI were also closing in? Hell, maybe they already knew who he was, but hadn't tried to capture him yet. He shook the thought from his head. *No, this isn't 'our' Flying Guy.*

Bernie turned on his computer and pulled up his email. He sent an email to Cindy Hill. He thanked her again for the help on the three vehicle searches she had done and then asked another favor. This time, he felt the need to provide some back-up reasoning. He thought about what he'd say,

777

but couldn't come up with a plausible story. He didn't want to lie and then be caught in it. He enjoyed both the personal and professional relationship with Cindy, and didn't want to ruin either.

He decided to just ask for the address and hope she didn't ask why. He typed the names in, told her they were all around nineteen or twenty years old, attended UW – Eau Claire, and he needed their home addresses in Aston. He was sure she'd be able to get that information. He hit send.

Bernie lay in bed awake until late that night. The names of David Anderson and Jeremy Liggit repeated over and over in his head. But he kept coming back to one more than the other, the one that gave him the feeling it was him. *David Anderson. A couple houses down from the gnome.*

*

Bernie left for work a little earlier than normal the next morning. Instead of heading right to his office, he took a detour to the east side. Minutes later, he was creeping down Ninth Ave. He found the Miller's house, and then the Anderson's. He crawled by looking at the area. No flying going on today, he determined. Then he swung around the corner to pass the Liggit's house. No signs of anything there either. He wasn't sure what he was looking for in particular, but, he thought, as he pointed his car toward downtown, this may not even be where these boys live. He needed to know for sure what their exact addresses were.

It wasn't until noon before Police Detective Cindy Hill responded to his email. She sent current local addresses of the parents of the eight boys. She didn't even ask why. Bernie went immediately to David Anderson and Jeremy Liggit. Bingo on both. The addresses were the ones he'd figured. He checked the other six, and only one lived anywhere near that side of Aston, and that one was outside of what Bernie considered the target zone.

So, he mulled it over, *it's David or Jeremy. Are one of you the boyfriend of Amy Kellerman?*

Bernie wasn't quite sure of how to find out if Amy did indeed have a boyfriend, and whether it was either of those two boys. This could all be simply coincidental. Then with a jolt, it came to him. His nephew had called him about the witch sighting two years back. He had graduated with all of the kids on his suspects list. Maybe he'd know. But what if he connected the dots, when Uncle Bernie, the newspaper guy, asked such a personal, yet seemingly random question? He thought of his nephew, Justin. He pictured him. No, he figured. He wouldn't connect the dots. He's a nice kid, but he's not the sharpest knife in the drawer.

Bernie picked up the phone and called his sister Laurie to get Justin's phone number. He explained that he just wanted to ask him a question, left it at that, and got the number she said he could be reached at. He dialed it, hoping he was available. Bernie checked the clock, seeing it was about noon and during most people's normal work hours. He didn't expect to catch Justin, but to his delight, he answered after only a few rings.

"Hey, Justin," he said. "It's your Uncle Bernie."

"Hi, Uncle Bernie," his nephew said. "What's up, man?"

Bernie made up a story about how he was investigating college age romances for a story for the paper, and asked if he knew of any kids who graduated with him who was dating someone else from Aston, while going to college. Both going to the same school, he explained. Justin couldn't think of any. This was a real fishing expedition, Bernie thought.

"Well, how about an Amy Kellerman?" Bernie went directly to the target. "I heard she may be dating a boy from Aston. Do you know her?"

"Oh, yeah," Justin said. "Forgot about her. Cute girl. I think she might still be dating a guy from town. They were thick as fleas in high school. Even when she lived in Rapids for a year."

Bernie's ears began to buzz. "Remember his name?" he asked. He held his breath.

"Yeah," Justin told him. "David Anderson."

Chapter 43

The sky was still dark gray and threatening more rain. The storm had passed through the area over an hour ago, but the aftermath remained. There had been an incredible deluge of rain in a short period of time and water stood in puddles everywhere. Many streets were partially flooded. There was considerable wind damage. Trees were down, and the landscape was littered with debris.

Amy was at the wheel of the car bringing her and David home from her uncle's house. The birthday party they had been at was brought to an early end by the weather. She expertly dodged deep standing water, keeping her speed slow as she wound her way through town.

"What a mess," David observed, as he surveyed the branches and trees lying everywhere. "Let me know if you want me to drive."

"I'm okay," Amy replied.

There weren't too many other cars on the road, and they were both thinking maybe they should have stayed the night at her uncle's. But David had work the next day that he couldn't miss, and the storm was over. They just didn't expect the damage to be so severe.

It wasn't long before they found the main reason for the light traffic. As they got to the center of the small town of Brookwood, they saw that the bridge on the main road in the center of town was closed. Actually, a part of it now was missing. Cars were parked along the few streets in the small downtown area. As Amy crept slowly closer, the swollen and raging Basten River came into view. The storm had dropped enough rain to send the usually slow moving creek over its banks. Enough debris had been washed and blown into the river to cause damage to the bridge.

Amy found an easy turn to make, to go back in the other direction they had come from, in order to go west a few miles to cross the river at another spot. As she turned, they both noticed people running to the small park nestled just downstream from the ruined bridge.

David rolled his window down and yelled to the people headed in that direction.

"What's going on that everyone is headed down there?" he pointed as he asked the woman.

"There's some people stuck in the river, I guess," she replied.

"Yow," David said to her as she headed off. Then to Amy, "Pull in over there and let's see what's going on. We have time."

Amy guided the car into the parking lot off the small park. It was on a slightly higher level than the grassy park itself, which was now partially flooded with the swiftly moving water. She parked in one of the last open spots in the back near where the woods started. They got out and hurried in the direction of the crowd gathered near the water's edge.

"Over this way," David told Amy. They moved to where they could get a better view, but Amy still had to stand on her toes to see over the crowd.

"There." Amy pointed.

The river had several small islands here. When the creek was at normal level, it looked like the trees sprouted from clumps of grass surrounded by water. Now, as the flood waters from the rainstorm surged, only trees could be seen jutting above the torrent. A few smaller ones had been knocked over by the current and leaned downstream.

Clinging to one of the downed trees was a woman. She had a tentative hold on a small child. It looked to be a girl of about eight to ten years old. The water rushed around and against them. It was obvious they were about to be swept away. If any of the debris swirling in the water were to brush against them, they most likely would lose their hold on the downed tree.

David looked around at the people up front to see who was helping out. There were three police officers there, two with cellphones to their ears, but none of them appeared to be doing anything to help.

"Gees," David said to Amy. "Why isn't anyone trying to get them? Doesn't the fire department usually do this? Or is someone in a boat?"

"You'd think," she replied. Her eyes scanned the on-lookers on the other side of the stream for signs of any assistance being given.

"The fire department can't get to them," said a man who had overheard their conversation. "They're stuck on the other side of the bridge." He pointed and they could see the flashing lights. "They tried to get the boat in," he went on, "but the current took it right down."

"They better do something quick," another woman chimed in. "They probably can't hold on much longer."

"Supposedly there's another boat coming," the man said, "but it's been awhile."

Amy pulled David by the arm, away from the crowd to the rear.

"Davey," she whispered, "you have to do something."

"Yeah, I think so," he agreed. "Come on."

They moved quickly back to their car, trying not to look conspicuous. They wove through the full lot to the back. Both were casually looking around as they walked, watching to see if anyone was around or watching. There wasn't. Everyone was at the water's edge, keeping an eye on the helpless pair marooned in the center of the river.

"Grab my stuff out of my luggage and keep an eye out for me," David said as he crawled in the backseat of the car. He ducked down on the seat, pulling his shorts down over his shoes. He pulled his tee shirt over his head. Amy had gone to the trunk and into the suitcase. She retrieved his black biking shorts and shirt. From the glovebox she got his ski mask and goggles. She handed them to him in the backseat. He put the black bike outfit on and then put his brown shorts back on over them. The tee shirt he had taken off wouldn't cover the black shirt, so he pulled on a sweatshirt he had taken off before. He stuffed the mask and the goggles in a pocket as he exited the car.

"Let's go back here," he pointed to the trees at the edge of the lot.

"Looks clear," Amy said as they walked about fifteen yards in to the trees. "Everyone is by the river."

"Okay. I'll be back."

With that, David rose and wove swiftly up into the upper branches of the tree. He stopped, hovered, and pulled his shorts and sweatshirt off, hanging them over a branch of the tree. He pulled the mask and googles from the pocket and slid them on.

He parted the branches at the top of the canopy and floated slowly out, looking around. It was habit. No one would be watching up there, but he always checked. He turned in the direction he would go downstream and went about fifty yards, stopped and looked back. He needed to establish a landmark of sorts, so that he knew where to return to. The woods itself had many large trees, and it stretched along the river. Many tall pines grew among the leafy trees, and from up here the tallest had spires rising above the level of the other trees. David saw three spires that formed a triangle, and would use that to pinpoint where he needed to return to.

He turned and sped away. He covered the half-mile he needed to go in just seconds. He banked right toward the river, and dropped down to a height about five feet above the raging waters. He flew upstream then, quickly, around the bend and toward the pair still clinging to the branch.

"Showtime," David said to himself softly, when he knew he was in view of the crowds.

He flew directly to the woman. Her eyes widened with amazement that temporarily replaced the fear. He stopped and hovered just above and in front of them.

"I'll take her to shore," he told the woman as he reached for the young girl.

"Wha..? How?" she stammered, not fully grasping that this man was flying to save her. She pulled her daughter closer to protect her. Instead, she almost lost her to the current.

David saw that he didn't have time to explain. He reached for the girl, taking her by the hands and pulling up, lifting her from the water and her mother's grasp. He awkwardly got his arms around her and headed toward shore.

He was met by a crowd of people who all wore the same dumbfounded expression. Eyes were wide and mouths agape. They parted like the Red Sea. David set the girl down, and without a word, turned and darted back to the woman.

"I don't think I can lift you from the water," he told her, as he stopped just above where she held tightly to the branch.

She had reached for him as he approached, and now fear crept back into her expression.

"Okay," was all she could say.

"Here's what we'll do," David told her. "You grab my wrists like this," he showed her, "then when I pull you away, you straighten out. I think I should be able to get you across the water."

"Okay," she said again and reached out a hand.

David grasped her wrists as she did his. He pulled back, flying backwards. She did exactly as he had said, flattening out, and he easily skimmed her across the water toward the shore. He brought her to the same spot in the park where the crowd and her daughter waited. He looked back to gauge where he was, slowing when they approached. She could see the shore and reached a leg out. It was slippery on the grass, but when David let go, she scrambled up and in a few moments her daughter was in her arms.

David rose up above the onlookers, hovering about ten feet over them, looking down at their faces. They didn't seem the least bit concerned for the pair just rescued from the river. All eyes were on him. A few had cellphones out, taking pictures of him. He didn't know what to say, so remained silent. No one else spoke. He had to make an effort not to make eye-contact with Amy.

He banked left, flying headfirst out over the river and back downstream, without a word from them. He sped away around the bend. When he was confident he was out of sight, he slowed to rise above the trees to the left, circling back toward the park. He spotted the triangle of evergreens standing above the canopy and picked a treetop he thought was the one he had ascended through. He guessed right and hovered where his clothes had been hung. He quickly put on the shorts and sweatshirt, and stuffed the mask and goggles in his pocket. Listening for signs of people below and finding none, David descended.

"Amy?" he called out in a hushed voice, when his feet hit the ground. She hadn't returned yet to where he had left her. Seconds later he spotted her walking back from the direction of where the crowd was. She was grinning.

"That was quite the show you put on back there," she said softly as she came near. "Someone said you're an angel in black. Or Superman."

"Hmph," David chuckled. "Let's get out of here before someone connects us to it."

They jumped in the car, this time with David at the wheel. He threaded their way through the cramped lot and back up to the road. As he pulled out he was nearly broadsided by a Channel 8 News van whipping into the lot. They were in a hurry.

"We'll have to watch the news tonight," David said.

"My hero," Amy smiled and leaned over to plant a kiss on his cheek.

"I still think I need a cape," he joked.

"And tights," Amy said.

They both laughed at that.

*

"Bernie!" Dan stuck his head in Bernie's office.

"Dan!" Bernie mimicked his tone. "What's up?"

"Your flying guy just rescued two people from a river."

"What? Where?" Bernie jumped from his desk.

"Brookwood," Dan told him. "Rain caused the Basten River to flood and a woman and her daughter got swept away trying to save their dog. The cops and fire rescue couldn't get to them and your guy swooped in and saved the day."

"Witnesses?" Bernie asked, grabbing his jacket and field case.

"A bunch, I guess. Should be some pictures or TV footage," Dan said. "Go. With your trip up north and now this, looks like your theory that he's a good guy has grown more legs. See if you can get pictures."

Bernie was in his car in seconds, headed out to the main road to Brookwood. Hopefully witnesses remained. He kept checking his watch as he raced off.

Fifteen minutes later he came into the small town. He didn't have to ask directions, as he could see the small park that was crammed with people. Television news vans stood out in the lot. He had to park two blocks away and sprint to the park.

"Better late than never, hey Bernie," a friendly voice greeted him. It was Alicia Heinz, anchorwoman for a Wausau TV station. She was both a competitor and a friend.

"You know me. Johnny on the spot," he replied. "Where's the witnesses?" He had his notebook and recorder out already.

"I started with the top police officer who was here." She pointed in the direction where a group of police officers stood, microphones still in their faces.

"This one's a good one, Bernie. I guess your stories were true all along."

"What would you expect?" Bernie feigned indignation. He offered his thanks and headed over to interview anyone he could find with information. Everyone seemed willing to talk.

He felt pretty good when he left Brookwood a couple hours later.

This made the front page of the newspaper. It also made the front page of many other newspapers, as well as the lead story on local and national television news. There was cellphone footage of the Flying Guy, and it would soon be seen worldwide.

Chapter 44

Artie Johnston was suffering through his recuperation. It wasn't the pain from his injuries. The headaches had lasted for about ten days, but it was now two weeks since he'd felt one. Initially, he'd experienced dizziness when standing quickly, but that had subsided also. He wrist was healing well, although he hated having the cast on. It would remind people of his accident. Even though he hadn't faced any other fellow agents since coming home, he still felt he may get some level of ribbing for being injured while jogging. It would take a long time to live that down.

To make the time go faster, he spent most of his days doing as much work at home as possible. He contacted Agent Jance and was able to have copies of the Northcentral Region Liaison reports sent to him, as well as copies of the newspapers he usually read. The only difference was that he read everything from the comfort of his favorite over-stuffed chair, located in his home office. That comfort only accentuated his desire to get back to work at the FBI office.

Catching up on his reading had enlightened him to the fact that his replacement, Agent Jance, had completely missed what Artie had hoped he'd get back to him on. There had been two days where the Aston Police had gotten calls on a Flying Guy sighting. Bernie Fredder, at the newspaper, had comments on the flyer in his Tuesday column. Agent Jance must have thought that this was silly and didn't deserve the time of the FBI. He didn't have the history of the issue to add context. Unfortunately, it hadn't been an option to give him the whole scoop.

Artie wrote a short report for the Director and Special Agent C. Randall Whiting. He had planned to go out that afternoon for some grocery shopping. Being a bachelor required him to do this on his own and just after getting home from the hospital he had not felt well enough to get out. The cupboards were now getting bare. He'd drop the report off then. It was a hike from home to his office, but he needed to get outside and get some fresh air.

He was about to turn off the TV that he always had going in the background. There wasn't much on daytime TV, so he stayed mostly on the news channels. Just before hitting the off button on the remote, the news announcer caught his attention.

"And just after the break, we're going to show you something you're not going to believe," the female newscaster said. "A superhero was caught on camera, flying in to rescue a woman and her child from a river where they had been stranded."

In the background Artie saw the snippet of the story that they used as a teaser to get people to come back after the commercial. It showed a black clad figure flying in from the side, and stopping to hover over what looked like someone clinging to a fallen tree in the middle of an obviously flooded river.

Artie sat down on the edge of his chair, his eyes glued to the screen. When the commercial was over, the newscaster went through the details of her report. In the background there was the additional footage of the dramatic event. The view wasn't real clear, as it came from a cellphone camera, but the grainy, wobbly footage clearly showed a flying person come into view, pull a child from the water, bring it to safety, and then go back and drag a woman to shore. The end of the footage was the most startling. The person taking the shot was barely ten feet away, with the camera pointed over the heads of the other onlookers. Artie clearly saw the black clad person floating there. He was so shocked at seeing it that he dropped the remote.

He sat listening to the newscaster making light of what happened. She thought it was surely a hoax. Anything could be done nowadays with computers and photo-shopping, she said. Artie knew better. Now he really wanted to get back to work.

His cellphone rang suddenly, startling him. He pulled it out and looked at the number that was calling him. He didn't recognize it, although it was an Arlington area code.

"Hello," he answered it.

"Agent Johnston. Ed Gorman. How are you feeling?" the Director of the FBI asked him.

"Fine, sir," Artie told him. "Even better after just catching the news on CNN. Have you seen the report on the flying person rescuing the people from the river? They have film of the flyer."

"Yes. That's why I called. When were you scheduled to get clearance to get back to work?"

"Hopefully next week, sir," Artie said. "I'm not anticipating any issues with passing the physical requirements."

"Are you okay to work now?" the Director asked.

"Yes, sir. I feel fine," Artie told him.

"I can get your physical waived. Can you come in this afternoon?"

"Yes, sir. I don't see an issue with that." Artie felt like he was being rescued. He could get back to his office.

"Good. Can you be in my office at two o'clock?" the Director asked.

"Yes, sir. I'll be there."

*

Artie hung up and took the shower he realized he probably otherwise wouldn't have taken today. It felt good to get back into his work routine, especially getting out of the sweatsuit he'd started getting accustomed to. The only problem was that he couldn't get his left arm into a suit coat sleeve. The cast was too big. He thought he looked ridiculous with the coat just hung over that shoulder and his cast sticking out in front. He put it on that way to get in to the office, but left the coat on his desk chair before leaving to see the Director.

"Agent Johnston. Come in," Ed Gorman said as he came to the door to greet him.

"Sir," Artie said, shaking his hand. Then he saw Special Agent Whiting standing to greet him. "Agent Whiting." He shook the offered hand. He knew his seat and took it before the Director said to sit.

He didn't seem to mind.

"So," the Director started, "the Flying Guy hath appeared." He smiled.

Artie looked at him and tried to gauge the smile. It didn't seem sinister, as he thought it might. In fact, it was an amused smile. C. Randall Whiting chuckled. Out of the corner of his eye Artie saw him smile also. His wasn't so much an amused smile though. His smile said '*I gotcha*'. He looks like the cat that caught the canary, Artie thought.

"Yes, sir. And in a pretty dramatic fashion, I'd say," Artie responded.

"Yes, indeed," the Director said. "Flying in to save the day. At least he was doing something helpful and not trouble for us. His motives have been, and are, our main concern."

"Yes, sir. Our flyer seems at first impression to be a good guy, not a bad guy," Artie stated. "Although, through the years all of the information we'd gotten gave an impression he wasn't a threat."

"Still, sir," Agent Whiting chimed in, "we need to find out who this is and what their ultimate intentions are." He squirmed in his chair.

"Yeah, the ultimate intentions," the Director said to him. "What do you think they are?"

"I don't know, but we need to determine whether a flying person is a threat to the United States, regardless of this public, but still lone... heroic incident." Agent Whiting stopped short of saying he also wanted to see what made him fly, and if he could duplicate whatever caused that anomaly.

"Based on this recent incident, I'm no longer convinced that he'd be a threat," the Director said.

"I agree, sir," Artie quickly added.

"It looks to me like we may have a superhero on our hands, right out of the comic books." Ed Gorman leaned back in his chair and crossed his legs. "What have you got from the blanket surveillance?" he asked Agent Whiting.

"A lot of chatter, sir, but nothing that we can pinpoint as coming directly from the flyer. Everyone in Aston talks about it, so there has been a significant amount of information to be digested."

"Hmm. I was hoping that would have caught something," the Director told him.

"We did get some satellite footage that caught him though," Agent Whiting said.

"Really?" Artie spoke up. "What did that show?"

"I had asked for infra-red scanning over Aston and areas nearby whenever one of the NSA satellites passed overhead. They go over an average of twice a day, and only have about a ninety minute window where they can capture imagery of one certain point. Then the satellite moves on and, well, that's it. But whatever the satellite sees, gets stored in their database. So all we ever need to do is access the memory storage. It's easier to see infra-red dots moving than normal camera footage, that's why I have them concentrating on that."

"What did you get?" the Director asked a little impatiently. He was leaning forward now.

"We clearly got footage near Brookwood before the satellite moved out of range. We traced the heat signature of the flying person as it just suddenly appeared above the forested area behind the park where the rescue occurred. This person flew in the opposite direction, at a pretty good clip too, before turning and following the river back to where the civilians were stuck in the water. Then it just showed the same activity that is now also seen from the cellphone footage. The satellite passed out of range just as the flyer took off to go back down the river in the direction it came from. It was just luck that we got what we got."

Artie looked at Agent Whiting. He thought he looked like he really enjoyed explaining that. He looked like he enjoyed being able to use spy satellites like toys. He waited for him to go on.

"What's our next step?" the Director asked.

"I think we should have Agent Johnston to back to Aston, and this small town where the rescue was, to see what else he can find. I'm sure the police and news agencies interviewed people, so we can get names and interview them ourselves."

"That's also what I was going to suggest, sir," Artie nodded in agreement. He wanted to check out the wooded area the flyer was seen at. Maybe there was still some evidence of his being there.

"Go," the Director said. "Take however much time you need to get as much information as you can."

"Yes, sir," Artie nodded again.

"But check in with me... one of us, daily," Agent Whiting added.

"Okay. Anything else?" Artie stood to leave. Ed Gorman and Agent Whiting stood also.

"Yes," the Director said. He held out a hand to Artie. "Good job, Agent Johnston. It was your intuition that there was something to this otherwise absurd notion of people who can fly, that has allowed us to have a jump on it. Otherwise this rescue might've been the first thing we'd seen." His praise was genuine. He put a hand on Artie's shoulder as he walked him to the door.

"Thank you, sir."

*

"Well," Ed Gorman said, regaining his seat behind the huge desk. "I didn't really think we'd come this far. Until now it was just a lot of people seeing things."

Agent Whiting was lost in thought and didn't respond at first. When he did, his eyes were smiling. "I agree, sir. But now that we're close, we should plan on what to do if we make contact with the flyer."

"What are your thoughts, Randy?"

"I'm not sure, sir. If Agent Johnston doesn't come up with something solid that we can use to track the Flying Guy, we're no further ahead than we were. And my worst nightmare is that the NSA or CIA wants to get involved."

"Except now we know that the flyer is the kind of guy who helps people, rather than someone who might give an indication that they're a threat. I think I can get them to back off. This is local. This our turf."

"That's true," Agent Whiting said. He didn't care about that though. If he had a flying person at his command, he'd have him doing more than just rescuing people from raging rivers. An idea came to him. He wondered if it would be possible to set up a fake rescue scenario. A trap to draw the flyer to. But that would take time to set up, and would be tough to get away with though. It would have to involve local authorities believing there was a legitimate situation. He decided to tuck that idea away for when it was one of few options left.

*

Artie returned to his office. The first thing he did was make travel arrangements to Wisconsin. He phoned the closest FBI branch office to the Aston area, which in this case turned out to be Green Bay, as they had a temporary command center set up for other reasons. He asked the Agent in Charge (AIC) to get the names and contact information of anyone who might have been interviewed at the scene of the rescue. Getting

285

that information would require two agent's time, the AIC complained. They'd have to contact the local news outlets to get that information. Artie disregarded his concern and asked that this information be available when he flew in the next day. He was assured it would be. It had helped when Artie mentioned he was there on Director Gorman's instruction.

Then Artie called Bernie Fredder at the Aston Daily Sentinel. He told him he'd be in town the next day investigating the Flying Guy. They set up a time to meet. Bernie would be available all day unless something unexpected came up. Like a Flying Guy report, he chuckled. Artie could just ask for him when he got there. If Bernie wasn't there, he was free to wait at the Sentinel office for him. Bernie would make all efforts to get back as soon as he could.

Chapter 45

"Agent Artie Johnston of the FBI," Bernie greeted him at the front counter of the Sentinel office. They shook hands.

"Ha," Artie said. "My brother calls me Agent Artie."

"Ah, good. I wasn't trying to be sarcastic. Come on back."

"No offense taken," Artie told him.

Bernie led Artie back to his office and closed the door behind them. Many sets of eyes, who knew this was the FBI guy back in town to see Bernie, had watched as he walked through. Artie noticed that too.

"So. Somehow I expected to see you," Bernie said. "How's the wing?" He pointed at the cast.

"It's healing," he said with a smile. "But I still can't fly,"

Bernie busted out laughing. Artie joined in. That lightened the mood, but Bernie still felt like he needed to be on his toes here. After all, this was his Flying Guy. Not the FBI's Flying Guy. He wasn't going to let Agent Artie schmooze information out of him.

"Now that the cat is out of the bag, so to speak, what do we do? What's the FBI's plans?" Bernie wondered if Artie could answer that, or whether he'd dance around the question.

"For now we're… I'm collecting all of the information we can, and I believe the plan would be to make contact with this flying person. The Bureau wants to know what we're dealing with here."

Bernie looked at Artie, trying to read what was behind his expression. Same answer as last time. There didn't seem to be a hint of malice or anything else that was sinister. Today, Agent Artie seemed to exude some excitement over the flyer. But then again, he wasn't just coincidentally in the area like he claimed to be the last time.

"I'd like to meet him myself," Bernie told him. "Haven't figured that part out yet. It's not like shooting up the 'bat signal' or anything." He didn't have a problem lying to the FBI. He wasn't about to hand David Anderson over to the government.

"Nor have we," Artie said.

Bernie continued to gauge everything Artie said. He was comfortable, based on the way Artie said it, that the FBI had indeed not determined who it was. He had to suppress a smile when it occurred to him that he had outsmarted the Federal Bureau of Investigation. Then that smile disappeared from within him, as he wondered if the FBI could, or would demand he turn over all of his information to them. He made a mental note to hide everything he had. He pictured a scene he was sure he'd seen in a million movies, of government agents rummaging through his house looking for documents. Opening drawers and dumping the contents on the floor. Slitting open the couch cushions. Nope. Don't want that.

"What do you need from me?" he asked Artie.

"Names of anyone you know who saw this would be good. I had our local office contact other media outlets for the names of those they had interviewed, but I don't know if they got everyone."

"I can get you that. I can give you what they told me too." There was no harm in that Bernie figured. The eyewitness reports matched the cellphone footage already seen on TV. He hadn't learned anything new from them. He thought he was appearing helpful to Artie.

"Great. That may save me some time," Artie told him. "Has there been anything else prior to this? I mean relatively recently?"

Bernie hadn't called Agent Johnston about the sighting a couple weeks back, when the Agent was still on leave recuperating. He told him now. He started by apologizing for not calling, as he'd misplaced the number, but it was just another of what was now routine sightings over Aston.

Artie just nodded. He'd found out about that anyway when at home reviewing the information Agent Jance had missed. It didn't matter that Bernie hadn't called. It did however, make him wonder if there was other information he was holding back on.

"Let me know anything that comes up," Artie told him. It came out like an order. He saw the corners of Bernie's eyes tighten. "I'm sorry," he said, trying to cover the demand with a smile. "I'm pressed to find the guy and it doesn't seem like he wants to be found." There was an awkward silence.

Bernie spoke first. "I don't think I'd want the FBI to find me either if I were him."

Artie chuckled. "I would guess not." Then to Bernie's satisfaction he added "Neither would I."

They shook hands after agreeing to keep each other posted, and Artie left to go to the scene of the river rescue. Bernie sat thinking. It may be better if he got hold of David Anderson sooner, rather than later.

*

Artie stood in the middle of the parking lot at the park in Brookwood. He looked out at the now tranquil creek. There was still evidence of the flood, but the water was now back to what looked to be a normal level. Above and to the right, he saw the road signs that blocked the traffic from going over the bridge. Work had already begun to repair the structure.

He looked at the satellite photos he'd pulled from the large envelope Special Agent Whiting had sent him. They were the infra-red shots showing where the heat signature of the flyer first appeared above the trees. Artie looked at the picture and then at the area around him. Everything in the photo to the right of the trees didn't exactly match what he saw before him now. The river's edge was way off, and the parking lot was now nearly empty. In the photo, it was full of cars and other heat signatures. People. He turned and looked at the woods near the rear of the lot. Based on his estimation, the heat dot started from over in that direction. He took one last look around the lot and headed into the trees. He walked to where he was sure the flyer had been.

Artie looked up at the insides of the trees. There were few gaps in the foliage of the upper canopy, but all he saw was branches and leaves. Maybe he flew from here to up there, and went out that way, he thought. He looked back toward the parking lot. That seemed logical. This spot was out of sight, and in addition, everyone would have been looking at the river. Not back here. He looked up again. Then he looked down on the ground around him. Maybe he left some trace of his having been there. The flyer would have walked here, and then gone up. Artie knelt on one knee and examined the floor of this wooded area. He saw a thin layer of pine needles from the few pines that were among the much larger and dominant maple trees. There were some leaves on the grass, but this far in where it was darker, the grass was thin. He walked around, looking for something that didn't belong. There was nothing. He looked up one more time, putting it together in his mind.

The guy had evidently been here on the ground, seen what was happening, came back here to make his unnoticed departure, flew up, then out in a downstream direction to throw off the people watching from the river's edge, then flew upstream to the people, pulled them from the water, and even though the satellite lost him then, probably returned to this spot and left. Or maybe he didn't leave, Artie thought. As stupid as it always seemed, he knew, many people do in fact return to the scene of the crime. They just have to see what they've caused. Maybe the flyer is in some of the interview footage. Hell, maybe he got interviewed. Artie made note to get all of the TV footage taken from here that day. He'd look for anyone who he thought seemed like they knew more than what they were letting on. It was a long shot, but anything would help.

Artie spent the rest of the day interviewing witnesses from Brookwood. All of the stories were the same. In the end, his call to Agent Whiting summarized it as exactly what was seen in the video footage. No one knew any more than that. He had reviewed the tape of the interviews and nothing had jumped out at him. He told Agent Whiting to advise the Director that he would stay one more day, in hopes that now that the flyer went public in a big way, maybe he'd come out again to say something.

Agent Whiting reiterated what the Director had said. Stay as long as needed. We want the Flying Guy.

Chapter 46

David had gotten out of work at five o'clock on the head. He pulled his parent's car out of the grocery store lot and headed for home. It was a Saturday and he had plans to go out with old high school friends that night. Like David, most of them were going to be sophomores in college and were home working for the summer. He was looking forward to seeing them. It was going to be a party.

When he pulled in the driveway, he saw his mother in the Meyer's driveway talking to Mrs. Meyer. They looked deep in conversation. David parked the car near the garage and walked to the back door. Mrs. Meyer saw him and gave him a wave. He waved back and yelled a hello. His mother turned then and waved also. He said hi to her too. He went in the house and directly to the refrigerator to fix himself a sandwich. He was going out for Chinese food with his friends, but that wouldn't be until eight. He hadn't had a lunch and needed to fill the hole in his stomach now. He poured a glass of milk to go with it and sat at the table. He noticed the house was silent and figured his father must be gone.

Just as he shoved the last corner of the sandwich in his mouth, his mom came in the door.

"Hi, Mom," he said around the mouthful of food.

"Hi, honey. How was work?"

"Samo samo," David told her. "You remember I'm going out with the guys tonight, right?"

"Yeah," she said. "That's okay. You're not taking the car are you?"

"No. Rick's picking me up." He noticed her face had a sad look. "You okay?" he asked.

"Mmm, no. Not really," she said, and then appeared on the verge of tears. "Phyllis said Emery isn't doing well."

291

"Oh, no," David said as he forced down the last swallow. He didn't want to hear that. He liked Mr. Meyer. He was like a grandfather to him. He knew he was old, not quite sure of the exact age, but didn't think he'd be on his last legs. "What is it?" he asked her.

"He has Alzheimer's," his mom said sadly.

"Oooh," was all David could say. He wasn't real familiar with the disease, but he'd heard enough to know that there wasn't a cure. Once Alzheimer's set in, there was no turning back. People lost their memories and eventually die. He knew that.

"Yeah," his Mom told him. "Phyllis said he had started to forget things. Easy things. Like how to shave. For now, that's all the further it's gone, but they went to the doctor and he diagnosed him with Alzheimer's."

"What are they going to do?" he asked.

"What do you mean?"

"I mean, keep him at home or does he need to go to a nursing home?" he said.

"No, they plan to have him stay at home as long as possible," she said. "He's still mostly the same as he always was, since it just started coming on. For now it's just little things he forgets."

A thought occurred to David. "I should go visit him."

"Yes, that would be nice," his mom said, after thinking for a second. "He'd like that. And Phyllis, too. Emery has always liked you." She was about to cry.

David felt tears starting to well up in his eyes too. He suddenly realized this was his first brush with death - well, impending death. Both of his grandfathers died before he was born, so he never knew them. Both of his grandmothers were still alive and in seemingly good health. Other than obituaries in the paper, he never knew anyone who'd died or who was even sick enough to die, until now. He didn't like the feeling.

Before his friends came to pick him up, David stopped over at the Meyer's. He whispered with Mrs. Meyer in the kitchen that his mom told him what was going on. He asked if there was anything he could do. She said no, other than stop over to see him once in a while.

David told her he would. His eyes were getting misty again. She told him he was in the den, going over financial stuff. He'd promised her that he'd make sure everything was in order "before I lose my mind." David smiled at that. Sounds like something he'd say. He evidently hadn't lost his sense of humor yet. He went in.

"Hi, Mr. Meyer," David said when he saw him.

"Well, Davey," Mr. Meyer turned with a smile. "I assume the missus told you of my dilemma?" He'd overheard them whispering.

"Yeah," David said, taking a seat in a chair near Mr. Meyer's desk. "Shitty thing to happen, hey?"

Mr. Meyer nodded. "Not much I can do though. Sit back, buckle up and see where it takes me. I guess I have to enjoy things while I can."

They were both silent. They looked at each other and unspoken words were exchanged. David felt like crying. Mr. Meyer seemed to sense that, so he broke the silence.

"So," he said, "have you been out saving more people lately?"

"No," David told him, glad to change the subject. "But I figure I might as well do that kind of stuff since I have the power to fly." He grinned to himself. *There's that word again. Power. I wish it was still just the ability to fly.*

"That was a wonderful thing you did, saving those people." He leaned over and patted David's knee. "I heard they would have been goners for sure, if you hadn't been there."

"Yeah, I guess so." David felt a momentary rush of pride.

"I'm looking forward to hearing of more exploits," he said. "Now that you've been outted, so to speak, there's plenty you can do."

"Yup, that's the plan," David told him. "I'm still hoping to keep myself anonymous though, but we'll see how that goes. The newspaper guy, that Fredder, seems to be pretty interested in me. Sometimes I see him around, and he always looks like he's looking for something."

"Well, I'd think you could make a getaway if you needed to."

They both laughed. Then there was more silence. David wanted to say he'd give up his ability to fly, if it would save Mr. Meyer. He looked at him. He didn't look sick. He looked like he always did. A thought struck him then.

"Hey, Mr. Meyer," he asked him. "How would you like to go for a ride? In the air? You know, flying. I can do that. I could take you up."

"You can do that?" Mr. Meyer said. He looked astounded. Evidently David's parents hadn't told the Meyers that David had taken them up, and that he takes Amy on a regular basis.

"Yeah." He leaned forward. "What do you think?"

"Is it safe?" Mr. Meyer asked.

David explained how he did it. Mr. Meyer listened with a smile on his face. He knew what a tandem parachute was and exactly what David was referring to. He could picture himself hanging from the harness, scooting around the clouds. When David finished he added a wry comment.

"Well," he said, "what's the worst that could happen, I'd die?"

It took a couple seconds for that to sink in, but then David burst out laughing. Mr. Meyer joined him. David leaned over and slapped his knee.

"Yeah, I guess you're right. Might as well go out with a smile on your face."

"Exactly," Mr. Meyer said. "Tell me when and tell me where, and I'll look forward to it."

"Okay," David told him. "I'll figure something up and let you know."

*

When David went back to his own house, he told his mom what he planned to do. Ever since the river rescue, going out flying was no longer considered something to hide. The plan was to help others, and this qualified.

"That's a wonderful idea," she said, wrapping her arms around him in a brief hug. "I bet he'll love it."

"I'll make sure he does." He hugged her back, feeling a tear finally escape the corner of his eye.

*

David watched the weather report closely for the next few days. There was rain forecasted for the short-term, but then they predicted warm and sunny for a stretch. He figured the coming Saturday would work best for him, and asked Mr. Meyer if that fit his schedule. Hell yes, he was told and the plan was made.

At eight o'clock on Saturday morning David went over to the Meyer's house. Mrs. Meyer, who had been skeptical about the flying idea until Margaret convinced her it was safe, had made them a big breakfast before their aerial adventure. David noticed Mr. Meyer had not shaved. He put the thought out of his mind. Today was about being alive and feeling good.

Emery let David drive the car out to Woods Flowage. Thankfully, the parking lot was empty and there was no one to be seen. He grabbed the bag with the harness, and he and Mr. Meyer walked down the trail a bit, away from the parking lot. They stopped in a piece of cool shade.

David explained how the harness worked. He put his section on first and then stood behind Mr. Meyer while he strapped in. He appeared to know what he was doing, as he fastened the belts before David even told him where they got hooked to.

"I'm familiar with parachuting," Mr. Meyer told him. "I did some while in the service."

"Really?" David said. He handed him the extra ski mask he'd brought and helped him slip it on. "I didn't know you did that. I knew you were in the army, but not that you were a paratrooper."

"I wasn't, but we used to do that just for fun. I was stationed at an airfield and they gave lessons really cheap. A bunch of us guys gave it a try. It was fun."

"Well then," David said, as he rose slowly off the ground and pulled him up with him, "you may remember the view."

David turned them in the now routine readjustment process and they hovered horizontally, pulling on the straps to adjust the comfort level. They started off down the trail. David had planned to cruise the trails first, as long as no one was there, and then go up. Now that he'd been seen in Brookwood, he didn't need to be so concerned. All he needed to do was get far enough away from Mr. Meyer's car, so that no one would connect that with the flying guy. Bernie Fredder would be sniffing around the neighborhood then.

"Ha ha ha!" Mr. Meyer let out a laugh as they went. "Davey, my boy. I'm really glad you asked me to go."

"Well, don't speak too soon. We're not done yet."

With that he turned upward toward the sliver of open sky showing through the trees. He shot straight up, feeling the weight of his passenger pulling down. Mr. Meyer was a thin man, weighing less than David's father, and there was no problem pulling him up. He barreled into the blue sky.

In seconds they were over four thousand feet above the ground. David slowed to a stop. He turned horizontal so that Mr. Meyer had a better view of the earth beneath him.

"Are you doing okay?" David asked him then.

"Oh, yeah. I'm doing just fine." He was looking around. It had turned out to be just as the weatherman had predicted, warm and pleasant. A few puffy cumulus clouds floated just above them. "Wow, what a view."

They stayed there for a couple minutes. David was familiar with the area from the air now, but this view was new to Mr. Meyer. This was his day, so he let him be the gauge on when to go again. For now, he seemed to be enjoying pointing out significant and poignant landmarks that had punctuated his life. David was happy to watch him point and listen to his stories. He was good at that. He pointed to a stand of trees, telling him he'd lost his virginity there.

"There?" David pointed and began descending to the spot.

"Oh, don't go down there," Mr. Meyer protested.

"Oh, come on. Let's take a little trip down memory lane. Who was the girl?'" David asked.

"I can't tell you that. Well… do you know the Windsors over on Pine?"

"Yeah," David said. "Oh. You're not saying it was her? Mrs. Windsor?"

"Yeah, but you gotta promise you don't say anything to anybody. Least of all Phyllis."

"Sure, it'll be our secret," David told him. "You old dog, you."

They hovered over the exact spot, as Mr. Meyer filled him in on the sugar-coated details of his first tryst with a girl. It was actually a sweet tale, and David wondered if he carried a torch yet for Mrs. Windsor. His memory spoke very fondly of her now.

"Can we go higher?" Mr. Meyer asked, craning his head around. "Up to those clouds?"

"You bet, Casanova," David told him. "I like buzzing around the clouds."

He turned them into a horizontal position, zooming around in a banking maneuver that curved up toward the closest cloud. He saw a bulb shaped corner to the cloud and flew into it. They both lost visual contact with everything but the whiteness surrounding them. They could feel the mist on their faces. Then they popped out the other side, into the sunshine.

Mr. Meyer held his arms out like wings. David smiled. He told him how Amy steers him around by dipping one arm for the direction she wanted to turn, while raising the other, a banking maneuver. Soon, he was being led around the cloud again and then off toward the city of Aston.

"Show me my house," David heard him say.

David pointed out various landmarks along the way that he figured he didn't know. He didn't add stories as Mr. Casanova Meyer had done though. They went down to a level of about two thousand feet. He was sure they'd be seen at this height, but it no longer mattered. And this was after all, for Mr. Meyer's benefit. They spent over fifteen minutes circling town, pointing things out to each other.

"How about we zip over to Wausau and buzz Rib?" David asked.

"Zip away, Davey. Zip away!" he was told.

They sped off and in just minutes were circling the big hill that dominated the landscape around the city of Wausau. David took them down one of the ski slopes at a height barely five feet above the ground. To his surprise, he saw small patches of snow still remaining in spots, even now in June. Mr. Meyer was letting out a loud *whoo-hoo*, when they cruised down the hill.

Then David shot straight up, further than he'd taken anyone before. The ground was now just a patchwork of green and brown parcels of varying shades. Rooftops were tiny specks along the roads. He leveled off, then dove toward the ground. They screamed downward. At about a thousand feet he curved up and increased their speed as they headed back to the north side of Aston, and then on back to Woods Flowage.

"Thank you, Davey," Mr. Meyer said once he was untethered from the harness. "That has to rank up there as one of the best things anyone has ever done for me."

David felt the tears again and he didn't hesitate. With the harness dropping to the ground, he took Mr. Meyer in a warm embrace. They stayed that way until he was able to wipe the tears away. He noticed Mr. Meyer wipe his eyes too.

"Yeah. Me and Mrs. Windsor. We made you happy." They both howled with laughter.

When he was home and had recounted most of the story to his parents, David's dad asked for another ride sometime. David decided then, that he was going to enjoy the new version of freedom.

Chapter 47

The phones were ringing off the hook at both the Aston Police Department and the Sheriff's Department, as well as the Daily Sentinel. Bernie had barely made it in the front door that morning, before he overheard people talking about the sighting the day before. The Flying Guy was the hot topic.

"Hey, Bernie," someone yelled from a desk in the rear of the Advertising Department as he walked past. "Looks like your flying guy is going to stick around and give rides."

"What are you talking about?" Bernie asked.

One of the advertising executives up front filled him in on what was now evidently common knowledge to everyone but him. A lot of people had seen the Flying Guy the day before. He heard one girl in the advertising group saying she was going to figure out how to use the flyer in some way, in her advertising for any client who'd be interested.

Bernie almost ran the last twenty feet to his office. Just as he expected, there was a stack of pink message slips in the middle of his desk. He dropped his briefcase in his chair and started going through them. He scanned their content, disregarding the names of the people who called. Where the witnesses lived, or who they were, wasn't as important as it used to be. He didn't need to verify that the witnesses weren't drunk or pulling something on him. When he read the last one, he shuffled them in a neat stack and idly flipped them with a finger.

So, he thought, *David Anderson seems to have thrown all caution to the wind*. He grinned when he thought of 'thrown to the wind'. The flyer was seen by all of these people, Bernie didn't bother to count them, out in the open sky. He'd played around some clouds, flown around the city, and the part Bernie liked best, the flyer again had a guest with him. All of the eyewitness's messages indicated there were two people. They were attached somehow, one on top, one on the bottom.

Bernie thought about it again. He pictured some kind of strapped contraption that would hold one person securely to another. He didn't get a good view of the straps up north. The clothing was dark, and he couldn't see very clearly from his vantage point hidden in the weeds. The strap thing wouldn't be hard to do though, he figured. He'd seen parachutes like that. Bernie again felt that adrenalin surge he'd experienced when he'd seen the flyer with what appeared to be a girl suspended beneath him, flying around Andy Cook's cabin. He again thought of getting a ride. And he'd need to hurry before the FBI got their hands on him.

He put the briefcase from his chair onto his desk and sat thinking about he should do. If everyone here had already heard about it, so had others. With the sighting in Brookwood and the footage on TV, everyone in the world has seen it. Bernie had expected more calls from people saying they've see something, even when they hadn't. He'd expected the prank calls to start increasing. Aston was definitely abuzz over their hometown hero.

Dan Powers, the Editor, showed up in his doorway. "Got a minute?" he asked Bernie.

"Sure. Come on in," he said.

Dan closed the door, slid a chair over, and dropped into it. "Looks like Superman not only saves the day, but also is open for business giving people rides," Dan said.

The way he said that made Bernie want a ride even more. He was suddenly jealous that other people could get rides. He wanted to contact David Anderson now to schedule one. He pictured himself talking into the phone *"Hey, David, can I set up a time to go flying with you?"* He shook his head. It wasn't that easy. Agent Artie would want a ride too, back to Washington D.C. and some dark, windowless room. He was going to have to figure something out, and so far, contacting David Anderson was the obvious course of action.

"We need to make contact with the flyer," Bernie said. "I'm not any closer to figuring out his identity," he lied, "but maybe we should run a story and ask the flyer to give us a call. Maybe he'd read it and call."

"Until yesterday, I was under the impression the Flying Guy wanted to remain anonymous," Dan said.

"Me too," Bernie said, flopping back in his seat. "I was hoping he'd remain a little more... I don't know if anonymous is the word. More like... discreet. The FBI has been looking for him too."

"Oh, yeah," Dan raised an eyebrow. "I forgot to ask how that went. I heard there was someone here the other day from the Bureau."

"Yesterday," Bernie nodded. "I don't think they know any more than we do. But I do know I don't want them to catch the guy. There's something unsettling about the way Agent Johnston refers to the situation. This isn't just a really cool phenomenon to them, like it is to us. They want him for something else."

Dan looked deep in thought as he nodded. "Maybe it's an FBI experiment and they're following up on how it's going, especially now that it's public. You know, maybe they secretly impregnated some woman with a flying baby and waited for it to start flying around."

"You watch too many movies," Bernie laughed. "Unless Agent Johnston is a really good actor, I don't think he knows a thing." He again thought of how he had evidently outwitted the feds.

"Maybe they sent someone who wasn't aware of all the details so that they could get an objective assessment of the situation," Dan went on. His eyes were smiling, so Bernie knew he was mostly joking.

"I never thought of that," Bernie said. He considered it for a second. Dan's point may be only half serious, but at the same time it could also be plausible. The whole concept of a flying person was crazy. So why wouldn't the possibility that the flyer was created by scientists, government scientists, be one scenario? It could. *No,* he thought. *No. That's not the case. David Anderson is the son of Mark and Margaret Anderson. They are otherwise completely normal people.* He'd checked them out since discovering David's identity. The FBI is not involved.

"Let's think on how we can try to make contact," Dan said then, as he stood to leave. "We could just come right out and ask them to contact us, you know, by running something in the paper. Who knows? Maybe they'd respond. We're too late for today's paper, but if that's the route you think we should take, let's figure out something for the next edition."

"Sounds like a plan," Bernie said almost too eagerly, to get Dan out the door. "I'll let you know."

"Okay. Later," Dan said and left.

*

Bernie sat at his desk considering his options. He had hoped to quietly try to make contact with David over the next few days. He hadn't figure out what he'd say yet, but thought he had some time to work on that. He'd hoped that Agent Johnston would have gone back to wherever he operated out of, and the Flying Guy issue would again subside. There was plenty of chatter about the rescue yet, but included in that, at least on the national news level, was the possibility it was a hoax. It still strained everyone's credulity that a flying person existed. But now the flyer, David Anderson, Bernie was sure, was no longer trying to stay out of sight. He wondered then how many calls had gone to the law enforcement guys. That's what would get Agent Artie's attention. He picked up the phone and dialed Police Chief Mike Bresky's number.

"Mike Bresky," came the answer.

"Hi, Mike. Bernie Fredder," he greeted his friend.

"Bernie. I expected you to call sooner."

"I would have, but I got into another conversation on the hot topic," Bernie told him.

"The Flying Guy?" Chief Bresky asked.

"Yup. When it rains, it pours. I'm wondering how many calls you've got about a sighting yesterday."

"A lot," the Chief said. "Not as many as the Sheriff has, but quite a few."

"Any change in official plans on what you'll do?" Bernie asked him. The last time they had discussed it, both the Police Chief and the Sheriff didn't think there was anything to be done. No laws were broken and this was at that time, a matter of people, a lot of people for sure, saying they've seen someone who can fly. There weren't any established guidelines for that.

"I'm gonna have to sit down with the Sheriff and talk this through. Like before, no laws are being broken. The kicker now of course, is that the Flying Guy appears willing to help other people out. It's not lost on me how great it would be to have someone like him around to help when needed."

"Yeah, I can imagine that," Bernie agreed. "It'd be nice to have our own homegrown, hometown superhero around."

Bernie and the Police Chief discussed what they'd do in the short-term. The Chief indicated he'd meet with Sheriff Lippman to figure out what, if anything, law enforcement needed or wanted to do. As of now, he wasn't sure. He'd never run into anything like this before. Bernie said he was trying to figure out who it was, but was reaching dead-ends. It hurt a little more to lie to his friend than to the FBI, or even Dan, but the identity was safe for now.

Bernie asked if Agent Johnston had stopped to talk to him about the Flying Guy after he'd been to see him. The Chief said he did get a visit and thought when Johnston had broached the subject, it seemed to be just in passing. He had downplayed it then too. Just small-talk, that was it. Bernie told him the FBI is more than a little interested, and they could expect to see more of them if the Flying Guy becomes more regular. He told him that Agent Artie could still be in town. The Chief commented that he'd keep an eye out for him.

When he finally put the phone down, Bernie was more convinced he'd have to make contact with David sooner rather than later. If the FBI convinced the local law enforcement to get involved, things could get out of hand.

Motives for making contact with the Flying Guy had evolved for him, Bernie realized. At first it was the journalistic instinct, the thrill he considered it, of exposing something. That subsided as it became obvious that the Flying Guy, David, didn't want to be caught, hadn't done anything bad, and was actually a pretty good source of entertainment as a news item in the paper. Since Bernie saw him flying with the attached person up north at the lake, he now wanted nothing other than meeting him to ask for a ride. That was the best motivation. That had looked like fun.

Now it appeared he needed to contact him to warn him that the Federal Bureau of Investigation was looking for him. The police reports would make their way to Agent Johnston. If he'd already left town, he'd be back again.

Bernie wanted to keep tabs on the FBI agent's actions. He pulled Agent Johnston's card out and dialed the cellphone number he'd written on the back. He figured he may as well go through the recent sighting and see what Artie was thinking. Maybe he'd let on. He had to leave a message on Artie's voicemail, but less than ten minutes passed when he got a return call.

Agent Johnston thanked him for the information. He already had gotten the police and sheriff's department blotters, and since he was still in town, had planned to go talk to the Chief and the Sheriff again. His original plan of leaving to go back to Washington was now scrapped. He'd be staying in town for at least the next few days to see if the Flying Guy appeared again. He was most interested, he reiterated, in just making contact. Any help in that would be greatly appreciated.

Bernie told him he'd stay in touch and let him know anything he thought relevant to finding the guy just as soon as he had it. When they were done talking, Bernie slid the keyboard from his computer over and summarized the recent events for a front page article. As he wrote, it occurred to him that this was no longer an ODDS & ENDS tidbit. He now wrote for the front page.

Then he thought about what he was going to say to David Anderson.

Chapter 48

C. Randall Whiting sat in FBI Director Ed Gorman's office discussing what Agent Johnston had told them. Evidently the flyer appears to be much less concerned over being seen, and was now even taking – what ? tourists for a ride? This could make it easier to catch, they thought. Their hope was that someone, the passenger perhaps, would talk. They could catch the conversation on the continuing blanket surveillance program in place. It would be better yet, if someone came forward with information. They discussed offering a reward, but the Director wisely declined what he thought would surely turn into a public relations nightmare. The flyer had turned into a hero. You don't put him on the "Ten Most Wanted Heroes" list.

Agent Whiting however, was still eager to catch the flyer. He had commented on the recent sighting with the passenger along. If he was their guy, working for them, he said, that could be some sort of equipment he could carry. Or weapons. His imagination was constantly working on how this could aid the government.

As Director of the FBI, Ed Gorman's duties and responsibilities were pretty well defined. But as with any high level government official who ran an agency, he had some latitude on determining how or when things got run. He had a job to do, in this case run the FBI, but he could do it his way. He listened to C. Randall Whiting salivating over the prospect of having flying G-men. He suppressed a laugh, as it would have been a condescending one, and decided he needed to ratchet Randy back a bit. He wasn't sure how. While bordering on being a conspiracy theorist, Agent Whiting was the kind of agent you needed around. If things ever went to hell, the Director had long ago learned, Agent Whiting was one guy you wanted working for you, rather than against you. He needed to humor him for now.

"Randy," Ed Gorman told him, "let's have Agent Johnston stick around up there in Wisconsin. We'll see if more turns up by the end of the week."

"Ed," Randy said, "I think we need to send more assets to the location." He rarely used the Director's first name while on the job. He sounded like he was pleading.

By assets, Randy meant people. The Director wasn't sure more people was the answer. If they already knew the identity of the Flying Guy and needed assistance to locate him, then that may be appropriate. For now, no, Agent Johnston was enough.

"The blanket can run yet and we can see what Agent Johnston can turn up," the Director told him. "Until we get a solid line on who the Flying Guy is, I don't want federal agents combing the northwoods."

"I understand, sir." The informality of calling the Director Ed ended when he was given an order. "Perhaps with an increase in flying, we can pick him up on satellite again."

The Director nodded.

*

When C. Randall Whiting left the Director's office, he felt like he had been knocked down a peg. He didn't like the feeling. For now, he had no choice but to wait and hope there was a break somewhere.

Chapter 49

The Andersons always made a habit of eating their nighttime meal together at their dining room table. It gave them the time to catch up on whatever the others were doing.

Today there was only one subject. It centered around how David planned to make contact with law enforcement people to let them know, not his identity, but what he wanted to do. His newfound fame over the river rescue, then subsequent sightings over town with Mr. Meyer, had people pressing to find out who he was. The conversation the Andersons were having now was on how to try to let it be known he was here to help, but that he wanted to remain anonymous. Remaining anonymous was the key. Neither David, nor his parents, wanted the publicity that would come with him being found out. They had often thought through many of the changes in their lives that this would bring, and were envisioning a few now.

"Your life will never be the same," Margaret said to David. "This will even affect Amy. You two would never have a normal life."

"I know," he said. "I was hoping it could always stay under wraps, but I guess I knew that eventually someone would find out. I'm more concerned in what this'll do to you guys."

"We'll be fine," his dad spoke up. "You're the one who will be in the brightest spotlight. They won't leave you alone. You'll only be known as the Flying Guy, not David Anderson."

"I've always been aware this was coming and hoped that maybe I could convince them to not say who I am."

"How are you going to do that?" his dad asked.

"I think tomorrow I'll call the police and talk to them," David said. He twirled his fork in his food, staring at the plate. "Maybe I can convince them."

"They could trace the call," his mom said.

"Mmm, yeah. Maybe I should just go there. Drop in."

"Ha," his dad laughed. "That'd really freak them out."

"But they have guns," Margaret said to her husband. "They could shoot him."

That hung in the air for an uncomfortable time. It hadn't been discussed that they'd try to hurt him. They always figured someone wanted to catch him, but not cause him any harm.

David spoke first. "I don't think they'd do that. I could always go in with my hands up to let them know I'm… not dangerous. I didn't commit any crimes. If something looks threatening, I think I could get away. I couldn't outrun a bullet, but I know they'd have a hard time hitting me."

Mark looked at Margaret. She looked uncomfortable. "Is there any other way to do this?" he asked her.

"No, I guess not," she said. "But be careful. I don't think they'd shoot, but you don't want to get caught and handcuffed or something. They could throw a net over you. Keep a distance."

"I will, Mom," David said. He didn't think they'd have nets ready for him.

All three jumped when the phone rang. Margaret was closest to the kitchen extension and leaned over to answer it. Mark and David resumed eating for the moment.

"Hello," Margaret answered the phone.

"Uh, hello," the caller said. "Is this the Andersons?"

"Yes, it is."

"Can I speak to David Anderson, please?" the caller asked.

"He's eating supper right now. Can I ask who's calling?" she looked at David as she spoke. He had a puzzled 'who is it?' look on his face.

"Bernie Fredder. From the Daily Sentinel."

Margaret couldn't speak. Her jaw dropped. Mark and David looked at her. Then she covered the mouthpiece with her hand. "It's Bernie Fredder. From the newspaper."

David and his dad looked at each. Then David held his hands up in resignation, before reaching for the phone his mom held. She gave it to him. He took a deep breath, feeling his parent's eyes on him.

"This is David Anderson," he said.

There was a moment of silence, and that silence told David everything he needed to know.

"Hi, David. This is Bernie Fredder at the Daily Sentinel. I'm sorry to bother you at suppertime," Bernie told him. "Would it be better if I called back a little later?" Bernie didn't want him to say yes. What if he called back and David had figured out what the call was about and took off? Like really seriously took off.

David looked at his parents. He felt some comfort that they were together for this fateful moment.

"No, that's okay. Now is fine," he told Bernie. He somehow felt like there was a balloon with the air being let out. Slowly. Hissing softly. "What can I do for you?"

The question didn't sound so much like it required an answer, as much as it was giving an opening for Bernie to pop the balloon.

Bernie had rehearsed a few opening lines to broach the subject, but they eluded him now. His tongue seemed tied. If all his reasoning was correct, he was now talking to the Flying Guy. He felt uncharacteristically nervous.

"I was wondering if I could meet you somewhere to talk," he finally said. "I don't want to talk over the phone." Maybe some of Agent Artie's friends were listening.

There it was, David thought. Bernie hadn't said specifically what he wanted to talk about, so it could only mean one thing. *He knows who I am.* He couldn't think of another reason. The not wanting to talk over the phone gave him an uneasy feeling though.

"Does anyone else know?" David said flatly. He held his breath, hoping to hear he was the only one. He felt a surge of relief when Bernie said as far as he knew, he was the only one who knew.

"Okay," David said, thinking. "Do you know where Wood's Flowage is? Just east of Polar?"

"Yeah, I think so. You turn by White's mink farm, right?"

"That's it," David told him. "How about nine o'clock tomorrow morning?"

"Okay. I'll be there," Bernie told him. He felt a rush of excitement. Finally, he'd meet him.

"You'll be alone, right?" David asked. He might decline this meeting if it involved others. If there was going to be a group meeting, like with police being there, he'd prefer a public place.

"Yes. Alone. I'll be alone," Bernie said quickly. He didn't want this opportunity to slip away on him.

"I'll see you then. Bye," David said and hit disconnect.

*

Bernie hung up his phone and leaned back slowly in his office chair. It gave him a very satisfying squeak. He rubbed a wavering hand through his hair, then suddenly thrust his fists up in the air. *Yes,* he thought to himself. *Yes! I've found him.* The feeling overwhelmed him. By agreeing to the meeting, and asking if anyone else knew, David Anderson had tacitly admitted he was the Flying Guy. Just as he had figured. Just as he had outwitted the Federal freaking Bureau of Investigation. He settled back in his chair with a smile. Then a thought occurred to him and his smile faded. David had suggested a deserted park setting to meet, just after he had verified Bernie was the only one who knew about him. What if he planned to silence Bernie? It was a seldom used park in the middle of the woods. *No,* he thought. *Now I've been watching too many movies.*

On his way out of the office that night, Bernie stopped in Dan Powers' office. He told him he had some things going on in the morning and wasn't sure what time he'd be in. Maybe not until noon. Dan asked if it was something on the flyer and he told him yes. He hoped Dan wouldn't ask specifically what it was, and was relieved when he didn't.

*

Mark looked at David as he handed the phone back to his mother to hang up. He'd heard the conversation and wondered why David had chosen Wood's Flowage as a place to meet the reporter. He asked him why.

"If he's the only one who knows, I want to try to convince him not to say anything," he told his father. "Maybe he could help convince the police, too."

"You think he'd keep quiet?" his mom asked.

David nodded, thinking over his idea again. "I think I might have a way. That's why I chose Wood's Flowage. I'll offer him a ride and see if that'll be enough. He's mentioned in his newspaper column a couple times that he wished he could fly like me. Maybe that'll persuade him to keep the secret."

His father looked at him, nodding. He looked in agreement. David looked at his mother. She looked to be comfortable with the plan. All of the years of concern were now being put aside. There was almost a slight look of relief on her face.

"So, this is it," she stated.

They ate the rest of their meal in silence, lost in thought over what the next day would hold. If David could convince Bernie Fredder to stay quiet, things could go the easy route for them. If he decided to expose David, then they would all need to make drastic changes in their lives.

"I almost feel like staying home from work tomorrow," Mark broke the silence, as he put his dirty dishes on the counter next to the sink.

"Me too," Margaret said as she joined him.

"No," David told them. "I'll be fine. I can meet you here at lunchtime. I have to work in the afternoon anyway. At least I hope I still have a job tomorrow. In the same place."

They agreed to be home around noon to see how it went. They'd reluctantly agreed to go into work since they'd just be sitting around waiting anyway. Plus, David noted, it could be their last normal day of work. Ever. They should take advantage of that.

Chapter 50

At eight thirty the next morning, Bernie Fredder pulled his car onto Highway 64, heading east out of Aston. The sun was warm and it was supposed to be a nice day. The air was still cool at this hour, but Bernie cracked his window open a couple inches as he drove. He enjoyed the feeling of the wind on the side of his face. He imagined himself flying, with the wind buffeting him.

He was anxious for his meeting with David Anderson. This was it. This was the culmination of his years of wondering if the flying person was real, and finding him if he was. He was happy, and he was nervous. Agent Johnston of the FBI was still in town, seeking to do the same thing he was doing now. Bernie wondered if he'd be in trouble with the FBI for not telling them. He didn't think so. He wasn't aiding and abetting a criminal. As far as he knew, David had not done anything that was against the law. He didn't care. He was on his way now to meet the Flying Guy.

David was a little behind Bernie in getting ready. Being able to fly to Wood's Flowage made the travel time considerably shorter. His plan was to depart from his own backyard and head east to their rendezvous spot. He'd determined he could get in the air from behind the Meyer's garage without being seen. His mom had called Phyllis Meyer to let her know David's plan. She had expressed concern over getting caught and his mom had been heard agreeing with her.

The tandem parachute harness was in the bag he usually carried it in when he went by car to a departure point. Today he needed to carry it while flying, so figured a regular backpack would do. He still had a couple around home that he'd used when he was at school in Eau Claire. It was a tight fit to jam the harness in, but when he folded it, he was able to get it inside and zipped.

David stood behind the garage, fitting his goggles and ski mask over his head. He was thinking about what he was going to do. It may all be over today. Now, in a couple hours. Or maybe there's a reprieve. He hoisted the backpack around his shoulders and strapped the front straps together so it didn't fall off while flying. *This is it*, he thought. He looked around, listening, determined it was safe and rose over the garage, over the trees, and was gone.

*

Bernie turned off the highway onto the gravel road that lead to Wood's Flowage. He remembered it was about a half mile down on the left. His heart was thumping in his chest.

"Jesus Christ!" he suddenly blurted out. His thumping heart nearly stopped.

Out of nowhere, the Flying Guy appeared at his driver's side window, flying next to his car. He was so startled, the steering wheel jerked in his hands and he felt the car fish-tail ever so slightly on the gravel. He gripped tight to maintain control and looked out the window.

The Flying Guy was right there, not three feet away, on the other side of the glass. He didn't have his hands out in front of him as Bernie might have expected. They were down along his side. He wore a black mask over his head. What had startled Bernie the most were his eyes. They were black bubbles, and it took him a second to realize they were goggles he was wearing under the ski mask. Then he noticed the backpack. The thought he had the night before about being offed in the seclusion of the woods came back then. No, he thought. I'm okay. *This'll be okay.* The Flying Guy zipped ahead of him and banked into the parking lot area.

David Anderson had landed and was now standing at the back edge of the small gravel lot. Bernie pulled in next to him and turned off the car.

He was barely breathing when he got out and stood before David. They looked at each other for a long moment. David shrugged the backpack off and dropped it to the ground. To Bernie's surprise, he then reached up and pulled off the mask and googles.

Gees, he is just a kid, Bernie thought. David Anderson was twenty years old, he had learned once he'd figured out it was him. He looked to be a little younger than his pictures indicated. He hadn't looked this young when seeing him at the camping trail up north. A nice looking kid though. Wavy brown hair and a friendly face. He looked like a completely normal person, the kind you see every day. Bernie couldn't remember if he'd ever seen him around town before.

David held out a hand. Bernie shook it.

"So," was all David could say.

"So," Bernie said, nodding. They stood taking the measure of the other. "What's in the backpack?" He pointed down.

"A bribe," David told him.

"A bribe?" Bernie raised an eyebrow. What did he have? A backpack full of money? At least he didn't say it was something he was better off not finding out about.

David nodded. "You said you were the only one who knows, right?"

"As far as I know," Bernie nodded. "I haven't told anyone, and no one I know seems to know."

"Are you going to tell?" David said, right to the point.

"I... don't think so," Bernie told him. He thought about it again. *No.* He didn't want to tell anyone. Not Dan. Not the public. Not Agent Arthur Johnston of the FBI. "No," he said.

"Good," David said. "I'd prefer it was kept a secret." He believed Bernie. He felt a wave of relief sweep over him.

"Well, unless I need to be bribed," Bernie smiled at him then. "What's the bribe?" He pointed at the backpack again. He felt good he was keeping the secret.

David bent down and picked it up. He looked at Bernie, up and down. He was a little bigger than him, but thin and lanky. He looked to weigh just a little more than maybe what Mr. Meyer weighed.

"If I remember right, you had expressed a little interest in being able to fly. I recall an article where you commented you thought it would be cool to fly like Superman."

Bernie felt lightheaded. *Man,* he thought, *it doesn't get any better than this. I get to meet him, and Christ, I don't even need to ask for a ride. He's ready to give me one. Now. Right now.* He nodded, grinning.

"Yeah. Yeah, absolutely," he clamored. "I'd love to go flying." This was too good to be true.

"Well, how about we go up first and talk after, or during," David suggested. He could tell by the look on Bernie's face that he was very excited about going up. He figured if he gave him the thrill of a lifetime, he'd be even more willing to keep his identity private. Bernie seemed like a nice guy, at least so far, and he was thinking it may work.

"Let's do it," Bernie eagerly agreed.

David explained how the harness worked as they strapped themselves into it. Bernie was obviously thrilled about this. He did everything as David showed him and in a matter of minutes was standing, waiting to be taken up. Up in the sky. *Up, up, and away,* he grinned. David rose slowly, and when Bernie felt his feet leave the ground, he thought his heart would stop. He felt himself turning and then hanging, face down, about two feet about the path below. David told him why he was doing that and he fidgeted a little to get comfortable.

"Ready to go?" David asked him.

"Oh, yeah. I'm ready!"

David turned slowly and headed down the trail. He went slowly as he always did, to make sure he didn't meet anyone else out using the park. He wanted this location to remain a secret. They wound down around the bends and over the gentle slopes of the terrain.

"Doing okay?" he asked Bernie.

"Yeah!" Bernie almost yelled. "I can't believe this!"

"Want to go faster?" David asked. He knew Bernie did, but he wanted to give him a ride he wouldn't forget, not scare the crap out of him. Not that it was likely he'd ever forget this anyway. He just wanted him to be ready when he poured on the jets.

"Yeah. Faster!" was all Bernie could muster. He was lost in the experience of being airborne.

With that, David tore down the trail. He took it faster than he ever did before, hoping no one was around to spot them. He knew the entire length of the path back to the flowage, and it was easy to navigate at the increased speed. He banked around the corners, letting Bernie swing out in the harness, as he smoothly made the turns.

The path ended abruptly when it came to the largest of the ponds in the flowage. David turned out over the water where there were no trees. He arched his back and shot upwards. He went faster even than when he had taken Mr. Meyer up. When he was just below the level of a passing cloud, he leveled off horizontally before speeding out in a wide circle around the city of Aston.

Bernie had his arms out. David grinned. He eventually slowed to a stop, and they hovered over the center of town.

"So, what do you think?" David asked Bernie.

Bernie laughed then. "I don't know what to think. This is so cool. I can't believe it. I didn't know it would be like this."

"Good enough to keep a secret?" David asked.

"Definitely!" Bernie told him. This was more than worth the simple task of keeping his mouth shut. Way more.

*

An hour later they disengaged themselves from the harness. When they were out, David began stuffing it back into the backpack.

"You need to know something," Bernie said to David. His face was solemn.

David looked at him.

"No, I'm not going to say anything," Bernie told him when he saw the look he got. "Don't worry about that."

"What is it then?" David wondered what it could be. It sounded like he was going to say something he didn't want to hear.

It was.

"The FBI is looking for you. There's an FBI agent in town trying to figure out who you are." Bernie felt awful having to tell him that, especially after just having one of the greatest experiences of his whole life. But David needed to know. Maybe then he'd have some idea of what to do to avoid being caught by them.

"The FBI?" David was stunned. This is what his parents had always warned him about. Bad guys from the government coming to find him. Capture him. Take him away. He felt a knot in his stomach.

"There's an Agent Artie Johnston who's been following your exploits," Bernie told him. "He's been here before and he came again after the rescue. Evidently, the Federal Bureau of Investigation is interested in flying people."

Now David felt like vomiting. *The FBI. Wow.* His mom was going to have a heart attack when she hears this. Suddenly the prospect of Bernie divulging his identity started to pale in comparison to the Federal Bureau of Investigation finding out who he was. He stared at the ground. *Shit*, he thought. *Shit. Shit. Shit.*

Bernie saw the look on David's face. He wished he hadn't had to tell him that. A thought occurred to him though, and he told David.

"This Agent Johnston doesn't seem like a bad guy," he told him. "I'm sure he's following someone else's orders. Maybe you could take him for a ride and he'll stay quiet."

David thought about it. He didn't like the idea. Giving Bernie a ride was one thing, but he didn't want to have to deal with anyone else if he could get away with it. Still, maybe there was a way to get him to back off too. Maybe if he was able to talk to Agent Johnston to get an idea what he wanted, he could figure out what he'd need to do.

"No, I don't know if I want to do that. Can you arrange a meeting with him?" David asked.

"You want to meet him?" Bernie was surprised. "Unless you want to give him a ride, I'd have thought you'd want to avoid him."

"If they're going to try to get me, eventually they will. You managed to figure out who I was. I'd think eventually the FBI could too."

"True," Bernie said. "Okay. How about I call him and ask him to meet us somewhere today? This afternoon? Is it okay if I'm there too?"

"Yeah, that's okay, but I can't today anymore. I have to work this afternoon. How about outside your office at nine tonight?" David offered instead.

"Outside? Downtown?" Bernie looked at him. "You sure?"

"I'd rather meet him in a public place. One where I can get away if needed," David said.

"Yeah, I think you're right. Good thinking," Bernie nodded.

"Don't tell him I'm coming. Just have him there, out front, at nine. I don't want him to know ahead of time and be able to set a trap or anything like that."

"I think I can do that," Bernie said. "If not, I'll call you."

"Call my cell number," David said and gave him the number.

They shook hands with Bernie grinning. "Thank you," he said sincerely. "That was by far the coolest thrill of my life."

"Well, now I'm hoping it's enough to help keep FBI agents off my ass," David responded.

"I'll do whatever I can," Bernie told him.

*

David was sitting at the kitchen table eating when his parents came in. They'd both arranged lunch at noon, so they could get home together to find out how it went with his meeting with the newspaper reporter from the Daily Sentinel.

"So, how'd it go?" his father asked anxiously, when they walked in the kitchen.

His mother pulled out a chair and sat. His father followed suit. They watched David take a gulp of milk before he answered.

"Well," he said, "not so bad. Bernie Fredder said he wouldn't tell anyone. I believe him."

"Well, that's a good thing, isn't it?" his mom asked. She looked relieved.

"Yeah, but there's a downside to this."

"What's the downside?" his father asked with a puzzled look on his face. He'd have thought the goal was just to remain anonymous and he'd said Bernie Fredder would keep it that way.

"Evidently the FBI is on to me," he told them. They both looked alarmed then. His mother turned pale.

"The FBI?" she said.

"Yeah. There's an agent from the FBI who'd been following the newspaper articles and the police reports about me. He's in town right now."

"Oh, no," his mom said. "What are we going to do?" She looked at her husband.

His dad was silent, his face serious. David looked over at his mom. They both looked scared.

"I'm going to meet him tonight and talk to him. Bernie is arranging it," he told them. "I'll try to see what their plans are. What they want."

"What if it's a trap?" his dad asked. "What if they try to catch you?"

"Bernie said he isn't going to tell the guy that I'll be there. He's just going to get the guy to meet him at nine tonight down at the newspaper office. Then I'll meet them there."

Mark and Margaret looked at each other. It seemed so simple last night when it was just David meeting the reporter. Now the FBI was involved. They were scared. The old fears came back. But they noticed that David didn't seem as concerned as they were. He was calm, just wolfing down lunch before work as he's always done. Maybe it wasn't as bad as first thought.

"What are you going to tell the FBI?" his dad finally spoke.

"I don't know yet," David said. "I'll play it by ear and see what my options are, I guess." He drank the last of his milk. "I'll be okay." He felt oddly at ease with the way this was playing out. This was a giant step for him, but he felt ready to take it.

The three of them talked for a while before David had to leave and they had to get back to work. His mother remained concerned, even though David tried to convince her that everything would work out. After he left with his friend who'd picked him up, David started wondering what Amy would say. He hadn't told her yet, since she was out of town for a couple days. He had talked to her just before getting Bernie's call, but wasn't planning to call her again until the following day. Hopefully he'd have everything figured out by then. He knew she'd support him no matter what. She was the one who had started the ball rolling over going public. David's main concern about her was the same concern he had for his parents - if he was identified, their lives would then be in the spotlight of the world. This could, or would for sure, affect her too. She'd become known as the Flying Guy's girlfriend. He didn't want to put her through that.

Chapter 51

David had hoped his work day would speed by. He wasn't so much nervous, as he was anxious to get this meeting over with. This could very well cast the die for the rest of his life. The life the Andersons had managed to live so far was pretty much as normal as anyone else's. They were a quiet middle-class family, in a small town in Wisconsin. He was about to step foot on the world stage. Well, David thought, maybe that's a bit too grandiose of a way to say it, but that's as good of a description as any. He had to make an effort to talk to his co-workers. His mind was elsewhere, and he didn't want anyone to wonder what was troubling him. He and Bernie had talked about whether Bernie was going to make it known he'd met with the flyer. David was feeling a little paranoid that his friends at work would tie his uncharacteristic moody silence today, to the report of the contact with the flyer. It was a stretch he knew, but he needed to appear as normal as possible. He thought he did an adequate job.

When he left work at seven o'clock, he declined the offer to go out with a group of his co-workers. They knew his girlfriend was out of town and had invited him out with the guys. His friend who dropped him off at home called him a leaker when he got out of the car. David smiled, gave him the finger and walked to the house.

David sat for a while, talking to his parents again about the meeting with Agent Johnston. They asked that he come right home afterward, so they knew he was safe. He said he would. He didn't think he'd be up for joining his friends that night.

At quarter to nine he was ready to go. His mom and dad joined him in the back hallway as he pulled on his goggles and mask. His mother even adjusted the mask because there was skin showing. David told her that a view of his neck would not reveal his identity. His dad said he was better safe than sorry. They shared a group hug before he left. Those were getting to be common occurrences.

Chapter 52

Bernie Fredder had called Agent Johnston's cellphone number earlier in the afternoon. He hadn't called immediately when he got back from meeting David, as he needed time to think about a ruse to use to get Artie to come down to his office that late at night. He didn't come up with one until after he had taken the time to fill Dan Powers in with a white lie about what he had done that morning. Then he spent time with his office door closed, replaying the aerial treat he had gotten. He never wanted to forget that experience.

Agent Artie had accepted Bernie's invitation to meet him at the Sentinel office. They'd go out for a beer and talk about the current status of the Flying Guy. Bernie had gone home for supper, but was back to his office by eight o'clock. He was anxious for this meeting to take place.

At five to nine, Bernie heard a knock on the front glass doors of the office. By the time he got up front, one of the few other newspaper workers working late had opened the door to let Agent Johnston in. Bernie checked his watch when he held out a hand to Artie.

"Right on time," Bernie said. He noticed Artie was dressed casually. No one would ever guess he worked for the FBI.

"In the FBI, promptness is next to godliness," Artie quipped. "So, ready to go?"

"A couple minutes," Bernie told him. He needed to leave as little time as possible between when he told Artie the flying guy was coming, and David's actual arrival. He didn't want to give him enough time to formulate some kind of plan to capture David.

He didn't have to wait long. In the soft light that was given off by the outside lights in front of the office building, a dark shadow came into view.

It came down from above and Bernie made out the figure of David landing in front of the door. He was again dressed in all black.

"Someone else is coming too," Bernie said, pointing out the door.

"Oh," Artie said, turning to see who Bernie was pointing at.

It took a second for what he saw to sink in. He raised his eyebrows in a look of disbelief. A man stood there, dressed in black from head to toe. He knew immediately who it was. He had never really expected to meet the Flying Guy, at least not like this, yet there he was on the other side of the door, looking at him.

"C'mon. Let's go outside," Bernie said, opening the door for him. He half expected Agent Johnston to pull out his cellphone to call for assistance. Or maybe to pull his gun. Artie didn't look like the stereotypical tough-guy FBI agent, especially with the cast on his arm, but Bernie didn't know what he might do. Like David, he wanted this meeting to be where there was an escape route and in view of others, to make a capture attempt less tempting.

"Holy shit," Artie said under his breath as he walked out. He stood in front of David, eyes wide.

Bernie broke the ice. "Agent Arthur Johnston of the FBI," he said pointing to him. "Meet the Flying Guy."

They shook hands, eyeing each other up. The silence felt awkward.

David's anxiety started dropping when he realized the FBI agent probably couldn't make a grab for him with an obviously wounded left arm. More than that though, he could read in his eyes that he wasn't considering it. Bernie had kept him in the dark on the meeting, so he wasn't prepared to do it if he wanted to. Now all David had to do was talk him out of any potential plans he had to expose him, or any other nefarious plots they may have to catch him eventually.

"Let's go around the corner to the parking lot," Bernie said, waving for them to follow. "We might draw a crowd out front." The lot was out of sight of the street, but still afforded the escape route for David if it was needed. They followed Bernie to the back.

Bernie took over.

"I got a call from the Flying Guy... is that what we should call you?" it dawned on him to ask. David didn't have an official public name. He was only known as the Flying Guy in conversation and in the newspaper, so that name has been used most.

"That'll do," David said. He smiled. *The Flying Guy*. He noticed Agent Johnston didn't take the opportunity to ask him his real name. That was a good sign.

"Anyway, I got a call from... the Flying Guy here, this morning," Bernie lied. He'd come up with this story just before Artie had shown up at the office. "He said he wanted to meet, so we met this morning. I told him you would also like to meet him, and here we are." He left it at that. Whatever happened this morning wasn't discussed.

"Well. Wow. I wasn't at all prepared for this," Artie said. He looked at David. He wasn't sure what to say.

"Mr. Fredder said you have been following the reports of me, and were hoping to make contact with me," David said.

"Uh, yes. Yes, I was," Artie said. "Well, the FBI was, I mean is, hoping to make contact." Artie realized he was on his own here. He couldn't just call Director Gorman or C. Randall Whiting for direction.

"What is your... the FBI's interest in me? What do you want?"

"Um, well, primarily to insure that you aren't in any way a threat to our national security," Artie said, as he finally got his bearings on what to say. The shock was wearing off. "This is all... new to us - flying people, and we're concerned about your abilities and intentions. I'm sure you understand."

David nodded. Sounds logical when stated that simplistically. "I can assure you that I have no intentions to cause anyone harm, and that includes national security or whatever you're afraid of," he told Artie. Artie nodded back at him.

"In fact," Bernie chimed in, "the Flying Guy had expressed his desire to me to have his identity remain unknown, and to that end would be, uh, acting accordingly. Behaving, I guess is the way to say it."

"Yes," David said. He looked Agent Johnston squarely in the eyes. He always thought he was a good judge of a person's intentions by reading what their eyes said. That was always a telltale sign.

Artie was silent as he considered what to tell the Flying Guy. He had just now come to the conclusion that he'd be okay with not knowing the real name of this man, but was almost certain that C. Randall Whiting would feel otherwise. He didn't know how he'd work around that.

"I'm not sure if that is possible," he finally said. His eyes looked sad for having to say that.

"Why?" David asked. "Why do you need to know who I am?"

Agent Johnston gave a somewhat abbreviated explanation of who he answered to on this in Washington and how they had been approaching it. Both David and Bernie listened in fascination as they got a picture of the internal workings of the Federal Bureau of Investigation. It didn't make David feel very good though, when he found out he was a hot topic of the upper echelon in the federal law enforcement agency.

"I personally don't need, or want to know your real identity," Agent Johnston said. "I have to answer to higher powers, so may not have any choice in what I will be doing after this. I can pass on word that you want to stay private and see what they say. If you don't cause any trouble, they may agree. I can't guarantee it though. I know they'd like to have a flying person working for them."

"Work for them?" David asked. "How so?" Artie had made him feel a little better.

"I'm sure they'd find things for you to do," Bernie spoke up. He hadn't liked the sound of what Agent Johnston had said. The Flying Guy belonged to Aston. He belonged *in* Aston. He was 'our' Flying Guy, not yours. Not the FBI's.

"Well, there are a number of ways that I could think of using someone who could fly," Artie said. "The scenarios are unlimited really. Surveillance. Reconnaissance. Rescues, like you did."

David thought for a bit. This the part he had found himself considering all afternoon while he'd been at work. The shock of knowing the FBI was after him had spurred him to consider options that had never come up before. How to get the FBI to leave you alone, when they may not want to, isn't an easy question to answer. David had come to at least one solution though.

"Tell them if I agree to help them out once in a while, they'd need to leave me alone. Not look for me, or try to figure out who I am."

Artie looked at him. While it sounded like a reasonable request, Artie was sure it would be a tough sell to get Agent Whiting to back off. Maybe the Director would agree, but even then that probably wouldn't stop Agent Whiting. He had too many tools at his disposal.

"I'll convey your message to my superiors in Washington," he told David. He looked at Bernie. "If you have any documentation that may help lead to knowing his identity," he said pointing a thumb at David, "you should put it in a secure hiding place. We may come asking for it."

"I will. Thanks," Bernie nodded. He'd already done that.

"You didn't hear me say that though," Artie looked serious.

"Gotcha," Bernie agreed. Maybe Agent Artie wasn't such a bad guy after all.

"Okay. Here's the deal, and this is for both of you," David began. "First, I am not going to hurt anyone, or anything like that. I think you know that by now."

"I do," Artie said. Then he smiled. "I loved the flag stunt by the way. That was you, right?"

"Yup," David chuckled. "That was fun. But that was a harmless prank, so you know I'm not a threat, doing stuff like that. I'm not doing any more of that sort of thing anyway."

"Oh, come on," Bernie protested. "You have to do stuff like that. I have a newspaper to write, you know."

"Ha," David chuckled. "Okay, once in a while. Just for you."

"What else?" Agent Johnston steered the conversation back.

"I plan to stay here in Wisconsin. I'll do things here. Maybe I'd do something further away, but I'd have to have the time. I know this ability allows me to be able to do things others can't, like rescuing the lady and her kid from the river. I'll do that kind of stuff. If the local cops need help with something, I will do what I can, as long as it doesn't put me in danger. I won't carry a gun and I won't shoot anyone. I'm not joining the FBI or the army or any other organization."

"That sounds fair," Bernie said. "Do you want to make contact with the police to discuss this or do you want me to pass it on?"

"You," David told him. "I'll explain in a minute. Agent Johnston, I'll help the FBI whenever I can. I don't want to become a super top secret agent for you. Or for any other agency. Not the CIA. Not anyone. When you need me, ask. Don't order me. Ask me. I'll do what I can."

"Okay," Agent Johnston nodded. "I'll pass that on."

"And remember," David emphasized with a finger pointing at the FBI agent, "I want to remain anonymous. If my name is discovered and leaked or anyone I know is affected, then everything is off the table. Okay?"

"Yes. I'll pass that on."

"How do we get a hold of you?" Bernie asked. He was feeling pretty good about the way this had turned out so far. He needed to make sure to ask this question in a manner that didn't look like he already had the phone number for David.

"Ah, yes. The method of contact," David said. "I guess I'd like to have a front man to deal with. Bernie, I was hoping maybe you'd be willing to be my contact. We'll figure out some way for you to reach me without that divulging my name."

"Yeah, that works for me," Bernie eagerly agreed. Gees, he was going to be the go-to guy for the flying guy! That's a pretty cool thing to be known for. Dan Powers would be more than happy to have one of his newspaper guys doing that. It was like being a superhero's sidekick.

"Okay by you?" David asked Agent Johnston.

"Sure. I think that could work. If anything else is needed, we can figure it out when it presents itself." He paused. "Of course, everything on my end needs to be run up the flagpole." He grinned when he said that.

"All right," David started to wrap it up. "You, Agent Johnston, ceck with your bosses on whether that'll work. When do you think you'd get a response?"

"By tomorrow, I'm sure," he said. "I'll talk to them first thing in the morning."

"Good. Let Bernie know and we'll meet again to go over any concerns or expectations they may have, and whether I'm going to be good with them or not."

Artie nodded.

"Bernie," David pointed at him, "talk to the police and let them know I'm available to help. Same restrictions and guidelines."

"Yup, got it," Bernie told him. He thought he could agree to just about anything right now. So far today he'd been taken flying and that had been absolutely great. Tonight, he was asked to be the contact guy for the Flying Guy. He'd never even considered that a scenario like this could happen.

"We'll work on a way to contact each other after we meet again. For now, let's plan on me getting hold of you Bernie, tomorrow afternoon sometime. That'll give you, Agent Johnston, time to talk to your boss. Sound okay?"

"Yes. And call me Artie from now on," he said as he offered David his hand.

"Artie," David said, shaking it. "I hope in the future I can look back on this meeting and say it was a pleasure to meet you."

"So do I," he said.

"Yeah. I guess the jury is still out on that," Bernie added, almost sadly. "But I hope the same thing."

"Can I see you fly?" Artie asked then. "I didn't see you come here."

"Sure," David said. "Gentlemen, until tomorrow." He nodded at them, then slowly rose up and did a slow lap around the parking lot. When he went up and headed home, he left behind a grinning newspaper reporter and a very amazed agent from the Federal Bureau of Investigation.

"I could use that beer now," Artie said.

Bernie nodded. "Yup. My sentiments exactly."

*

David landed in the usual spot he had departed from near the Meyer's garage. He pulled off the mask and goggles and stood thinking for a bit. He thought the meeting had gone pretty well. The FBI agent seemed like he understood David's concerns, sympathized with them, and would put an honest effort into helping keep his identity a secret. But he was feeling a little anxious again. He had to wait on another meeting to find out what will happen.

When he came in the back door, his parents heard him and came to join him in the back hall. They both wore expressions of anticipation.

"So how did it go?" his father asked David.

"Okay so far, I guess," David told him. He came up the stairs to the kitchen, where they all took seats at the small table.

"So far? What does that mean?" his father asked. He looked more concerned now.

"Well, I met the FBI guy and we had a talk," David began.

"He didn't try to catch you?" his mother interrupted.

"No. He didn't know I'd be there and since we met outside, I don't think he could have tried even if he wanted. Plus, he had a broken arm or something. He had a huge cast on one arm. He wasn't threatening at all."

There felt to be a slight easing of tension when they heard there was no capture attempt. And besides, David had made it back without any trouble. He still was much calmer than they were. It had a calming effect on them.

"Did you talk about keeping your identity private?" his mother then asked.

"Yes," David continued. "I told him I could help out on things when needed. Well, I told him more like help out when I could. I didn't promise anything. But I told him it would all depend on my not being bothered. If my identity is revealed, then everything changes."

"What did he say to that?" his father asked. Both of his parents looked eager to hear the answer.

"He needs to talk to his bosses in Washington. At the FBI Headquarters."

His mom looked pale again, like she did when she first heard him mention the FBI that morning. They sat in silence, digesting what David was telling them.

"Oh my gosh," his mom finally said. She looked at her husband.

"So, we're waiting on what they say?" his father asked.

"Yeah. Agent Johnston, an okay guy by the way, will talk to his bosses tomorrow morning. We're going to meet again tomorrow afternoon to find out what they said."

"Another waiting game," his father said after a moment. "What do you think will happen?"

"I don't know," David told him. "It seemed certain that he had no idea who I was, and he didn't seem to be fishing for clues either, so at least we might have him in our corner. But, he said one of his bosses was a real dick and he might want to continue trying to figure out who I am."

"We'll find out tomorrow then?" his mom asked. "Will he, Agent Johnston, be able to tell you whether they'll keep trying to find you?"

"I think he might be honest about that. He even told Bernie Fredder to get rid of his evidence about me in case the other guy keeps looking. Then it wouldn't get confiscated, I guess."

"What about the newspaper guy?" his mom asked. "He won't tell, will he?"

"I don't think so," David replied. "I get the impression he likes having the Flying Guy around, doing good deeds and all that. He jumped at the chance to be my go-between."

David explained how the rest of the meeting had gone. He told them that Bernie Fredder would contact the local police to let them know the same thing he'd told the FBI about helping under the condition of privacy. His parents appeared to relax as he spoke. With the meeting set for the next day, they still had some anxiety, but David could tell they were getting used to what was going on. Now all they could do was wait.

Chapter 53

Artie got up early the next morning. He wanted to try to catch the FBI Director as soon as possible to have the discussion. With the difference in time zones, and with Ed Gorman's well known propensity for being in his office by seven o'clock, Artie had to be ready to call by six o'clock Wisconsin time. He waited until six on the head and dialed the direct number he'd been given.

The Director's assistant, Carol, told Artie he'd need to hold while the Director finished up a short meeting with someone else. Artie told her to try to get C. Randall Whiting and see if he can join in for the call. She put him on hold.

While waiting to be connected, Artie ran through what he was going to say. Usually, he just gave them the information he'd gathered and wait for their instructions. Today, he would be asking them to do what he felt was right. This conversation would be different, and the instructions he'd get would be crucial to whether the Flying Guy would work for them.

When Carol came back on the line it caused him to jump.

"Agent Johnston? Are you still there?" she asked.

"Yes, I'm here."

"I have the Director on the line, and Agent Whiting is also teleconferencing in," she told him.

"I'm here," Agent Whiting said. He was in his own office taking the call.

"Thanks, Carol," the Director said, and then a soft click indicated she had disconnected. "Agent Johnston. You're calling bright and early, so I assume there is some break on the flying guy."

"Yes, sir," Artie told him. He paused a second, suddenly wondering how Agent Whiting was going to react.

"And?" the Director prompted him.

"I met him, sir. I met the Flying Guy."

"You what?" Agent Whiting exclaimed.

"I met him yesterday," Artie told them. "Evidently the Flying Guy caught wind that the newspaper reporter was looking for him, so he met with him early yesterday morning. The reporter, Bernie Fredder, the guy from their local paper, told the flyer that we were also interested. So, he agreed to meet with me. It was all arranged beforehand and I didn't know about it. Fredder asked me to meet him, but didn't tell me the Flying Guy would be there."

"Did you get his name?" Agent Whiting jumped in.

Artie figured that would be his first question. Agent Whiting was only interested in one thing. This gave him a transition into the issue that needed to be resolved.

"No," Artie went on. "The guy wore a mask. It's like a ski mask. And goggles. So I didn't see his face. He never said who he was, and it was clear that he didn't want to be exposed. Asking him his name would have been useless."

"Did you get any clues as to how we could find out," Agent Whiting persisted.

"No," Artie replied. He didn't know what all Bernie Fredder had for information, but he didn't want to offer up the thought that they could put heat on him to get any. He felt guilty for withholding information from his superiors, but with Whiting involved, he thought it was the best course of action.

"What did the Flying Guy have to say?" the Director asked.

"Well, sir, one thing is clear. He absolutely does not want to be caught. Identified. He doesn't want anybody to know his identity."

Agent Whiting was quiet and Artie was glad for that. He'd prefer to deal just with the Director when he expressed his opinion of what they should do.

"Hmm. So what do think we should do, Agent Johnston?"

Artie was surprised he asked him that question first, and not Agent Whiting. He was ready with his answer, but needed to lay it out the right way. He started out with the same position he planned to end his discussion with.

"I think we should leave him alone, sir," Artie told him. "This guy seems to be just an otherwise average, normal guy, who just… has the ability to fly. He doesn't have any other powers. He seemed young, I'd guess twentyish. The river rescue sort of inadvertently brought him out, and now he is willing to do things like that. I believe he recognizes he has this special power and needs to use it for other people's benefit."

"A superhero," the Director said.

"Yes, sir, sort of, and actually, that's pretty much how he wants this to be handled. He'd be available, as best he can he said, when summoned to do something. He's willing to do that with the local law enforcement and said he would also help us if he can. When he can."

"This is sounding like a dream come true," the Director said. "What needs to be done now? Randy, any ideas?"

Artie didn't want the conversation to switch to C. Randall Whiting. He wasn't sure what he'd say, but Artie knew he needed to steer the conversation in the direction he wanted.

"Sir, first there's a catch to this," Artie quickly interjected before Agent Whiting was able to respond.

"A catch?" Agent Whiting spoke up.

"Yes, sir," Artie told them. "The Flying Guy said he will only help us out if we back off trying to identify him, and if we leave him alone. He said if it goes public who he is, he'd bail on us. I believe he'd probably disappear somewhere. That would certainly be easy for him to do."

"I see," the Director said. "So we'd have to… what? Shoot up the bat-signal when we need him?" He chuckled.

Artie laughed. "I guess so, sir. Something like that."

"Sir," Agent Whiting joined in. "We should still take some efforts to find out who he is. We could keep that to ourselves. We need to find out how he flies. That was one of our main purposes."

"I know, Randy. But according to Agent Johnston, this guy won't help us if we do. They already have seen Agent Johnston there in Aston. We can't send more agents to the area. People would notice. They'd talk. The Flying Guy could get word and then that would be it." Ed Gorman was looking at the bigger picture. "I'm thinking a bird in hand is worth two in the bush, if you know what I mean."

"Yes, sir. I do," Agent Whiting said, a hint of resignation in his voice. "But we would still prefer to find out how he flies."

"Yes, I know," the Director said.

There was silence then and Artie wanted to speak. But it was looking like the Director was siding with him, so he let them dwell on it a little longer. It felt too long then, and Artie didn't want to let the decision slip away.

"Sir," he said, "It's my opinion that the guy is sincere in wanting to be an asset to us, and if it all hinges on keeping his identity a secret, then I believe we should." He left it at that. He waited for the Director and was surprised that Agent Whiting didn't speak up.

"I agree," the Director said finally. "How do we proceed?"

"I'll be meeting him again later today," Artie told him. "I'll advise him of your decision. Bernie Fredder and the Flying Guy were going to work out the logistics of communications between everyone. The Flying Guy wants Fredder to be his contact, so they will work that out. But like I said, this has to work out so that no one knows who he is and no one is looking."

"Let us know what the final arrangements are," the Director told him. "Good Job, Agent Johnston. Hell, you could end up in the history books one day."

"Thank you, sir. I'll keep you posted. Goodbye."

"Randy, hang on the phone after this, okay?" the Director told him.

When they heard the click of Agent Johnston disconnecting, Agent Whiting spoke up.

"Ed," he said, deciding on the less formal route. "We should find an opportunity to get more information on the flyer. Maybe we could ask him to come here and meet with us. Or I could go there."

Ed Gorman thought about that. The only problem, he figured, was that Randy would get overzealous and scare the Flying Guy away. No. As much as it seemed like a great idea to have flying G-men, especially the interesting ways Randy has suggested in the past, they were probably better off just going the route the Flying Guy has offered. He thought about how the flyer must be considering this. Anonymity was obviously important.

"Randy," the Director finally said, "Let's back off and see how this plays out. Having this guy working for us, even if only on a limited basis, is better than losing him altogether. Plus, think of how this will look to the public.

The FBI will have its own superhero working with us. This'll be a feather in our caps. And that includes yours."

"Yes, sir," Randy said, back to formalities. "I assume you want me to terminate the surveillance program?"

"Yes. Pull everything," he said. "And Randy, we did good here. Agent Johnston has landed us a plum. Let's not screw it up."

"Yes, sir," Randy said, and they ended the call.

*

The Director had been clear, and while C. Randall Whiting didn't completely agree on the plan, he wasn't in a position to disobey the instructions. After he had hung up from that call, he called the Deputy Director of the NSA who helped set up the blanket surveillance over Aston. He told him to end the program immediately. When asked if they should delete everything they had gathered so far, Agent Whiting told him no. It should be saved in case they needed it. He asked to be put through to the analyst that worked the program for him. Agent Whiting instructed the analyst to store all information related to their flying person activities in an electronic file that only he could access, and that any access to this file needed explicit permission from him, Agent Whiting, and no one else. He told him that it would likely be needed in the future.

For the short-term, since they could reach the flyer now if needed, it didn't matter.

Chapter 54

Mid-afternoon of that day, David parked his car next to the public phone booth at the end of the BP gas station parking lot, on the far west side of Aston. He pulled out Bernie's phone number. Not knowing whether the FBI guy was going to back off or not, he didn't want to use his home phone or his cell. They could be tapping Bernie's phones now and tracing incoming calls. The FBI had plenty of time since yesterday to set that up. The pay phone was the only option, other than going directly to the Sentinel office. He wasn't prepared for the first daytime public appearance yet.

Bernie answered on the first ring. He told David that Agent Johnston had called earlier and could meet at any time, to just let him know where, and when. He'd talked to his superiors, and while not coming right out and saying, he'd left Bernie with the impression it was all set as hoped.

David suggested they meet at Wood's Flowage again. If it all worked out, he'd take Agent Artie for a ride. Bernie eagerly asked for another one also. They set a time of four o'clock, and when David hung up, Bernie called Artie to arrange it. He told him to meet him at his office and he'd drive.

*

Everyone was early for the meeting, and when four o'clock finally came, there were already smiles all around. Bernie was elated that the FBI had agreed to David's terms. That would keep the Flying Guy in Aston - well, in Wisconsin anyway. He knew David had a few years of college left.

David was pleasantly surprised. Very pleasantly surprised. It looked like it could all work out. He saw the sincerity in Agent Johnston's face, and was more than happy to take him for a celebratory spin around the town. Artie was very appreciative and promised to stay in touch. He told David, if there were ever any issues with the FBI, call him and he'd connect him to whoever was needed. He offered to run interference if there were ever any problems. He was more than happy to help. It hadn't been lost on him, that he had just gained an as yet unmeasurable stature within the Federal Bureau of Investigation. As Ed Gorman had said, this was historic.

Bernie had done some research and found he could purchase a simple electronic paging system for contacting David. He would have a device that would send a low frequency electronic signal to a device David would carry. There was no voice features to it. It simply buzzed and vibrated when Bernie hit his button. He wasn't going to tell Agent Johnston about it, and figured the FBI couldn't intercept that signal and trace it, if they didn't know specifically what they were looking for. It would work in Aston, though Bernie told David they'd need to figure something for when he'd be back to school. This signal wouldn't be strong enough to go that far.

The Police Chief and the Sheriff were dumbfounded when they were told they now had the Flying Guy at their service. That meeting with Bernie had left them both speechless. Bernie told them that whenever they wanted the Flying Guy for something, just call him on his cell and he'd contact him. They were amenable to that.

*

David told his parents and they were ecstatic. His mom fought misty tears of relief. His dad was smiling again. They both felt a faint sense of what they'd experienced when telling Emery and Phyllis about David, a sort of relief from having to keep the whole secret.

"It sounds too good to be true," his dad commented, "but maybe this will all work out." He was pretty proud of his son. His son, the Flying Guy.

"Oh, I hope so," his mom said.

*

Amy was happy too. She was surprised that all this had taken place while she was away.

"Oh, my gosh, Davey," she said to him when he called. "That must've been pure hell to go through. I'm sorry I wasn't there."

"Yeah. I wished you could have been here," he said. "But it all worked out okay. At least so far anyway. We'll see."

When Amy returned to Aston, she came for dinner at the Anderson's. Mark and Margaret suspended one of the cardinal rules and they all held up a glass of wine.

"To saving the world," David said.

"To saving the world," they all replied.

Epilogue

Bernie Fredder had told David he wanted to write an article about meeting him. He wanted to formally introduce the Flying Guy to Aston. Of course his name was safe, but since he was going to be seen more publicly and more often, Bernie wanted to let the world know. Plus, Bernie thought, he was able to bask in some of the glory. Dan Powers was overjoyed with the whole idea. He'd pretty much left Bernie, and everyone else, with the impression he thought Bernie walked on water now. Bernie fully intended to milk that for all it was worth.

David was fine with the idea. He did ask to see the final draft of the article before it was printed. Bernie gave him a copy during a clandestine rendezvous at a downtown restaurant. He silently passed an envelope as he walked past David's table. They both enjoyed their secret ways of communicating. They laughed about how they felt like they were spies.

The city of Aston, as well as virtually the entire rest of the world, was captivated by the phenomenon of the Flying Guy. It was all anyone talked about for weeks after the announcement. News agencies from around the globe came to Aston hoping to get a glimpse of the flyer. For now, David stayed away. He had to think through his stepping into the spotlight, to reduce the chances someone would try to catch him.

Bernie came up with an idea, and David readily accepted it. Since gaining fame, he'd become more comfortable with having to deal with the public. Bernie's idea was for the Flying Guy, as he was now officially known, to make an official, public meeting with the people of Aston. Actually, he had told David, the whole world will probably be there.

The Fourth of July holiday was coming up, and the parade they held was always a big event in Aston. The city prided itself on holding one of the largest parades in the northern part of Wisconsin. This year would likely be, by far, the largest ever.

This year, the Grand Marshall wasn't riding in a car.

"That's pretty hokey, Bernie," David had commented. "I'm going to be a float in a parade."

"Hey, maybe we'll dress you all up in red, white, and blue."

About the Author

John Baraniak has been writing short stories for over 30 years and is near completion of a book for publication. This is his first full length novel.

A native and lifelong resident of Northern Wisconsin, John has worked primarily in corporate finance. But his love for reading and writing has produced a number of well received short stories.

He was a private pilot in the early 1990s and from that experience has developed an eye for viewing the world from the air. Like many, he has had the wish that he could fly and has put those ideas into this novel of a small boy who was born with that special ability.

Printed in the United States
By Bookmasters

Printed in the United States
By Bookmasters